King Of The Wood

Valerie Anand

St. Martin's Press
New York

All characters in this publication – except the obvious historical ones –
are fictitious and any resemblance to real persons, living or dead, is
purely coincidental.

KING OF THE WOOD. Copyright © 1988 by Valerie Anand. All rights reserved.
Printed in the United States of America. No part of this book may be used or
reproduced in any manner whatsoever without written permission except in
the case of brief quotations embodied in critical articles or reviews. For
information, address St. Martin's Press, 175 Fifth Avenue, New York, N.Y.
10010.

Library of Congress Cataloging-in-Publication Data

Anand, Valerie.
        King of the wood / Valerie Anand.
            p.   cm.
        ISBN 0-312-02939-X
        1. Great Britain—History—William II, Rufus, 1087–1100—Fiction.
    I. Title.
    PR6051.N34K56 1989
    823′.914—dc 19   89-30082
                                                                CIP

First published in Great Britain by Headline Book Publishing PLC.

First U.S. Edition
10 9 8 7 6 5 4 3 2 1

This book is for

KATE MORTON

who helped so much with the
research and who, from the
beginning, cheered the project
on.

Author's Note

According to *The Anglo-Saxon Chronicle*, King William II of England, otherwise known as William Rufus, was shot dead with an arrow by one of his own men, while hunting in the New Forest on 2nd August 1100.

This is all that is known for sure about his death. Whether it was accident or murder remains a mystery. If the latter, there is more than one possible murderer. A man called Walter Tirel, Count of Poix, who was visiting the court, is popularly credited with loosing the fatal arrow, whether intentionally or not, and, if the latter, whether on his own behalf or that of someone else.

Other names have been mentioned. Tirel's brother-in-law Gilbert Clare, Earl of Tonbridge, is thought by some to have been involved, with arranging Tirel's escape if nothing else. Gerald of Wales, writing many years later, also names a man called Ranulf des Aquis as having been concerned. He was writing in Latin and 'Ralph des Aix' is a reasonable Anglo-French rendering of the name. I have christened my character accordingly. For bringing Ranulf des Aquis (and much else besides) to my notice, acknowledgements go to Duncan Grinnell-Milne's informative book, *The Killing of William Rufus*.

The place where William Rufus is traditionally said to have died is near a small community called Canterton. At the time of the Domesday Book this was known as Chenna's Tun, which is the name I have used. Similarly, Truham was the eleventh century name for the district now called Fritham Plain.

I am indebted to the historian Catherine Morton for her theory about the real nature of the relationship between William Rufus and Count Helias of Maine. Their recorded exchanges have an intense quality which is extremely puzzling, except in the light of this theory.

vii

I am also indebted to Professor Frank Barlow, for patiently answering queries about Count Helias, and above all, for the goldmine of information in his biography of William Rufus.

Finally, the rare commodity which Richard Debrouillard grows on his manor was known in England before the Conquest but then faded out and was not officially reintroduced until the 14th century. But it continued to be known in Cornwall and who is to say that in England no entrepreneur ever tried producing it between the 11th and 14th centuries? My thanks go to the Spice Bureau for their helpful advice on this subject.

Prologue

His story ended on an August evening, in the forest. The trees were in the dark green leaf of mature summer, and shafts of golden light from a declining sun slanted through the boughs. To look westwards was to be dazzled. The air was soft. Almost, one could hear the earth breathing deeply in gratitude for the warmth of this fine day after a long affliction of rain.

And then: the shaft that came out of the sun but was not made of light. And under the trees where a moment ago had been a calm and lovely evening, with a stag in antler running superb and graceful through it, there was squalid pain, and death.

That was the end of the story. But the beginning?

Ralph des Aix sometimes thought about that beginning. It seemed that one could trace cause and effect back for ever. Yet there were certain events, concerning different people in places far apart which although small in themselves, were nevertheless like the seeds from which grew the forest where William Rufus died.

Perhaps, Ralph thought – a little wryly, since he was himself involved – the earliest seeds were planted in 1068, when two boy-children were born. (There were girl-children too, but Edith and Sybil came later.)

One of the boys was the future Henry I, brother of William Rufus who was king before him, both being sons of that stark ruler William Duke of Normandy and King, by conquest, of England. Henry was born in Winchester, the only one of the Conqueror's children to come into the world after their father became a king. It was a bad labour, so report said and, although Queen Matilda survived, there were no more babies.

The other child was Ralph himself and he was born in

Normandy, the second son of a man called Peter Long-shanks and he too gave his mother trouble as he forced his way into the light.

So much trouble, in fact, that unlike Queen Matilda, she did not survive.

And that, as it turned out, was important.

PART I

IN WHICH THE SEEDS ARE PLANTED
1068–1087 AD

One

Untimely Death
1068–73

Peter Longshanks' second son came as an unwelcome surprise. Peter was nearly fifty when Ralph made his disruptive appearance, and his wife was well past forty. Their elder boy was twelve and Cecile had not conceived in all those years.

Who, Longshanks asked himself as he stood in the upper room under the slanting rafters, looking down on his wife's still face, would have expected this?

The sun, shining through a roof louvre, showed the dancing dust motes. Seeing them made him angry, for they looked as if they were alive, while Cecile was not.

He was going to be lonely. He had been that, he admitted, even while she was alive. But now it would be worse.

His home was in southern Normandy but he was not a Norman. Peter Longshanks was English. He had followed his exiled lord to Normandy, long ago. But when the lord made up the quarrel which had sent him into exile, and went home, Longshanks had stayed behind.

He had stayed because by then he was married and Cecile, cut off from her smallholding and her own language, would have been far more lost in England than he was in Normandy. She had married him believing that he would remain with her on the holding of Aix, and he would not break even an unspoken agreement, not when it would cause her so much anguish.

But he had suffered. Cecile had limitations. She was dumpy and swarthy and her conversation was restricted to practical matters. 'I think the pig is ready for killing.' 'Reggie is growing out of his tunics.' 'Peter, I think I'm *enceinte* again . . .'

She had spoken only Norman-French and he had never known, until his English lord had gone, how much one's own language meant. Even the dullest remarks would

3

have sounded like music, if he could have heard them in English.

But she had cared for him and Reggie, worked like a demon to make the holding productive. She had tried hard to be company for him; she had *bothered* about him. He drew the rug over her face and turned away to descend the ladder to the ground floor, trying not to cry. It wouldn't bring her back. Only, he would not have thought her going could leave him so desolate.

The room below was sunny and spacious. Aix was an old name borne by many places large and small and most of them had springs of good water. The local priest, who was interested in such matters, said that the Romans had settled in these districts, being appreciative of the springs for bathing (he didn't approve of too much bathing himself and managed to make it sound like a dubious heathen practice). He thought the name Aix had something to do with Aqua, the Latin word for water.

Peter thought he was right, for Aix had a fine spring, and in one corner of the paved downstairs room there were traces of mosaic. As he stepped off the ladder, he saw that the sun was picking out the bright chips of purple and pale green. The floor was clean because Cecile had swept it only half an hour before her pains began. The need to grieve overwhelmed him and he blundered, eyes flooding, to a stool, ignoring the two people who were already in the room – three, if one counted the child in the cradle. The others were the midwife, who was clucking over the mewling newborn bundle which was his son, and the priest, who had given Cecile the last rites and baptised the baby, just in case, though the brat seemed healthy enough, Peter thought with bitterness, burying his face in his hands.

But although he didn't want to be pestered with any of them, it was clear after a few moments that something was expected of him. The priest was clearing his throat. Peter raised his head and became aware that somebody was missing. 'Where's Reggie?'

'We sent him to the village,' said the priest. 'The child needs milk. We have sent for Elise.'

'*Elise*? Without asking me?'

'There is no choice,' said the priest shortly. This female,

4

carnal matter embarrassed him. 'As the goodwife here says, there is no one else who will do.'

'But *Elise*! And where did her baby come from, I'd like to know? Devil's spawn, if the tales are true. They say she's a witch.'

'That won't affect the milk,' said the midwife, 'or if it do, there's no help for it. There ain't no one else.'

'And no proof of sorcery, either,' put in the priest. 'That's just the talk of jealous old women.' He did not like or trust women, but he did his duty by his female parishioners and was shrewd enough about their mistreatment of one another. 'A widow with a pretty face is easily led into sin, and there's a good few without pretty faces, who'd like the chance! So tongues clack. They'll say anything. They'd do better to say their prayers instead. And Elise'd do better to marry again.'

'Well, don't look at me,' said Longshanks.

The priest looked through the open door instead. 'Here's Reggie with Elise now.'

Longshanks sighed and then, because he sensed that they thought he should, he went across to the cradle and looked at his new offspring. The comment about clacking tongues had reminded him of something. There had been just one real cause of dispute between himself and Cecile. She wouldn't let him teach Reggie to speak English. She'd feel shut out, she said, if father and son got to chattering in some foreign tongue.

Well, he could teach this new child, Ralph, to speak it. He could learn from babyhood.

It was a plan for the future, something to look forward to, that he could think of as important. It made him feel a little better. He turned quite amiably to greet the woman Elise as Reggie brought her in, thinking that after all, the spare-time occupations of Ralph's wet- nurse were hardly of any consequence.

He was wrong.

By the autumn of 1073, Ralph des Aix was five years old. Over in England, the Conqueror's last-born son Henry had also turned five and was in the process additionally of turning into a handful.

5

The royal hunting lodge at Brockenhurst in Hampshire had belonged to the Conqueror's predecessors and was English in construction. This meant that its fortifications were derisory by Norman standards until King William ordered a moat to be dug round it, and also that it was built of timber. It was conventional for its Norman users to comment disdainfully on its rusticity. But more than a few of them secretly admired the subtle, intertwined patterns of carving on the doorposts and the similarly adorned furniture within. And all of them valued the warmth. The timber walls were double, with brushwood packed between. It was more flammable than a stone castle but infinitely drier and much less draughty. The Conqueror liked it. In search of a few days' hunting and relaxation, after a successful campaign across the Channel in Maine, to the south of Normandy, it was to Brockenhurst that he went.

Most of the court accompanied him. There was room. In the English fashion, the lodge was surrounded by small editions of itself, thatched apartments where guests and their servants could be accommodated with more privacy than most castles afforded, and where business could be conducted in peace or small boys tutored.

'Only,' said Henry, staring mutinously at the slate on which his tutor had drawn an outline of Normandy, 'I don't see why I have to stay in and look at maps. My brothers have gone out hunting with Father. It isn't fair.'

Some instructors might now have administered a sharp rebuke, either verbal or physical. But Henry, even at five, was capable of meeting verbal disapproval by folding his mouth into an obstinate shape which meant *I won't listen*, and of withstanding any kind of chastisement suitable for his years, in a silence still more obstinate, until the chance came to kick the perpetrator's shins, when he would do it.

Besides, the tutor sympathised with his charge. It was a glorious September morning and the hunt setting out had been something to see; the horses pawing and tossing their heads and the coupled hounds all but pulling their handlers over as they smelt the first frost of autumn. The colours had been dazzling too; brilliant tunics, scalloped reins of scarlet against the neck of a dapple grey horse, the

6

leaves of a chestnut tree turning golden-brown, spread against a sky so purely blue that it would surely feel smooth to the touch.

Britnoth was a monk and ought not to be moved by such worldly things. He also knew that he should disapprove of the king's passion for the chase. King William valued the beasts of the forest above the lives of men and it was a disgrace.

But that morning, holding Henry's hand as they watched the hunt set out, he had longed to be part of it all, just as much as Henry.

Who was now regarding him with smouldering brown eyes, from under a very untidy black fringe. No doubt Henry had liked the bright colours too. Children did. 'Looking at maps need not be dull, Henry. I'll show you.'

Half an hour later, he was congratulating himself on the success of his stratagem. Where charcoal lines on a slate did not appeal, pigments on scraped sheepskin could enthral. Henry, his tongue poking between his lips, was industriously filling in the blue outline of England, dipping an interested brush in water and paint, and asking intelligent questions about whether the land was really that shape.

'More or less,' said Britnoth, with strict regard for the truth. 'The real coastline is more jagged but this is near enough. Now, we'll put some wavy lines for the sea – thus – and put in Normandy. What colour shall Normandy be?'

'Red,' said Henry. It was his favourite colour.

'All right. I'll do the outline and you can fill it in presently. I'll put some other places in first. Wash that brush for me. Now, what's this place I'm drawing in a red dotted line below Normandy; to the south, that is? You ought to know. Your father has just come back from there.'

'Oh, that's silly old Maine.' Henry had heard the word bandied about all summer while his father was away, and since the king's triumphant return with the keys of Maine's capital, Le Mans, in his possession, it had been bandied about still more.

'Excellent, Henry.' Britnoth held out a hand for the brush, which Henry had been dipping in water. 'Now I'm

7

going to make a new colour, green. I mix blue with yellow
for that – there. And I'm drawing a new outline, still
further south. Where would this be? Do you know who its
lord is?'

'No.' Henry was interested in the paint-blending process but bored by the questions. He kicked the bench-leg
beneath him, warningly.

'That's called Anjou. It has a lord with a funny name.
Men call him Fulk the Surly. He was disputing with your
father over which of them should be called the overlord of
Maine but your father won. Now here on the eastern
border of Normandy – I'll show you how to mix purple for
this – we have France, whose king is Normandy's own
overlord . . .'

Hoofbeats went past outside, at speed. The water jar
slopped with the vibration, fortunately on the table and
not on the map. 'Mop it up with this rag, Henry, quickly.
Come along, what are you waiting for?'

'I'm not waiting, I'm listening.' Shouting had broken
out somewhere nearby. 'What's all that noise?'

'A messenger, I expect. If it concerns us, we'll be told.
You mustn't be inquisitive.'

'I mustn't be inquisitive. I can't go hunting with the
others. It's not *fair*.'

'You'll be able to ask more questions, and go hunting
too, when you're older.'

'Robert says I won't ever catch up. He says I'll never be
on equal terms with him and Richard. He says all my
father's lands will go to them and there'll be nothing left
for me.'

Britnoth was forty-eight, had led a sedentary life and
had never been athletic even when young. The king's
eldest son Robert was nineteen and tough; he could have
picked Britnoth up from the ground, or felled him to it,
with one hand. Notwithstanding any of this, Britnoth
frequently had a wild desire to box Robert's ears. He was
for ever teasing and provoking his small brother. Britnoth
thought he did it because he himself had been thus provoked, usually by his father, who never praised him but
often gibed at him for things he couldn't help, such as his
short stature. Curthose, *Shortlegs*, was the Conqueror's

preferred nickname for his firstborn, spoken jovially but with the lion's claws not entirely sheathed. But one could hardly expect Henry to understand that.

That Robert's remarks had been perfectly accurate, did not help.

Mildly, Britnoth said: 'It is the custom for the eldest son to inherit his father's lands intact. When a man spends a lifetime gathering a great estate, he doesn't like to think of it being broken into fragments the moment he's dead. Normandy and England are so very separate in the way of nature that perhaps in this case the two eldest sons may benefit instead of just the first, otherwise Richard would be no better off than you. In fact, Henry, you're the fourth son. You've never met your brother William because he is being educated in Normandy while you were born here, but he will share what you regard as the unfairness. Both you and he will have to make your own careers. It isn't a disaster. To make a successful life for yourself, to gather possessions by your own efforts, there are great satisfactions in that. But you'll need your education. You must understand the world you live in, the better to seize your opportunities . . .'

'That *noise*,' said Henry persistently.

The clamour outside had increased. Doors banged and running feet sped by. A man's voice was raised in shocked exclamation and a woman near at hand had burst out crying. Henry, regardless of the value of education, scrambled off his bench and made for the door. Britnoth went after him.

People were streaming across the paved inner court, towards the gate. A woman clutching a bucket and broom went by, followed by a fat baron whose hangover had kept him from hunting that day. After him ran a cook with dough on his hands. All their faces were distraught. 'What's happened?' Britnoth cried as he and Henry, drawn by the ancient magnetism of calamity, fell in with the rest. 'A hunting accident! They say it's the king himself!' The woman with the bucket quavered an answer. 'And what'll become of us all now . . .!'

'It ain't the king!' the cook contradicted. They were through the gate now and jostling across the muddy outer

9

court, towards the gatehouse. The drawbridge was down and a grim procession was already making its way across. Britnoth had caught Henry's hand, but Henry dragged him forward, pushing between massed bodies. They were in the front as the hunting party which had gone out so bravely in the morning, came home.

It came sombrely, led by King William himself, on foot. He was obviously not dead but he carried in his arms something that was. Robert Curthose followed him, mounted and leading his father's horse. Behind Curthose, a huntsman led another riderless animal. The Conqueror's face was set like granite. As he stepped off the drawbridge, he paused to adjust his burden and with a gesture that seemed strange in a man normally so harsh, he lifted the head that lolled over his forearm and cradled it against his shoulder. Those who were nearest could see its face. Britnoth looked round for a way to get Henry out of the crowd but in vain. Someone let out a wail and someone else cried: 'What did it?'

It could be seen now that the body had a smashed red band across its throat. The Conqueror glanced round and called an answer. 'He was galloping to reach a good position for shooting. A low branch got him across the neck. He died before he hit the ground.'

Then Henry, who had been standing on tiptoe, recognised the dead face and with a screech of: 'Richard, it's Richard!' broke away from Britnoth, flinging himself at his father.

Britnoth lunged after him. 'Not now, Henry! I'm sorry, my lord, my apologies; Henry, don't . . .'

'But it's Richard! He's dead!' Henry knew what death was. One did not reach even five years of age in the Conqueror's household and remain unfamiliar with the concept of death, with the sight of dead stags and with talk of dead men.

'Bring him to the chapel later, when his brother has been made seemly,' said the Conqueror, and walked on. Henry fought to follow, pummelling Britnoth's chest as the tutor picked him up. 'It's Richard, it's Richard, I want to go to Richard!'

'Hush!' said Britnoth desperately. The woman with the

10

bucket said: 'Poor little soul.' Curthose, who had pulled up when William stopped, jumped down, threw the reins of his two horses into the nearest pairs of hands and with the first sign of fraternal affection Britnoth had ever observed in him, removed Henry from his tutor's arms. 'You poor bloody little tyke,' said Curthose. 'Big brother Robert's still here. Don't cry.'

Next day, because it was customary, Britnoth admonished Henry on the importance of quiet and dignified conduct and took him to the chapel to say farewell to his brother, who lay before the altar, tidily disposed upon his bier, candles at his head and feet. Henry clutched his tutor's hand tightly and seemed to be puzzling out what the meaning of this solemn new thing would be to himself.

He considerably startled Britnoth when at length he voiced his conclusion. Having touched the white waxen forehead with a small forefinger, he stepped back and said: 'Poor Richard. Is he in heaven now?' And then, before Britnoth could answer: 'I only have two brothers ahead of me now, haven't I?'

Two

Lives Alter Course
1073

'I'm thirteen,' said the boy to himself and his recalcitrantly pounding heart. 'I'm nearly a man. I'm the son of King William. I've slept in this room every night for five years and I know every stone of it. There are people all round me. I'm William the Red, son of a king and there's *nothing to be afraid of.*'

His mentors at St. Stephen's Abbey in Caen would have been both astonished and scandalised to think there was, for the young boys at St. Stephen's, most of them prospective priests and monks, were protected as far as humanly possible from all harm, either physical or spiritual.

By day, they went to church, studied, took exercise and dined, all under the eyes of their superiors. Some, whose parents had not finally decided their future, took lessons in riding and the handling of arms, but also under careful supervision. And at night they slept in a long dormer, each boy alone on his rope cot, although in the homes they had left behind, their brothers and sisters huddled like puppies, three and four to a pallet, to save space and keep warm. Two monks guarded them, sleeping in the two end beds, to watch over their charges' safety, health and morals.

But in the interests of health, recreation times were needed. So during the day, there were interludes for games and stories; decorous games and improving stories. The machinations of a cunning sinner in a tale might inspire a little laughter, but the spectres of mortal corruption, the demons of Hell, must at the end of the story clutch him with their gaunt fingers. It had occurred to no one that these specifications might allow an unsafe amount of scope to those of the brethren with raconteur talents. Even wise old Abbot Lanfranc, who had laid down the rules for the boys, before departing for greater things – to cross the Channel and become Archbishop of Canterbury, no less – had underestimated the potential of the talents in some cases. That of Brother Philip, for example.

Of *course* there was nothing to fear. The boy slowly scanned the sleeping dormitory. Brother Philip's bed was only four feet away, at the end of the row. It creaked as its occupant stirred. The windows were shuttered but a small oil lamp burned at each end of the room. The building was new, for the Abbey had been founded by the Conqueror after his marriage. But the shutters didn't all fit well and the low flames flickered in small draughts. Shadows, enlarged and distorted, moved on the pale stone walls. The clothes chest facing the end of his bed, its dark bulk blended with its elongated shadow, looked like an animal with a stunted head and neck.

That evening, Brother Philip had told them a tale about a youth who spoke ill of St. Stephen. It was summer, Philip had said impressively, building his effects, and when the lad went to bed that night, his window was wide to the air and the moonlight. As he lay there, restless in the heat, he noticed that in the moonlight, the shadow of his own bed looked a little like a bear.

And for three nights thereafter, said Philip to his breathless hearers, as the moon waxed to the full, the likeness grew more and more pronounced. Until on the third night there was no more doubt and as the wretched blasphemous youth lay trembling on his pallet, staring at the shadow on the floor beside him, he felt the mattress move under him, and grow warm and thickly pelted, and then mighty, furred paws encircled him and steely claws entered his flesh . . .

A few feet off, Philip raised himself on an elbow. His whisper just crossed the space between them. 'Still awake, Red?'

The boy turned his head. 'Yes.'

'Scared? Come on, then.'

He was a king's son and might yet be a knight one day. His terrors shamed him and he was more shamed still that he had once, incautiously, admitted them to Philip. He knew, though dimly, that Philip had stepped up the horror of his stories since then, to maintain a hold on him. For all these reasons, he wished to stay where he was. But fear drove him in the direction of comfort and besides, with the promise of safety there was mingled an unholy delight.

He yielded, slipping soundlessly from his bed and sliding into Philip's. He pressed his face into Philip's smooth, warm chest and Philip pulled him close. He felt the pulsating heat begin in the man's loins and the queer, molten feeling that always answered in his own. Under the rugs, Philip felt for the boy's right hand, and guided it.

When he woke, he was in his own bed again, innocently ready to rise with the others for Lauds. At this season it meant getting up before daybreak but the cold dark that preceded dawn never, oddly enough, had midnight's power to frighten. He went to church with the rest, himself again, young and tough, afraid of nothing, somewhat bored by the monkish chanting.

Then came breakfast in the refectory. After that, there was a summons from the abbot.

He followed the brother who brought the summons, wondering what it portended. He could think of nothing he had done recently which merited a rebuke from the abbot himself. Unless . . .

Unless someone knew about him and Philip. That occurred to him when he was halfway up the narrow steps to the abbot's door, and turned his inside liquid. If they had been found out, what might happen next would be beyond imagining. Human authority outraged by *that* would outdo the fiends of Hell with ease. As he entered the room, the first thing he saw was the chest in which he had brought his personal belongings to St. Stephen's five years ago. It lay on the floor with its lid thrown back and he could see his clothes already folded inside. He was to be expelled, then? His head came up and inside his clenched hands, his fingernails cut into his palms. He would deny the accusation. (He hoped he wouldn't stammer.) He would pretend he didn't understand what it meant. He would find out who had laid the information and say whoever it was had a grudge against him. He would . . .

14

'No need for that fiery expression, my son,' said the abbot calmly from his chair. 'Come here to me. Whatever you have on your conscience just now – plenty, I don't doubt – I'm not concerned with it. If you've given another bloody nose to a fellow pupil over the tangled question of whether your father is or is not the rightful overlord of Maine, don't tell me about it. I shall hope not to hear it officially until after you've gone.'

'Gone?' But if they didn't know about him and Philip, why?

'You're leaving us, William. Your father has sent an escort to bring you to him in England. You are not to be a bishop after all, it seems. Not, to be honest, that I ever thought you had the makings of one. I would call you warrior material.' And getting more so every day, the abbot added to himself, taking in the short, strong build of the boy in front of him, the round light eyes in the square freckled face, and the thick, pale ginger hair that topped it. Even a trace of ginger made for aggressiveness in the abbot's experience, and there was more than a trace of choler in this boy's temperament. He flushed so easily with anger that he had been given nicknames about it. He answered as readily to a shout of *Red* or *Rufus* as he did to his given name of William.

He had flushed now, although this time with pleasure at being called warrior material. It was a pity, after that, to have to upset him. Breaking this kind of news was one of the harder tasks which devolved on those in authority. 'Your father has sent for you for a special reason, William, not on account of any recommendation I may have made. Your family has suffered a bereavement and you are being called to England to fill an empty place. Your elder brother Richard – I am sorry, William – recently met with an accident, hunting. A fatal accident.' He went on, speaking steadily, explaining the circumstances of the death, allowing the boy time to assimilate the news. When he had finished, he waited, but William said nothing. 'Were you close to him?' the abbot asked.

'No, not really. Five years is a long time.' It was difficult to take in, William thought. Richard was far away, a tiny figure at the end of a tunnel of memory. The abbot was speaking to him again.

15

'Before you leave, you can spend an hour alone in one of the chapels. You'll want to say goodbye to your fellow pupils, of course. Is there anyone else you would like to bid farewell to?'

'I. . . yes.' This was easier than answering questions about his own feelings. 'Can I say goodbye to Brother Philip?'

'By all means.' Excellent, thought the abbot. It was so satisfactory to know that Brother Philip was able to win his charges' affection.

'He tells such interesting stories at recreation,' said the boy. And added, with an ironic depth of meaning which quite escaped the abbot, 'I'm sure I shall never forget them, or him.'

The weather broke while he was on his way to England. A gale delayed him at the coast and when the ship finally sailed, it was on a very rough sea. But he was not afraid and found that he had a reliable stomach. The men of his father's escort were pleased with him.

The gale was mighty. It blew for several days and nights all across the southern half of England. It brought down hundreds of trees. One, a huge uprooted beech, blocked a track which for certain reasons was of interest to folk in nearby communities, especially that of Chenna's Tun, twenty miles south-west of Winchester. A squad of men from the locality therefore went out in secret one moonlit night shortly after, and removed the obstruction.

The gale also did damage in a wooded Sussex valley near the nothern edge of the downs, where a woman called Wulfhild, English by birth but married to a Norman, had just borne her third child; a son. It brought down a tree across the roof of the resthouse (which stood alone, English fashion) where Wulfhild and her child were lying. They were not directly injured but the damaged thatch let in rain and the baby, which had been baptised Simon after his father Sir Simon of Fallowdene, took cold and a few days later died. Wulfhild in her grief railed against God and shocked her family by crying out that they would do better to propitiate the old gods of forest and sky.

*

16

They sailed up the Thames to Westminster in a slashing downpour which turned the river to the likeness of pockmarked lead and hid the walls of the great Tower which William's father had built. The rain was so heavy by the time they landed that he saw hardly anything of the outside of Westminster either. His escort hurried him from the landing stage and up some steps to an archway where a guard clashed pikehandles on the floor in salute. Then they went at a run across a courtyard and climbed some more steps. There were more guards and more salutes and then, squelching and dripping, they were passing through a vestibule to an inner door and suddenly there was brightness and heat, the scent of woodsmoke and rosemary, and the rustle and babble of a multiplicity of people.

They were in a pillared hall, with a raised dais at one end and a long central fireplace where logs blazed, pouring smoke through a roof louvre and hissing occasionally as the rain found its way in.

The flagstoned floor was thick with rushes and it was from these that the scent of rosemary was rising, for sprigs of the herb had been strewn there to release its essence as it was trodden underfoot. It was being subjected to heavy trampling now, for the lowering sky had driven everyone in from the outdoor pursuits most of them preferred.

Whatever activities could be followed under a roof were in progress. On the dais, where a brazier supplied a private source of heat, half a dozen well-dressed men sat talking, feet stretched towards the warmth, brown hands absently reaching down to scratch between canine ears, for every man had a hound beside his chair.

In the body of the hall, a couple of merchants were displaying readymade cloaks for sale and, beyond them, an intent circle of men squatted on their heels betting noisily on the fall of a dice.

And at the far end of the hall from the dais, a number of youths stood round a man who seemed to be showing them different patterns of arrow and sizes of bow. A monk (one never got away from them, thought William) stood listening, with two small boys at his side.

He and his escort had come in unheralded and for a

17

moment stood unnoticed. Then, because they were so wet and the fire was welcoming, they moved instinctively towards it. One of the youths, taking aim along an imaginary shaft at an imaginary target, found himself staring straight at William's pale ginger hair. He lowered the bow and spoke to his companions. A moment later, they were all round the newcomers. 'You,' said the lad who had been holding the bow, 'you're my brother William, aren't you?'

William's escort was speaking to the youths' instructor. The men on the dais were turning their heads. The instructor and the escort knights made for the dais. For the moment, William was alone with his peers. 'You're Robert,' he said. 'I remember you.'

Memory was aided by the fact that at nineteen, Robert was much as he had been at fourteen when William had last seen him. He was strongly made with a head of thick dark hair, and he stood with feet firmly apart. He was still nearly as short as William remembered him and the hands holding the bow were small. 'I was *christened* Robert,' he said, 'but most people call me Curthose. Shortlegs if they're speaking English. Have you got a nickname?'

Another youth, cutting in as William opened his mouth to answer, said: 'He ought to be called the Red. Look what the sea wind's done to his face.' This boy was about Robert's age but he was taller, with high cheekbones which gave him a wooden expression, and blue eyes in which there was a disconcerting ring of yellow. When he spoke, he drawled.

'I've been called the Red for years,' William said. 'Or Rufus. That's not new. The escort called me Rufus on the way here.' They had meant it kindly and he had warmed to it. 'You can call me that if you want.' He wondered if the uncomfortable drawling youth was the hall bully. There always was one.

'It'll be up to Father,' said Robert Curthose. 'If he thinks you should have a nickname, then you'll have one and you won't have any choice. If he doesn't, you won't. Well, do you want to know who people are? These two are both called Hugh . . .'

William, gently steaming by the fire while Curthose

18

performed the introductions, had already assumed that most of these boys must be the sons of his father's friends, being educated at court to fit them for the illustrious futures their own fathers expected for them. He looked at them with interest, for he was mature enough already to realise that some of them would probably be his lifelong associates.

There were two Hughs, two Rogers, an Aubrey and a plethora of Roberts. Most, to avoid confusion, were not known by their first names but by their fathers' names or the lands their families held. The uncomfortable boy with the blue and yellow eyes was a Robert but he was called Belleme after his mother's lands in southern Normandy. 'He gets his eyes from his mother,' Curthose said, 'and one or two quirks of character as well.' There were some dutiful-sounding sniggers. Curthose did not enlarge and William asked no questions. The murderous reputation of the Belleme family was already known to him and besides, he had sensed at once the aura of menace round Robert of Belleme.

Another Robert, known as FitzHamon because his father was Hamon, Sheriff of Kent, also in adolescence foreshadowed the man he would become. He had a bull's physique, with thick, forward-angled shoulders and massive features. His hazel eyes were intelligent, however; he looked as though he might be more capable of fine feeling than his crude bodily build suggested. More, perhaps, than the third Robert whom Curthose brought forward, the future Count of Meulan.

Meulan resembled nothing so much as a pugnacious mouse. He had alert round eyes and a pointed nose, and a short upper lip drawn up to reveal two bright front teeth. But it would be unwise, William knew instinctively, to comment on the mouselike features, unless one wished for a prompt demonstration of the pugnacity. Years later, when they were grown men and close friends, he spoke to Meulan of that first impression. 'And I haven't changed,' said Meulan, amused. 'Not in that way,' William Rufus agreed. 'In another, you have. You were grubby then.'

Meulan in adulthood had become a dandy, his tailor's bills a byword and his barber a well-rewarded personal

19

friend. He laughed, because William's friendship was precious to him, and William was therefore one of the few people who could with impunity have suggested that Meulan had ever, even long ago, been grubby. As boy and man alike, Meulan, though as intelligent as FitzHamon, reserved his sensitivities for his own easily hurt feelings.

'That's the Roberts,' said Curthose, finishing with Meulan. He turned to the monk and the two small boys. 'This is Brother Britnoth and this goldenhaired angel with the curly halo is Gilbert Clare. He's only five. His father is the Earl of Tonbridge. If you annoy Gilbert, he bites.' The angelic child pulled a frightful face and Curthose sidestepped with a yelp of mock terror. 'Hold on to him, Britnoth, I don't want his pearly teeth in my elbow again. Gilbert's new; he's to be a companion to our little brother Henry. This is Henry. Henry, come and say hello.'

'Henry?' William dropped to one knee to get on a level. The second little boy regarded him suspiciously from brown eyes half hidden behind a black fringe, as though he were peering out of a thicket. 'You won't remember me because you were born in England and I've never been out of Normandy until now. But I'm your brother William.'

Britnoth gently pushed Henry forward. He resisted, favouring William with an inimical and silent stare. 'Greet your brother, Henry,' said the monk encouragingly.

The small face became mutinous. '*Not* my brother. Richard was my brother. Don't want any more brothers. Don't know you.'

'Now, Henry . . .'

'You'll get to know me.' William adopted a coaxing tone. 'I'll be living here. Tell you what . . .'

'Don't know you! *Don't want you!*' Henry turned scarlet. 'Go away!' With a gesture of surpassing impropriety, probably learned from the older boys, he twisted out of Britnoth's grasp, and ran. Britnoth uttered a scandalised exclamation. Henry, charging blindly through a forest of legs, crashed headfirst into a pair of shins striding the other way. Two strong hands came down and plucked him into the air. 'Now that's not the way to welcome your brother. What do you mean by it?' said the

20

Conqueror, and brought Henry with him as he came straight on to William.

William, who had started to rise from his kneeling position, changed his mind and decided to stay there.

Frightened, in the dormitory at St. Stephen's, he had told himself that he was the son of a king, but it was a long time since he had seen his father and only now did he remember what this King was like.

The Conqueror was physically a tall man, becoming heavy as he grew older, but his stature was far more than bodily; it was a quality of the mind. Many men were as big and as finely dressed. But what was the secret of wearing clothes with such an air, so that the swing of the mantle expressed haste or anger or satisfaction in tune with its owner's thoughts, and the shoulder brooch continually flashed to draw the eye? He put Henry down with a little shake and the small boy, awed, muttered some kind of greeting to William after all. 'Take him away now,' said the Conqueror, handing him to Britnoth, and set his warm, padded hands on William's shoulders. His black falcon's eyes saw everything, William thought. His voice was genial but had a grating timbre. 'Welcome to England. Up you get, let me see you. Christ, you're wet; we'll have to wring you out before you sit down to supper. Turn round. Not as much height as I'd like to see but never mind, you're sturdy enough. Show me your hands. Good. Callouses in the right places. I gave orders that you were to learn fighting skills. Forget the church. You'll make a soldier. We'll try you out against Curthose and the rest tomorrow.'

Curthose said mischievously: 'He tells us he has a nickname too. Some people call him Rufus, he says.'

'Rufus?' The Conqueror stood back, hands on hips, taking in the wind-reddened skin and tawny hair of his second surviving son. He laughed. 'Can't have him at a disadvantage compared to you, can we? Rufus it is. It suits him very well.'

He had his nickname. He kept it, for life.

The rain had stopped. Curthose and Belleme were told to show him round, an indication at once of the pecking order among his new companions. These two were at the top and roughly equal. This was confirmed as the tour proceeded. Belleme showed no special deference to Curthose the king's son, but Curthose on his side interrupted Belleme's drawl with casual ease whenever he felt like it. They were courteous to the now officially named William Rufus but with an air of secret appraisal. His place in the boys' hierarchy was yet to be decided and he might well have to fight for it. Even at St. Stephen's, hedged by rules of Christian forbearance which wouldn't apply here, he had once or twice had to use his fists to prove that he couldn't be bullied.

Westminster itself was interesting and unexpected. On the way over the Channel, questioning his escort, he had somehow got the impression that it was a single huge building, like a castle. But this old palace built by Edward the Confessor was more like a haphazardly arranged small town, with buildings dotted about anyhow within the containing wall. They stood at odd angles to each other, some of stone, with slate roofs dully gleaming under the grey sky, some of timber, roofed with dripping thatch. The dormitory where the boys slept, from which the tour started after he had changed his clothes, was a fair walk from the chief hall. 'When it's raining, we have to sprint,' said Curthose.

Much of the palace was very old and his guides took turns in telling him stories, mostly lurid, of its past history. There had apparently been any amount of murders in Westminster and Belleme claimed solemnly that the place was haunted by a number of restless ghosts.

Trumpets eventually called them back to the main hall where he found that the others would have to serve their seniors at dinner before being allowed any themselves. 'You can be excused this first day, William, but in future . . .'

'I'll join in with the others if I may, sir.'

'Good,' said the knight-instructor, and handed him over to a steward. Serving at table proved more nerve-racking than he expected, however, for he did not know the routine or the people. He had served the monks in the refectory at St. Stephen's but that had been on a much smaller scale. He tried to do as he was told but soon proved conclusively that at St. Stephen's he hadn't been told nearly enough. He apologised for his errors ('Put the napkin over the *other* arm, boy, and I hope you know you've just spilt gravy on the Earl of Shrewsbury.') and found to his annoyance that the stammer he had developed when he first left home and went to St. Stephen's, but thought he had mastered, had now reappeared. He was tired, and hungry.

The boys dined afterwards, separately. Britnoth joined them with Henry and Gilbert Clare. They had also helped with the serving, and more competently than Rufus. Gilbert irritatingly insisted on telling the others about the incident with the gravy. 'I *only* spill things on important p . . . people,' said Rufus as crushingly as possible, and applied himself ravenously to the food. It was excellent, especially to a monastically educated palate. The bread was white, the roast meat fragrant with thyme; there was an exotically flavoured stew, and beans in a sharp sauce. They were just leaving the table, and he was feeling better, when a manservant he recognised as the one who had brought him a change of clothes, arrived in haste. 'You're wanted in the boys' quarters, my lord William. I believe it is to try on some mail for arms practice tomorrow. Do you know the way?'

Rufus nodded and the manservant, clearly concerned with some further errand, hurried away. 'Haven't you got your own mail?' Henry asked. It was the first time he had spoken to Rufus since their initial encounter. He had spent most of the meal staring at him as if trying to decide what he was.

'Yes, but I'm g . . . growing out of it.' Inwardly, he cursed the stammer. 'I said so on the way here. It must have been r . . . reported.' He made purposefully for the door, to counteract the bad impression of his hesitant speech.

Belleme said: 'I hope for your sake you soon g . . . grow out of that stutter too.' The two Hughs laughed sycophantically. Rufus, deciding not to hear, marched on. The others drifted after him. They passed into the vestibule, torchlit now that night had fallen. A cold wind blew in through the outer door.

'Chilly,' remarked Curthose. 'I think we'll stay here. If you know how to get there, off you go. We'll see you when you get back. There's usually music in the hall before bed.'

They had halted, letting him walk on. The outer door stood half-open. He stopped dead on the threshold. In front of him, the courtyard steps went down into nothingness.

He stood still, peering into the dark. There were in fact torches fixed here and there on the walls of various buildings. But the pools of light they cast were isolated and in between them were gulfs of blackness as deep as oceans. At St. Stephen's he had feared the dark but never had to challenge it. Never, that he could recall, had he had to face a dark room, an unlit courtyard, alone.

Plenty of people, all ages and both sexes, were afraid of the dark. But among boys, it was a conventional pretext for jeers. They looked out for it and pounced on it. He had claimed he remembered the way but he had forgotten that it was now night. His companions had not forgotten. Behind him, Belleme laughed softly and little Henry giggled. 'What's the matter?' asked Curthose. 'Not scared of the bogles, surely? Want someone to come with you?'

He was a king's son. He must prove himself.

'D . . . don't be a fool. I was just wondering if I really d . . . did recall the way. I've got it now. No, I don't need anyone to show me, thanks.' He reached up, snatched a torch out of a wall bracket and stumped off down the steps.

Turn left, he thought, forcing himself to call to mind the route he had memorised earlier. Cross the courtyard, go under an arch and across a bigger courtyard, and he would be there. Look for landmarks in the pools of torchlight, not for weirdly shaped shadows, and don't think about Brother Philip's stories, or the earthbound ghosts of Belleme's tales this afternoon.

There had been an ugly story of a girl walled up with her baby, whose ghost still sometimes cried for help . . .

He was a king's son. The Conqueror's son.

He could keep one hand on his belt knife, for reassurance.

24

He had sensed his erstwhile companions drawing into a huddle as he set out, probably to laugh at him. Let them laugh. He held the torch high and it shone back from a wind-rippled puddle. He veered left, angling the torch to make sure that he was now walking parallel with the side of the hall. The arch loomed up, yawning darkly, and a cresset over a nearby doorway shot his shadow grotesquely out ahead. He wished his shoes didn't echo so much.

The flagstones of the next courtyard swam up as he passed through the arch. In a tall building on his right, lamps had been lit, and two unshuttered windows, close together like yellow eyes, watched him pass.

Somewhere in the distance there was music but immediately around him, all was still. He saw a faint gleam ahead, which must be a candle or a lamp in the building for which he was making. But in the shadows under the wall on his right, somebody was whispering.

He glanced sideways, hesitating, and a thin, quavering wail rose in the air, stopping him short, the hairs prickling on the back of his neck.

He froze, his eyes moving this way and that. He moved the torch in a slow circle, to see all round him. The wail was repeated, this time ahead of him, between himself and the safety of his quarters. He drew two deep, slow breaths and took a step forward and as he did so, into the wavering edge of the torchlight came three white things, bending and swaying and ululating.

His heart gave a single terrified lurch and his mouth went instantly dry and then he knew what he must do. Raising his hands high, the torch blazing and sparkling in one and the fingers of the other curved like talons, pulling the worst face he could manage and hoping that the torchlight would do it justice, he uttered an eldritch yell and sprang at the largest spectre.

At the last moment, he turned the talons into a fist and it contacted something satisfyingly solid, producing an entirely human yelp. The three spectres wheeled and fled, vanishing at once into the deeper darkness of the courtyard's remote corners, except for the smallest one which unfortunately fell over its shroud. As Rufus seized hold of it, it began to shriek piercingly.

25

'What's this uproar?' The monkish tutor, Britnoth, was suddenly there, brandishing a torch of his own, shining it in Rufus' face and then on the sheet-entangled entity on the ground. 'What in the world do you think you're doing, Henry?' There were more whispers in the shadows and the sound of swift feet retreating. Somewhere, a door banged. Britnoth did not seem to notice, which was understandable, since Henry was still screeching like a damned soul and Rufus only heard the sounds because he was listening for them. Britnoth picked Henry up and half-patted, half-shook him. Henry, still loudly bawling, pointed at Rufus. 'It's all right, it's only me. You tried to scare me so I scared you back,' said Rufus impatiently.

'Tried to . . . oh, I see, he's dressed up as a ghost. Henry, be quiet! Come with me,' said Britnoth, and bore Henry off indoors.

In well-lit and familiar surroundings, Henry, though shiny-eyed and red in the face, stopped screaming. 'Now explain yourself,' said Britnoth to him sternly. 'Trying to frighten your brother, is that it? And ruining a good linen sheet while you were about it?'

'It wasn't only me,' said Henry, hiccuping. 'And he attacked me!'

'You fell over. I was trying to grab one of the others,' said Rufus. 'I can guess who they were.' He was fairly sure that he had recognised Belleme's voice in the wailing and suspected that it was Belleme with whom his fist had made contact. It must have left a mark; he would know tomorrow. He looked at Britnoth. 'The older ones made him do it; don't be angry with him. It doesn't matter. It was just a silly joke. I didn't mind.' No one must ever know about the very real terror he had known in the dark courtyard. 'I'm sorry I gave you a fright,' he said to his small brother. 'Look, I think I'm going to ride horses tomorrow. I'll take you up in front of me for a gallop. I expect they'll let me. Would you like that?'

Henry nodded. Britnoth said approvingly: 'That is a proper spirit. We can't have all you brothers at odds with each other before you've been here five minutes.'

Rufus grinned and held out his hand to Henry. 'I know I'm not Richard. I'm sorry about him, too. But . . . friends?'

26

'Friends!' agreed Henry and bounced off the couch where Britnoth had placed him, chanting: 'Silly old Curthose! Silly old Curthose!'

'Yes, isn't he?' said Rufus, under Britnoth's interested eye. He put Henry back on the couch and solemnly shook his brother's small hand, complete with the mud and grit it had picked up in the courtyard. Henry, unwittingly, had just confirmed his private guess that Curthose had been the third spectre and that the scheme had probably been his, rather than Belleme's.

It was the start of a pattern. In it, outsiders such as Belleme (for all his power and ruthlessness) and Gilbert Clare who bit people (for all his uncertain temper) would be supporters, catalysts, stalking horses but never more than that, always subsidiary elements in a design whose centre was a fraternal triangle.

Three

Brotherly Love
1078

In the summer of 1078, Henry was rising ten. Far away in Normandy on the smallholding of Aix, Peter Longshanks was worrying over the future of his younger boy, Ralph. Rufus had turned eighteen and no one now played tricks on him.

The Conqueror himself came to watch Rufus' first testing in arms. He saw his third son unhorse the future Count of Meulan with a lance, be unhorsed by Curthose and then pick himself up to try again and this time keep his saddle though Curthose won on points. As Rufus was six years younger than his opponent, this was highly creditable. To the friends who had accompanied him, the Conqueror said: 'He'll do.'

And: 'Reckon you'll do,' said the beefy FitzHamon between gusts of laughter after an incident in which, on account of a dispute over the ownership of an ornamental dagger which had formed part of a complicated barter transaction, Curthose and Belleme lay in wait for Rufus and dumped him in a pond.

The next day, Rufus waited in ambush on the roof of a barn and slid down the thatch to land on Curthose's shoulders as he rode past, carrying him straight out of the saddle to the ground and winding him so that Rufus without difficulty could lug his elder brother to a convenient horse trough and duck him.

Belleme, who had been riding just behind Curthose, chased the loose horse and brought it back. Its owner, massaging bruises and wiping water out of his eyes, thanked him. But Rufus, seemingly indifferent to any bruises of his own, eyed Belleme in a way which said *you next* so unmistakably, that Belleme judged it politic to apologise for the pond.

He was building a reputation as one who if attacked would hand you back your investment, doubled. His peers said – after a time it was with affection – that young Red wasn't frightened of anything.

It gave him confidence, as did his sound health. He needed that. People said of Rufus that 'he would do' and 'wasn't easy to frighten' but they never said 'he's handsome'. He was not.

He would have liked to be. But comb his ginger hair as sleekly as he would, and dress as richly as he might, he would never attain the good looks which Curthose took for granted and Henry was already developing. Their skins tanned smoothly in summer; his turned ridiculously red. They had dark eyes with depth; his were 'like water', Henry once commented with the tactlessness of immaturity, not intending to wound, and they were trimmed, moreover, with white eyelashes.

None of the trio would ever be tall but Rufus knew early on that he was the worst proportioned of them all, too broad for his height, almost barrel-shaped.

'But you just remember,' said Meulan (who wasn't handsome either), 'no one's going to laugh at you once you've knocked them off a horse, and no one of common birth is going to laugh anyway. If you're a knight, even a landless one, churls have to respect you and if you're a king's son, even knights have to.'

'So I should hope,' said Belleme, strolling up and joining in. 'Especially the churls. Imagine the chaos if we weren't here to control things. They're there to do our bidding so don't ever let one get away with impertinence. *Has* anyone been impertinent?'

'Not yet,' said Rufus.

'If any villein offered insult to me.' said Belleme, 'I should . . .' He enlarged. They listened, impressed by his inventiveness. Henry came up with little Gilbert Clare and listened to Gilbert Clare make the only comment, a suggested improvement on one of Belleme's more sordid recommendations. 'Dear saints,' said Meulan, surveying him, 'listen to the child. And he looks like a cherub.' After which, the conversation dissolved into laughter.

Curiously, the Conqueror never gibed at Rufus about his personal appearance, reserving that for Curthose. Rufus was grateful. He had admired his father from the beginning and by the time he was eighteen, he had come to love him. It was for the Conqueror that he strove to be always the foremost in the charge when they practised war tactics, the strongest swordarm, the longest-enduring through the struggle and swelter of their exercises.

From his father and from the knightly instructors whom the Conqueror chose, he learned that it was his duty as a king's son to be the most relentless foe in the siege, the most magnanimous when an enemy sued for peace, the swiftest to the aid of any vassal who called on him. And that he must never give his word unless he meant to keep it and that then he must keep it until he died.

The tales of valour with which his instructors illustrated their lessons kindled his powers of fantasy in a more healthy way than Brother Philip had, but very strongly. His imagination was more vigorous than most of his associates knew. He *saw* the world that he inhabited, in his mind, as peopled with splendid figures such as his father, all moving about within a golden globe of light, the radiance of nobility.

Occasionally, when wine had loosened his normally hesitant tongue, he would try to put this vision into words and his friends did not laugh, for their own vision of the world was similar if fainter (except for Belleme, whose mental world was full of images of torment and faces twisted in terror or agony).

But of the horrifying darkness which surrounded this radiant globe, the blackness which engulfed people when they died, and spawned the monsters which haunted his worst dreams, he did not speak. They *would* have laughed then.

Certainly Curthose would. Curthose occasionally allowed jealousy to surface. 'Why does Father sneer at me and never at you?' he said once, resentfully.

'By the time I came along, you'd got him used to stumpy sons. I was less of a shock,' said Rufus, and prepared to dodge a punch or parry a retort.

Curthose, however, only shook his head. 'No. I've never been what he expected. Only I've never been able to work out what it is he expects. But if I had,' said Curthose discontentedly, 'he'd let me hold land in my own

30

right now. God knows I'm of age. One of these days, he and I are going to quarrel badly.'

In the summer of 1078, they did.

The root of the quarrel lay far from England, in Anjou, to the south of Maine. Where tradition, handed down for years after the event, insisted firmly and hilariously that the disgraceful events of that summer owed their origins to Fulk the Surly of Anjou's bunions.

That was certainly over-simplification. Maine – from the Conqueror's point of view – was consistently troublesome, full of disobedient vassals who at frequent intervals embattled themselves in their castles and refused to acknowledge his lordship or send him their dues. Matters were due to come to a head again soon, anyway.

But chance, the flick of a cosmic penny, decreed that the precipitating agent in 1078 should be a restless and hard-ridden horse stepping heavily on one of Fulk's deformed feet as he dismounted after a day's hunting.

Fulk was not then very old but he was far gone in misanthropy already, with the humourless facial lines and grainy skin of a much older man with a lifetime's practice in sullenness behind him.

He was not immune to passion; in fact, he was susceptible and had a wife whom he had married for desire as much as for her dowry. Unfortunately, his wife, who was a pretty, cuddlesome thing with small gleaming teeth and a sharp wit like a kitten's claws, had not desired him in return, had been married to him against her will and never changed her attitude. Seeing Fulk limp as he entered the hall, she exercised her wit at his expense with an unfeeling remark about waddling ducks.

Fulk said that if she were any sort of a wife, she would bring him hot water with salt and medicinal herbs in it, to bathe his feet.

His wife said that she was not a servant, but with frigid courtesy called a page and passed the instruction on.

Fulk said further derogatory things about his lady's short-comings as a wife and the lady complained about his bad temper. Old scores were dragged up and the quarrel grew furious. The page brought the footbath and Fulk's

31

wife, making a distasteful face at the sight of her husband's admittedly unlovely feet, withdrew to her private bower, her maidens and her embroidery. Fulk soaked his feet, fulminating, until an unexpected guest was announced.

The guest was a man called Count Rotrou of Perche, which was a Norman province adjacent to Maine. Rotrou was bound on a visit to relatives in Anjou and was seeking a night's lodging. In the course of the evening they spent together, Fulk, directing his unassuaged rage into the channel which most conveniently presented itself, became bad-tempered about politics.

He spoke disparagingly of King William who in his capacity as lord of Normandy was Fulk's rival for Maine, and demanded to know why Rotrou remained faithful to him. 'His tide's ebbing in Maine. He's in England too much. Absentee landlords never prosper. I could take the place over tomorrow if it wasn't for the likes of you, sitting next door waiting to rush in on its behalf. What do you get out of it?'

'Peace and quiet,' said Rotrou, who was not a bellicose man.

'What kind of talk do you call that? I'm talking about real rewards. Land, wealth! I'd see anyone was paid who'd as much as promise to keep his nose out of Maine while I move in. As for anyone who'd actually put men at my disposal, he could expect riches. Can't you see,' said Fulk with a snort of angry laughter, 'that I'm making you an offer?'

If Rotrou agreed, he thought, Maine would fall into his hands like an apple in October. And his wife wouldn't dare sneer at the feet, however noisesome and misshapen, of a man who'd taken a province away from mighty William. She'd kneel and kiss them.

She'd fall in love with him, at last.

He bribed and bullied halfway through the night. And when his visiting was done, Rotrou went home, formally switched his allegiance to Fulk, and demonstrated the same by sending fifteen fully accoutred knights to Anjou.

William, with an army, was across the Channel in what to Fulk and Rotrou seemed only ten minutes.

*

'Only,' grumbled Henry, 'when are we going to do any fighting? We ought to have seen blood by now. Father said we'd learn from being at a real war. *What* war? He's just brought his army across to scare the enemy, if you ask me. He spends all his time in council trying to negotiate a peace.' Henry, though young, was politically sophisticated. The situation annoyed him but he understood it. 'This place,' he complained, 'is so *boring*.'

The remark was justifiable. The town of L'Aigle, where the Conqueror had grimly planted himself just to the north of Rotrou's territory, Perche, was small and dull. Even the castle was small so that as men came in to join him, the Conqueror had moved himself and his immediate entourage out, and into lodgings in the town. As Henry had observed, he was spending much time shut away in council meetings from which his sons were excluded, which meant that they were left to their own devices.

Curthose, who considered himself more than mature enough to join the councils, and was accordingly offended, had attempted to retrieve his slipping dignity by forming a miniature court of his own, consisting mainly of the older boys. He had withdrawn to separate lodgings and was rigorously keeping his juniors at bay.

Which at least offered opportunities for diversion.

'We could go round and see Curthose again,' Rufus suggested.

'The last time I went, he said he'd skin me alive if I annoyed him again,' said Henry. 'You'd think his rotten lodgings were a palace. It's only a merchant's house. He's just a show-off.' In his small sunburnt face, the brown eyes lit up with mischief. 'Yes, let's go round there and irritate him *properly*,' he said.

It was afternoon and in a sky of intense continental blue, the sun was blazing. Their father was in council yet again and everyone else was apparently asleep. The merchant Cauchois' house, where Curthose was staying, was only a hundred yards away along the dusty street. The gate was languidly ajar and within it was a small paved court with a fishpool. Beyond this was the house. It had a terrace and here their brother, on a high-backed settle which had been dragged out of doors, was snoozing, chest bared to the sun. His host, Messire Cauchois, solid and bald, scalp flaring scarlet in the heat, was seated at a table, playing a very slow game of backgammon with Belleme. Others of Curthose's circle lounged or sprawled on the warm stone of the terrace itself. A second small table held a jug, and goblets.

'Oh, no,' said Curthose, opening one eye at the sound of their footsteps. 'You're not here. I'm hallucinating. It's the sun.'

'We're come to see you,' said Rufus unnecessarily. Cauchois glanced round, decided to let the Conqueror's offspring sort out their own disagreements and turned back to the game.

'I thought,' said Curthose, 'that I'd make it clear that you weren't wanted. I'm too lazy to throw you out today but behave yourselves if you don't want me to wake up. You may have a drink.'

Henry was already inspecting the jug. 'It's fruit juice,' he informed Rufus. 'Would you believe it? Curthose our big brother is drinking apple juice like a lady.'

'Shut up,' said Curthose, 'and sit down.'

'My game,' said Belleme. Cauchois, who had let it happen because he was distracted, said irritably: 'I've got dice and some more backgammon sets upstairs. I suggest our visitors find a game to occupy them. Go up and help yourselves, Messires. You know the way. You've been here before. Stay out of my bedroom next door.'

'And off this terrace. Stay up there,' said Curthose.

The staircase led up from the end of the balcony. Rufus and Henry, who had indeed seen the upper room before, clattered up enthusiastically. It adjoined Cauchois' bedroom and had once been his wife's solar but since her death it had become a storage and amusement room. Its wallhangings depicted lively hunting scenes and there was a table with a backgammon board let into it. Chests contained an enthralling mixture of old clothes, dog leashes, falconry tackle, tallysticks and the like, and a tall cupboard held a fascinating miscellany of backgammon and chess sets in gleaming wood and walrus ivory, several pairs of dice, a box of polished shells which were of no apparent use but looked and felt pleasing and squeaked agreeably when rubbed together, some spare candlesticks and some earthenware bowls in colourful designs. Because they had been told not to, they poked inquisitive noses into Cauchois' bedroom but found nothing interesting there beyond the evidence that his servants were well-trained. The bed was made up neatly and a silver water ewer already stood in place beside it. They wandered back to the cupboard.

'It's too hot for chess or backgammon,' said Rufus. 'How about dice? They're all torpid on that terrace so we may as well play here. What shall we use for stakes?'

This was a problem. After some thought, they produced a silver penny, a brooch, an ornamented belt and a gold ring between them, and laid them out on the table. Henry said his shoes had cost a lot and offered them but Rufus said they wouldn't fit him and he didn't propose to set up a footwear stall in L'Aigle market. 'Let's start with my penny against your brooch,' he said.

Half an hour later, when the stakes had moved back and forth between them with a pendulum-like regularity for some time, and each had ritualistically accused the other of cheating but not bothered to make an issue of it because of the heat, they tacitly broke off and roamed to one of the small arched windows. Nothing had changed below. 'How scarlet Messire Cauchois' head is,' Rufus whispered. 'I bet it's sore. He must long to pour cold water over it.'

There was a pause.

They gazed at each other. For a moment, despite the differences in age and feature and colouring, their faces were stamped with the selfsame diabolical intent. They were visibly brothers.

'There's water in the bedchamber,' said Rufus.

'I dare you.'

'Let's throw dice for it. Lowest score does the deed.'

'Done.'

The dice they were using were wooden, painted red, with white spots. 'Me first. I thought of it and I'm the elder,' Rufus said. 'Double six. That's it. You can't beat that.'

'Do it properly! I want my throw.' Henry joggled the

dice in their cup and tossed them on to the table. 'See? Another double six. Do we throw again?'

'There're bowls in that cupboard. A bowl of water each? Fetch that ewer.'

A moment later, the peaceful scene on the terrace was shattered as a double cascade of water from the windows above curved through the air to drench not only Cauchois' bald head but the backgammon game, Robert of Belleme, the slumbering Curthose and little Gilbert Clare, who was allowed in Curthose's coterie because (according to Henry) he was such a crawler.

Cauchois swore and mopped his head but did not seem disposed to retaliate. Curthose and Belleme, on the other hand, leapt up with a simultaneous yell. 'It's those young devils upstairs!' Belleme glared at Curthose as though the outrage were his fault. 'They think they're above you and not only because they've climbed a staircase, by the look of it.'

'Rufus and Henry?' Curthose spun round, craning his neck. 'Listen, you up there . . .'

'Quick, Rufus, while his mouth's open.'

A second stream, aimed expertly at Curthose's protesting upturned face, described a glittering arc. Indignant speech changed to wild spluttering, while Curthose's fashionable hose darkened with wet. Meulan, propped on an elbow on the terrace, exclaimed: 'I'd get them for that!' and beside him, FitzHamon laughed. Cauchois, alarmed, began to say: 'Just a moment . . .' but Curthose, shaking his fist at the upper window, was already making for the stairs. The others followed. Cauchois, exclaiming anxiously, brought up the rear.

Upstairs, Rufus and Henry took up hasty battle stations behind the table and used what was left of the water to hurl at the foe as Curthose and his companions burst in. Then they hurled the earthenware bowls and the silver ewer. Curthose, declaring his intention to cripple Rufus for life and wallop Henry's behind so that he'd eat his meals standing for a fortnight, braved the missiles, flung the table aside and closed in. Belleme and little Gilbert joined in. The rest, half-laughing, crowded at the door to watch.

After that it was a fight, an explosion of fists, knees, feet, elbows, oaths. Gilbert Clare, who retained some childish proclivities along with his angelic appearance, sank his teeth into somebody. Rufus hauled Curthose off a kicking, screeching Henry and was instantly grabbed by Belleme and thrown back against the wall. Lowering his head, he charged like a bull and drove Belleme back across the room to collide with the cupboard, which burst open, showering its contents round them. Belleme hit out. Rufus punched him back and the blow went through Belleme to send the cupboard crashing sideways. It caught in the wall-hangings and brought them down on top of the fight. Simultaneously battling Belleme and the enswathing folds of tapestry, Rufus heard as if from afar Cauchois' voice shouting to someone to *fetch their father*.

The servant thus despatched was lucky, arriving at William's lodgings just as the council finished. Brought up short by crossed pikes at the gate, he gasped out that Duke William's sons were at Cauchois' house, killing each other, and it seemed that William was with him instantly. The duke's long legs outstripped him on the way back and the uproar was still in full flower when William raced, three at a time, up the stairs to deal with it.

The scene was now one of dramatic devastation, the furniture in ruins and the combatants fighting each other not only with fists and feet but with candlesticks and wrenched-off tablelegs, tripping and swearing amid the rucked remains of the tapestry and the scattered hazards of backgammon counters and little shiny shells. There was a good deal of blood about, from an assortment of injuries. FitzHamon, who had been in the crowd of onlookers at first, was now in the melee, having been hit by accident and lost his temper. Meulan had been drawn in too, and his sharp nose was streaming scarlet.

The duke opened his mouth to roar. As he did so, he saw his son Rufus barge a shoulder into Belleme and then the situation switched in an instant from the merely violent to the potentially deadly as Belleme wrenched out his dagger, the first to draw steel. Rufus' eyes widened and then with a crackling surge of energy (the kind you sweated to teach your sons to produce and when you finally got it you boasted about them for days), he sprang, tore the dagger out of its owner's hand and hurled it accurately through the nearest window. It splashed into the pond below to scatter frightened fish. That was enough. 'Stop!' bellowed Duke William, in the voice that never went unheeded.

They froze, struck into an instantaneous, gory tableau. 'What the devil do you think you're doing? Messire Cauchois, my sincere apologies. Curthose, you are the senior. What is all this about?'

Explanations came tumbling and not only from Curthose. The duke's black eyebrows rose as the facts emerged. 'All this . . .' he gestured at the wrecked room '. . . for a splash of water? And who do you suggest should compensate Messire Cauchois?'

'It wasn't just a splash of water,' said Curthose furiously.

'No? Then what was it, pray?'

'It's what was behind it.' Curthose glared at his younger brothers. 'They have no respect. I'm their elder and supposed to be your heir but they have no respect. They started it. Well, let them compensate Messire Cauchois. I can't. What with?' demanded Curthose, and his eyes met his father's with a sulky defiance which had to do with a dispute quite unconnected with a splash of water or even the pretensions of a couple of younger brothers who didn't know their place.

'You attacked *us*!' With a defiance equal to his brother's, shaking all over and stammering with rage, Rufus exploded in his turn. 'You'd have thought we'd thrown b . . . boiling lead over you instead of w . . . water, the way you came at us. It was nothing but a prank. We didn't want all . . . all this!' He waved an arm at the surrounding mayhem, a stocky, defensive boy, crimson with exertion and heat and violent feeling.

'I had provocation!' Curthose flung back at him. He turned to his father. 'Well, are you going to deal with them for this? Or just say it doesn't matter and make me look a fool again?'

'Again?' The black eyebrows went up still higher.

'Yes, again! They despise me! And whose fault is that? I

can't expect them to look up to me, can I, when I'm the eldest son but I haven't as much as a beanfield to call my own. I'm your heir but I live on your charity. I'm even shut out of councils though I've been a man for years.' There was a silence. 'You despise me yourself, don't you?' said Curthose at last. He sounded, incredibly, near to tears. 'You always have. Always sneering at me, calling me Shortlegs. I ask you again, Father, are you going to deal with them for this? They haven't even apologised!'

Sheer weariness unexpectedly descended on Duke William. What did one marry and raise up sons for, he wondered? They fought each other and their own sire for power, like young wild stallions. Vassals who were no kin to you could be more reliable than your own relatives. Sons or brothers, they were as bad as each other. (He had a half-brother, Odo, whom he had left in England to guard his back but who would assuredly stab him in it one day, when it looked advantageous.) Now there was this. 'Rufus,' he said. 'Henry. Apologise if you please. My sons should be on good terms with each other.'

Rufus shook a vigorous head. 'No. I would have at first but not now, not after all that about respect. We're his brothers, not dust under his feet.' He glanced at Cauchois. 'I'll apologise to you. But not to Curthose.'

'Come.' William's voice was persuasive and even unhappy. One was vulnerable to one's children. Men he had defeated at war, whose limbs he had lopped, would not have believed their ears. 'It is very proper to apologise to Messire Cauchois and I shall myself see that he is recompensed. But you must also set yourself right with your brother, both you and Henry. And you, Robert, must accept the apology. That's an order.'

There was a fiery pause. 'Very well,' said Rufus at length. 'Sorry, Robert. Come on, Henry, say it too.'

'Sorry,' said Henry, as one who recites a lesson.

'Robert,' said the duke. 'Rufus is offering you his hand.'

'I can see.' Curthose looked at the extended hand and knocked it aside. 'So it doesn't matter.' His voice shook. 'It was just a drop of water and it doesn't matter. I told you why it matters but you never listen. It's the insult, what they must think of me before they could behave like that, but you won't see, will you? I'm your eldest son but I've *nothing*.' His head came up. 'Well, that's it. What you won't give, I'll take. I've waited long enough. I'm old enough to have made friends of my own, Father, perhaps you didn't know? There are plenty of men who don't care for you much, or the way you treat your sons, and they aren't all paupers!'

'*You* threaten *me*?' William roared. Conciliation vanished as if it had never been.

'I'm saying goodbye to you,' said Curthose. He glanced round. 'Anyone's welcome to come with me except my brothers.' He marched across the room and tramped noisily down the stairs. As if released from captivity, three or four of his friends slid away from where they had placed themselves against the walls, and followed.

'Where's he going?' asked Henry.

'Not far,' said William with a snort. 'He won't go far. You'd better set to and clear this mess up. And you, Rufus.' He glared at his second son, who was still flushed and somewhat shaky. 'Calm yourself. What's the matter with you? You've given your temper a good gallop. That's enough.'

It was one of the few times when William of Normandy was in error. He did not know it, but he had reached the time when his elder sons at least were beginning to grow beyond him. He had misinterpreted Rufus' state of mind altogether. As for Curthose, it was two years before peace was made between him and William, and it was William who had to do the making.

Four

Wild Love
1079

The troubles of that alien Norman, their king, did not interest the inhabitants of Chenna's Tun near Winchester, or the neighbouring communities of Truham and Minstead.

They had their own preoccupations, some of which stemmed from certain laws lately imposed upon their district, which was in the middle of what William called his New Forest and had been made subject to the full rigour of his game laws.

Other troubles sprang from the wet, raw winter which set in early in the October of 1078 and was still drearily in force the following April.

But the May Eve of that year was mild and clear, arousing hopes of betterment. There was an atmosphere about the three communities that day, an undercurrent of restless excitement. As evening drew on, people came often to the doors of their wood and wattle cottages, to see how near darkness was. Suppers were prepared, but they were small and eaten quickly.

In Minstead, fourteen-year-old 'Ditha could not eat her beans and rye bread though her mother tried to persuade her and her grandmother, who had a nutcracker chin and the most outspoken sense of humour for miles, recommended her to 'stoke your fires well, wench, you'll need them'. Her father was silent, leaving her to the women. Once, his mother-in-law looked at him sharply and said: 'Perk up, lad, you're not about to be bereaved.'

'Ain't I?' he said shortly.

In Truham – which was not a village but a scattered group of smallholdings – a garrulous woman paused from sweeping her floor to say: 'It'll be grand knowing our daughter's there but you be careful this time, old man. That first child of hers is that sickly and I reckon I know why. It's because . . .'

'That's the fourth time you've said as much. And it's the third time you've swept that danged floor.'

41

'I can't keep still, waiting.'

'Can't keep your tongue still, neither.'

'You're as restless as a hare in March yourself,' said his wife, chuckling, and went to the door yet again, still carrying her broom, to look at the sky as the sun went down behind the forest. The fan of a great elm, the tall spikes of fir trees, were outlined in black against burning gold and warm saffron. 'How long till we can start?' she said softly.

Minstead was the largest of the three communities, but in certain respects Chenna's Tun was the most important, and knew it. The Tun lay in a wide clearing, with a stream curving round the northern edge of its two fields. On one side of the stream stood four small dwellings and their outhouses. On the other side was a house somewhat larger although similar in fashion to the rest, with a couple of barns of its own.

In one of the smaller dwellings, the young woman whose mother in Truham had just spoken of her looked worriedly at the baby girl coughing on her cot. 'I know Goda's staying to see to the little ones since it's the wrong time for her to go to the Wood, but I don't like leaving her.'

'There's always things folk don't like about these nights,' said her husband. 'But it's the friction strikes the flint, they say.' Like the woman in Truham, he pushed open the door to look at the flaring western sky. 'I hope that there's a good omen,' he said. 'We need one.'

Across the stream in the bigger house, Old Chenna, the head of the village, although not grand enough to call himself its lord, chaffed his son and said to the young man who was their guest: 'It's none so often we have a stranger who's also a friend with us on these nights. It's good. You're welcome.'

In difficult English, for he was a Norwegian, travelling alone through England (for what purpose no one ever knew), the young man said: 'What would you do – no, have done – if I were not a friend, as you put it?'

'Turned churlish and sent you to the priest at Minstead for a night's lodging,' Chenna told him.

In Minstead, a blind cripple in one of the humbler

42

houses sat mumbling and monotonously cursing by the fire, because he knew that tonight he would be alone and he was at once jealous and frightened.

And in the priest's house, Father Ilger sat, shutters closed against that majestic sunset, preparing a sermon for the next day, hoping his flock were also decently indoors for the night and knowing perfectly well that they were not.

In the Tun, Old Chenna said: 'Time I was on my way.'

Darkness came. The moon rose, near to the full, turning new thatch from gold to white, and the moist young leaves of the forest to glistening silver.

Under the trees, however, the darkness was intense. The figures in the rough hooded cloaks who now set out from the three communities carried horn lanterns.

The direction they took was southwards; those who lived north of the broad track from Winchester to the coast slipping quietly across it in the moonlight.

North of the road lay the Hoar Woods, tree-grown tracts separated one from another by wide grassy glades or stretches of heath, called Hoar because the trees were so ancient and ivy-enswathed.

But south of the road was a district where the trees were just as old, and grew closely and continuously for miles. The forest here was so deep and tangled that even the Foresters rarely came there. The king's huntsmen beat through it perhaps once in the year, when the king was at Brockenhurst, and charcoal burners used a clearing there occasionally; that was all. The tracks, such as they were, were made by deer.

On one such track the hooded figures now moved, in twos and threes, and single file. They went, however, with more boldness than they could have mustered on most nights of the year. This night, they were privileged and need not fear the stealthy rustlings in the undergrowth, or the enmity of the non-human sentience which pervades all woods by right from dusk to sunrise. Tonight, they were themselves a part of that sentience.

They went silently, for the winter rains had soaked last year's fallen leaves, and the leafmould was soft enough to

43

deaden footfalls. They went unhindered for though the path was faint, it had received unobtrusive attention, a bough pruned here, a rough place smoothed there, or a fallen tree shifted out of the way. They walked for a long time. The trysting place was deep in the woods.

The clearing opened up with a flicker of firelight (the ash pile that lay permanently in the charcoal burners' clearing was not all due to the manufacture of charcoal). They were glad to see the fire for despite their conviction that tonight the perils of wolf and demon were withdrawn, the lanterns had done no more than show the ground just before their feet and they had come all that way with invisible companions. It was all too easy to let one's imagination slip, to think that the presence breathing just behind you might, in the darkness, have . . . changed . . . into someone or even some*thing* else.

And yet they had come here to change into other creatures. Where the path entered the clearing, a curious heap of objects lay. As each figure came in, it snuffed its lantern and, stooping, set it down, taking an object from the heap in exchange. Shadowy hands were raised to shadowy heads. And when they walked out into the firelight, their human faces were gone.

They had the heads of goats, crowned with stubby horns. Their eyes gleamed through the slits of leathern masks. As they went, they loosed their cloaks and dropped them. And so came, naked but for the masks, past the fire and to the feet of the Being they had come to worship.

On the far side of the clearing, there was a fallen log of elm, its bark gone years ago, its wood bleached with weather. On it as on a throne, hands at rest on thick thighs, sat their Lord.

His worshippers were as goats. But He, above the throat, was stag. The firelight sparkled on the fourteen ivory points of his spreading antlers. They tipped in acknowledgement as each worshipper kissed his king's bare feet.

Having done so, the worshippers sat on the ground in a semi-circle before Him, old folk and children (though none younger than about ten were present) at the back.

44

When all were seated, the royal Being said: 'Does any challenge the right of the King?'

No one answered. The fire whispered and crackled. At length a second ritual question was asked. 'Before this Feast of Beltane begins, are there any declarations?'

This was answered. 'Bloody forest laws,' said a broad Hampshire voice, oddly mundane in that fugitively lit clearing and in that gathering, which was part human and part beast and yet touched with something that was neither.

'Yes,' said the King, and his voice was deep and hollow. His accent too was rustic but ceremonious phrasing garnered through centuries lent him dignity. 'Not only can we lose eyes or hands for taking a deer. Now we learn that we cannot even fence our land. We shall be hard put to it to defend our corn from the deer this year. As if the weather of the past year were not trouble enough. Let us then dedicate this Beltane to the confounding of the Norman and his laws. The forest has its own powers when it cares to use them. The Norman lost his son in it, five years gone. Remember that while you dance. Remember that while you love. Bring forth the Maiden.'

There was pushing and giggling and a figure was thrust to its feet. The slender childish body under the goat mask was that of a girl. She was shivering.

'There is nothing to fear,' said the King and the smile in his voice drew a ripple of laughter from the rest. 'We all come to it but for monks and nuns and they do not attend Beltane. It's a rare May Eve when the Maiden is truly so but tonight she is and this is her Initiation. And not only hers. Chenna the Young, my one living son, who one day will wear the antlers and sit upon my throne unless my house is cast from it by challenge, also tonight becomes truly one of our company. In recognition of the future, I yield the Maiden to him. Stand up, my son.' A youth rose, nervously. At the back of the assembly, one of the older folk began a low, disturbing rhythm on a drum. 'Where is the goat?' asked the King.

A goat – it was in fact a young kid – was carried over to him. A knife was handed to him. He slew the kid with the blade across its throat and in the blood he baptised Young

45

Chenna and the Maiden. 'Take her hand,' said the King, 'and stand by my throne until the dance begins. I will join it tonight. Remember that our seed renews the corn and that if your union is fruitful then will our fields be blessed, free of blight and ill-weather. May the God of the Wood show us mercy in this year to come. One more thing. We have with us tonight a stranger to our forest though not to our observances. May he too plant a seed and leave something of his strength among us to be nurtured. Herne Huntsman, Lord of the Forest, hear us! Take your places!'

The gathering rose. The King joined it. It formed a double circle, men outermost, facing an inner ring of women. A second drum began. A pipe joined in. The beat quickened. The two circles began to revolve in opposite directions. The music quickened yet more. Someone began to chant: someone else cried out, in excitement. Swifter still grew the rhythm; feet stamped, the dancers sang, flinging out their arms. There was yearning in the music. If any had feared the embrace of a faceless partner, the drums and the dance overcame it now. Moonlight, flamelight, flowed over sliding muscles, sweat-beaded skin, matted chests and polished young breasts, swinging used dugs, shoulders wide or sloping, bellies flat or heavy. The dancers whirled, swaying. Suddenly the circles closed together and became a single ring of wildly gyrating pairs.

The pairing was not quite left to chance. There were evasions and attractions. But there were no rules. Brother had met sister and parent had met child in the dance before now, and would again.

By the throne, Young Chenna caught up the Maiden and half-running, bore her to the clearing's edge where the light did not follow. Still spinning, the other pairs danced away from the firelight also and vanished among the trees.

Round the fire, the old people who no longer danced or coupled exchanged chuckles and a ribald jest or two and set food to cook. The lovers would come back hungry.

Four times a year they met and three times a year the ritual was of this fashion. At these feasts, the act of love was sacred and with whom one coupled did not matter. If children were born of such unions, they were blessed.

46

Tonight, the normal world was left behind. They had withdrawn to their origins when they were part of the wild wood themselves and there were no marriages, only matings.

The Feast of Beltane, 1079, had begun.

Five

Beyond the Curtain
1080

'. . . and so,' said William of Normandy from behind the white-draped table in the hall of Rouen Castle, 'we call on you to rise for a toast. At this Eastertide, the traditional season of peacemaking, our son Robert Curthose has mended his quarrel with us and comes under his father's roof once more in love and amity. We in turn confirm him our firstborn son, heir to our dukedom of Normandy. Raise your goblets.'

He raised his own, to a face as harsh as a hatchet. The assembled guests stood up obediently and drank but few ventured to smile, least of all Robert Curthose.

'Listen to him!' he muttered to Rufus under cover of a minstrel who now stepped forth to sing a syrupy lyric in praise of family solidarity. 'You'd think I'd come bareheaded, suing him for peace. *He* sued *me*. It took,' growled Curthose, 'the King of France, half the Norman baronage and His Holiness the Pope to get me to agree. I fought a battle with Father and personally unhorsed him. And still he sneers! He's even still using that damned nickname.'

'You're saddled with that for life,' said Rufus cheerfully. 'The whole world uses it.' His sympathies were with the duke. What father took kindly to being unceremoniously shoved off his horse by his own son, after all? He also knew how much William had resented having to spend good money buying Rotrou off in order to concentrate on Curthose and the Norman vassals who had regrettably chosen to side with him. Fulk of Anjou, having lost his bid for Rotrou, had withdrawn his threat to Maine but it had been a near thing. 'Once lose territory that used to be yours,' the Conqueror had said to Rufus, on this very subject, 'and your reputation's dented. Every restless lord in your domains will start to wonder how to evade his own obligations. What you have, you must hold.

Never forget it. Believe me, I'll never forget that Curthose endangered that policy for me.'

Yet he had also said to Rufus, earlier that day: 'Be pleasant to your brother. I know you gained a scar fighting against him, and fighting your own brother's a bad way to get your first wound. But he's still your brother, and my son. I want this peace to stick.'

Twelve-year-old Henry, speaking across Rufus, said: 'You hurt Father's feelings, quarrelling with him, Curthose. But he means it when he says he wants to mend things.'

'I know. I said, he sued for peace. I also know why. A rift with me puts him at risk. I took a lot of his vassals with me.'

'He minds about you as well,' said Rufus, and respectful of his father's wishes, he rose as the minstrel finished and proposed a toast of his own, to the future accord of father and son. He was rewarded by a grimly approving glance from William. Belleme, further along the table, murmured: 'Well tried,' in his malicious way, and young Meulan of the bright round eyes and bright front teeth, observed: 'You're an optimist. I give this peace two years at most. If I were you, I'd just enjoy the food and get drunk.'

On the whole, Rufus suspected that this was good advice and he therefore took it although he went on trying, albeit in a manner increasingly fuddled, to make polite conversation to Curthose. As a result, although he could never quite remember afterwards how it came about, he found himself, after the feast, outside, actually arm in arm with Curthose, with Belleme and Meulan on his other side, in the midst of an amiable argument as to whether Henry was or was not old enough to accompany them where they were going.

'No. S'only twelve.' Curthose was fairly drunk, too.

'He can watch, can't he?' said Belleme.

'No, not decent,' said Curthose reprovingly.

Rufus shook a woozy head, remembered that to please his father he ought to side with Curthose and agreed that Henry was too young to go to . . . 'where *are* we going, anyway?'

Belleme answered, but his reply was lost in the clatter as their horses were brought to them. The flank of a horse complete with saddle and stirrup was presented to Rufus. He mounted and rode out of the gate with the others.

It was a mild April dusk with the stars coming out as the sky dimmed between the rooftops. They rode through a number of streets and round several corners and then under an archway into a courtyard where they dismounted and the horses were taken by shadowy, obsequious grooms. Curthose, who seemed to know his way, led them up some steps to a door which he simply pushed open, clearly certain it would not be locked. Inside was a vestibule paved with black and white and lit by candles in what looked like gilded candelabra, attached to walls covered with murals in soft colours, pink and gold and powder blue. Their subjects were explicit. Small lit tapers, also in wall brackets, perfumed the air. The scent was pleasant but obscurely worrying. 'It's sandalwood,' said Curthose, amused, as Rufus' nostrils visibly twitched. 'Exotic, isn't it?' Belleme, who seemed to have been here before as well, went to a small gong which stood upon a table, and sounded it.

A curtain hung across an arched doorway opposite them. The curtain rings rattled and Rufus concluded that he was even more drunk than he thought because the woman who stood there was apparently a giantess and he didn't believe in them.

She was as tall as his father and much fatter. She billowed. Thick plaits of unnaturally black hair hung forward over mountainous shoulders. The latter were clearly visible because although her sanguine-coloured dress swept the floor, its upper regions left astonishing and unconventional acreages of flesh exposed. Her bulging breasts were going to escape from it altogether, at any moment. There was no guessing her age for her large round face was painted, thick as enamel. But there was brown mottling on the backs of the fleshy hands she extended as she came to meet them.

Curthose was introducing those of them who were strangers. The giantess, in a voice that boomed like the gong, was overwhelmed at finding *two* of Duke William's sons in her house. She swept them a colossal curtsey, which put Rufus instantly in mind of an undermined castle wall collapsing.

Rising, she beckoned them to follow her beyond the curtain. Two minutes later they were in a small stuffy

50

chamber with more inflammatory murals, sitting on wide padded couches of a kind he had never seen before.

Two more minutes and they were being introduced to girls. The wine-mist parted. He knew now where he was and why.

If he hadn't been afraid that the others would laugh at him for evermore, he would have leapt to his feet and run.

Girls. He had hardly ever met any. There were few women at court, since his mother was no longer there. Those who were to be found there were mostly humble, maidservants and the like. Like his friends, he had made a few experiments with them, but only because the others did and because they kept boasting about it. He had made two experiments, to be precise, and both had been embarrassing failures. One of the girls was sorry for him and the other had been amused and he didn't know which was worse.

He sat stiffly, still fully clad when the others had cheerfully disrobed and were briskly establishing intimate relations with partners now equally unclothed. Belleme was buried in the cushions with his girl, who was emitting sharp little cries which sounded as though they were more of pain than pleasure, which was probably the case. For Belleme, all his life, the best enjoyment was founded on someone else's suffering.

Meulan was running his hands through the honeycoloured hair of his girl and Curthose had balanced his companion on his knee and was asking where her Madam had got the idea for these couches.

'Pilgrims bring back other things from the Holy Land besides relics,' she told him. 'Folk sit on these in outlandish places and not only sit on them, either.'

'Really? I'm so ignorant, you must show me,' said Curthose, and rolled over on to the couch, taking her with him. Everyone but Rufus seemed perfectly at home. Yes, he said desperately to the young woman who was nestling against him with professional languor, yes, I like you. She felt over-soft – *squashy* was the word that sprang to mind – and what on earth was the blue stuff round her eyes? Curthose would know; he knew all about this sort of thing. He was said to have a regular, well-born mistress already. Belleme's girl suddenly shrieked out loud and the line of his back, just visible amid the cushions, undulated serpentlike as a great shuddering spasm seized him.

Rufus' girl glanced at him sidelong and said encouragingly: 'I think you're nice.'

'Th . . . thank you. What's your name?'

'La Belle.'

'The Beautiful. And it's true,' said Rufus awkwardly, 'but . . .'

'You ain't comfortable,' said La Belle, with perspicacity. 'Some aren't, not when they're among others. You want us to go somewhere by ourselves?'

Rufus nodded. At least, alone with her, he could make a fool of himself without the rest knowing. Even Meulan, who had advanced on his objective more slowly than the others, was now nothing but a pair of briskly rising and falling haunches. He let La Belle take his hand and lead him out.

In private, he felt better. She was kind. She did not show pity, or scorn, or impatience, but gave him skilful help. After all he did not disgrace himself although it was all oddly unreal as if his body were a machine. For La Belle herself he felt only a little gratitude: he had no curiosity or desire for conquest. And she was not deceived. 'You're the duke's son,' she said concernedly, lying at his side. 'I want to look after you right and I don't think you've had your money's worth. Would you like a different girl? I'm fair, maybe you'd like someone dark, or with red hair . . .'

'No, no,' he said hurriedly. 'It isn't that. You're very sweet.' He couldn't say outright that he hadn't the faintest idea what to say to a woman, even her sort of woman, and that every time she looked at him he was sure she was hiding her distaste for his reddened skin and unnatural white eyelashes. He said feebly: 'What if I get you with child?'

'You won't,' she said, amused. 'And if you did, it 'ud be my problem and Madam's. Would you like some wine?'

'Yes.' The wine he had had at the feast was wearing off rapidly and he yearned for its anaesthetic properties. Thank the saints – if there were any saints who protected

52

whores' clients – that the others hadn't witnessed the way she had had to help him. If they had, he would have crawled out of this place on hands and knees and drowned himself in the Seine.

She was ringing a handbell. Presently, robing herself, she answered a tap at the door and spoke softly to someone outside. A few minutes later the tap was repeated and La Belle admitted a boy of about sixteen, with a tray. 'This is Rayner,' she said. 'Rayner, this is my lord William Rufus, son of the Duke. Entertain him for a while. I must leave you for a few moments, I think my lord will excuse me.' She gave Rufus a smile and a curtsey, girdled her robe more firmly about her and was gone. Rayner set the tray on a little table and said: 'This is an unexpected honour. I welcome the chance of meeting you, my lord.' His accent was more educated than La Belle's. 'May I pour for you?' he enquired.

Rufus nodded and watched as Rayner filled a goblet. The boy had graceful movements, which looked as though he had practised them for years. Just, Rufus thought fascinatedly, as a young knight might practise swordstrokes. He was self-possessed and very clean. His brown hair was longer than most men wore it but it was glossy as though he washed and brushed it often. Within his smooth red wool tunic and his russet hose, the lines of his body were hard and male.

He handed a goblet to Rufus with a little bow. The fingers round the goblet stem were long, with a boy's broad knuckles. Rufus took the wine and Rayner's released hand went up to rest on the other's naked shoulder. In the act of drinking, Rufus stopped.

It was what he had wanted, without knowing it. This hard body, this smooth flat chest devoid of squashiness, these deeper accents, speaking to him in a way he could understand because the mind behind them was masculine like his own. It was a kind of homecoming, reviving memories of Brother Philip. But Rayner, in his youth and candour, had more to offer than Philip. He could initiate without patronising.

And he knew more, far more, than Philip had. He knew all the gates to Paradise, it seemed.

Afterwards they lay talking. Rayner was interested in the details of the war against Curthose, able to ask the right questions. Rufus was emboldened to ask questions too. 'Rayner, how did you come here? Where were you born?'

'God knows, I don't,' said the boy casually. 'In Maine, I think. I was found there when I was tiny, crying in a street in Le Mans, lost. There was fighting going on at the time. There often is, in Maine. Some people took me in. Then Madam came by. She travels a lot, looking for likely girls and boys. I think the people I was with sold me. I must have been about seven by then. I can just remember coming here. She had me educated and I used to put out seat cushions and whatnot and run errands till I was old enough to earn. She's been good to me; I've had a chance to save. That's important. One can't work for ever. One's youth doesn't last. But if I go on as I am, I'll be able to open my own place one day.'

'Tell me,' said Rufus, aware that the wine was talking but unable to stop it, 'am I attractive?'

Or am I only a job of work? He wished he hadn't asked Rayner about his past. Till then, they had been talking like friends who had chosen each other out of all the world. Now Rayner, with that word *working* and that other, mercenary, little word, *save*, had spoilt it. And didn't even seem to know there was anything to spoil. 'Well?' he demanded, suddenly aggressive.

'My dear!' said Rayner, startled, and propped himself on an elbow to examine his client's face. His own was like a picture Brother Philip had once shown Rufus, of a mythical half-human being called a faun; wide mobile mouth, ears a little pointed, eyes almond-shaped. But he was taking the question seriously. 'How can I answer? You are . . .'

'A client. Forget I asked.'

'Yes, a client. So if I say yes, you are attractive, you will think perhaps I'm only saying that to please you. My lord . . .'

'Yes, well?' He knew he sounded surly.

'You have no need to ask that question,' Rayner said earnestly. 'You are the son of Duke William of

54

Normandy, King of England. You can take what you desire from the world. Few will refuse you. If I were you, my lord – and believe me, I wish I were you – I'd simply enjoy it.'

'And enjoy you, you mean?'

'My lord, it's what I'm here for.'

Yes, thought Rufus, out of a sudden puerile anger born from the disappointment of a puerile hope, this boy was as cold as one might expect a half-human creature to be.

But he was excellent at his work and he did it most graciously, when Rufus took him at his word.

Six

Daughters and Brothers
1081–2

Edith of Scotland was born in the January of the year 1081, in a stifling chamber in her father King Malcolm's fortress at Inverness.

The room was stifling because the weather outside was bitter, the sky full of snowflakes spinning horizontally before the east wind that men called the black wind, because a night in which it blew seemed blacker than any other kind of night, and because there was something in its vicious edge which darkened all one's senses. To offset it, the room where Queen Margaret bore her daughter had been thickly hung with curtains and tapestries, and the bed piled high with the best and softest furs: beaver, seal and marten. There were two braziers. The effect in the end was that the heating had been overdone. Even the child seemed to think so, for when she was wrapped in the white woollen cloth the midwife had ready, she became scarlet in the face, and screamed.

'That's a bonny pair of lungs that's come with her,' said Malcolm of Scotland admiringly. 'It's a fine princess you've given me there, Margaret. She's welcome. We've boys enough, the quarrelsome brutes.'

'How do you wish her to be named?' asked Margaret.

'I suppose,' said Malcolm, half-humorous and half-disparaging, 'ye've some saint's handle in mind?'

The room, apart from being hot and rich, was also very much Margaret's room: pious, learned and feminine. A small shrine faced the end of the bed, with candles burning and a golden crucifix giving back their light. Malcolm thought it a disquieting sight for a woman facing the dangers of childbed, for as the candles flickered, the figure on the cross seemed at times uneasily to move. But Margaret apparently derived strength from it, and her husband let it stay. On a table by the bed were signs of the other pastimes which Margaret liked and had employed as distraction until the last moment: an exquisitely illuminated Life of St. Withburga of Ely, in Latin, and a strip of gold and silver embroidery. Probably for some churchy purpose, Malcolm thought, though not necessarily. Margaret embroidered all his tunics herself and the half-finished strip might be for him. He realised that under the blanket-like mantle which was essential everywhere in the fortress just now except for this one room, he was sweating, and shrugged the mantle off, revealing the splendours of one of the tunics, stretched taut across his barrel chest.

'I mind,' he said, 'when you were carrying Edward and green as ill-cooked cabbage with it, I told you you could have the naming of the bairns. You have the trouble of bearing them; you're entitled. Call her how you like. You like English names,' he added, 'and why not? As long as it's naething oot of date.' He glanced sideways at the illuminated book on the table. He could not read but he recognised the cover. 'Not Withburga. Even in England, they're no naming their lassies that ony more. Call her after you, maybe?'

'My grandmother was named Edith,' said Margaret. 'That's a good English name. I like it. The wife of the Confessor was an Edith too. She was a most pious lady. What do you say to Edith?'

'Imph. Short, royal and makes a nice noise,' said Malcolm. 'But mark one thing. I'm no against piety in a lass. It keeps them honest to their husbands and forby it's maybe an interest in a woman's life. But she's to be reared as a wife for a prince. I'll no have her turned into a nun.'

'She'll need an education. That will mean a stay in an abbey where there are learned women to instruct her. It would be hard for me to do it. I have so many duties.'

'That ye have. And I'm no against learning, either. It's never been but an ornament to her mother. But no matter what she learns or where, in the end she's to be the bride of a man, a flesh and blood yin, and none else.'

Gently, Margaret said: 'That will be as God wills.'

'No it won't,' said Malcolm, grinning. 'It'll be as *I* will, my lass!'

*

Sybil, the last child born to Wulfhild and Simon of Fallowdene, arrived at Candlemas, on 2nd February in that same year, but under very different, not to say melodramatic, circumstances.

That Candlemas morning was hushed and grey. But as ever, there was work to do. Their twelve-year-old son Richard, who was being educated with one of Simon's friends in London, was home on a short visit and Simon had bought him a new horse. Father and son were up at daybreak, gulping a few mouthfuls of food the sooner to rush out to the entrancing pastime of grooming and training their mounts.

Wulfhild, who had noticed that Richard was growing out of his clothes, had also despite the weariness of being eight and a half months gone, risen before dawn and stirred up the rest of the household. She put out their sewing gear in the hall but while they all waited for the feeble daylight to grow, she set the other women to livening up the fire and preparing the day's bread dough, and herself went out to feed the poultry. Richard and Simon, erupting back into the hall, almost knocked her over. 'Warm water!' said Richard, urgently.

'And ginger! Is there any in the kitchen?' Simon demanded.

'Ginger?' Wulfhild pushed away a couple of the dogs, who had been disturbed from a snooze by the sudden noise, and were trying to jump at her. 'What's wrong? One of the horses?'

'Yes, my Hammerfoot. Restless, dull coat, keeps looking at his flanks,' said Simon tersely. 'I think it's colic. That horse cost me a fortune and I've just bought Richard's; I can't afford another. There's no ginger left in the physic stores; Alric Steward couldn't find any last time he went to Chichester. Whoever goes next has *got* to find some. You bought a little from that pedlar who was carrying it, who came by at Christmas, didn't you? I've sent Gurth to the village to see if anyone there bought any and hasn't used it all up yet, but surely we've still . . .'

Editha had heard and came hurrying through the curtained door to the kitchen, a pail in one hand and a small earthenware jar in the other. 'There's hot water here. And some ginger but only about half an ounce, powdered . . .'

'That'll have to do. My thanks,' said Simon. He grabbed jar and pail and vanished, accompanied by Richard. Wulfhild glanced anxiously after them and then followed, the dogs prancing round her.

The poultry came cackling to meet her as soon as she stepped into the yard. Daylight had broken fully by now but there was still not much of it. The thatch of hall and outbuildings was dewed with fog and the trees which filled the lower part of the valley, and grew close to the hall palisade, were shadowy outlines in thin vapour. On a clear day, one could glimpse the hearthsmoke from the sub-holding of Westwater at the far end of the valley, and see the smoothbacked downs to north and south, parading a long the skyline like the porpoises Wulfhild had once watched from a ship when as a young woman she had travelled to Normandy. Today none of these were to be seen, no smoke, no sign of the hills, only the clammy, windless mist.

On the other side of the yard, the difficult business of drenching Hammerfoot was in progress. Simon's bay stallion was a warhorse trained to trample down his rider's foes, from which ungentle skill he got his name. He was not an amenable animal at the best of times. At present, tormented and frightened by stomach-ache, his principal desire was to savage every living thing in sight and he was not taking kindly to the indignity of having his mouth forced open with a clamp while Simon, standing on a bench, poured ginger and warm water down his throat through a hollowed oxhorn. He was tied to a ring in the stable wall but it was still taking the united efforts of four grown men as well as Richard to control him.

Wulfhild scattered the meal for the poultry and then became aware of two things. Firstly, that the gate to the outside world had been left ajar, probably by Gurth, when he ran out to the village, and secondly, that a white and tan canine rear was just squeezing through it. She let out a down-to-earth curse and shouted: 'Patch!' The dog squeezed on, disappearing. Wulfhild cursed again, threw down her basket and lumbered after him.

She had reason for concern for once out of that gate the dog could roam anywhere in the valley and up on the downs there were ewes in lamb. Patch was a young dog who was proving unreliable with sheep. He had tried to chase them, more than once. She trudged to the gate and shouted his name again but although there was a faint bark from the direction of the track to the south down, he did not come back.

She did not want to call anyone else to help. Hammerfoot, still plunging and rolling his eyes, needed all the attention he could get and the entire male population of the hall was by this time clustered round him. She did not wish to disturb the women at their doughmaking either. And besides, Wulfhild was in the habit of doing things for herself. She was, as she often said, the daughter of a plain man. At one time in her life, she had been a lady's companion, devoting her time to embroidery and conversation, but when she came to Fallowdene with her father, she had taken to the farm life again as if she had never known anything else. She was sturdy, her skin rough with weather and her startlingly blue eyes accustomed to long distances as much as to embroidery. She was used to walking. If the dog had gone to the down, it must be fetched back and it seemed to her that just now she was the best person to do it. She plodded, therefore, in pursuit.

The chalk path was easy to see even in the mist and though the vapours closed round her as she left the hall and the clustered village behind her, she was not afraid of losing her way. She walked steadily for some time, uphill, skirting one of the great fields, calling Patch at intervals, usually standing still to do so because she was somewhat short of breath. She wished she could see ahead. Grass and ploughland blended into the fog only a few feet off. She reached the top of the field, where the sheep pastures began, and stopped to call once more.

Again, Patch barked in answer and sounded closer. He also sounded excited. 'Come here!' Wulfhild shouted. Her voice was muffled in the cloud. 'Come here at once! Patch!'

And then she heard the sound for which she had all the

time been listening, to the accompaniment of a silent prayer that she would *not* hear it: a frightened bleating and a convulsive scampering. '*Patch*!' Wulfhild screamed. She pressed a hand to her back, which was aching, and trudged forward. Hideous noises broke out ahead: furious snarls, a terrified, agonised baa-ing and a wild scuffling which caused Wulfhild, despite her bulk and lack of breath, to attempt to run. Sheep were half at least of Fallowdene's assets and a killer dog could mean ruin.

Panting and lumbering, she came to where a gorse bush loomed greyly in front of her. Ugly, distorted growls came from the other side of it. She stumbled round the bush and Patch, crouched in the wet grass, lifted a bloodstained muzzle and regarded her warily as, nauseated, she took in what he had done: the ewe with its torn throat and a tiny, savaged, premature lamb half out of her, and the blood oozing into the soaked grass and the gorse spines.

'You foul, filthy dog, I'll cut *your* throat for this! I'd do it now if I had a knife!' Wulfhild gasped and lunged for his collar. He sidled away, growling. She lunged once more and then the pain in her back intensified, invading her entire body. She straightened, but the agony sliced through her again. Patch plunged away into the mist.

The child wasn't due for two weeks, at least.

What of it? Richard had been a month early. It could be.

There was nothing to fear. It was no more than half a mile to home and she wasn't lost. She could see the track perfectly well. One walked, anyway, during the early stages of labour. She would just walk home, downhill. She wondered irresolutely if she should try again to capture Patch but another murderous slash of pain stopped her. The sheep must take their chance now. She must get home at once. She would send someone out after him. She started down the path.

It was true that in the early stages of labour, one walked. But within the confines of a room, with the couch at hand and Editha to lean on. And the floor didn't slope, wasn't made of wet, slippery chalk. She managed about a furlong and then the ground slid from under her. She was down and could not get up again. She didn't believe that

61

at first, not until she had tried several times and been foiled by a wrench to her knee which kept her slithering feet and unwieldy body from getting on balance again, and by the onslaughts of pain . . . *pain*. If only she had been able to see the roofs of home, she could have pulled the scarf from her head and signalled with it, but grey silence closed her in. Hall and houses might have been a hundred miles away. Suddenly terrified, she screamed for help. The earth and air were unbearably dank and her teeth were chattering, and she was alone out here and somewhere in the mist was that horrible dog which had . . . she thought of the ewe, helpless as she was and for the same reason and screamed again, still more wildly, as from close at hand in the fog Patch, either in duet or competition, gave tongue in a wolflike howling.

When she heard the sound of a human voice calling, she began to sob with relief. A figure strode up the track with a smaller shape prancing beside it. 'Oger Shepherd! Help!' Wulfhild wailed.

'Ma'am!' The shepherd, a wiry lad with a tangle of untidy flaxen hair, broke into a run and came to kneel beside her. 'I heard you from down the hill. How did you get here? Did you fall?'

'Yes. I got here by walking; how else?' Relief made Wulfhild acid. 'I was after that dog.' The sheepdog which had been at Oger's heels was now engaged in a barking contest with Patch. 'He's killed an ewe and a lamb, higher up.'

'What!'

'You'll have to catch him but help me up first . . . it's the baby . . . ahhh!'

Oger, with alarmed exclamations, hauled her to her feet. 'My dog'll bring your hound down with him.' Once up, she found she could stay there by leaning heavily on Oger's shoulder. The wrenched knee was painful but could take some weight. They started downhill. Oger whistled and Patch fled past them, heading homeward with the sheepdog close behind. A warm wetness was flooding out of her, soaking the skirts that clung round her legs. She tried not to moan aloud but could not help it. But the moan turned to a wavering cry of thankfulness as

62

Simon, on foot, came half-running out of the mist. 'Oh, thank God. Simon, the baby's coming!'

'Editha asked where you were. Gurth said he'd seen you going out of the gate, just as he came back from the village. Are you out of your wits, wandering away up here? Oger, what happened?'

'I found her, sir, I've just this minute found her.' Simon's thick French accent always flustered his villagers. As their lord he was fair in his treatment of them but his voice reminded them that he was Norman and they didn't trust Normans, not even this one. Oger was almost babbling, afraid that in some mysterious way he would be held to blame.

'It's not Oger's fault. He can't be everywhere at once,' Wulfhild panted. 'It was the dog, Patch . . .'

'Help me pick her up, quick,' said Simon to Oger.

'Your horse, Simon; you've left Hammerfoot . . .'

'They're walking him for me and he's got enough nursemaids. I wanted to find you. Wandering off into the mist like that . . . all right, not long now. Come *on*, Oger!'

Wulfhild was still explaining as she was carried into the hall, where a flour-dusted and expostulating Editha took charge. 'Oger's to be rewarded,' said Wulfhild between gasps. 'And that dog must be killed, he's dangerous. Simon, do you hear me? The dog . . .'

'Yes, Mother, we know.' Richard had run to them as soon as his mother was borne through the gate. He regarded her with the same expression of slightly exasperated alarm as his father. Richard was already very like his father, with the same neat facial features, and he was beginning to be aware of himself as Fallowdene's future lord. 'Now let Editha take care of you.'

'You always think no one can attend to anything except you,' said Simon rebukingly as Wulfhild was placed on her couch in the resthouse. 'You could have called someone to fetch that damned dog.'

'. . . your husband is right, you take too much on yourself and always did,' said Editha, shutting the door on the men and setting to work to strip off Wulfhild's wet garments and wrap her in warm, dry blankets. 'You'll learn different one day but it's a shame you can't grasp it now. Sir Simon's terrified for you and the baby, I suppose you realise that? And it'll be a wonder if it gets safe into the world after this!'

But Sybil, born an hour later, was none the worse. She arrived, on the contrary, bawling more noisily than Patch had howled on the hillside or the infant princess Edith had cried in her overheated birth chamber; and without causing her mother ('You're luckier than you deserve,' grumbled Editha) more than minimal trouble. She was in fact a being of great spirit, not to mention vocal powers.

She was also, from the moment of her birth, quite simply beautiful.

King William had known that one day his half-brother Odo would stab him in the back; the only question in William's shrewd mind was: when?

In 1082, when both Sybil and Edith were in their second year of life, he found out.

The common parent between Odo and William was their mother. Odo was not therefore part of the Norman ducal house and he felt it. He had position certainly; he was Bishop of Bayeux and after the Conquest, William had made him Earl of Kent. But what was either, compared to the Conqueror's dukedom, the Conqueror's throne?

If someone had presented Odo with a kingdom on a platter, however, most people who knew him doubted if he could have made good use of it. He resembled William physically and like him was getting corpulent in middle-age. But those who were acquainted with them both said that Odo was 'like the Conqueror with something missing'. He lacked William's mental stature.

But he did not know this, and being denied a secular realm of his own, he looked round for advancement as a prelate. And conceived the idea of campaigning to be Pope. Which meant going to Rome to create an impression.

'Which he was welcome to do,' William said to Rufus, explaining his reactions, 'but not if he insists on cutting a dash by taking several hundred trained knights with him. I

64

can't spare that number of professional fighting men out of this kingdom. He's a fool anyway,' he added. 'If I wanted to steal an entire army from an overlord for my own use, I wouldn't assemble it in a castle – no matter how handy a place for setting sail from – where I was preparing to host a major council for the same overlord. I wouldn't be stupid enough to think that no one would notice my swollen garrison or wonder what all those ships were doing in my harbours. I suppose he thought that with so many lords and knights gathering for the council, the crowd would mask his own muster. It didn't. Also,' he concluded, 'I don't think Odo has ever realised that I have my own paid informers in every great household, including his.'

Odo's suffused and bulging countenance was a startling spectacle on the last day of the council, when, with the agenda complete, the Chief Clerk asked formally if there was any other business and William, rising majestically to his feet, said: 'There is. We wish to order the arrest of Odo, Earl of Kent.'

The actual business of the arrest proved difficult. No ordinary guard captain could be commanded to arrest a man of such eminence and when William looked at a group of senior barons, they looked at each other and at Odo and did not move. Odo was vindictive. He would not forget a man who had arrested him. And one day, he might be free again.

'Splendour of God! The greatest men in my realm and you look like frightened hares,' said the Conqueror furiously, shoved his heavy chair backwards so that it crashed into a pillar, strode round the table and grasped Odo's meaty upper arm himself.

'I would remind you,' said Odo, 'that I am an anointed bishop and as such have ecclesiastical immunity from arrest.'

'You're the Earl of Kent, my vassal, and it's a treacherous vassal I'm arresting, not a bishop. You're also,' said the Conqueror, in a lower tone and through his teeth, 'my *brother*. I knew you'd try to do me an injury one day and I was right. I knew you'd fail, as well. But it doesn't make the offence less. Brothers of all people should be able to trust each other.'

65

With the formal arrest completed, the guards could be called. Odo, shouting threats and claiming ecclesiastical privilege at the top of his voice, was removed. William stared at his silent and embarrassed baronage, made an explosive and derogatory noise and stalked out of the hall. Only Rufus, who had been sitting beside him, ventured to follow and even he did so with caution, a few paces behind.

Mantle swishing furiously round his calves, the Conqueror strode down a spiral stair to a small stone landing where brightness poured in from the sunlit outer world, through a narrow slit. A narrow segment of the English Channel glittered beyond. William stopped, slamming a hand flat on the deep ledge below the slit. 'If you're ever able to trust your closest kin, you'll be lucky, my boy. There's no end to the trouble I'm having with mine. Look at Curthose.' As Meulan had pessimistically predicted, Curthose's peace with his father hadn't lasted long and Curthose was once more making a freebooting nuisance of himself in Normandy. 'Now it's your uncle. Can I trust *you*?'

Rufus, as always in moments of emotion, annoyed himself by turning pink and stammering as he tried to assure his father that he at least was reliable. He was relieved to be interrupted by rapid footsteps, as a young man came running up the stairs towards their landing. He checked at the sight of them. He was a tall, strongly-made individual, moving athletically inside a priest's dark garb. His tonsure was dark brown, tinged with copper, and his eyes virtually matched his hair. His eyes caught their attention at once, for they were ablaze with an anger as magnificent as William's own. The young man's whole being was ablaze with it, in fact. He was a sight no wise farmer would want anywhere near his hayricks. 'Ranulf!' said William. 'What's the matter?'

The young man tried to remove the scowl from his face and failed. 'It's nothing, sir. I beg your pardon.'

'Nonsense. I said, what's the matter?'

'I've had a . . . a disappointment, sir. That's all.'

'Personal or professional?'

'Professional.'

66

'Indeed? Come in here.' William led them into a small room off the landing. It was an archive chamber, with rolls of vellum arranged on shelves, and nothing to sit on but a couple of chests. William rested a foot on one of the chests and turned to his son. 'This is Ranulf. He's a clerk in my secretariat. He was born in Bayeux and came to England in your uncle Odo's household. Since then, he's transferred to me but he kept up his contacts among your uncle's followers. I'm indebted to him for the information he has given me about your uncle's plans to travel to Rome.'

'It sounds shocking,' said Ranulf frankly to Rufus. 'As if I were guilty of treachery. But I'm on your father's payroll, not Bishop Odo's. And what Bishop Odo tried to do – that *was* treachery.'

'What the Earl of Kent has tried to do would be a better way of putting it,' said William. 'The arrest has just been carried out, by the way.'

'Yes. I saw them taking him away.' A bleak expression crossed Ranulf's face.

'It's all right,' said Rufus. 'My uncle broke one of the first rules of knighthood,' he added stiffly, knowing that he sounded boyish and pompous but nevertheless meaning what he said. 'Fidelity to one's overlord. It matters.'

'Quite,' said William. 'We all regret these necessities. But necessities is what they are. And now, Ranulf, what about this disappointment of yours?'

The young man grimaced. 'The Chancellor, Maurice, promised to obtain a promotion for me. I'm suitably qualified and I thought it was settled.' The Conqueror nodded. 'Now,' said Ranulf bitterly, 'it's fallen through.'

'Why?'

'My background isn't good enough, that's why! I'm a priest's son to start with, though what that has to say to it, I can't understand. My father was a village priest in Bayeux and when he was young it was the custom for priests to marry. I also have a . . . a common law wife myself. The Chancellor went nosing into my business before he made my promotion final, and found out. He says I won't do on either count. And on top of that, there's my mother.'

'Your mother? Even the most austere prelates I know,' said the Conqueror, 'including the Archbishop of Canterbury and my saintly old friend Abbot Anselm of Bec, admit that priests have to have mothers, though most people agree they shouldn't have wives. What was the objection to your mother?'

'The Chancellor had heard she was a witch, my lord.'

'And is she?'

'Of course not!' said Ranulf violently. He recovered himself and added: 'my lord.'

'Never mind that,' said William. 'Go on. Why does Maurice think she's a witch?'

'Chancellor Maurice,' said Ranulf, 'couldn't tell a witch from an archangel.' William grinned for the first time that day. 'My mother understands herb remedies and she can charm warts. That isn't witchcraft! When I was small, we were very poor. She used to sell love potions and things to silly girls in the village, just to make ends meet. The girls used to bring her presents, honey and eggs. It helped us and as for the potions, they were just harmless concoctions brewed from flowers. But what with that and the warts, she gained a reputation. In fact,' he added thoughtfully, 'once or twice I have known her . . . guess at the future in advance. She'll say she dreamed so and so – that someone is coming home unexpectedly, for instance – and she turns out to be right. But that isn't witchcraft, either. There were seers in the Bible. It's a gift from God. But the Chancellor . . .' He bit off what was probably an outright criticism of Chancellor Maurice's intelligence.

William said: 'You've served me well over today's business. You may not be an ideal priest, perhaps. The Chancellor isn't altogether wrong. Your parents are neither here nor there but I can't approve your wife. I didn't know about her and I would prefer not to hear of her again. But there are other, non-ecclesiastical posts in which you could be very valuable, which would be an equal promotion for you. Leave this with me, Ranulf.'

Recognising dismissal, Ranulf bowed and went.

'I suggested that promotion to Maurice,' William said to his son, 'as a reward to Ranulf for services rendered. As I said, I didn't know about the woman. I don't wish to override Maurice on that. But I must find Ranulf something else. He's too able to waste. They call him Ranulf Flambard, the Cresset, because of his vitality. Any suggestions, Rufus?'

Rufus said thoughtfully: 'The Keeper of the Seal has died lately, hasn't he? Or would Ranulf be too young for that?'

William considered him with a glint of appreciation in his hard dark eyes. 'No, not with the ability he has. A very good suggestion, Rufus. My thanks.'

Continuing downstairs with his father, Rufus said casually: 'I wonder if Uncle Odo could ever have made himself Pope?'

'I doubt it,' said William over his shoulder. 'And just as well. Popes tend to regard themselves as the High Kings of Christendom, you know. Odo as Pope would have gone about claiming that I was accountable to him. He would soon have learned otherwise but now there's no risk at all that I'll be put to the trouble of instructing him. I really am *very* grateful to Ranulf,' he added thoughtfully.

Seven

Leaving Home
1083

Odo was arrested on a day of clear weather, which in 1082 was unusual, for it was a wet, cold year. Sheltered Fallowdene, where Sybil had begun to toddle, did not fare too badly. But in Scotland the little Edith was scarcely allowed to step out of doors, and in Hampshire, Chenna's Tun and its neighbours suffered a poor harvest, which brought hunger and sickness in its wake. The next summer was equally poor, the bad weather extending even to southern Normandy near the Maine border, where on the little holding of Aix with its two hundred acres of only moderately productive land, Peter Longshanks was at last brought to the point he had tried to delay. His younger son, Ralph, must leave the home which could no longer support him.

It was not uncommon. The boy was fifteen now; many lads left home to enter other men's service when they were much younger. But all the same, on the morning in the August of 1083 when Ralph and his father set out from Aix on the first stage of Ralph's journey into the world, conversation was stilted.

'I've done the best I could for you,' Longshanks said earnestly as they went. 'Better than I hoped at one time, in fact. If your mother's cousin hadn't been a chaplain on this estate you're going to in Maine, you might have ended up in some border fortress full of God knows what kind of riff-raff. But La Fleche has a good reputation and so has the Seigneur Helias. You'll have chances to learn as well as serve. Not that he'll take notice of you personally, mind. You'll be just another trainee soldier, don't forget.'

'No, Father.'

'Your bowmanship won't disgrace you, but keep in practice with all kinds of weapon. Take care of your pony. Not that I need tell you that; you've always been

70

good about looking after anything that's yours. I wish I could send you off with more, but . . .'

'No, Father, I know we're not rich. It's all right. Really.' Ralph's voice held a trace of a quiver.

His father said heartily: 'The man I came to Normandy with, he left home young, like you, because he was a second son. He made his way. The last I heard, he'd become a thane back in England. Serve your lord well and he may reward you with land one day. It's what you should aim for, what every man really wants. You can marry and raise a family then. Fallowdene, Brand's place was called,' said Longshanks reminiscently. 'Somewhere in southern England, in the county of Sussex, I think. I wonder if he came through '66? There'll be visitors at La Fleche, coming from everywhere. If ever you hear news of Brand of Fallowdene, let me know.'

'Yes, Father. Of course.' There was a fidgety pause and they broke into a trot to cover it.

He was to travel under the protection of a bishop who was passing near Aix en route to visit La Fleche himself. In a few minutes they would be at the abbey where the bishop had lodged the night, where Peter Longshanks would hand his son finally into someone else's care. There was no more to say, or at least no time for saying it.

Longshanks would have liked to say: I'm sorry we haven't been closer. I'm sorry there isn't land enough for you as well as Reggie. I'm sorry your birth killed your mother.

Ralph would have liked to say: I wish I didn't hate Reggie for being older and luckier. I wish I didn't think I'd be a better master for Aix one day than he will be. I like taking care of things and he doesn't. And I'm sorry I was short when I said goodbye to him this morning. Inside my head I can still see the patterned paving in our downstairs rooms. I can't believe that maybe I'll never see it again. I can see Elise too. I know she's sobbing her heart out because I've gone. I never knew my mother; Elise was my mother. I won't forget you, Elise, or the things you taught me. I wish I were staying. I wish my home were mine . . .

But none of it would go into speech. It was a time to damp feeling down, not to fan it. In another fifteen min-

71

utes, they had parted. Ralph des Aix (for so he was always known although Aix was never his) was on his way.

He took with him the ability to speak English, a bundle of clothes, a somewhat scruffy pony, a yew-wood bow he had made for himself, and some arrows to go with it.

With him also went an intangible donation from Elise, who had been his nurse and was now his stepmother. She had borne children of her own but none had lived long. She had given her love to her nursling and to him had passed on all the advice and guidance that she could, to protect and nourish him out in the perilous world.

Some of Elise's lore would have met with considerable disapproval from Ralph's prospective lord, Helias of La Fleche, who was a pious man. And the man with whom Ralph travelled to La Fleche, the honest Bishop of St. Evreux, it would certainly have scandalised.

In the castle of La Fleche in Maine, light and air penetrated the living quarters in unusual quantities. Helias' father had decreed that they should, to the horror of the architect and the chief mason hired to change the original slits into windows with some width.

'But, Seigneur!' protested the architect. 'The defences!'

'Round this castle,' said his employer, 'is a moat. The moat encloses a steep mound and on top of that is a battlement wall seventy feet high. Inside that again is another ring of walls. The only approach, up the only adequately sloped part of the mound, is guarded by a gatehouse in the outer wall and two more towers in the inner one. No one capable of hammering his way through all that will be deflected by the mere width of a window. I am a cultured man, Messire. I am sick of living in quarters as dismal as my own dungeons. *Les fenêtres, Messire, s'il vous plait!*'

And *les fenêtres* there were and the young Helias (who now, at eighteen, so closely resembled his late, debonair sire that people who had known the older man often repressed an exclamation when first encountering the son) was glad. It pleased him to descend, brisk and lithe, from his tower chamber on a summer morning and not feel that he had left the exhilaration of the burgeoning day behind.

Above all after such days of rain and cloud as they had just had, he liked to see the sun make golden patches on the hall rushes, and to smell the wind blowing in from the misty forest.

And in August, the stags were in antler and when the day's business was done, there would be hunting in prospect. 'So *please* don't present me with any major tasks,' said Helias beguilingly to his steward. 'The hounds are spoiling for a run after so much wild weather, and so am I.'

'Michel wants to see you,' said the steward. 'He's been here since cockcrow, in fact. Shall I fetch him?'

'Did he say what it was about?'

'No, sir. He was rather mysterious in his manner, to tell you the truth. He's got a leather bag with him, full of something or other, and he keeps on, well, hugging it.'

'You intrigue me. Bring him in,' said Helias.

Michel, the head huntsman, was lean and quiet-voiced, with the faded eyes of men who scan horizons. He was not given to wasting words. Without delay he opened the drawstring of the bag he was indeed carrying close under his arm, and tipped the contents on to a table. Helias gazed in surprise at two bundles of flat wooden tallies, ten inches by three, marked not with notches but by upright strokes in chalk.

'What's all this?'

'They're scores, sir,' said Michel. 'The boys in training had a shooting match yesterday. Those two new boys who arrived in the bishop's train a few days ago were being tried out against the others of their age. I watched.'

'And?'

'Look, sir.' The huntsman sorted the tallies deftly. 'This bundle is the scores for the last round. They were shooting at a still target, from sixty yards. With the bows the lads use, that's the maximum for accuracy. Each boy shot six arrows and each had his own tally with his mark at the top. They got three points for a bull's eye, two for a shaft in the ring nearest the centre, one for the next ring to that. Eighteen points is the most anyone can score.'

'I know. It's not so long since I was training that way myself. Go on.'

'*Look*, sir,' said Michel, pulling one of the bundles apart. 'No one scored more than two bull's eyes – except for one of the new lads; this one. See? Four bulls and two near misses, sixteen points all told. And now look at this.' He undid the second bundle. 'These are the scores for when they used a moving target. Someone was throwing a board in the air for them. Some didn't score at all. But this lad – it's the same one – he hit the board every time and twice dead centre.' Suddenly the faded eyes were bright and the huntsman's calm deserted him. 'Sir, I lost my apprentice in that outbreak of plague last month and you promised me I could take my pick of the lads, bar the ones destined for knighthood. I'd been looking at them, I'd almost made my mind up . . . then this boy came and he's a marvel! Can I have him?'

'My own personal force of retained archers would be none the worse for a marvel or two,' Helias pointed out. He ran his fingers through his crisp dark hair. It was as springy as a bush and in frosty weather it crackled.

'Sir,' said the huntsman pleadingly, 'when an archer goes to war, he has to be able to shoot a long distance, so that he can keep himself well back from the enemy. But he need not be that accurate. If he's shooting into massed ranks what does it matter which man he hits? He's bound to hit someone. But in my business we have to bring down wounded deer, we have to shoot wolves and suchlike vermin. Accuracy matters. Their instructor knows I'm here. He gave me the tallies. He says the boy isn't one of the future knights.'

'I'd like to see this prodigy for myself. Where would he be at this hour, I wonder?'

'They ride after Mass on this day of the week, sir. Practise with lances at straw targets. All of them, future knights or no.'

'Those are my orders. A man-at-arms who can grab a loose horse and replace a fallen knight if necessary is a man who can help win a battle,' said Helias. 'Come with me.'

The horsemanship training could be worth watching. It was common enough to find the paddock gate clogged with interested onlookers. It was also common to find among them several who shouldn't be there, such as the spitboy and three of the maidservants. But on this occasion, their intentness on whatever was happening within the paddock, and the unanimous gasp as Helias and Michel appeared and pushed through, indicated that something special was happening.

Then, before they had reached the gate, they saw an equine profile, roman-nosed and foam-bespattered, with a white-ringed eye and a tossing mane, show briefly above the intervening heads. It vanished, to reappear almost instantly, facing the opposite way. The crowd gasped again. Erratic hoofbeats could be heard.

'Elbow of God, I gave orders forbidding this!' Helias shouted, and thrust the last two people out of his way so roughly that they fell. 'Where's their instructor? *Gilles*! What's the meaning of this? Get that boy down! *Jump, boy, jump!*'

They were in front of the crowd now and could see. The blue roan horse in the middle of the paddock was bouncing stifflegged, the head with the angrily flattened ears now somewhere about the level of its fetlocks. The rider appeared to be attached to the saddle by witchcraft.

But as Helias shouted again, the boy heard and obeyed, releasing the reins, sliding his feet out of the stirrups and toppling backwards. He fell rolling but came straight to his feet. The horse bounced away and then ceased to plunge. It stood still, head hanging and flanks heaving. The blue-grey hide was dark with sweat. The boy, shaking himself as if to make sure he was unhurt, went up and caught the dangling rein. The horse took no notice of him. He patted its neck and spoke to it. There was a cheer.

'The last lad they played that trick on broke a leg,' said Helias furiously to the knight instructor, who had stepped out of the crowd to face him. Sir Gilles was rather white. 'And there's another whose right arm'll never straighten again. I'm training soldiers. One-armed bowmen and expensively drilled cripples I wish for as much as I wish for an attack of smallpox. I don't like seeing good horses ruined, either. Boy!' He swung to face the paddock once more. 'Put your hand under the saddle!'

The lad did so. He drew it out again and looked at

75

something in his palm. He came across to Helias, leading the horse, and extended his hand. The sharp-edged nut that lay there told its own story. 'If I'd realised, I'd have jumped at once, sir. I'm sorry.' He was slightly out of breath but not too much. He was a thin, olive-skinned youth with long wrists that suggested imminent height. His sweat-soaked hair was black and his eyes so dark they almost qualified for the same description.

The instructor said: 'I came a little late this morning. This was in progress when I arrived. I too must apologise. But my rapscallions like to take a rise out of newcomers and this particular newcomer has put their noses out of joint with his shooting scores. He's good with a bow.'

'And on a horse, apparently. Where did you learn to ride like that?' said Helias to the boy.

'I used to help one of my father's neighbours break in colts. He bred destriers. I like horses, sir.'

'What's your name?'

'Ralph des Aix, sir.'

'It's him!' said Michel in Helias' ear. 'It's the same boy!'

'But you're not going to be a knight, Ralph?'

'No, sir. Well, my father isn't, you see.'

'You have a horse of your own?'

'No, sir, just a pony.'

'So when someone offered you a ride on a goodlooking horse, you were eager to accept. Who owns this blue roan?' Helias demanded.

There was an awkward silence before another boy, a thickset lad a little older than Ralph, came forward. 'He's yours?' Helias asked.

'I . . . yes, sir.' The youth, like Gilles, was rather white.

Helias was not easily made angry; his temperament was sunny. But his wrath when it did happen could be devastating. Those who instructed the lads of La Fleche used him as an example. 'Don't waste your strength. Be like Helias. When you strike, strike to kill.'

'You mean,' said Helias, 'that the horse used to be yours. He's Ralph's now. You can manage on borrowed mounts till your father provides you with another. It's your own fault. Take that animal to the stable and rub him down, Ralph. I want no more of this.' He was addressing

76

Sir Gilles and the other boys now. 'Ever. Be quiet.' The blue roan's erstwhile owner was attempting to plead for some other penalty. 'Take charge of your class, Sir Gilles, and make them work. I want every single one of them too exhausted to stand by the end of the day.'

He walked away. Michel came with him. 'I want him. I *want* him!' said the huntsman ravenously. 'No one rides like that unless he can think like a horse. If he can think like a horse, he can think like a hound, or a deer. I *want* him!'

'Grilled, with a wine sauce?' Helias laughed. 'His training as a huntsman isn't to interfere with his training in arms, mind. But he might be better living to some degree apart from the rest for a while. I daresay he can look after himself, but nevertheless, it might be wise. He can share your quarters. Make your arrangements with Sir Gilles so that he attends training sessions. Apart from that, he's yours.'

Eight

Visitors by Night
1087

The weather was kinder for a few seasons but in 1086
came more storms and men said it was heaven's wrath on
the unseemly inquisitiveness of the Conqueror, for that
was the year when he held the Great Survey of all the
manors in his kingdom. As a prelude, it soon became
clear, to raising taxes. Chenna's Tun suffered considerable privation from them. The following spring was cold
and a sense of foreboding set in, which even the fires of
Beltane could not lift.

Four nights after Beltane, a barking dog roused the
Chenna household.

Struggling up on his elbow, Young Chenna was aware
that his wife was already sliding her feet to the floor and
that beyond the curtain which roughly divided the house
his father too was scrambling up. 'Get out there and see
what it is! Brindle don't carry on like that for nothing!'
Old Chenna shouted. His son, yanking on hose and jerkin
in the dark, plunged out.

The dog stood on stiffened legs, at the full extent of his
chain, barking steadily and pointing towards the west,
where the track along the stream vanished into the
water-laced tract which they called the Brook Wood,
which faded at its southern edge into the Hoar Woods.
'Quiet, Brindle. What's the matter? I can't hear nothing.'
The moon was high and full, riding clear of the treetops,
casting a cold and even light on the thatched roofs of the
Tun, turning the stream to silver. Among the other
cottages on the far side of the water, another dog yelped
and a door banged. Brindle burst into renewed clamour
and now, at last, Young Chenna felt it, the vibration in the
ground; horses, coming through the Brook Wood.

The riders cantered in along Chenna's side of the river.
They pulled up and swung out of their saddles, three of
them. Young Chenna gentled the dog again and faced

78

them. One held the horses; the others came up to him. 'Inside,' one of them said shortly, in guttural English.

He led them in, silently. He knew them; everyone for miles knew them. They were the King's Foresters, tough, Norman-bred men whose fathers had come to England in someone's following at Hastings or soon after, who'd found themselves employment as the king's bullies, enforcing his Forest Law. Inside the house, rushdips had been lit. Old Chenna stood defiantly beside his daughter-in-law. 'Ditha had pulled a gown on and thrown a shawl round her, and was in the act of tying her straw-coloured hair roughly back. She looked terrified.

'What's all this, disturbing folk in the middle of the night?' Old Chenna demanded belligerently.

He used the broadest local dialect but the Foresters understood it. They needed to, for from the very first, from the day after Hastings, almost all the English had been resolutely stupid, to the point of idiocy, about learning their new masters' tongue. Though, as the Foresters said to each other, they were cunning enough about evading the law.

'It's news to us,' said the senior Forester, in his own crude accent, 'that being out of bed of a night worries the likes of you. Especially when it's moonlight. Someone took a deer last night, not a mile from here.'

'Did they now?' said Old Chenna sourly. 'And how'd you know, if you weren't there? And if you *were* there, why don't you know who did it? Coming here in the middle of the night, trying to catch honest folk out . . .'

'Hark at Messire Clever,' said the younger Forester. 'We found the bloodmarks on the ground in the morning and the trail into the wood, where something was carried, in this direction, by a man with boots on. *And* we found an arrow, where somebody missed his shot and couldn't find his shaft afterwards. Misleading thing, moonlight. Stand back against the wall, all of you. We're going to search. If we find nothing here, we'll search the other houses.'

'And you'll find nought in any house here,' said Old Chenna angrily. 'Where could folk like us hide anything?'

He yanked back the leather curtain behind him. The curtains divided the house into three. In the front was the

79

space where they cooked and ate. It had a stone fire trough with a roof louvre above, benches and a table, hooks on the wall for field implements and ox-harness, shelves for pots; 'and them rows of earthenware jars on the floor have oil and flour and lard in, and not enough of any of 'em just now,' Chenna informed the intruders.

At the back were the two stuffy compartments used for sleeping. The one where Young Chenna and 'Ditha slept was cluttered, with 'Ditha's personal chest on the floor by the bed and her loom and the rush basket she used for weeding in a corner. There was a wooden cradle too, full of unspun wool. 'Ditha had never quickened, not as the Maiden, nor since she and Young Chenna had been wed. Nor had anyone else been kindled by Young Chenna in the Wood. As yet, there was no new generation to succeed him.

'But we're young yet. There's time,' he had said when his father grumbled.

Was there time still? He stood beside 'Ditha as the search proceeded and wished she had not tied back her hair, because he would have liked, just once more, to bury his face in it. He had begun to tremble.

The search was carried out without heed to noise or destruction. The Foresters had brought torches which they lit at the embers of the fire, to illuminate their work better than the rushdips could. The pallets were hauled off the beds and ripped open with daggers, chests were opened and their contents flung out on the floor. The men plunged grimy hands into the storage jars and prodded the thatch with broomhandles. Every time they passed close to 'Ditha, Young Chenna pulled her away, although they regarded this manoeuvre with obvious scorn.

None of the Chennas would have given them credit for it, but the Foresters were respectable men in their own eyes. The English, thought the senior Forester as 'Ditha was jerked away from him for the third time, were not only stupid, cunning and lawless; they had minds like cesspools too. He had a perfectly good wife of his own, thank you very much, and Mabille at least washed her hair occasionally. Under his tread, he felt the texture of

80

the floor beneath the thickly strewn rushes change. Stepping back, he kicked the area clear. 'Oho, what have we here?'

'We keep our salted pigmeat barrels down there,' said Old Chenna sullenly.

There was a stout wooden lid and a plank-lined cavity beneath. It was about four feet by six, and five feet deep. It did indeed contain barrels. The younger man jumped down to examine them while his colleague squatted on the edge and held a torch for him. 'Empty . . . some salt pork in this one . . . empty again . . .'

'Satisfied?' Old Chenna asked.

'Not quite.' The older man, crouching on the lip of the hole, leant down and banged the plank wall with his fist. He edged round and banged another wall. It sounded hollow. The man in the cavity used both hands to drag at the planking. It yielded easily. 'Ditha pressed close against her husband and felt the tremor in his body. 'Well, well, what's this, then?' said the man in the pit, and out into the torchlight he dragged the deer carcase which had been snatched from the hook where it hung and thrust into hiding by Old Chenna and 'Ditha when Brindle gave the alarm. After it, he brought out the possession which was illegal for anyone living within forest jurisdiction, unless the king officially employed him to use one; a bow in working order. He handed the damning evidence up, and climbed out.

'We were hungry!' cried 'Ditha shrilly. 'Grain's nearly all gone and you can see we've hardly a mouthful left of the winter's meat. We were hungry, I tell you!'

Young Chenna stared at the Foresters and thought that their faces were different in feature, but amazingly alike in their expression of mingled satisfaction and implacability.

He knew what it meant, but he could not yet believe it. A few minutes ago he had been safe in bed in 'Ditha's arms. In his mind, he still was.

They were going to take him away. If ever he returned, he would be blind or a cripple. Or both, like Blind Edric of Minstead who lacked eyes and hands alike since he was caught with a dead hind over his shoulder. His son and daughter-in-law had to feed him and lead him about, not that he went about much. He had become afflicted in his head and spent most of his days mumbling and cursing to himself by the hearth.

If what they did to him didn't kill him, he thought wildly, he would kill himself. And then he saw beyond the immediate horror, to its wider implications. He would never make love to 'Ditha again, never have children now. Would never go swearing into the rain again to chase the pig out of the onion patch, never . . . the enormity of his loss, of the things that were going to happen to his body, swelled up in him. The muscles melted at the backs of his knees. He longed again, with humiliating desperation, to clutch 'Ditha and hide his eyes in her hair. His mouth worked.

His father said: 'Got it wrong, as usual. Don't make me laugh. My son's a good boy but shoot straight enough to kill a deer by moonlight? He can't drive a nail straight. Always hammers his thumb. I shot that buck.'

His mouth was drier than ash but Young Chenna heard himself croak: 'Dad, you can't even string my bow.'

The senior Forester regarded Old Chenna wearily. 'He thinks we're criminals like him. Listen, old one, we're here to take in the guilty, just the guilty. So you shot it, did you? Very well, then, if you shot it, string the bow you shot it with. Catch!' He threw the bow at Old Chenna and his companion, in response to a nod, handed over the bowstring to go with it.

Young Chenna stood three inches taller than his father and he was, indeed, young. Old Chenna's muscle tone was fading as the years went by and the rheumatism had invaded his right shoulder. He wrestled with the bow, sweating, veins standing out on his forehead and tears pricking his eyes. The bow was in any case obviously meant for a taller man. The Foresters watched, cynically. 'Enough,' the senior said at last, taking the weapon away. 'Bring the youngster.'

Young Chenna had held on to his nerve just long enough to defend his father but now he broke. He fought, babbling, as they lifted him from his feet and carried him out, dangling between them. They trussed him and dumped him like a sack over the withers of one of the

82

horses. 'Ditha ran after them and tried to tear their hands away from her husband but one of them caught hold of her and half-ran, half-threw her back into the house.

She sank sobbing to the rushes, banging impotent fists on the floor. Her father-in-law slumped down beside her. The tears were running down the furrows in his face. 'He'll die, they nearly all die. We'll curse the Norman at Lammas but what use'll that be to us or to him? And who'll follow me now? You quickened, yet, girl? Any life in you yet?'

She shook her head. She would have turned to him for comfort or tried to offer it but in his misery he only wanted to be alone and he threw her out that night. Her old home had been in Minstead and she stumbled back, through the forest paths, by herself. Her family were as hungry as all the rest in the district and when she came pounding and wailing at their door at dawn, another mouth that would need feeding, they weren't best pleased to see her, though they took her in.

Young Chenna, as he had wanted and as his father had said would happen, died of his mutilations before the harvest was ripe. He was allowed to come home to die. When the Yule of Lammas was held in the forest, the worshippers gave form to their anger, asking Him who ruled in the Wood to avenge them, to destroy the Norman king whose laws had done this.

But next day, lying on his pallet too heartsick to rise, Old Chenna knew that all the curses and invocations were only foolishness, that there was no power in the world to aid the humble and the weak, not Christ and not the Horned One either.

Like the Christian God, the Horned One was a trinity, at different times king-god, or sacrificial victim or huntsman of souls. But in no aspect had he true power, Old Chenna said to himself, nor could he lend it to others. If you had no power in your own right, then you had none at all and that was that.

He turned face down on the musty pallet and wished he hadn't thrown 'Ditha out after all; he could have done with human company, someone to talk to him, clean the place up and cook for him. But he hadn't even let her know when Young Chenna came home and he'd been told that when she found out, too late to see her husband before he died, she'd been very bitter. She wouldn't come now and besides, it was said that at the year's end she intended to marry a man from Minstead.

The news that the Conqueror was dying reached Fulk of Anjou when he was in session, adjudicating on the disputes of his tenantry like any other feudal lord, except that his tenants were lords themselves, albeit less powerful than himself, and his manor currently included not only Anjou but, more or less, the province of Maine as well. The Conqueror had tried to settle the affairs of Maine and patch up a peace with his contentious eldest son at the same time. Fulk was to be overlord of Maine and Robert Curthose, on his father's death, to hold the province under Fulk. Curthose, who wanted his lands immediately, had taken a less than grateful view of this arrangement.

And when a young Angevin lord who had been travelling in Normandy when the news broke arrived in Fulk's hall and interrupted a busy agenda with the tidings that William was in the monastery of St. Gervais, near Rouen, on his deathbed, Fulk was on suspicious alert at once.

'Dying men have overset their existing wills before now,' he said to the nobles who were with him, some of them because they were seeking his judgement, others because as his vassals they were obliged to grace his court from time to time. 'They get people crowded round their beds, all pressing their own claims to this and that. I'm going to St. Gervais.'

Helias of La Fleche was among those who were in routine attendance. It was he who said: 'It will make a great difference to the world if William dies. He's held England and Normandy together. He's held whole tracts of land quiet and under a single man's control for years. What will happen when he's gone? He must have a remarkable personality,' Helias added, 'I wish I'd met him.'

'Now's your chance,' said Fulk. 'I'm taking companions, obviously. You can come to St. Gervais with me. You'll see him, after a fashion. Not that any man's himself *in extremis*.'

84

Helias went gladly, interested by the prospect of actually looking on as great a man as the Conqueror, and of being present at the time and place when his world entered on an era of change. He liked the prospect of a journey, too, and the chance to meet new people.

But the one who was really going to matter to him he did not see face to face.

In Chenna's Tun, in Minstead, in Truham, they said, marvelling: 'The Norman is dead. Only three months since we cursed him, and he's dead!'

Old Chenna sneered at them and pointed out how often they'd cursed the Normans before, without result, but they took no notice. They had no doubts. The Horned God of the Wood had shown His power, they said. He had it, when He chose. Here was the proof.

It gave them a sense of strength. Perhaps it was only a coincidence, and a genuine accident, that one of the Foresters who had taken Young Chenna away was found shortly afterwards lying dead after his horse had apparently thrown him headfirst against a tree.

But on the other hand, to believe that one has power is to gain courage.

The soil is fertile and the seeds are planted. They are already growing.

PART II

IN WHICH THE SAPLINGS GROW APACE
1087–1091 AD

One

The Old Order Changes
1087

The custodians of the Royal Treasury at Winchester had never been so outraged. There were things to which they were accustomed and things to which they were most emphatically not, and this intrusive and undignified inquisition into mundane detail on the part of exalted persons who ought to know better unquestionably belonged in the latter category.

It was perfectly natural that the new King William (who was now called Rufus to his face only by close friends like the Count of Meulan and the bull-like FitzHamon but was still called it behind his back and would be for ever), should wish to establish his right to the Treasury.

It was perfectly natural that on leaving his father's deathbed near Rouen, he should make for Winchester even before descending on Canterbury and its Archbishop to demand a coronation. The Treasury keys were the keys of the kingdom and he would have been a fool to do otherwise, since without them no ruler could pay his army or make supporting him in any degree worthwhile.

And it was entirely reasonable that he should want to know precisely what the Treasury contained. In any case, it was September and they were just getting ready for the Michaelmas audit. *But* . . .

But there was a time-hallowed method of conducting audits. Underlings, humble men but men nonetheless of sound probity, each with an equally trustworthy scribe trotting at his heels, would count everything in the vaulted store rooms under King Edward's old palace, writing down descriptions and quantities.

Then senior clerks would match the returns against last year's, carefully accounting for all incomings and outgoings in between. The finished product, complete with details of debtors and creditors and careful annotations to forestall queries, all exquisitely penned on vellum with section headings in coloured inks, was presented to the Treasury's three senior officers who would examine it, make a lot of queries which their subordinates had after all failed to forestall and at length, in turn, present the outcome to the Sheriff of Hampshire. Who, having requested and got answers to queries of his own, would present them formally to the king.

It was as clearcut and dignified and in its way as beautiful as a church ritual. And it was nothing whatsoever to do with the Keeper of the Seal, whose province was to ensure the authenticity of documents issued from the royal secretariat; that and nothing else.

Certainly, no Keeper of the Seal had ever hitherto arrived hotfoot on the second day of the operation, bearing written authority (complete with the current king's seal) empowering him to oversee the audit personally and shepherd it officiously through all its stages from the very beginning, upwards to the crown.

Ranulf Flambard had done just that. Furthermore, having got the authority to interfere, he had made it clear that this was no mere theoretical right; he meant to use it.

Scribes and clerks, their indignation almost strangling them, went about the work while this crass young man, his dark copper tonsure fairly aglow with vitality ('and the joy of noseyparkering,' said an angry scribe) and his voice offensively confident, strode about the vaults peering over people's shoulders and carrying out random recounts of silver coin ('does he think we're pocketing it on the side?' enquired an offended clerk sarcastically). He had bullion ingots heaved off the scales in the middle of weighing, so that he could check the counterweights and at one point brought in a panel of Winchester merchants ('outsiders!' exclaimed a horrified Chief Clerk) to give independent valuations of the jewellery and the costly robes in the hooped oak chests.

'All these items have been valued already and the records are available,' one official ventured to protest.

'Values change. We want to begin our reign with accurate information on the worth of the Treasury,' Flambard said.

'Who's we?' said the official, under his breath.

90

It was plain that Flambard was hugely enjoying himself, that his strong, shapely fingers liked handling precious metals and rich fabrics. It was an additional irritant that his enthusiasm was somehow catching; despite their fury they finished the counting half a day sooner than usual because of it.

The final insult which he added to the injury he had already done to their self-esteem was that he handled an abacus better than any of them. When all was done and the accounts ready for Rufus, who had just returned, straight from his crowning, to receive them, Flambard retrieved the sheets from the Sheriff's office for 'a final check'. The Sheriff of Hampshire, annoyed, asked what his own staff were supposed to be for, but: 'I'll save them the trouble. It's a pleasure,' said Flambard with a maddeningly sunny smile, the one to which the exasperated clerks had more than once unwillingly responded.

Recalling the stir he had made caused him to smile again as he sat alone, late into the night, validating totals on the abacus. He liked working at night. It was undisturbed; one could concentrate. Flambard needed less sleep than most and his excellent eyesight was not inconvenienced by candlelight. Nor was he nervous. His chamber in the old English palace had three slender glazed windows as well as shutters and he had left the shutters open because he liked a glimpse of starlight, and he did not, as so many people did, think of darkness as something inimical to be held precariously at bay by the circle of man-made light. There was nothing out there, he had sometimes said when talking to the superstitious or the imaginative, but the ordinary world which in daylight one could see.

He was astonished at himself, therefore, when as the door of his room opened suddenly and quietly, a bolt of alarm shot through his stomach, bringing him half to his feet with the abacus gripped firmly in his hand.

Rufus, a square and not notably royal figure, wrapped in a heavy mantle for the purpose of roaming through the cool September night, stepped into the room. He was carrying a lamp. 'My lord?' said Ranulf. 'You startled me.'

91

'I woke and saw a light. Sit down.' Flambard did so and the king set the lamp on the table. A loose fold of the mantle showed a patch of barrel chest fuzzed with pale red hair. 'All my chamberlains were snoring so I came myself to see what you were up to, awake at this hour. Still clicking your beads, eh? Something wrong with the audit?'

'Not that I can see, I'm glad to say. Your Treasury staff are admirably honest and competent. But I like to make sure.'

'Imph. I picked you for efficiency. So did my father.'

Nothing was wrong, surely. Certainly Rufus' pale round eyes held only approval of this late-night perfectionism. It was strange that the sense of impending menace which had come through the door with him should linger, and so strongly. It was ridiculous, Flambard thought, that he should be wishing that someone else were within easy call. He shook himself, and made the abacus beads rattle. Rufus came to lean over his shoulder and look at the device more closely. 'I was shown how to use one of these things as a boy, but I can't remember much about it. Let me see it.'

A square, reddish hand reached out and flicked at the beads. The king was standing so close that Flambard could feel the heat from his body. 'My lord, take care. Those wires are fragile.'

'Am I so clumsy?' Rufus enquired, rhetorically. 'If I wanted to multiply seven by eight, how would I . . .?'

'Like this.' Flambard demonstrated. 'Forgive me,' he said, having sensed annoyance in that comment about clumsiness. 'My wife is careless sometimes and breaks things. She is always having to buy new pots and goblets, which I have to pay for. I've got into the habit of warning her when things are delicate. It's so ingrained now that I warn everyone.'

'Your wife, eh?' To Flambard's relief, Rufus seemed to lose interest in the abacus. He moved away to a settle. 'You're a priest but you're married. You've no guilt about it – or her?'

'It was usual in my father's day. I can never see why it can't be usual now. Why should a man who is called to serve God have to cease from the ordinary business of being a man? I serve the priesthood adequately, I think. I am also a perfectly normal man. I find no clash between them.'

'What if there were a direct clash between your wife and your ambition? Would you put her away?'

'It almost did come to that, once, my lord. No, I should not. I might pretend to do so but no more than that.'

'Humph! I suppose that's an honest answer. But you *are* ambitious, aren't you? Did you know that on his deathbed, my father released my Uncle Odo, Bishop of Bayeux, from prison?'

Flambard rode the sudden change of subject like a good horseman on a restive mount. 'Yes, my lord. I had heard.'

'Do you think it was wise?'

Flambard understood. Taking on the office of king had given a new air of authority to this solid young man. But beneath that forced toughening, Rufus still needed advice and knew it, and he preferred to seek it privately, not in a hall full of older men some of whom might try to take advantage of his inexperience. Whatever else he had had in mind when he came here tonight, a desire for counsel was at least part of it. Advise him well, and there would be reward. The atmosphere of menace had mercifully faded. Flambard knew where he was now. 'No, my lord, I don't think it was wise. Bishop Odo was my patron once but I have to say – as I said once before – that his offence was grave. Your father's act of forgiveness was admirable in its way but wise – no.'

'My father was worked on,' said Rufus violently, 'when he was dying and in pain. He was worked on by priests talking about hell and calling on him to repent of his sins. I was there. I threw them out of his room more than once. Worrying him, taking advantage of him. You can't know what that r . . . room was like.'

It was the worst memory he possessed. The weather had been so hot, a bad summer turning suddenly to blistering sun just when it was wanted least. The chamber had been stuffy and it stank with the odours of his father's body, the nausea and excreta which as time went on grew more and more uncontrollable and offensive. The aromatic herbs the physicians burned to sweeten the air only seemed to

93

thicken it, and the brazier raised the temperature to the tropical. And in the midst of it all, helpless as he had rarely been before, the man who had once been the Conqueror had lain, breathing short against a pain he could not conquer and facing eternity in cold blood instead of on the battlefield where he had always expected to meet it. Had lain facing concepts like God and damnation. Had confronted the knowledge that in the past he had done things which other men spoke of only in whispers, and that he could not now go back and undo them. Had faced the bleak truth that he was afraid.

And the priests had been in there like carrion crows pouncing on a dead donkey, to exploit the situation.

'My father didn't make his own will at all,' Rufus said aggressively. 'The priests made it for him, backed up by a few obliging barons. I tried to help but he needed someone with the Church's authority and no one there who had that authority was on his side. The Archbishop of Canterbury was his friend but he was here in England. My father's old friend Anselm of Bec was ill himself and couldn't come. So they did as they liked with him. Uncle Odo to be freed, in a kind of payment for past sins, along with a few less important captives. They wanted him to reinstate Odo as Earl of Kent as well but that was one of the times I threw them out. Them and some of the b . . . barons and counts who kept clustering round him, w . . . worrying him . . .' His stammer had reappeared as it always did when he felt emotional. 'He n . . . never had any peace. There were always people round his bedside. You can't *know* . . .' His voice faded. There was a great deal that Ranulf Flambard could not know, or ever be told, not all of it directly concerned with the Conqueror's death. When he entered the candlelit chamber, he had realised very quickly that there were certain things against which Ranulf Flambard would instinctively raise defences, would avoid even discussing if he could, by talking about his woman . . .

The death-chamber, the day he ordered Fulk of Anjou out. Fulk had gone, tight-mouthed, stamping off down the stone stairs. Rufus, glad to see the back of him, spoke with the doctors and knelt for a few minutes by the bed,

94

anguished as always in this room by a mixture of pity and disgust. It was not disgust with his father but with the dreadful disintegration of his father's body. He tried, silently, to pray for the Conqueror and it turned into a prayer that nothing like this should ever happen to himself. This shocked him and hearing the noise of hooves and voices below, he rose and went to the window for distraction.

Below, an angry Fulk was taking his leave, but was holding his horse roughly back because although most of his suite were in their saddles around him, someone appeared to be missing. A groom held a saddled horse and looked anxiously towards the door into the abbey. Fulk cursed, loudly, and demanded to know where that insouciant young devil had got to.

And then, running from the door and down the steps towards his horse, the insouciant young devil came, light summer cloak flying from his limber shoulders, cheerful voice calling an apology in which there was a considerable amount of laughter and no subservience whatsoever. A young deerhound pranced at his heels. The young man put a hand on his saddle pommel; and was up, as if he had wings.

In that moment, Rufus' soul too took flight, straight out of the window towards that blithe young man. He had been taken by surprise, because he had not known that such things could happen. It had never occurred to him before that one glimpse of a stranger could change the whole world, could impress itself on one's mind and spirit like a seal upon clay.

Then the party was gone, jogging and clattering under the archway. He remembered a strong, co-ordinated body, crisp dark hair and the intonation of a voice and nothing more. He did not even know the young man's name.

He could have asked. He could have gone down to the courtyard, and said to someone, a groom, the guards at the gate: who was that who came out late and annoyed Fulk of Anjou? But he was afraid that his yearning would show and he could not think of any mundane excuse for the enquiry.

95

So he had done nothing, said nothing, let it go. But it had left a mark. Since that first encounter with Rayner, he had been schooling himself to a life in which one gratified desire with one set of people and sought friendship with others. One staggering moment of revelation, standing at his father's window with death in the room behind him, while he looked out upon the springs of life, and he would never be quite satisfied with that compromise again.

But the first time he had moved, timidly, towards an attempt to combine the two, Ranulf Flambard had at once spoken of the woman he called his wife. If he wished to keep Ranulf's friendship, he knew he must not repeat the attempt.

Or allude in any way to that revelation at St. Gervais. He must continue in a political vein. 'They've started on me too, about reinstating Odo in Kent. I don't know what the outcome will be. I tell you, Flambard, the priests forced my father to forgive Curthose, who'd done nothing for years but rebel. They made Father ratify the arrangement about Maine, and present Curthose with Normandy. But when he sent for C . . . Curthose he c . . . couldn't even hurry himself to g . . . get there before Father died. My father didn't want to do any of it, he said Curthose was too irresponsible, but they made him agree, to buy the goodwill of Heaven.' Being angry about Curthose and the priests was a way of channelling another kind of feeling, he found. 'My father hadn't the strength to resist. So . . .' he hurt himself with the next words but did it as if lancing a boil '. . . priests can have wives as far as I'm concerned, Flambard. I've seen what the virtuous priests are like!'

'I think,' said Flambard in a calm voice, aware that they were once again in a conversational quicksand and apprehending by now something of the reason – he knew a good deal about Rufus by hearsay – 'that the bequest to your brother Robert Curthose may have something to be said for it. It is customary to pass on inherited land to the eldest son. Normandy was your father's inherited estate. After all, he confirmed Curthose as heir, years ago.'

'I know. But my brother rebelled again just the same. As far as I'm concerned, that should have put him out of the running. My brother Henry agrees.'

Flambard, who knew quite well that Henry had also complained that he had been swindled out of England, to which he was entitled because he was the only son born there, and the only one born during his father's kingship, said nothing. Rufus eyed him sharply.

'You're thinking that I'm the one who's ambitious. You're saying to yourself: ah, he wants all that his father had before him, all for himself and to hell with his brothers.'

'I see nothing wrong,' said Flambard, feeling his way, 'in a son wishing to resemble his father. Your father was a great man. He gathered vast possessions and that always leads to complications when there is more than one son to follow on. Looking at it from a purely practical point of view,' said Flambard thoughtfully, 'there's no avoiding complications. If your father had cut Curthose out in your favour, as I suppose you wish he had, or divided his estates between you and Henry, do you think Curthose would have accepted that meekly? You'd have been at war already.'

'We'll probably be at war anyhow, before long. Curthose thinks he should have had the lot!'

'Yes. As I said, complications are inevitable. Many men hold estates both here and in Normandy and therefore owe allegiance to both you and Curthose. We can only pray that the matter resolves itself smoothly.'

'Oh, pray.' He had made a sorry mess of that at his father's bedside. 'Well, I'm no use at that. That's your job. You're a priest, even if you're an odd one.' Rufus looked up the wall behind Flambard, where a silver crucifix hung. 'Tell me something, Flambard. Do you believe in it?'

'Believe in what, my lord?'

'All *that*.' Rufus made an impatient gesture at the crucifix. 'About the Resurrection and saying prayers and hell and heaven and angels and all the rest of it. Do you think it's true?'

'We're assured by the Church that it's true, my lord. It does no harm to believe in it, certainly. Some men would keep no laws at all but for the fear of God. If it's not true, if when we die there's nothing . . . well, we'll never know,

97

will we? But a mistake in the opposite direction could be disastrous.'

'I keep thinking about my father. If the priests are right, where is he now?' In the death chamber, there had been sprinklings of holy water, and endless praying, as well as the scented herbs. And they had been just as much use, which was none. Another reason why he had not run down to the courtyard and asked who that young man was, was that as he turned from the window, he had seen his father's sunken, waxy yellow face again and it had come between. Death was stronger than life, it seemed. 'I think myself,' said Rufus, 'that he isn't anywhere.' And against all likelihood, the startled Flambard saw tears glitter in the pale eyes and knew that he was in the presence of mourning.

Priestly consolations were obviously useless. He offered the sympathy of silence instead. After a moment, Rufus recovered himself. 'There were other things I disliked in that will, that the prelates insisted on,' he said. 'I'll carry them out. I promised. But I don't approve. Too much giving away, too many grants to too many abbeys and whatnot. I'll be wanting to recoup.' He glanced at the vellum sheets on Flambard's table. 'Any suggestions?'

Flambard, who had already totted up the awe-inspiring figure to which the Conqueror's financial bequests amounted, had had similar thoughts. 'There are ways and means,' he said. Despite the opinions Rufus had just expressed, he still felt inclined to caution. 'Income is at a good level just now. There have been some recent deaths among abbots and bishops,' he said. 'The revenues of their estates revert to the crown, of course, until their successors are appointed. Together, they're worth about seven hundred and fifty marks a year. Naturally, the new appointments must be made. But it is vital in these matters to choose the right appointees and this can take time. Meanwhile . . .'

He was interrupted by a roar of laughter, gusty enough to blow the candle flames about. The sense of menace evaporated finally and completely, so that Flambard wondered if it had ever been real.

'Ranulf, you're priceless! And so bloody tactful!' They

98

were conspirators now, brothers in arms. 'I should have thought of it for myself,' said Rufus. 'Why didn't I? It's a jewel of an idea. Take time to appoint replacements? It'll take till Judgement Day if I can manage it.' He thought it over, chortling. 'Archbishop Lanfranc's getting on. Canterbury'll fall vacant one of these days. Now there's a profitable concern if you like. He read me a lecture a mile long at my coronation, Ranulf, all about leading a pure life. I had to listen to priestly prating all the time the crown was being put on my head. Canterbury can pay for that, one of these days.'

Two

And the New Order Is Unwelcome
1087

At Michaelmas 1087, Brand of Fallowdene, the father of
Wulfhild, died in Ely Monastery and his daughter took to
her bed. To Editha's astonishment and horror, she stayed
there for three weeks.

Wulfhild had known widowhood by then and had
mourned Simon deeply. But her father's death struck at
her in a way even more fundamental.

Outwardly, they had not been close. She was his natural
daughter and she was almost twenty before they met.
After that, her Norman marriage had kept them estranged
for years at a time and the last five years of his life he had
in any case spent in Ely. Yet in the short time they had
had together, a bond had nevertheless formed, all the
stronger for being continually under challenge. Now she
grieved for the years they had so irretrievably lost.

It was unlucky that her son Richard was away from
home when the news came from Ely. He was Sir Richard
of Fallowdene by then, young and earnest, taking his
responsibilities as knight and landlord seriously. He had
gone off in good time to attend the October Shire Court at
Chichester. He had taken with him, among others, Ufi,
the young Fallowdene man who had succeeded Editha's
husband as steward, old Alric having died the previous
winter.

As a result, poor Editha, with the weight of the hall on
her shoulders until such time as those to whom authority
properly belonged should see fit to resume it, spent much
of that October shaking her head and sighing to anyone
who would listen that she'd seen others turn their backs on
the world like Wulfhild and if it went on too long, her
lady'd die too and then what would become of them all?

She undoubtedly had cause for despondency but
happily it proved to be misplaced. There came a night
when Wulfhild, instead of lying awake to weep as she had

done for twenty-one nights in succession, slept quickly and woke, late, to find her sorrowing done, as though a loud and discordant noise had suddenly ceased.

Her father was dead and she would not forget him. But for her, life must begin again. She got out of bed, annoyed to find herself weakened by inaction and by the sharp pain in the stiff knees which were the principal sign of her forty-three years. The trouble had begun in the one which was wrenched on the hillside, the day Sybil was born, and had gradually spread to the other. Richard had made a handsome carved stick for her and she reached for it impatiently. Her brain, unlike her body, seemed the better for its rest and was teeming with sudden ideas, which she wanted to put into effect at once.

She summoned a thankful Editha. 'Hot water, please. I want to wash. My hair too.' While she washed, she thought about lapsed land. After the Conquest, Fallowdene, like everywhere else, had been desperately short of men and a certain amount of land had gone wild again for want of hands to till it. But a new generation was growing up now. The hall had absorbed some of them as had always been the custom. Surplus young men moved into it to form the warband which every lord must train in arms; surplus girls or widows worked for their keep on the myriad tasks of a big house. But soon there would be too many for the hall to accommodate. Some of that land must be reclaimed. While Editha towelled her hair, she went over the map of Fallowdene in her head.

The manor actually consisted of three holdings. There was Fallowdene itself, with its fields and church and mill, at the eastern end of the valley. Then there was little Westwater, the subletting at the western end, and over the down to the south was Little Dene, which was actually bigger than Westwater. Little Dene still had enough land . . . her first objective, Wulfhild decided, taking the comb away from Editha in order to ply it more vigorously, should be the lapsed acres of Fallowdene land on the south down. The first steps might also be taken towards clearing some new land on the north down. Fallowdene had ample timber and there were some oaks which could with advantage be cut. Once seasoned, they could be sold for shipbuilding and the land they had occupied could eventually come under the plough.

'There's still hardly any grey in your hair, lady,' Editha was saying. 'Will you wear colours or mourning? Reckon you've mourned enough, myself.'

'So do I. I'll wear the blue overdress and the tawny undergown.' Since Simon's death, Wulfhild had reverted to English styles. 'And a clean white headshawl.' All her clothes were old, she thought. Some of the oak timber could be sold green, for a quick return of good silver. They could do with it. Money had been on their minds lately, with the bad weather of the last few years. They hadn't actually gone short of food but they had had to deplete their stores. The land taxes hadn't reflected the poor harvests, Wulfhild thought grimly. Eighteen shillings the tax gatherers had wanted last Lady Day. And there was still the matter of Sybil's dowry. In fact, one way and another, there was the matter of Sybil . . .

In the hall, breaking her fast, she sat by the fire and watched her six-year-old youngest child 'help' Editha and the other women make bread dough. She continued to make plans. Her elder daughter, Blanche, was settled at Withysham Abbey, five miles away. She had been sent there for an education but said she wished to stay, as a nun. Her portion had been set aside already to be paid to the abbey but was modest in amount because the abbess was her aunt and was not asking much. But Sybil would never make a nun and anyhow, it would be a waste. Only, to make a worthwhile marriage, a girl must have material accompaniments in land or money and where was it to be found?

Sybil ran across the hall to show her mother a shape she had moulded from the dough. She stood on tiptoe, beaming, oblivious of the gap where she had lost a baby tooth. As always, Wulfhild looked at this lastborn child of hers with something close to wonder.

She and Simon had been neither goodlooking nor ugly; merely ordinary. Their elder children were much the same. Both had inherited Wulfhild's somewhat heavy eyebrows, which gave strength to Richard's face but were a drawback to Blanche. Both too had Simon's light build.

102

Richard would have liked to be chunkier. But neither he nor his eldest sister were in any way remarkable.

Sybil was quite otherwise. In Sybil, some trick of heredity had worked a miracle, combining Simon's fine brows and agility, and the smooth black hair he had possessed in youth, with her mother's brilliant, almond-shaped blue eyes, and she was going to have Wulfhild's good width of brow and cheekbone, too. The overall effect was breathtaking, and as if that were not enough there was in Sybil a sparkling spirit which was all her own. Even her naughtinesses were inventive. Many little girls ran off and hid when threatened with the boredom of lessons in spinning, but few were discovered in the sheep pasture solemnly doing a dance, 'to amuse the lambs', or leading half a dozen friends among the village children into the woods, 'because we're going to be hermits and live on nuts'.

When Sybil was grown, one glance from those merry eyes would topple knights from their saddles like the swing of a mace and drive monks whimpering out of their vows. She would have to be married somehow. Yet although Fallowdene was prosperous compared to many places, most of what it produced, it consumed. Any dowry it might yield, certainly at present, would be derisory.

But there was a possible answer. The idea popped into Wulfhild's head as though it were the result of long deliberation. Fallowdene was held on condition that it furnished two knights and four men-at-arms to its overlord for forty days each year and at other times as necessary. The men-at-arms had never been a problem, since Simon had brought his own and now that most of these had gone away or retired into domesticity, there were the young men of the hall. What had at times been difficult was providing the knights.

While Simon was alive, he was one of them himself, and now Richard had replaced him. The second knight had been supplied by various stratagems over the years until, just before his death, Simon had let Little Dene to a young and impoverished knight called Sir Brian FitzWaleran, who had lost an inherited manor in a lawsuit and was very glad to get under a roof he could call his

103

own, for he was a widower with a small son. The boy was between one and two years older than Sybil. In all probability Brian would agree to their betrothal. Fallowdene's goodwill would be part of the deal, after all. He was a dull and worthy man whose conversation was limited to harvest prospects and his personal obsession that the crossbow was superior to the common bow, and his son already resembled him, but although Wulfhild would gladly have given Sybil the moon, in this matter she recognised limitations. Sybil would be lucky to get any husband sound in mind and body; she couldn't expect him to be interesting as well. With Brian's son, she would at least be safe.

Yes, that would do. As soon as Richard got back from Chichester, she would tell him. He would be relieved to have the worry of Sybil dealt with. Something must be done soon about a wife for Richard, too. Not that he'd be hard to settle, since he'd have Fallowdene to offer. Revolving candidates in her mind, Wulfhild finished eating, gave various orders to the women and went out, moving briskly enough with the aid of her stick, to see how much replenishment the woodstack would need before winter set in. It was on its way; the woodlands were turning russet and the wind had a restless gustiness which spoke of autumn. She glanced up at the southern escarpment of the down, trying to judge whether the racing clouds above it would thicken or lighten as the day went on. On the white path over the downcrest, the same path where once she had pursued a rogue dog, there were horsemen.

Even at this distance she knew them. Richard's horse, the one his father had bought him, was a dapple grey, visible miles away. She turned, shouting for the household.

She was so busy chivvying them that the arrivals were drawing rein in the yard before she looked at them properly. When she did, it was first of all to make sure that all who had set out, Richard and Ufi, the men who had accompanied them, their mounts and the three pack mules which carried purchases made in Chichester, were safely there.

Only when she had assured herself of that, did she

notice that the three pack mules were now four and that there was an extra rider, hooded, cloaked and anonymous, sitting on a lightweight bay mare and hanging back, half-shielded from view by the rest.

Her mind jolting with a fearful premonition, Wulfhild turned to her son. 'Richard, who . . .?'

Richard smiled down from his saddle. He turned and held out a hand to the stranger, who now rode forward. The mare halted beside him, tossing her pretty head, and Richard, jumping down, helped the mare's rider to alight, putting back the hood with a brush of his hand which was more than half a caress.

Wulfhild looked into a small, pale, precise face: blue eyes, charmingly modelled nose (*prissy* small mouth, said a scathing commentator inside Wulfhild's head) and a slightly receding chin. The owner of these doubtful attractions could be no more than seventeen. She did a beautiful little curtsey and drew off her gloves. They were of fine, supple leather and the hands they revealed were perfectly white, with small, gleaming, evenly-filed nails.

She raised one of them to tidy the hang of a plait and the plait, though mousey in colour and too thin, was clean and neatly threaded with silver cord.

'Mother,' said Richard, his voice quivering with pride, 'may I present to you my wife, Alice?'

105

Three

Opening Moves
1087–8

'Who is she?' Wulfhild demanded. 'Where did you find her? To bring someone back to Fallowdene like this and without a word of warning . . . what were you thinking of?'

'Thinking of?' Richard sounded amused. He saw that Alice's mare was eating her feed, patted her and came out of the stall, bucket in hand. 'What does a man usually think of when he takes a bride, Mother? And why did you need warning? Fallowdene's ready for her and she'll be company for you. You'll love her once you get to know her.'

'Will I indeed? She doesn't look strong enough to pick up a hoe, let alone pull her weight at harvest-time. Would she even *recognise* a hoe?'

'Where is she now? I think we should walk for a while and talk.' Richard put the bucket down, took his mother's arm and led her out of the stable.

'In the hall, nibbling a meat pasty, sipping elderberry wine and looking round her as though she'd never seen anything so rustic before,' said Wulfhild.

'Nonsense. Alice wouldn't be thinking that. She's just interested to see her new home, that's all.' Richard steered them out of the gate and turned on to the path to the down.

'She's a lady. Over-refined.'

'You've been a lady yourself in your day, Mother.'

'Who *is* she?' Wulfhild demanded again. 'And,' she added, coming to the point, 'what's her dowry?'

Richard, still displaying that maddening amusement, gave her a sidelong glance. 'Oh, is that what's worrying you? It need not. I've done well for the dowry, I promise you.'

'Who is she?' said Wulfhild for the third time, through her teeth.

106

'Her father's Roland of Warburton.'

'Roland . . .? The Chichester merchant?' Wulfhild had not been off the manor for years but she knew the names of all with whom Fallowdene did business. Roland of Warburton owned three ships and traded in Europe and the Mediterranean. He was versatile; his ships carried anything he thought he could sell at the other end. But he specialised in exporting hides and cheeses and bringing wine and spices back. He was wealthy. Wulfhild looked very slightly mollified.

'The same.' Richard said. 'After we had that trouble with Hammerfoot, the day Sybil was born, and we hadn't enough ginger, Father made an arrangement with Roland to supply us regularly with that and some other things . . .'

'Yes, I know.'

'Well, I've got to know him quite well over the years. I call at his warehouse whenever I'm in Chichester. This time he asked me back to his hall. He's half-English and half-Norman and his wife is English. Alice speaks both tongues. It's a very mixed kind of household, like ours. I felt at home. And Alice was there. I went into the house as one man,' said Richard simply, 'and came out as another.'

'You don't look like your grandfather,' said Wulfhild exasperatedly, 'but you take after him, just the same.'

She knew the story of her own conception. Her father, wildly, desperately in love for the only time in his life, discovering that the girl had encouraged him only to spur on someone else, had stumbled strickenly away from that revelation, and relieved his frustration on the floor of a cow-byre with a blue-eyed thrall woman. Hence Wulfhild. She knew too the story of how he had first fallen into love, walking round a corner and coming face to face with a young woman and passing instantaneously from one mode of life to another.

Exactly as Richard had apparently done in the hall of an Anglo-Norman dealer in cheese, hides, spices and Loire valley wine. It would probably have made little difference to Richard if Alice had had no dowry at all. Wulfhild's face darkened again.

107

'The dowry,' Richard was saying. 'There's fifteen pounds of good silver coin in the mules' saddlebags. That's just to begin with. It ought to solve our tax problems for a few years. Then, I can buy ginger and other things at half-price for the rest of Alice's life. And I've a half-share in one of Roland's ships. *And*,' he said with emphasis, putting a hand to his belt-pouch, 'there are these.'

Wulfhild stared disbelievingly at the handful of small objects he held out for her inspection. 'Have you gone mad, Richard? *Onions*?'

'Wrong. Guess again.'

The tap of Wulfhild's stick was a storm warning. 'Don't play games with me, Richard. *What are they*?'

He had changed. He was no longer quite her son. Her indignation could not reach him; he was teasing her from the security of some private fastness. She recognised it. It was the assurance of manhood and Alice, that prim, pale, skinny intruder who was now sitting in the hall and drinking Wulfhild's best elderberry wine, had given it to him. Her fury made her speechless. When Richard told her the name of the curious little pale corms in his hand, she could not at first answer and thinking the name unfamiliar to her, he began to explain. Brusquely, she stopped him.

'I know. I've served in great houses in my time. In the Lady of Wales' household it was used in the cooking on feast days. Once at a bardic festival, her husband had it sprinkled in the rushes to sweeten them instead of rosemary; to honour the bards, he said. But it was hard to get and expensive; they gave up using it before I left Wales. I haven't heard of it for years.'

'You're hearing of it now,' said Richard with a grin.

'I'm offering you a gamble,' Roland had said, standing in the little back room at his warehouse. He had emptied a small pouch out on to the table between them. 'There's maybe fifty of these little bulbs here. It will take years to grow enough to be of any use. The yield is low. It means investing time and land and only wealthy customers will buy it – I import a little for the court and so on – so you wouldn't call it a buoyant market. But it could be worth its weight in gold if you can produce enough and *if* you can find buyers. What about it? You can have these as part of Alice's portion, or a mark of gold instead. The choice is yours.'

'Where do they come from?' Richard asked, picking up a corm and feeling its papery skin with his thumb.

Roland chuckled. He had married late in life and was already ageing; his angular shoulders beginning to stoop and his scanty hair now grey. But his veined eyes had a boyishly wicked gleam. 'Moorish Spain. I've a contact there who is honest in his dealings with me – I pay him well – but less respectable in his attitude to some others, especially those he actively dislikes. He stole a couple of corms for me, from a man he had a grudge against. That was several years ago and these are the outcome. I've proved it will grow here, as you see.'

'But don't you want to go on growing it?'

'I thought I did,' said Roland frankly. 'But it's more nuisance than it's worth. I'm a merchant, not a farmer. Most of the land I hold, I let. I keep a few acres for myself, just outside the town, but I want them for corn. I haven't the ground to devote to this and besides, the enterprise needs to be kept secret so I have to keep on going out there to tend the plants myself. I haven't time. My son feels the same. I'd be just as happy if Alice's husband took over the task and gained the advantage, if any, instead. Well? A problematic profit one day many years hence, or a mark of gold now? By the way, if anything happens to you and there are no children, the revenue from these, if it exists, must revert to Alice, you understand?'

'Certainly. She would take out of the marriage all she brought with her, in accordance with normal custom. I should regard the crop from these as part of that.'

'That's what I wanted to hear. I think you'll treat her fairly. I've turned down some other men because I doubted them. Well, what's your answer? These or the gold?'

'I notice,' said Richard, 'that we're having this talk very privately, all by ourselves in this little back room.'

'Quite right. The rest of the settlement we'll discuss openly in the hall, in the usual way. But this is between you and me.'

'I'll take the gamble,' Richard said.

It was somewhat disconcerting to find that his mother had not only heard of the plant but thought little of it. 'The Lady of Wales told me it takes thousands on thousands of flowers to produce anything saleable and then who'll buy it? You've been cheated, son.'

It wasn't the moment, clearly, to mention the gold mark. 'I'm looking ahead,' he said. 'Perhaps one day Alice's son and mine will get the benefit.'

This morning she had thought that they must find Richard a wife. She had even thought of one or two names. She had also thought that the matter must be approached with care, for Richard's wife would be a permanency at Fallowdene.

It was only just being borne in on her that pale prim Alice was going to be that permanency. That she, Wulfhild, was Lady of Fallowdene no longer.

She would see about that.

'I hope you do have a son,' she said shortly. 'I hope Alice can manage it. She looks narrow in the hips to me.'

'Mother,' said Richard evenly, 'I hope you'll be kind to Alice. I promised her father I would take good care of her. Shall we be getting back?'

Waspishly, as they turned in at the gate, Wulfhild said: 'While you were so busy wooing and negotiating the most extraordinary dowry I ever heard of, did you remember by any chance that you are supposed to ask your overlord's consent to marry?'

'Of course. De Warenne was at the Shire Court. He agreed quite willingly.'

He would, Wulfhild thought with fury. De Warenne had only lately become their suzerain. There had been a change of overlords in their part of Sussex. They had been on bad terms with his predecessor but just at this moment Wulfhild positively regretted the change. De Warenne was much too amiable. He had condemned her to Alice. She walked into the hall beside her son, in an unfriendly silence.

*

'I know I've sprung Alice on you, Mother,' Richard said patiently later the same day, 'but really, she is very sweet and pious and you'll find her all that a daughter should be. It's true she's never chopped wood or scythed corn. But she can weave and sew. She wove and stitched every single thing she's wearing. She can make bread, too. You'll see!'

It became clear as the days went by that besotted though he was, Richard's assessment of his bride was perfectly correct. It was just unfortunate that her very virtues were her most irritating characteristics.

She was, for instance, docile and well-mannered. Her manners were so pretty that when the betrothal was mooted between Sybil and Brian of Little Dene's son, it was Alice who did most to persuade a slightly dubious Sir Brian, who to Wulfhild's annoyance had clearly harboured greater hopes for his boy, into agreeing. She could see Brian thinking that if Fallowdene suited a lady like Alice . . .

'Who does he think he is?' fumed Wulfhild afterwards and really meant: 'Who does *she* think *she* is?' only she did not say it because Richard was capable of being very unpleasant indeed to anyone who upset his Alice.

Then there was the preciseness, her most distinct trait, so marked that when she walked she seemed at each step to place her foot on *that* piece of ground and no other. This characteristic was the source of her formidable gift with a needle. A needle steered by Alice slid accurately between those two threads and no others. It was an admirable accomplishment and should have been an asset. But Editha and the other women had picked Wulfhild's sense of dispossession out of the air and they were loyal to their mistress; on top of which, the finish of Alice's plainest clothes made theirs look like sackcloth. Far from admiring, they were resentful.

Her effortlessly even spinning and weaving won her no acclaim either. Gunnor, one of the young women who worked in the hall, had formerly been recognised as the best weaver in Fallowdene. Dethroned, Gunnor sulked without concealment. As for Alice's undoubtedly competent breadmaking, she demonstrated it only once. On

111

that embarrassing morning, while Alice kneaded dough, Editha – who could outdo Gunnor in sulkiness whenever she had a mind – crashed pots together in a tub of hot water and violently scoured a pinewood table with sand, muttering audibly that old and lined she might be but ripe for burial she wasn't quite, not yet. Thereafter, on Wulfhild's edged advice, Alice's breadmaking skills were left to moulder away unused.

Richard had been right about the piety, too.

'You can't sew and weave all day,' Wulfhild said, trying to sound good-humoured although the vegetable patch needed digging over and half an hour with a spade would leave Alice worn out, with blistered palms. 'You'll hurt your eyesight. What else did you do, at home? Can you,' asked Wulfhild, inspired, 'make cheese, or milk cows?'

'No, Mother. I usually spent two or three hours at my devotions.' She prefaced the second sentence with a small *tch* sound as though assembling her thoughts and positioning her tongue just so before speaking. Richard had once unwisely remarked to his mother that he found this mannerism charming. Wulfhild, who hadn't noticed it before, had since then been driven to the verge of insanity by it. She clenched her hand at her side as she said: 'Here, we go to the church on Sundays. There's work to do the rest of the week and never hours enough to do it in.'

'Tch. I expect I could learn to make cheese and to milk,' said Alice pacifically. 'I'll gladly try.'

She did try. Perversely, she performed well. Wulfhild could with the utmost enjoyment have killed her.

But almost the worst thing about Alice was her effect on Richard. 'He's gone completely beyond my control,' said Wulfhild to Editha, her sympathiser. 'I came here to Fallowdene with my father when it was falling to pieces and between us we brought it back to life and now Richard won't listen to a word I say. He's agreed to clearing the wild land on the south down but he will *not* consent to cutting any wood. It's true we don't need the money now but you never know, and cut logs are as valuable as silver in the coffers. If we have another harvest like last year's, we could still be glad to know we've something extra in hand. But he's got so wilful . . . he even hummed and hawed before he'd put Sybil's betrothal to Sir Brian.'

'He's growing up,' said Editha, trying to comfort her.

'He listens too much to Alice,' said Wulfhild. 'Does he even *see* anyone but her, these days?'

So often, when they all sat by the fire at the day's end, conversation would drop away and Wulfhild would see Richard and Alice looking at each other and feel the air between them tauten and sing. And a few minutes later, murmuring their excuses, they would slip away to bed.

'And much good *that's* done,' she said to Editha. 'Christmas has come and gone and she's still bleeding every month. She's caught three colds in the head since she's been here but catch a baby, oh no! Too bloody refined, that's what she is!'

But in early February there were signs that in this respect at least Alice was mending her ways. She missed a course. She then began to be extremely sick and could not keep down any at all of the salted meat which, apart from bread, was their staple food at this season.

Nauseated, green-blotched, whimpering with exhaustion, she threw up meal after meal. Wulfhild, responding in desperation to Richard's pleading eyes, sacrificed a good laying hen to provide Alice with fresh meat and then another hen and finally an orphaned lamb for which she would normally have found a foster mother.

She even sent to Withysham Abbey for a few wrinkled last year's apples, because Alice said she longed for fruit.

A cold, hard March, beset by east winds, yielded to April, blowy and fresh but with gleams of sunshine between the rainstorms and the hail. There were days when it was at last pleasant to be out of doors. 'Where is Alice?' Wulfhild demanded as Richard hurried into the hall early on what promised to be a fine morning. 'She should be up and moving about. Is she being sick again?'

'No, but she's not well either. She's asking for you.'

Alice's face, peering over the top of a beaverskin rug, was wan. The cynical voice in Wulfhild's mind, which would not stop passing derogatory comments on her daughter-in-law, observed that with that receding chin,

113

the girl looked like a skinned hare. 'Mother,' said Alice dismally, 'I'm bleeding.'

And Wulfhild, roundly ignoring her daughter-in-law's shocked expression, swore.

By midday it was all over. Alice had been made as comfortable as possible and the pitiful bloodstained blob which would have been her child and Richard's had been disposed of. Alice was crying, wretchedly and persistently, like a querulous child.

'It happens.' Wulfhild did her best. 'Richard was early and so was Sybil and there were others I lost altogether. Worst of all is lasting the nine months and then losing a baby after it's born.' She told Alice about her small son who had died, during a storm. 'There's plenty of time,' she said, encouraging Alice as Editha had once tried to encourage her. 'Richard will want to see you cheerful. Drink your broth.' It was good fresh chicken broth; they had sacrificed another hen. Alice, however, sensing anger beneath Wulfhild's outward sympathy, cried harder and asked to see the priest.

'I've sent old Wenenc to her,' Wulfhild said to Richard. 'No, no, she's all right. She wanted to talk to him, that's all. God knows what help he'll be to her; he's as old as Methusaleh and half-blind and all he'll do is mumble prayers with her but that's what she wants, I suppose.'

'Wenenc may be old, but he's kind,' said Richard. Had that been pointed, Wulfhild wondered? 'I'm going to her,' he said, and left the hall.

Wulfhild, shrugging, took up her stick and made her uneven way out. The crops on the flanks of the downs were showing well. If only they could have a few weeks of sunshine at the right time and no more hailstorms, the harvest might be good. If Alice conceived in the summer, she would have a better chance of bringing the next child to term. At least she had proved she could conceive.

Sybil came dancing towards her, a puppy bounding at her side and a woolly toy which Wulfhild had made for her under her arm. 'Mother! There are horsemen coming, with banners! Are we expecting anyone? Who are they?'

114

'Banners?' Wulfhild swung round to look at the chalk track at which Sybil was pointing. The child was right. And she knew the colours of the banners. They were those of de Warenne and when one's overlord sent his men unexpectedly and bearing his official devices, one possible explanation sprang instantly to mind.

'It's a rebellion,' said de Warenne's messenger, standing in the hall with the household clustered round him. 'In Kent, mainly. The king's uncle, Odo of Bayeux, has taken to arms.'

They had come by way of Little Dene and scooped Sir Brian up with them. 'I was in Chichester at Christmas and there were whispers then,' he said. 'It's no surprise.'

Sir Brian always claimed that things were no surprise, however amazing they might be. If a dragon had appeared and set fire to the woods of Fallowdene, he would have said it was no surprise. 'He doesn't like surprises,' Richard once remarked caustically. 'They make life too interesting. Excitement will catch him up one day and it will serve him right.'

On this occasion, however, the statement in Sir Brian's monotonous voice was probably correct. There *had* been rumours.

'My lord Odo got his English estates back last year,' the messenger was saying. 'But the king was reluctant; it was the prelates on the Council who pressed for it. And the king chose other men for his advisers, not Odo . . .'

'Very wise,' said Richard crisply. He had already lifted down his sword from where it hung on the wall. 'In his place, so would I.'

'Perhaps, but the lord Odo resented it,' said the messenger. He had his story off pat; no doubt he had told it in half a dozen houses already. 'Nearly all the great barons hold land here and in Normandy; he kept pointing out to them how hard it is to serve two masters, and he found plenty to agree. Now his idea is to shrink the two masters down to one – Duke Robert of Normandy. He's taken fealty on behalf of Robert Curthose from a lot of barons and they're on the rampage in Kent and they've fortified some of the Sussex coastal castles to protect the malcontents and receive the duke when he lands. But de Warenne is loyal to the king. Fallowdene is called to arms to assist him.'

'I can be ready in an hour,' said Richard.

Wulfhild nodded. She had been through all this before. 'I'll pack your gear. Pick the men who go with you and say goodbye to your wife. I'll have the horses saddled.'

'Alice,' said Richard. His expression had gone bleak. 'I'd as soon not be going from home just now. And so suddenly.'

'Go and tell her,' said Wulfhild shortly. 'Leave the rest to us.'

He was shut away with Alice almost until the last moment and when he came out, his face was grey. 'Try to comfort her,' he said to Wulfhild, who was waiting by his horse.

Wulfhild said: 'God keep you,' and, 'the saints grant you victory,' and with the others watched the party ride away: the messengers, Sir Brian, Richard, and four young men from Fallowdene hall: Asa, Harold, Gurth, Swithin. Swithin was the eldest. He had been born out of wedlock and under protest to Gerda the miller's daughter, the year that Wulfhild and her father came to the manor. He was the fruit of an assault by an unmannerly housecarle, long gone from the place. Gerda had sworn she hated all men and would never marry but in the end surprised herself and everyone else by consenting to wed one of Simon's Norman companions. Simon had given him the tenancy of Westwater and Rollo had made a good stepfather. Swithin was a powerfully built man now, expertly trained in arms. The youngest of the four was Gurth, who had looked after the stables. He was only fifteen. The brothers Asa and Harold might well be missed most of all; Editha relied on their goodwill to get her land strips tilled. They did it for her in return for a share of the produce. Fallowdene would seem very empty until they all came back.

If they came back. That cruel possibility was always there. Wulfhild had known them all since they were babies.

She made herself watch them go with a steady face. She had had practice at this in the past and had long since

116

terrorised the other women into doing the same because men fought better and were more likely to keep safe if their minds were not distracted by worry over those at home. But it was hard.

She was still holding her features rigid against the longing to let them crumple into grief when she went to Alice. Alice lay on her back, weeping hopelessly, tears running down her narrow temples into her mousey hair. Her nose was an unpleasing pink.

'This won't do,' said Wulfhild. 'It's unlucky to send your husband off with tears. Sit up. You must get strong so that when he comes back . . .'

'What if he doesn't?' wailed Alice, putting the unmentionable into words. 'I haven't even got the baby, now.'

No, thought Wulfhild, her repressed dislike of Alice the intruder surging up through her with astounding force and suddenness. No, you haven't and nor have I. If Richard doesn't return, what will de Warenne say is to be done with Fallowdene? What if he looks on it as *yours*, Mistress Wheyface? If he does, he'll make you marry again so that Fallowdene can still have a resident knight, of his choice, and the whole manor will pass to that man, for ever, not even in trust for a child of my blood. And where shall I be? *What* shall I be? A leftover, a pensioner, living on sufferance here at Fallowdene when I'm the one who for twenty-five years has loved it and slaved for it and, yes, sold my body for it. All because Richard wouldn't let me choose him the right wife. All because you've bewitched him with your proper ways and that maddening little *tch* though you can't hold a pregnancy and can hardly even get one to start with. Oh God, or Woden Skyfather, anyone! Bring Richard safely home and help me to have patience with this . . . this creature!

'Mother!' Sybil danced in. One always thought of Sybil as dancing rather than walking, or running. Her feet made sprightly patterns on the ground wherever she trod. 'Mother, where has Richard gone? Is it Chichester again? Will he bring me back another red ribbon?' Richard had last year brought Sybil a length of scarlet silk ribbon which she thought looked so wonderful in her dark hair that she wore it till it was worn out, regardless of attempts to dissuade or even forbid her.

Anger melted at the sight of her. 'No, darling. Not to Chichester this time. You shouldn't be in here. Off with you, now. Go and look at the fields and see if the corn is long enough for the ryedogs' paws to show when the wind blows.'

Sybil danced away. 'Ryedogs?' queried Alice listlessly.

'When the wind blows across the corn, it looks as if something invisible were running over it. Some say it's the hounds of the Wild Huntsman, out for a run.' Sybil's intrusion had been beneficial; she managed to speak to Alice quite pleasantly. Which was as well, since this was Richard's wife and there was nothing to be done about it. 'Haven't you heard the legend?'

'The Wild Huntsman?' Alice, who had not sat up when told to, did so now of her own accord. Her tears ceased, apparently shocked out of existence. 'Yes, of course I've heard the legend. It's that old tale of the heathen god Woden hunting the souls of the dead. Some call him Herne . . . but Mother, surely you don't tell pagan tales like that to Sybil? What would Father Wenenc say? Our priest at home was very angry when a minstrel sang a ballad about Herne.'

It was too much. Wulfhild turned on her after all. 'Where's the harm? It's just a story. Or perhaps it isn't, perhaps there's some truth in it. Who knows? Do *you* know, my lady? Are you so sure? You're always very sure of yourself but how much do you know, really know, of anything?' Alice recognised the loathing in Wulfhild's voice and shrank against her pillows, eyes wide and lips trembling. 'Before you tell me how to rear my children,' said Wulfhild fiercely, stabbing home, 'you'd best have some of your own!'

Four

The Sybaritic Duke
1088

In August, the stags' antlers were fully grown and hardened, the velvet peeling off. The stag whom Helias of La Fleche had dubbed the Old One because he was not only old in years but possessed all the wisdom and cunning which were traditionally supposed to go with age, had sixteen points this year, ivory coloured dagger tips on horn branches stout as seasoned oak.

The Old One knew that the packs of two and four-legged carnivores which from time to time infested his forest did not always hunt in the same way. But whether they were trying to drive him on to the arrows of marksmen in ambush, or flushing him into the open for a chase, his favourite method of self-protection was much the same. He made a younger stag take his place.

He had been flushed out this morning, his initial attempt to lie flat under a tangled bush while the beaters went past having been spoiled by the questing noses of unleashed hounds. Now, as he sped across a stretch of open heathland, he heard the horns and the baying behind him and knew they were on his scent.

But he was on familiar territory. He veered to his left, seeking lower ground and the shelter of the bushes in the valley. Plunging into them, following his own nose which was as sensitive as that of any hound, he veered again and came headlong into a dell where another buck was lying. The other came to his feet at once and lowered his head, but six points were no match for sixteen. The Old One charged him, his weapons making contact while the other's were still hopelessly far away from doing any damage. The smaller stag wheeled and fled. The Old One turned at right angles to the line, made several mighty leaps which put an astonishing amount of ground behind him, arrived at the banks of a stream and began to wade upriver.

*

'What on earth are you doing?' the huntsman Michel panted, spurring up as Ralph des Aix was calling the hounds off the line. 'What are you about, Ralph? There's the stag; God's Teeth, I can see him!'

'It's the wrong one,' said Ralph. 'That's not the Old One, look at the slots! He's put up a substitute; his own slots are half that size. If my lord wants a sixteen point head above his seat in the hall, he won't find it in this direction. We've got to make a back cast.'

'The old devil!' said Michel, meaning the Old One.

'Well, it's natural. If I thought a pack of hounds were on my trail, I expect I'd switch them on to someone else's if I could. There's a stream down there; we'd best try that way.'

They brought the Old One to bay at the foot of a hill, where recent rain had caused a landslip and made a sheer face for twenty feet. With the hill to guard his hindquarters, he used his antlers to account for three deerhounds before Helias rode up to despatch him with a single arrow. 'Magnificent,' Helias said, looking down on the spread of the antlers. 'Almost a pity to kill him. He might have sprouted eighteen points next year, though I doubt it. They don't very often.'

'We'd have lost him but for Ralph here,' said Michel, with a meaning look at his lord. 'He spotted where the old fellow tried to set the pack off after another deer.'

'Ah. Yes,' said Helias. 'Ride with me going home, Ralph, if you please. I want to talk to you.'

'. . . Michel tells me,' said Helias 'that you intend to leave us.'

'Yes, sir,' said Ralph uncomfortably, looking straight ahead between his horse's ears.

'May I ask why? You are free, of course. You have a right to go where you will. Michel says you have some idea of adventuring off to England. But I must point out that if it's adventure you want, in due time you'll get that with me. And if you're off to seek your fortune; well, you'll get advancement here in time. Michel will retire eventually from active work. You'd be in line for his post, and it carries a good rate of pay, and land.'

One could not say to a lord as good, as likeable, as Helias that 'in due time' seemed a long way off, nor express regret that one's friend Michel, from whom one had learned so much, looked fit enough to hold his post for ten years yet. Fortunately, there was another reason which he could offer.

'I badly want to go to England, sir. My father died recently . . .'

'Did he? I didn't know. I'm sorry.'

'Yes, it was sudden.' And had taken away some kind of foundation from under him. His father was dead and if he were to go back to Aix now, his brother Reggie would not fail to welcome him . . . but his brother would be Reginald of Aix, the master of the holding, whereas he, Ralph, would be no one except to his stepmother. 'When I left home,' he said, 'my father asked me to let him know if I ever heard news of an old friend of his, someone who lives in England. I never did hear any news. Now I wish I'd tried harder to find out. And I thought, perhaps, I could go myself and look for this friend. Perhaps he might like to have the last news of my father, might like to know the friendship wasn't forgotten. I'm not putting this clearly. I've got some savings. I can buy a passage and keep myself for a while.'

'I know you've got savings. You've been training horses in your spare time, for other people.' Ralph glanced round in surprise and Helias laughed. 'Oh yes, I know. I know what goes on on my estate. I know what's going on in your head, too. You've had bad news, it's shaken you out of old habits. Suddenly you want to see new things, find out what's on the other side of the horizon. The horizon of the English Channel, in your case. I'm not unsympathetic. I've always longed to go on pilgrimage to the Holy Land and although I would most truly like to see Bethlehem and Jerusalem, that's not the whole of it. I'd like to see far countries, too. I'd be lying if I said that that wasn't part of it. Perhaps in some ways I'm not unlike you.'

'It won't be quite a strange country. England, I mean. My father was English and I speak the language.'

'I see. All right, Ralph. I won't say any more. I'm sorry

121

to lose you and so is Michel. It was he who asked me to talk to you. If you decide to stay in England, you shouldn't have much difficulty in finding employment as a huntsman, with some new lord. Perhaps in a more senior position than you hold here.' Tactfully, Helias pretended not to notice Ralph flush. 'One thing, Ralph. Be careful whom you pick as a lord. Open-handedness is a virtue but sometimes it isn't as open as it seems.'

'I will be careful,' said Ralph, after a pause. He did not quite understand the warning, but it seemed necessary to say something. Helias did not enlarge. In fact, he did not quite understand it either. He had spoken without intending to, as though prompted by some misty prescience. The boy was young in some ways for his twenty years, and he was setting out alone . . .

There were no forebodings in Ralph's mind, however, the day he sailed for England on a trading vessel bound for Dover, carrying a flag to assure patrolling English ships of her pacific intentions. Shipping from the direction of Normandy was suspect just then.

He embarked on a sparkling morning, with a high heart. He was off to adventure and new places, off to find people who had known his father and a new lord who would give him the land which his father could not, for which Helias would have made him wait. Land which would be his, to which his brother would have no title.

The weather grew heavy and sticky before the voyage was over and the wind failed. The seamen had to get out the oars, and complained about it. But Ralph had no complaints. He was exceedingly happy, and confident.

On disembarking at Dover, he found lodging in an abbey and there asked advice on how to find a particular manor in Sussex. The brother whose business it was to buy provisions for the abbey, told him to try a merchant who was that year head of the Dover Merchants' Guild. 'Merchants are good sources of that kind of information. If they don't know, they can tell you who will.'

Good luck was with him. There were several guild members dining in the merchant's hall that day and one of them knew of Fallowdene, had even bought wool from it.

'You take the Guildford road and at Guildford turn south for Chichester. But when you see the downs – that's what we call the range of smooth, bare-looking hills just inland of the Sussex coast – rise in front of you, look for a track to your left. These are the landmarks . . .'

He made the ride with perfect ease, although the land was strange to him and although it was technically at war. He saw traces of Odo's rebellion, signs of ravaging, once a group of refugees plodding wearily in search of shelter. But he himself was neither challenged nor delayed.

In after years, when he looked back on the strange affair that his life had been, it seemed to him that nothing in it was as strange as that; the ease with which he got to Fallowdene. It was as if it had been meant.

No one from Fallowdene died in Odo's uprising, though the brothers Asa and Harold came home with scars of which they were inordinately proud.

Richard came through unscathed despite – as he said when he reached home and regaled them all with his story – of having been in the forefront of all the action. He rode at his leader de Warenne's side as they chased the rebels across Kent, over blackened fields and past smoking farmhouses. He was one of those who actually laid hands on Gilbert Clare when he was taken. Gilbert Clare, now lord of Tonbridge, had demonstrated an adult version of his boyhood tendency to bite, abandoned the king and gone over to Odo. He was a catch and was sent to London to await trial, amid much satisfied rubbing of hands.

Odo, however, escaped to the sea and turned up next eighty miles away in Pevensey on the Sussex coast. Richard was in the force which cut across country as fast as their horses' legs would go and then, for the next six weeks, besieged Pevensey.

The castle was holding out in the hope of relief, but relief never came. Once, a handful of ships flying Normandy's leopards appeared at sea but Rufus had ships enough to discourage them. Richard, recounting to his family the history of that halfhearted invasion, said: 'We had two and a half vessels to every ship the Normans had. I saw the Norman sails retreat over the horizon.'

He then mounted to accompany de Warenne as part of the escort to a herald, who sounded a trumpet outside the castle and called on its inmates to surrender.

In later life Richard acquired the nickname of Debrouillard, the Resourceful. But some people maintained that luck played at least as great a part in his successful career and his survival to the age of nearly eighty. The response to the herald's summons was a swishing rain of arrows, one of which passed harmlessly and well-nigh miraculously between Richard's saddle pommel and the coarse grey mane of his horse, to bury its point amid the chain links of the mail on de Warenne's thigh.

Richard helped his leader back to camp and saw him taken away by litter to the priory where eventually he died, from blood-poisoning. Then he returned to his duty and was present when Pevensey, brought down at last by hunger, surrendered and its gaunt inmates marched out, and one of them asked the king quite candidly: 'Before you hang us, can we have a square meal?'

They were not hanged. Richard heard Odo make peace with Rufus on their behalf and his own and was in the royal escort when Rufus and Odo set out together to Rochester, the last stronghold of the rising, to announce that the war was over.

He had been told to include his own men in the escort, so Brian of Little Dene was with him when Odo . . . 'we christened him the Fat Fox,' said Richard afterwards, making them all laugh . . . astride the horse which Rufus had lent him, 'because that half-starved clothes rail you rode out of Pevensey on will drop dead before we get halfway to Rochester', went ahead to parley with the representatives who came out of Rochester Castle.

The parley lasted twenty minutes, out on the open no-man's-land between castle and king. Then Odo put spurs to Rufus' horse and in the midst of the men of Rochester, rode headlong for its gate.

'Oh, well, I'm not surprised, are you?' said Brian predictably. 'What else would you expect?'

Rufus hadn't expected it, apparently. 'By the Face!' bellowed the king, loudly enough to be heard by everyone within a fifty yard radius. 'By the Holy Face of Lucca, I gave him rope! If he wants to make a noose of it, then so he shall.'

'And that was the first time,' Richard said, not immediately after his return from that campaign, but some years later, 'that anyone ever heard him use that oath. It's famous now. He's made it his own. I believe his father the Conqueror used to swear by the Splendour of God and King Rufus wanted a private oath too. He always wanted to be like his father. The Face is the Italian carving of Christ's countenance, of course. People were talking about it just then; it was one of the marvels of Christendom.' Richard himself was slightly in his cups, showing off in a mild way because by then he was a friend of somebody close to the king. 'The second time I heard the king use that oath . . .'

The second time was in a different context. That time it was an exclamation of satisfaction. News was coming out of besieged Rochester, concerning the conditions inside it. That year, 1088, was a sultry summer, with a heavy, hazy sky for days on end, and the waters of the Medway sluggish and coloured like lead. And there were flies . . .

As a child, Henry had been prone to tantrums. As a man, he found himself subject now and then to black rages whose force even surprised their owner because they seemed to be actually bigger than he was.

He had one such surge of fury at his father's deathbed, when he learned that he was to inherit no land, only five thousand pounds' weight of silver. He controlled himself because he could hardly rave at, let alone attack, the mass of immobilised pain which was his father. William had sensed his anger, though, and tried to soothe it. 'Patience, Henry. Of all my living sons you're the most like me.' He said it huskily, because the corruption in his body was eating at his vocal cords, but nevertheless his tone carried conviction. 'I'd gamble,' whispered the Conqueror, 'I'd put money on it – one day you'll come into your own, and your own'll be all your brothers have now. Meanwhile,' William added, the hoarse voice changing timbre to something down to earth and cynical, 'take that sealed order there by your hand to Rouen Treasury and get your silver weighed out to you now. I wouldn't give a penny for your chances once Rouen's in Curthose's hands.'

He knew, when he had had time to think, that he had no right to anger; Britnoth had told him long ago that younger sons must make their own way, even when they were born to the purple and their elders were not. He was better equipped than some. He had five thousand pounds of silver, a first class education, and the Conqueror for a father. What was he, if he couldn't do something with all that?

Meanwhile, in order to live in any kind of comfort, he must give his allegiance to one or other of his brothers. He could lease land with that silver. Rufus showed signs of wishing to drive a hard bargain but the easygoing Curthose was willing enough to co-operate. He probably would have held on to Henry's silver if he had got at the Treasury first, but had no taste for haggling. In company with a number of knights bachelor, his friends, Henry settled down to the life of a Norman gentleman, oscillating between his rented estate and Curthose's court, and amused himself by wooing a couple of Curthose's lesser mistresses away from him.

Life was not disagreeable. But the next black rage was only just round the corner and when it arrived, it was Curthose who provoked it.

'There's a messenger from England – from Bishop Odo,' one of his friends said, ducking through the low door of Curthose's Rouen menagerie, and curling up a fastidious nose at the smell. 'The duke won't see him. He's asked for you instead.'

'From Odo?' Henry, who had been giving the keepers a hand in inveigling a panther into an inner den so that the outer lair could be cleaned, straightened up sharply from locking the cage. 'In Rochester?' His friend nodded. 'I'll see him in my chamber,' Henry said.

The messenger was a drawn-faced man, roughly clad but with a bearing that suggested that normally he dressed better. He was sitting wearily on a stool but rose as Henry came in. He then took in Henry's grubby appearance and rank aroma, and looked bewildered.

'My apologies if I reek of leopard. I've been helping to

126

look after one. I like them, handsome, sinuous, predatory beasts that they are,' Henry said. 'I've even called my horse Panther. You're from Rochester? Is the siege over?'

'No, sir. And I don't mind the smell of leopard. It's better than the stink I left behind in Rochester.'

'Stink?'

'You've had a little rain here, I'm told. There's been no rain in England for weeks on weeks. In Rochester, the salt meat's rotting in the barrels and the flour's full of maggots and your uncle Odo's men are taking turns to brush away the flies from one another so that they can eat even that. The flies are everywhere, on everything, great fat gorged buzzing things, and the bad food's poisoning the men. When I left, eleven had died in the castle and more in the town. It only takes hours once it starts. Their bowels turn liquid and they clutch at their stomachs and twist and twist and nothing eases them. They call for water all the time but the water's foul too and they only throw it up . . .' Suddenly, startlingly, the memories roused by his own words made him retch. He stopped, a hand to his mouth.

'You came to get help, is that it?' Henry asked. 'And Duke Robert hasn't been able to see you?'

'He won't see me, sir. But I must give the message to someone of position, so I asked for you. I got out of Rochester by stealth, a rope down the walls after dark and I escaped down the river in a stolen boat. I drifted half a mile so as not to make a noise with the oars. I bought a passage on a merchant ship at the estuary mouth. All to get word to someone who might help! The castle's being held for the duke, sir, but unless he sends aid . . .'

Henry seized his arm. It felt thin. 'Come with me.'

The room into which Henry hustled the messenger without ceremony could have been lifted straight from Araby. The duke's castle-cum-palace at Rouen had a marked Byzantine influence in its architecture, and this chamber, on the floor above the main hall, was the most exotic of all. It was wide and gracious. Sunlight, pouring through shapely windows, played on a high vaulted roof and elegant pillars of pale stone, and on a floor of polished boards strewn with rugs of spotted fawnskin. There were no tapestries but two carpets, brought from the infidel

127

east, marvels of complex design and rich colour, hung on the walls instead. And in the midst of it all . . .

Under Henry's hand, the messenger's bony arm went hard as if in rigor. Henry's own body clenched into an answering hardness.

He could not run amok here in the private quarters of the Duke of Normandy any more than at his father's deathbed. If Duke Robert Curthose chose to lounge sybaritically on a divan, flat on his lazy stomach so that he could hang over his baby son's cradle and croon nonsense to him, he was entitled to do so and he was entitled also to send urgent messengers about their business in order to wallow in fulsome paternity undisturbed. He was the duke.

And his mistress Biota, the baby's mother, had the right, as long as it pleased her lover, to sit curled beside him sipping in refined fashion at a goblet of fruit juice while a well-fed and well-dressed jongleur twanged the latest lovesong on a lyre and the other child she had given Curthose, the four-year-old Richie, sat on the floor learning backgammon from his nurse, with another pitcher of that same delectable fruit juice on the floor beside them.

In Rochester, Odo's beleaguered garrison and the people trapped with them in the embattled town below waited vainly for relief and if the messenger spoke the truth, there wasn't a man within those walls who would not have cut off his right hand for one single goblet of that clean-tasting juice.

No, he must not run amok but he wanted to. He wanted to tear down the carpets, empty the pitchers over them and over Curthose's well-barbered head as well, to seize the jongleur's lyre and smash it to bits, to hurl cradle and baby alike across the floor . . .

He dragged his companion forward. Curthose sat up, raising his eyebrows at the intrusion and began to ask the reason, waving the minstrel to silence. Henry got in first. 'This man comes from Rochester and I think you should hear what he has to say!'

Curthose's brows rose even higher but he closed his mouth. Henry prodded the messenger and the man drew in a nervous breath and went into his tale.

Curthose, to do him justice, listened. That, Henry

128

thought, was one of his most infuriating characteristics. Curthose was never unreasonable. On the contrary, once backed into a corner, he would be all charm and fair dealing until such time as he had escaped from the corner. He heard the man out and signed for fruit juice to be offered to him. The messenger shook his head. 'I've taken an oath to drink only water until Rochester is free and at that I'm privileged. The water they're drinking is no better than poison.'

'You put it strongly,' said Curthose, 'though I can't blame you. Sit down, man, you can hardly keep your feet, I can see. But tell me, what does my uncle hope I can do, at such short notice? I have a force in preparation but what it has to be prepared for is heavy fighting. I gather that my brother Rufus has ample support. I must have men and ships enough before I try to sail again. I sent a fleet earlier and it proved too small. That's a mistake I don't propose to repeat.'

'The campaign on your behalf in England started last April and was planned in January,' said Henry. 'You were informed by a messenger from Bishop Odo on the last day of January . . .'

'What a wonderful memory you have,' said Curthose coldly.

'How long do you need to mount an invasion? England would be yours *now* if you'd got to work promptly. You could have done far better, long ago, than a handful of leaky ships . . .'

'My ships don't leak, Henry.'

'. . . with timid maidens at the helm . . .'

'My captains aren't timid and few of them are maidens,' said Curthose with a grin. He dropped back onto an elbow and produced a coloured glass pendant on a thin chain, which he dangled over the baby's cradle. The baby gurgled and clutched. 'Look at him, grasping already. A proper little Norman lord. If conditions are as bad in Rochester as you say, my friend,' he said to the messenger, 'how did you get out?'

The messenger repeated his story, adding: 'I'm a merchant by trade. I deal with the Rouen bullion merchants. I was picked because I'm used to travelling and obtaining passages. Please listen, sir. If Rochester isn't relieved soon, the garrison will start cutting townspeople's throats to save food and if it still isn't relieved, they'll be cutting throats to *get* food. That is, if the rotten meat hasn't killed them all off first. My lord, in the name of all those I left behind, I implore you! Send help to Rochester.'

There was a pause. Biota (who was not a fool and furthermore was very attractive; Henry had not tried his luck with this one of Curthose's mistresses but had considered it), slipped quietly from her divan and signed to the nurse to follow her out with the children. Richie, annoyed at having his game interrupted, and displaying all the capacity for rage for which the Norman ruling house was famous, yelled loudly, snatched up a wooden sword which was lying handy, and assaulted his nurse.

Henry found a sudden, if inadequate outlet for his own anger. Stepping forward, he administered a backhander which sent Richie head over heels. Richie sat up and roared. 'Quiet, you're not hurt!' snapped Henry. Biota, running back to pick up her son, glared at him ('yes, *very* attractive,' said Henry's libido in between the pulsebeats of his wrath) and hustled Richie, nurse and baby out of the room.

'Really,' said Curthose, 'what disturbances you create, Henry. Have I refused to send help? I've every intention of sending it but not, I repeat, till the relief force is ready.'

'And I repeat,' Henry threw back at him, 'that you've had more than six months to get it ready. How long do you think Rochester can wait?'

'Oh, a call for help always exaggerates the urgency,' said Curthose easily. 'I know you're hoping for pickings if I get rid of Rufus, but I'm not so sure I want to get rid of him. You're very dirty,' he added, 'and you smell worse. What on earth have you been doing?'

Henry stood still, burning as if with fever. He was young, able, educated, and the Conqueror's son. But to his indolent eldest brother, he was nothing, could not even be given credit for a sense of loyalty or obligation. The blow he had just given Richie, he longed to give to Curthose, through the medium of a well-honed blade and

130

with his weight behind it. And all he was allowed to do was stand, and burn.

The messenger was watching him. The messenger had no knightly background; he was not a man with whom Henry would normally make friends. But their silent eye-to-eye communion now cut through that. They read each other's minds and found themselves alike in their impotence and hopeless anger.

'I was in the menagerie,' he said to Curthose. 'With the leopards. With your leave, I'll go back to them. Sometimes I find animals better company than men.'

In Rochester, someone had cautiously, in Odo's presence, uttered the phrase 'negotiate for terms'. Odo, who had hitherto shouted down anyone who dared to mention such a thing, this time said nothing.

Five

The Argumentative Homecoming
1088

Richard of Fallowdene, Brian of Little Dene and their followers came over the down from the north and drew rein on the crest. Fallowdene lay calmly under a patchy sky. A trailing grey shower drifted across fields of ripening wheat and rye, and darkly massed woodland. From the little patch of shaggy roofs which betokened hall and cottages, blue hearthsmoke curled lazily. Richard let out a sigh of relief because it was all still there.

He knew that Odo's ravaging had not come so far. But the illogical fear had still been with him, that he would return to find it like the homesteads he had seen in Kent, with fields burnt and buildings reduced to ash and rubble.

Brian, whose imagination did not work like that, said: 'Shall we ride on?' in a mildly surprised tone. They jogged on down the chalk track with Brian resuming a monologue, which the halt had interrupted, on the proper method of training men in the use of the crossbow. When the path forked, Richard said politely: 'Come in for some food before you go home,' but was relieved when the offer was courteously declined. Brian took the track for the south down and Little Dene, and Richard, with his own companions, rode for home without him.

As they passed the cottages, heads came round doors and there were calls of greeting. But when they came through the palisade gate, although the usual racket of barking dogs and cackling poultry greeted them, there seemed to be no people about. Puzzled, Richard pushed his reins into Gurth's hand, and made for the hall door.

It was only latched and he went straight in. He found himself behind a row of female backs. Editha, Gunnor and the other hall women were standing clustered with their attention on something in front of them. He pushed through and an impassioned declaration, in his mother's voice, that someone or other was a niminy piminy wantwit

132

who'd be better off with fewer airs and graces and much more commonsense, went past his nose like one of Sir Brian's beloved crossbow bolts. An unfamiliar voice, male and authoritative, replied that commonsense was beside the point. 'I can't believe, my lady, that you approve your daughter's behaviour!'

'There you are!' cried Alice's voice in triumph.

'Bah!' said Wulfhild.

No one had noticed his arrival because they were all in here enjoying the quarrel. His eyes, adjusting to the dimness of the hall, took in several people who should rightly have been outside. They also picked out faces he did not know. For one startled moment, Richard thought that his home was full of strange men. Then he saw that there were only two, a dark-haired young one who was standing back, a spectator, and a soberly clad individual, a little older, who appeared to be in the centre of things and whom everyone was taking for granted.

This one formed part of the tableau in the middle of the floor. On one side of this stood his mother, a protective arm round a wet-eyed and hiccuping Sybil. Opposite her, head up and arms folded, was Alice. The sober young man was standing beside her, shoulder to shoulder. They must all have seen the door open but they were too absorbed in their wrangle to take in who had opened it. No one even glanced his way.

Alice, unfolding her arms, made a dart at Sybil who screamed and clutched at her mother. 'I can't believe this attitude, it's shameful, shameful!' Alice cried, almost stamping in frustration as Wulfhild thrust the child behind her. From this secure position, Sybil made a face at Alice.

'What's going on?' demanded Richard, in the voice he used for ordering men up scaling ladders. Silence fell and heads turned. 'Richard!' Alice gasped and then she was in his arms and crying on his chest. Sybil, apparently in competition, burst into loud roars.

'You're safe home, God be praised!' Wulfhild exclaimed. The dark young man looked at him with interest but did not speak or approach.

The sober man said: 'Sir Richard? It must be, of course. Welcome home, sir.'

'I asked a question,' said Richard, still in his campaign voice, managing to embrace Alice so that her tears were muffled in his shoulder. 'I said: what's going on? And who are you, sir? And who is *he*?' He jerked his head towards the younger stranger.

'I can only regret having to introduce myself in the midst of a family fracas,' said the sober man. 'I'm Father Bruno, Fallowdene's new priest. Father Wenenc died in May, I'm sorry to say. Messire Ralph des Aix is a guest; I believe his family and yours were once acquainted.'

'I see. My apologies,' said Richard, 'to both of you as I'm sure that being forced to witness someone else's family fracas, as Father Bruno puts it, is most embarrassing. I should still like to know what it's about. All right, Alice, all right, I'm home and in excellent health as you can see. Father Bruno?'

Bruno made a deprecating gesture. Seen clearly, as he came forward, he was tall and ascetic of feature, with a high, polished forehead and a pale face in which all the planes were smooth and hard as though the flesh were as firm as bone. His eyes were the very pale blue which looks as though a layer of water or clear glass overlies the iris. His crisp voice spoke correct English, but with a French accent. 'It's perhaps a trivial matter, though I think it less trivial than the Lady Wulfhild does. I had been here in the hall, sharing a light meal with your wife and mother and their guest, sir. On my way back to my house, I went into the church. It has had a new roof lately, slate instead of thatch. I wanted to make sure that the work was properly done with no light showing between the slates . . .'

'I paid for the roof,' declared Alice, raising her head from Richard's shoulder. 'With some money my father sent me. I *respect* the church.'

'Yes, we know,' said Wulfhild disagreeably. Disconcertingly, the dark young man, who with his olive skin and dark eyes was so unlike Bruno that he could have belonged to a different species, grinned. Then he caught Richard's eye, looked apologetic and became serious again.

'Well, and?' said Richard impatiently.

'I'm afraid,' said Bruno, 'that I found your little sister

134

Sybil there in the church, sitting on the floor with some of the villeins' children . . .'

'Six of them,' said Alice, round-eyed with indignation, 'and all boys.'

'I thought it was the blasphemy that shocked you,' snorted Wulfhild. 'That isn't *blasphemy*! And she's only seven.'

'Father Bruno?' said Richard pointedly.

'They were boys, yes, but at their age . . .' Bruno dismissed this aspect with a shrug. 'The real point, sir, is that your sister was telling her playmates a story. I paused for a moment, unseen, and overheard some of it. It was an old legend of the Wild Hunt, a most unsuitable story for telling in a church. But that isn't all. Sybil was drawing pictures to illustrate her tale, drawing on the stone floor with a knob of chalk. When I went over to speak to the children, I saw the pictures. Some of them were most improper.'

'Horses mating,' Wulfhild informed him. 'She's seen it, this summer. Hammerfoot.' They had decided, last winter, that since the stallion Hammerfoot was retired from active service, they should breed from him. Richard had invested in some brood mares. 'So,' Wulfhild said with scorn, 'she wove it into the story and made a picture with chalk. How terrible! I wonder the sky doesn't fall in.'

'It *was* in a church. I thought it moderately undesirable,' said Bruno quietly. 'I spoke sternly to all the children and then sent them home. I shall see their parents later. I brought Sybil back here and your wife met us, sir. I explained what had happened. Perhaps I was at fault and should have told the child's mother first but the lady Alice asked me directly. My answer upset her and she spoke sharply to Sybil. Then the lady Wulfhild came in and the child ran to her pouring it all out and within moments the ladies were quarrelling.'

'So I heard,' said Richard dryly. Everyone in the hall was gazing at him expectantly, as if awaiting a judgement from Solomon. 'We're just back from a war,' he said abruptly and put Alice gently back from him. 'We're all safe. But we need food, drink, washing water, fresh clothes. I suggest that in honour of our safe return, you all

135

declare a truce. Father Bruno, I'm sure you're a conscientious confessor but for the moment I ask you to forget your priestly functions and simply stay to dine. Sybil, I'm sure you've made everyone justly angry but you're forgiven this time. And now,' said Richard, 'I should like to be properly introduced to my other guest, Messire Ralph des Aix.' He moved firmly towards the nearest settle. Behind him, his companions had come into the hall and were being joyously greeted by the womenfolk. 'Editha,' said Richard, 'bring out the elderberry wine. Sit here, Messire Ralph, and tell me who you are.'

'My father knew your grandfather, I believe,' said Ralph, coming obediently forward. 'I had hoped to find your grandfather still alive, in fact. Your mother remembers my father's name but I don't know if you know it. Have you ever heard of Peter Longshanks?'

'Oh yes, I remember Longshanks. I visited Normandy once. I was there with your grandfather and Longshanks was there too. This boy has a look of him,' Wulfhild said. Richard, making no pretence about it, had said he wanted to speak privately to his mother and walked her, regardless of her lameness, out of the hall and out of earshot of the rest. 'He's not so long in the leg as Longshanks was and he's dark, but there's a facial resemblance. He's been here for three weeks. Just rode in out of nowhere and said his father had wanted news of Brand of Fallowdene, had never forgotten him, and he thought perhaps Brand would like to know that. Longshanks died this year, it seems. I'm sorry about that,' Wulfhild said. 'They're mostly dead now, all the folk I knew when I was young.'

Richard nodded. His mother, however, said: 'You nod your head wisely but you can't *know* what it's like. I grew up in the old Confessor's time. It was a different world. I served in great houses that have been wiped out. There's times I feel as if I'm living in a foreign land, here on my own manor! I'd like to welcome this boy, Ralph, for old time's sake. But . . .'

'But?' Richard raised his eyebrows. 'Is there something amiss with him, then?'

'That's the trouble.' Wulfhild frowned and tapped her

136

stick. 'There's nothing wrong with him, that I can see. He's lent a hand round the farm and we've been glad of it; I fancy he's ambitious but I'd call that a virtue; I think he's got a kind heart. He's taught some of the lads to make bows and shafts and given Sybil a ride on his horse once or twice. But there's something about him that I can't make out and I don't like it. Alice says the same and for once,' said Wulfhild sourly, 'just for once, I agree with Alice.'

'And I call it nonsense,' said Richard roundly. He had taken to the young guest, responding, had he known it, to Longshanks' son as Brand of Fallowdene had once responded to Longshanks. He too had sensed a kindliness in Ralph, and something else, the presence of abilities he could respect. Ralph was modest in his bearing, but he moved and spoke, nevertheless, like a young man who knew what he was good for.

Wulfhild did not answer him. He said: 'Dinner ought to be ready by now. We'll go back. I expect you'll all want to hear my story. I don't suppose the news has got here yet, about what happened to Bishop Odo.'

There were undercurrents at the table, tensions between his wife and his mother, a tendency to impertinence on the part of Sybil. But over the wine and the hot capons and fresh bread, Richard controlled the conversation with the competence born of finding that he could control soldiers, and talked of the surrender of Rochester and King Rufus' not unnatural desire to hang all the malcontents – 'he felt it, being betrayed by his own uncle. To bolt into Rochester like that after pretending to make peace, that was outrageous. The barons talked him out of actually hanging Odo.' He laughed. 'We were treated to one of the toughest of them quoting Holy Writ in the effort to make the king be more forgiving. Something about King David having spared someone who'd cursed him. They all value family solidarity.' He eyed his own family reprovingly as he said that. Alice went slightly pink but compressed her mouth. 'The king,' Richard went on smoothly, 'quoted a story back at them, of a time when David *didn't* forgive an enemy. He said he'd spent his boyhood in a monastery and two could play at the quotations game. But in the end he agreed to safe conduct out of the country for Odo and his garrison, only he made them march out of Rochester to the sound of his trumpets.'

Father Bruno nodded approvingly. 'That seems to me a proper and correct decision. I've heard rumours about the king that I can't like but in this matter he seems to have behaved well.'

'Are the other rumours true?' Wulfhild asked her son, and Ralph des Aix, obviously intrigued, said: 'What rumours?'

'That he's reluctant to marry because he can't marry a man?' said Richard, answering his mother, ' I don't know.'

'I don't understand.' Sybil, who had been quelled into silence earlier in the meal, was now seized with a disastrous desire for education. 'What does it mean – because he can't marry another man? He can't get babies on another man, can he? Even women can't get babies sometimes.'

'You see?' said Alice furiously. Her eyes had gone hard and shiny. She sprang to her feet. 'That's what she's like. Unnatural, unchildlike, saucy. I want to go to bed.' She fled from the hall. Richard half came to his feet but she brushed past him unheeding. Wulfhild imperturbably took another piece of bread. 'You've married a fool, my son, but we shall all have to make the best of it,' she observed with her mouth full.

'I'm sorry, I'm sorry. It wasn't the welcome I wanted to give you.'

'It wasn't the welcome I'd hoped to get, either. There, there, it wasn't your fault, or not all yours, anyhow.' Her distress at his anger had touched him. He stroked his wife's hair.

'You don't know what these months have been like!' There was no considering *tch* between sentences now. 'I was terrified for you, day and night, and your mother gave me no peace. Nothing pleased her. The only thing that would please her would be if I had a baby but I lost the baby and she won't let me forget it. She keeps saying she had Sybil when most women are past childbearing so why

138

can I not manage it when I'm so young? She flaunts Sybil at me and Sybil makes use of it. She knows she can be as naughty and rude as she likes and your mother'll take her part. And it's bad for her, what will she grow up like? She's seven already and she runs wild with the villeins' children. She's completely out of hand. She hardly knows her catechism, though she can tell pagan stories that no Christian child should even hear! Your mother tells them to her sometimes and she'll talk anyone else into telling them that can. She's supposed to be going to marry that boy from Little Dene. They're a decent, well-conducted household, for all that Sir Brian's wife is dead. What good will Sybil be to them, if she goes on as she is?'

'Hush, darling, hush.'

Forget the quarrel, forget the sore places where hot chain links have rubbed through onto sweaty skin, forget the stench of burnt farmsteads, the buzzing of flies round the wounds of the casualties, the reek of Rochester when they entered it. He was home and despite his tiredness, his hungry body wanted his wife. He wanted peace in his home too. He was fond of his little sister but if she was causing dissension between Alice and his mother, then away with her, to perdition or a nunnery. Her education probably did need attention and no naughty child was going to do this to his Alice.

'It's time,' he said to his mother next day, 'that Sybil joined her sister at Withysham. She needs proper training. In seven years she'll be ready for marriage. Also, I think it would be best if she were not in this house. No, Mother, this is my idea, not Alice's. Leave Alice alone if you please. You want us to have a child, I believe. Well, how do you expect her to breed if you torment her? You were eager enough once to keep a dog from worrying breeding ewes. Do you think Alice has fewer feelings than a sheep?'

'It will break Sybil's heart to be sent away. Fallowdene is everything to her. She's like me,' said Wulfhild, for whom the manor had been the heart of the universe ever since she came there first at the age of twenty. Richard, looking at her, suddenly saw her as Alice no doubt did, a lame, shawled peasant woman, features hardening with age and chin growing whiskery, the horizons of her life narrowed to Fallowdene valley. As if she had read his mind, Wulfhild said: 'Your wife thinks I'm an ignorant old peasant that shouldn't be called lady, no matter that my husband was a knight. But I'm not ignorant. There are things I know.'

'Yes, there are. But you still look on Fallowdene as the beginning and end of everything and you think Sybil's the same. But she's a child, she'll adapt. She ought to see something outside the valley before she marries, *and* get a bit of ladylike gloss to her, too.'

'Airs, I take it you mean,' said Wulfhild sullenly. 'Like Alice.'

'That's enough. Sybil goes as soon as I can arrange it and there's no more to be said. *No*, Mother, I'm not discussing it any more. How are my new plants doing? Have you been to see?'

'No,' said Wulfhild sullenly. 'And how long is that young man des Aix going to stay on this manor? He came to see your grandfather, didn't he? Well, your grandfather's in his grave. So he's lost his errand. Time he was on his way.'

'It's time I was on my way,' said Ralph, without prompting. 'I've been glad of your hospitality here, Sir Richard . . .'

'You can leave off the sir.'

'Thank you. But we're not equals, or not yet. Perhaps one day.' Ralph, who had fallen in with his host as they were both going towards the stable, stopped and glanced back at the shaggy bulk of the hall. 'I like your home. One day I should like to have such a hall, such lands myself. But first I've got to make my way.'

'You'd be welcome to stay here as one of my household.'

'Your womenfolk don't like me.'

'My womenfolk,' said Richard, 'will do as they're told.'

Ralph shook his head. 'Forgive me. But if I stayed here as your man-at-arms – I am speaking very frankly now – what chances of advancement would I have? I need a wealthy lord. Do you understand? I'm a trained huntsman,

140

that's my trade. If I could find a post in some big house-hold – I was trained by Helias of La Fleche; that's a big place, it should be a recommendation of sorts – I think I might find the chances I seek. I'd like to think of you as my friend, and of Fallowdene as a place I could come back to, to visit, a sort of home. Your wife and mother might not mind me so much on that basis.'

'They don't really mind you now. They don't know you well yet.'

Ralph, with the toe of his boot, doodled a triangle in the earth of the yard. 'I doubt if that would make much difference. Richard . . .'

'Yes?'

'This isn't my business. Please don't think me dis-courteous. But I hear you are proposing to send your sister away.'

'Sybil? Yes. Well, it's time she went to get some schooling. A few years in an abbey is a good thing for a girl and we're lucky. The abbess of Withysham is her aunt. It won't cost us much.'

'But she's upset about it, isn't she? Sybil, I mean. I feel rather sorry for her and a little bit responsible.'

'Responsible? Why should you feel that?'

'She got into trouble for repeating a story about the Wild Huntsman. I'm afraid I told her that story.'

'Did you?' Richard was not disposed to take this seriously. 'Being a huntsman yourself, I suppose you'd hear all the legends of your own trade. She still didn't have to repeat it in a church, or be impertinent to my wife at dinner, in front of the whole household. There's no need for you to feel responsible. Or sorry for her. She'll soon settle down at the abbey. About this business of finding a wealthy lord for you. I understand what you mean. I haven't taken it amiss. My own overlord, de Warenne – it's the younger de Warenne now, since his father was killed – there might be an opening there. I can take you to see him and we can find out if you like.'

'Would you?'

'Certainly,' said Richard heartily. 'With the utmost pleasure. You'd rather do that than go back to Helias of La Fleche?'

141

'It was a good house, but there were no opportunities there within the next ten years, that I could see.'

'Then,' said Richard, 'we will try de Warenne.'

They walked on, towards the stable.

They tried to represent the sojourn at Withysham as an adventure and a privilege. But Sybil knew she was going into exile and retributive supervision and she displayed such terror at the thought of leaving the valley to go away beyond the great barebacked downs which had been the boundaries of her world, that Richard almost wavered at the last minute, and Wulfhild said: 'I told you so!' in accents of enormous satisfaction.

But Alice said: 'Give in now and we'll be giving in for ever,' and Richard after all refused to change his mind. Sybil wept, pleaded and finally screamed. They could do nothing with her and in the end left her to scream herself into exhaustion and surrender. Ralph, the bystander, was sorrier for her than ever. He hid his feelings from Richard, for their friendship's sake, but was less careful with the women, whom he felt were making the child a pretext for quarrelling. They sensed his disapproval and returned it. He was relieved when he and Richard left to ride to Chichester, to meet de Warenne.

In Fallowdene village too, there was sympathy for Sybil. 'Poor little thing, sent away like that. Come back as mincing and dainty as young madam in the hall, she will. Whatever made the master pick on that one?'

'She's embroidering lovely new hangings for the hall,' Gunnor said defensively, on hearing this. Alice's gift for weaving and stitchery had infuriated Gunnor at first but things were changing. Alice had proved willing to impart her skills and had also shown Gunnor how to make an ointment to keep her hands smooth for fine sewing. Pinkfaced, buxom Gunnor and slender, pale Alice had now struck up the beginnings of an alliance. 'She'll be all right. Master'll change whatever in her wants changing, given time. He's got sense.'

On the whole, Fallowdene agreed, this was true. Richard did have a lot of sense – well, if you ignored the

occasional oddity, like marrying Alice and making such a
to-do over the peculiar flowers at the edge of his rye field.
That was a funny idea to get in his noddle, if you like.
Wasting good soil on flowers was crazy enough but these
flowers! Whoever heard of autumn-blooming crocuses?

Six

Homesickness
1088

Henry arrived at Westminster in the July, before the weather broke. In London, where the after-echoes of the rising still reverberated in the form of trials and enquiries and panicky petitions from those who like himself wished to change allegiance, the air was like a muffling blanket. His chartered ship sailed up a Thames which flatly reflected a sky like dull copper.

They passed a ferry plying between the banks. A middle-aged burgher couple dozed in their seats while a young woman, their daughter perhaps, trailed a languid hand in the water. Henry and his companions whistled appreciatively and blew kisses. The companions could go no further because they only spoke French. Henry grinned at them in superior fashion and bawled a request for the young lady's name and address. The ferry bounced in the wash from Henry's vessel, the girl's parents woke up, clutched at the gunwale and glared at him and the young lady shook her head but laughed. Henry's brown eyes and square, tanned face were clearly a passport to female favour here as in Normandy and here he could not only make hello-darling signals; he knew the language, he could ask. England felt like home.

But then, he had been born here and none of his brothers had.

He had been born here and he was the son of an anointed king, England should have been his. The laughter went out of his face.

The royal residence proved disturbing. Some aspects of England had changed. In his father's day, the place had been richly appointed, certainly. The Conqueror had felt he owed it to his position to have gold and silver candlesticks about, fine hangings, murals, sweet herbs in the rushes. But now the fragrances were stronger and more exotic, there were . . . *cut flowers*? . . . in a niche

144

which Henry remembered as formerly occupied by a religious figurine, and the usher who came to lead the Seigneur Henri to his quarters was a staggering vision with curled brown hair sweeping sweetly from a centre parting to its owner's shoulders, and a sky blue tunic which waved about its ankles. It was, however, indubitably male. The tunic fitted glovelike over shoulders which had broadened since the garment was first acquired, and there was a fuzz of developing beard on its chin. 'Mother of God,' said one of Henry's companion knights in a shaken whisper. The nostalgia which had seized Henry as he sailed up the Thames took flight squawking and perched at a safe distance.

They followed the vision warily to a set of guest chambers, where he . . . it? . . . explained the system for summoning servants, assured Henry that his request for an audience would be conveyed to my lord king as soon as my lord king was out of his council meeting and asked languishingly if there were anything further the Seigneur or any of his knights required.

'No, thank you!' said Henry shortly, his nostalgia migrating altogether. The sense of unfairness, however, had increased. He would have done better for England than this. It was going to be hard to talk to Rufus in the necessary accents of persuasion and respect.

It was also, as it turned out, useless.

'No,' said Rufus bluntly. 'No terms. No land. Yes, I know we're brothers. If we weren't, you wouldn't be having this audience in private. You'd have got your refusal in the open hall where everyone could hear. I respect our relationship more than you do. You and Curthose between you would have had me off my throne and sh . . . shoved into a dungeon if you'd had your way.'

'I'm his tenant. I was in a difficult position.'

'You were, weren't you? Backed the wrong fighting cock altogether! Pity.'

'I didn't have much choice. You, if you remember, wanted the earth and the moon as rent for our mother's estates though it would have been fair enough to let me have them on easy terms, considering the size of the estate you got from Father! I had to go to Curthose. And that made me his vassal. When the rebellion started, I had to be on his side.'

'And why aren't you still on it?'

'Our brother Curthose,' said Henry candidly, 'is a lazy, vacillating, incompetent, smooth-tongued cretin . . .'

'What a lot of words you know,' said Rufus admiringly.

'. . . I couldn't make him get his army off its backside and into the field. Is there nothing I can say to make you reconsider? You've made your peace with others. You've come to terms with Gilbert Clare!' He kept his voice down with great difficulty, throttling his anger. Rufus was the king and had all the advantages. 'For the love of God, Rufus!' he appealed, 'I want to serve a better suzerain.'

'I'm not related to Gilbert Clare. See here, Henry, I'm not prepared to be stabbed from behind by my own family, uncles or brothers or whatnot. It's unknightly. I've thrown Uncle Odo out of England and all his worst supporters with him and you're one of them. That you're my brother *makes* you one of them, understand? And if dear brother Curthose has any sense, he'll lock you up when you get back to Normandy, to teach you not to turn your coat. But back to Normandy you're going.'

Henry stared angrily at the brother who had once fought beside him in the upper room at L'Aigle, but who had now grown so far away from him, into this odd-looking, tough and dangerous king.

Odd-looking, Rufus unquestionably was. Like the rest of his court, he had adopted shoulder-length hair and long gowns for informal wear. Clad thus, his chunky swaggering body looked extraordinary, and the girlish hair on either side of his ears made a startling frame for his blunt, wind-reddened features. Like his friend FitzHamon, he had a trick of lowering his head and hunching his shoulders as though he were a bull about to charge. He did it when annoyed or defensive and it was a warning not to provoke him. He was doing it now.

Henry read its significance.

'Thank you for your hospitality,' he said. 'I won't kneel to implore you further, Rufus. I wish you well.' He turned to leave. Over his shoulder, he added: 'You're not married yet, or considering it? You need an heir, you know.'

Rufus said, quietly but ominously: 'Get out.'

'Mother,' said Ranulf Flambard reprovingly, 'you're a lady now. I'm the king's Financial Adviser these days and I've hired this expensive London house and a legion of servants for you. Why don't you take to embroidery for a pastime? You've been at it again, haven't you?'

Flambard's mother was small and spry. Her hair had once had the same coppery tinge as her son's, and her bright eyes still matched his. She wore fine clothes with an air but the mesh of lines on her face witnessed a life in which clothes had not always been fine. 'Time was,' she said, 'when you didn't complain. Time was it kept you and your brothers in bread and shoes. Then I did it for pay. Now I do it for curiosity. Yes, I bin scrying. I sent the maids out; no one saw me.' She picked up the earthenware bowl at which Flambard's accusing finger was pointing, and tossed its contents out of the nearest window. 'Water and a spoonful of lamp oil afloat on it,' she said, 'but it was good enough. Maids couldn't see me but I saw you.'

'Saw me? Doing what?' Flambard, in some alarm, dropped into a seat. His disapproval was only half real. He was used to his mother's strange gifts and knew she worshipped no demons. This skill came to her naturally. But it tended to reveal warnings. 'I've done nothing I'm ashamed of lately,' he said. 'I've visited my wife but it's others who call that disgraceful, not me.'

'Tweren't that. But I saw something I didn't like the look of, all the same. Hounds running. I saw the pack all strung out, flowing like water and they wasn't chasing a stag. They was after a man. Not you, but you're in it somewhere. You're going to make a mistake, son. You won't pay for it; that'll be the man the pack was after. But you'll sorrow.'

'I think,' said Flambard, 'that this is one of the times I decide not to believe in your abilities, Mother. I sent a barrel of red wine round to you yesterday. Let's have some of it.'

*

147

Withysham Abbey was pleasingly placed, in a few acres cleared from Andred Forest near its southern edge at the foot of the downs. The downs were to Sybil one of the few homelike things to be seen, a secret source of comfort in a life otherwise so miserable that she woke every morning with a leaden lump in her stomach, and on most nights sobbed herself to sleep.

She dreaded the rising bell which started each remorseless day. She would open her eyes on the dorter she shared with the other little girls, stare at the stone walls and remember the cheerful chamber she and the other women at Fallowdene had used, with the soft fawn hangings covered in red and blue wool patterns. Her favourite toy, the stuffed animal her mother had made for her, which faintly resembled a fox and which Sybil called Woollypaws, was always on her bed then. They hadn't let her bring Woollypaws with her. She imagined him lying neglected and that was the point at which, every morning, the tears would scald her eyes.

Stiff inside with misery, she would stumble from bed to face another day of the Rule which like a great steel lattice imposed a rigid pattern on the abbey's life. In case some resourceful small person should succeed in wriggling out to freedom between its bars, its spaces were covered with a fine mesh of little rules. One could hardly breathe or move, it seemed, without infringing one.

She had learned very quickly not to speak or even whisper during the hours of prescribed silence. She had learned not to be late into church. Now she had found that she must not run on the way to church either, even to avoid the crime of lateness. In disgrace once more, she knelt on the stone ledge of a dorter window and gazed out northwards, not towards the downs but over the forest, although she could see little of it beyond some treetops which showed above the abbey's encircling wall.

She wanted to pray for release from this horrible place but it was no use to pray to Christ. The abbey was his and presumably he would favour it. In a way, Sybil thought resentfully, he could be said to have invented it.

She might try praying to Herne. He wouldn't favour a place where people put their hands over their ears at the mention of his name (she had been in trouble for mentioning it, twice).

She didn't know the proper way to pray to Herne so she would have to make do with the way she had been taught, the Christian way. She straightened her back and put her palms together beneath her chin. She shut her eyes.

'Please, Herne Huntsman, lord of forest and field and sky, save me from this place. Let me go home. Please don't mind if I'm praying to you the wrong way; I don't know what the right way is. But I want to go home. I want to go home. I want to go home.'

Seven

Lightning's Sudden Strike
February 1090

'Anarchy,' said the lean bishop angrily. He looked instinctively towards the Archbishop of Canterbury's seat, realised once more that it was vacant and fixed his eyes on the king instead. He banged the table with a palm-edge as if trying to dent it. 'Sheer anarchy. There's no other word for it. My parish priests, their parishioners throughout my diocese of Evreux, come to me *begging* for help. A man counts himself lucky to get a harvest in without a pair of private armies fighting out a feud across his corn, or his daughter married before some self-important lordling takes her husband's due.' He was fifty and had the authority which stems from a combination of years and position. He had been known as Cranelegs since his twenties because of his lankiness but it had long since ceased to be a personal comment and become simply a surname, and one held in respect at that. 'One noblewoman comments adversely on another's style of dress, and their husbands go to war. As ever, the innocent suffer. There is no law, no control at all. It's a *disgrace*. Duke Robert Curthose . . .'

'Is grossly incompetent,' said another bishop, Howel of Le Mans. He was plump and pink-tinged once more now that he had recovered from the hideous February Channel crossing which was the measure of the deputation's sense of urgency. He seemed flustered however as he added: 'This dreadful state of affairs has only arisen through his lax, pleasure-loving ways. It's an impossible situation, quite impossible. Lax and pleasure-loving . . .' he trailed off.

'Meulan,' said Rufus across the table to the Count of Meulan, who had accompanied the ecclesiastical deputation from Normandy, 'what's your view? You're one of the few men I trust to come and go between here and Normandy without risk to my interests.'

150

A glint in Meulan's round bright eyes indicated appreciation of the compliment. But he said soberly: 'Normandy is in chaos, that much is true. But whether all the trouble is due to the duke's shortcomings, is another matter. Count Henry, as he now styles himself, and the lord of Belleme are concerned too.' Belleme had been in England during the rebellion and had supported the wrong side. He had been ejected from England together with Henry '. . . they were both arrested when they got to Rouen but have since been released which in my opinion was an error,' said Meulan now.

'Another of Curthose's mistakes,' muttered Bishop Howel.

'. . . and since then they've been in virtual partnership as robber barons,' said Meulan. 'That's bred turmoil on its own. And then of course there is the matter of Maine. Bishop Howel can tell us more about that.'

The plump bishop made an exasperated gesture. 'I'd like to make it plain,' he said, 'that I am *not* in favour of the Maine secession. The leader of the insurgents, this Helias of La Fleche of whom we've all heard now, actually imprisoned me at one point, while a cousin of his was installed as independent head of the province. Mercifully, Helias is pious as well as headstrong and freed me in due course. I went at once to confer with my fellow bishops of Normandy and we are *all* of the view that Maine should continue to owe fealty to Normandy. Although that doesn't necessarily imply,' he added meaningly, 'to her present duke.'

'But for the moment,' said Cranelegs, 'Maine is claiming that from this year onwards, it is a state in its own right, owing allegiance to no one.' His tone said: *and if that isn't enough to make you intervene in Normandy and clear up the unholy mess your brother is making, I'd like to know what is*.

Four seats away from Rufus, Flambard cleared his throat. 'Flambard?' Rufus said.

'I understood that this Helias of La Fleche was represented in this deputation,' Flambard observed. 'But I'm not clear and I think a lot of us aren't clear, who precisely he is. Nor do we know who his representatives are or what their purpose is today. Can we have the answers to these questions?'

Cranelegs gave Bishop Howel what could only be called a malicious glance. 'You'll have to speak up sooner or later,' he said, in the manner of one pointing out to a defaulting schoolboy that his sins have caught up with him.

'Helias,' said Howel with feeling, as the Council fastened its attention expectantly on him, 'belongs to a leading Maine family and if he were the devil, he could talk his way into heaven. God preserve us all from such polished tongues. He launched this insurrection. He talked his cousin into taking control. And though he insists that the new Count of Maine should be his cousin and not himself because the cousin is his senior in the family – Helias is punctilious in these things – nonetheless, it is Helias who has the power. Yes, he is represented here and as for the name of his representative, he talked me into taking on the task. I was fresh out of prison and afraid of being sent back, to tell you the truth.'

The young Lord de Warenne of Sussex, a good-natured man, said: 'I feel sure we can understand that.'

'If I were you,' said FitzHamon cheerfully, 'I'd just say your piece like a lesson and be done with it. We'll forgive you.'

'Yes, come on, we're waiting.' Rufus was impatient. Opposite him, an arched window showed a segment of sky where the wind was chasing away the heavy clouds which had hovered since dawn. They could hunt this afternoon.

'I haven't had a good night's sleep since we left Normandy,' said Bishop Howel and then recited, in a dismal monotone: 'Helias does not wish to owe fealty to anyone, not to Normandy nor Anjou, but in particular he does not wish to owe it to Duke Robert Curthose. If Curthose were removed and replaced by someone else, he might – only might – be induced to come to some sort of . . . er . . . arrangement.' He broke off, sweating with embarrassment. 'I must reiterate, must reiterate that I personally disapprove as strongly as I possibly can of this abandonment of traditional allegiances, but . . .'

Rufus, grinning, spoke into FitzHamon's ear.

152

FitzHamon chuckled, deep in his chest. Flambard beckoned a clerk from the administrative staff, who were waiting about in case they were needed, whispered to him and sent him up the table to the king. Rufus listened to the clerk, grinned again and said: 'Tell Flambard we're ahead of him.'

A monk from the Norman abbey of Bec had taken up the argument. 'Our abbot, Anselm, wishes that for the sake of the friendship between himself and your father, my lord of England, you could offer help in restoring order to Normandy.' Like Cranelegs, the monk was eyeing Canterbury's empty seat with regret. The Archbishop, those wistful eyes seemed to say, would have known what ought to be done.

'We can't intervene directly,' said Rufus. 'My vassals aren't bound to follow me across water. My father promised when he crossed the Channel himself to come to England, that he wouldn't create a precedent. I hold by his word.' A number of baronial faces expressed approval and in some cases, relief. 'But . . .' said Rufus thoughtfully, and paused. Another grin, a smug small-boy expression of delight crossed his face. '*But . . .* what's the point anyhow of shipping an army over the Channel when as likely as not we can find men on the other side of it? If things in Normandy are as bad as our friends here say, we should be able to make the Normans take it for us.' He glanced at the window again. 'Our target,' he said, 'would be the place that holds the Norman Treasury. Once we have Rouen, we have the duchy. However, we need time to consider. Meanwhile, we suggest that this meeting be adjourned. I seem to remember, gentlemen, that we promised you all some hunting today.'

'What was all that about?' Meulan said to FitzHamon as they waited, mounted, to leave for the hunt. 'When Flambard sent his clerk round the table to whisper, and the king said you and he were ahead?'

'Oh, that. It was to do with what Helias of Maine probably means by coming to an arrangement. What Flambard said was: He'll want you to buy his allegiance.

153

Agree to nothing till we have discussed it. But the king had guessed what Helias was up to, already, and he won't buy Maine if he can get it by force of arms, believe me.'

Meulan laughed. 'I should hope not!'

De Warenne nudged his horse over to them. 'Politically speaking, we've a lively future ahead of us, wouldn't you say? It's an odd coincidence, but I've a young huntsman in my employ, half-Norman and half-English, who trained in this Helias' household at La Fleche in Maine. I must have a word with him and ask him what Helias is like. As well to know one's foe.'

'Is he with your men here?' asked FitzHamon.

'Yes. He's good at his trade,' said de Warenne. 'I thought it would be useful experience for him to work with the king's huntsmen so I put him in my entourage on this tour of duty. The king's Chief Huntsman's given permission for him to tag along. There he is, on the blue roan horse.'

'Quite a good horse for a junior huntsman,' Meulan said, not altogether approvingly.

'He's quite a good horseman,' said Ralph des Aix's current employer, with a grin.

They rode out of Winchester, a massed party of horsemen with the hounds and their handlers in the vanguard. The leashed pairs of lymers, who would put up the game, strained forward, all but dragging their handlers off their feet. Behind them, tongues lolling and sterns waving, came the pack of harriers who would follow the roused game by scent and run it to a standstill.

As the Old One in the forests of La Fleche had well understood, there was more than one way to hunt deer. One was static, the hunters taking up positions on foot to shoot deer which were driven towards them. The other was fast-moving with the hounds pursuing the quarry and the hunters following on horseback, to shoot whenever the chance presented itself, or else to bring the deer to bay, when the lord whose hounds they were, or one of his guests, would have the privilege of loosing the arrow for the kill.

The fast-moving hunt was not feasible in close forest but

there was enough open land round Winchester for the purpose and it was more exciting and warmer than standing about in the wind. On a February day, it was the natural choice.

The harbourer, who was short, taciturn and English, stumped ahead on foot. He knew on any given day where to find the deer and what they were: red deer or roe, hind, fawn, pricket stag with antlers not yet branched, runnable stag with twelve points to his crown. He was allowed to carry a bow for culling sick or injured animals.

He knew more about the forest than any of his masters, even his immediate superior, the Keeper of the Walk. He was one of the Children of the Wood, for he had been conceived in a firelit clearing on May Eve and he considered his parentage honourable.

He had a stag for them, he had said to the Keeper and the Chief Huntsman, in the terse Anglo-Norman pidgin which was their common language. It carried ten points, a good head. He showed them where to position the riders, downwind of the wood where the beast was lying. The lymers went in, long grey or fawn bodies sliding purposefully out of sight through a leafless hazel brake. The hunt waited.

A cold, brisk wind blew the horses' manes about. A jay went noisily up. For a long time, nothing else happened.

When the stag appeared it was undramatic. One moment there was just the brake, and then the stag was there, head up, frozen into stillness at the sight of the mounted men in front of him. Then he was swerving away and the harriers were yelping in pursuit. It was the season when the hinds were growing heavy with their young and horns were not therefore sounded; the young must come safely into the world to be hunted when they were grown. But there was a series of audible clicks as a number of elegant young men who had been showing off with expensively shod toes barely in their stirrup irons thrust their feet home ready for hard riding, and Rufus, eyes sparkling, stood in his own stirrups, cupping his hands round his mouth and let out a shout.

155

'He's anyone's who can shoot him! Permission for the lot of you, huntsmen included! If you can get him before I do! Catch me if you can!'

He sat down and used his spurs. His horse sprang from a stand into a gallop. In a drumming phalanx, the field set off after him, but as they swept round the eastern verge of the wood in the wake of the pack, Rufus was ten horse-lengths ahead and gaining, leading the way flat out among scattered silver birch.

He was happy. He was glad to be out under the sky instead of incarcerated in a council chamber where the fire billowed smoke at you whenever the wind blew, but never seemed to keep the place warm. He was glad to be on horseback. On a horse, he was always at home. His strong thighs and powerful forearms could control any mount. The hound music ahead faded and he drew rein, slowing to a trot. He found the harriers questing back and forth in a dip where trees drew close, with boggy ground between them.

The Chief Knight Huntsman, coming up, said: 'He's using the stream down there. But we'll pick him up,' and cantered on, whip cracking, collecting the hounds to try them where he guessed the quarry might have left the water. A moment later, a hound voice spoke and another joined it and in a few more seconds they were in full cry again. The field had caught up as well. Rufus waved an arm to show them their direction and spurred ahead once more.

Ten hard-riding minutes later, still ahead and now bent double to avoid low branches, he tore through a beechwood and emerged on to a grassy downhill slope. The hound music, somewhere below him, had changed note, which meant a change of direction. The stag was probably trying to swing in a circle and get back to its herd. He pulled up again, shielding his eyes with his hand, gazing out over a wide, shallow vale. Two or three miles away, on the far side, the ground rose again, clothed with leafless woodland, dimly brown with distance. Clouds were rolling swiftly across the sky; light and shade flowed over the landscape with them. An intermittent sun lit up the vale.

156

And there was the stag, a brown speck fleeing along the vale at right angles to him. Behind him, he could hear approaching riders. He drove his black horse forwards. It took the slope with a scramble and a slither, forelegs braced, hindquarters all but tobogganing. He gathered it at the foot, urging it on a path which closed with the stag's. Once in a while you got a chance for a shot like this, right in the open, no trees in the way. But he must first get into position; one must shoot from a standstill. Few men could manage bow, shaft and the reins of a galloping horse simultaneously.

The sun went in and a rainstorm swept down. Vale and stag vanished in a grey haze and the coldness drove through his clothes to his skin. Then the squall thinned and the stag, still running, was there again, coming into range. He reined back, unslung his bow, fitted the shaft in a single smooth movement, loosed and missed. He swore. The stag, which had seen him, was receding with redoubled leaps.

And then, out of the rain, which hid the top of the rise down which he had ridden so furiously, there appeared a marvel.

It lasted perhaps thirty seconds but it was a vision to endure in memory as long as life itself endured. The grey rain-curtain obliterating the wood at the top of the slope. The blue roan horse descending out of it, taking off from the foot of the slope, reaching for the good flat going, ears flat, nostrils wide. The zig-zag crest of its windborne mane. The reins knotted, in defiance of all custom and sanity, round the saddle pommel and the young horseman doing the impossible, controlling his steed with his knees, while he drew a bow and nocked a shaft at full and hurtling gallop. His aquiline profile. The strong, gathered movement of his shoulders as his right arm drew back. The taut gaiety of him, startling from Rufus' mind, as a buck is startled from covert, the memory of that other vision, that blithe, insouciant, nameless young man in the courtyard of St. Gervais. Then, the springing shaft and the calm olive-skinned face that watched it take the stag in mid-leap and fling it over into a tangle of antlers and kicking legs. The certainty, before the stag fell, that fall it must. The godlike certainty.

157

They met, horse's nose to horse's nose, across the stag's body. The Chief Knight Huntsman had come up and was whipping the hounds back, too busy to attend to the humans. 'Who taught you to ride and shoot like that? What's your name? By the Face, I never saw anyone shoot like that before!'

'I'm Ralph des Aix, my lord. I'm a huntsman in Messire de Warenne's household. I had permission to go with your huntsmen. I'm sorry I took your stag. I didn't see you. I know you gave leave to anyone to shoot, but . . .'

'I'd already missed, and I did indeed give leave.' This was not the young man of the St. Gervais courtyard. This was a younger man, dark of hair like the other, yes, but browner of skin and humbler of mien. But the other was gone, unnamed, lost for ever. This boy Ralph des Aix was here in the present.

The others were riding up. In the distance, the sky threatened another approaching downpour. The Chief Huntsman, his hounds now under control, had recognised the fortunate marksman as the junior hunt servant who was supposed to be tagging along and was regarding him with suspicion. 'Hunting's over for the day,' said Rufus. 'We'll be drowned in our saddles otherwise. Ride back with me, Ralph. I want to learn more of you.'

He was in his thirtieth year and since that shattering moment at St. Gervais, this experience had never, till now, repeated itself.

It might have done so with Ranulf Flambard, but Flambard had held him off and the impulse had died away into camaraderie, partnership, leaving no scar because no words had been said that could wound. It had left a warning. He had been careful not to lay himself open to rejection and as he had no shortage of money and could buy love when he needed it, he had not suffered too much. He might not be wholly content, but he had not wasted time and energy in yearning after the unattainable.

And then this young man with the olive skin and the aquiline profile came riding out of a rainstorm like a myth come into the daylight and overset for the second time in his life, here was Rufus of England riding shyly at the

158

wondrous being's side, stammering in hope and fear, heart banging with desire. In love.

And scarcely able to think of anything to say beyond the most mundane questions about his companion's history. He had established in the first half mile that Ralph had been born in Normandy, had an English father, had been only a short time in England, had been trained at La Fleche. He had felt bound to ask a few questions about Helias of La Fleche but had hardly listened to the answers. In Helias of La Fleche, Rufus could not at that moment have been less interested. And already the journey was ebbing under their brisk hoofbeats. Once back in Winchester, he could of course summon Ralph whenever he wished. But he wanted to woo, not give orders.

It was a hailstorm that saved him.

The sky, as he had seen, was darkening again. There was a new chill in the wind. The riders turned off the path to seek shelter in the trees on either side. Rufus shepherded his companion rapidly between the trunks of oak and chestnut and halted them out of sight and earshot of anyone else. There was a sudden rattle as the storm descended and a shower of hailstones swished down through a gap in the foliage to bounce on the damp earth. The horses started. Ralph slipped from his saddle to hold the roan's bridle and soothe it. Rufus followed his example and stood holding his own mount. 'Wild weather, eh?'

'Yes, sir. Wilder than I thought English weather would be, somehow.'

Above them, the wind tore through the branches with a sound like the roar of the sea. The gloom became livid. He could hardly see Ralph's face. But his presence was there, felt if not visible. The longing to reach out with his own square red paw and touch the other's slender, olive-tinged fingers was all but irresistible, a continuous twitch of unrealised movement. 'Do you like England? Will you stay here?' he heard himself enquiring inanely.

'Yes sir, I think so.' The boy was awkward, shy of being alone like this with a king. He probably imagined that Rufus was talking to put him at his ease. Much he knows,

159

thought Rufus in agony. 'My father missed England, I think,' Ralph said nervously.

The gloom began to lighten. He could see the boy's profile again, turned aside as he gentled his restless horse. It was a beautiful and well cared for animal; probably the centre of Ralph's life. Ralph's pulses weren't hammering with longing. Perhaps they never would. He must go carefully. What did he know of this boy? Nothing beyond a few plain details of birth and training, a glimpse of a wonder riding out of a rain-haze. He must stalk the quarry with care, not frighten him. What would win him? What was he like? What kind of things interested him? What did he know?

'You come from Maine,' said Rufus suddenly. 'And no doubt you've heard all the gossip about this present deputation; I suppose you know what it's about. What do you think of it all? Should England intervene in Normandy?'

'My lord, that's not for me to say!'

'You're part of the household of an English lord now. Your allegiance is to me, just as his is. Are you able to think as an Englishman yet? From all I've heard, an honest Norman might not think so differently, anyway. What if we took a hand? We'd look for supporters in Normandy. Who would be the likely men to approach?'

'My lord, my opinions can't possibly have any weight.' Ralph was distressed. The storm was passing; Rufus could see the boy's expression of earnest embarrassment and the reluctance to forget his position. Rufus yearned simultaneously to embrace him for his modesty and hit him for his obtuseness. Did he not understand that Rufus desired only to hear his voice, and to search out a way into his mind?

Ralph seemed at last to grasp that a reply was required. 'I used to hear hall gossip in Maine,' he said, 'and I saw who got the most respectful treatment among the guests, and those who had high places at table weren't great lords every time. I heard my lord Helias talking sometimes, too. I once heard him say that the most influential men in Normandy were the burghers of Rouen.'

160

'That's a good answer. Any particular burghers?'

'There's a man called Conan who's wealthy enough to hire mercenaries to guard his shipments. He deals in gemstones and bullion,' said Ralph unexpectedly. 'My lord Helias had dealings with him. I've been on escort duty when deliveries were brought in. I did other things besides act as huntsman, sometimes, you see. But I know so little of political matters. I understand horses and deer and archery. I oughtn't . . .'

'If I ask you a question, I, the King of England in my own country, you do no wrong in answering. And if I gave you an order, you would do no wrong in obeying it.' He watched Ralph's face but saw no sign that the boy had understood any double meaning. He was pensively engaged in drawing a pattern in the leafmould with the toe of his boot. 'I'd like the chance of giving you orders frequently.' Still no sign of comprehension. Rufus gambled. 'One of the huntsmen on my court staff will retire soon. His second will take over. That will leave a vacancy below. Sixpence a day and all found and a land grant before too long if you please me . . .'

With pleasure, he saw the boy raise his head at that, saw the dark eyes flash. 'You would have the chance of acquiring knight status, even,' he said. 'You'll be called to war as well as to the hunting field. Acquit yourself properly and you could win your spurs from me. You'd live at Winchester part of the time but travel with the court for the rest of it. Quite often, in fact.'

All the time, if things go well, my beautiful one, my love.

He waited, looking casual, looking bored, and not daring actually to look at Ralph.

'My present lord, Messire de Warenne, did a great kindness in taking me on,' said Ralph slowly. 'I wouldn't like . . .'

Rufus, staring at a tree root and willing himself not to be sick, swallowed and said: 'I will put it right with de Warenne. I will request you to be released from your service. You need not ask anything.'

Ralph stopped drawing patterns with his toe and rubbed the design out with it instead. He glanced up,

161

shyly. Those dark eyes were like the eyes of a falcon. A shy, wild passager, but he would come to the glove yet, and take meat from the falconer's fist. 'I think I should like to enter your service, sir.'

The sun blazed out.

Eight

Substitute for a Duke
November 1090–June 1091

From the walls of the castle in the south-east corner of Rouen, the old Roman layout was still visible, the north-south and east-west roads chopping the city into four mathematical quarters, the four gates set with military precision in the centre of each wall.

One could also see the congestion. The castle and the archbishop's palace between them took up huge tracts of ground, forcing other buildings to spread beyond the walls into a broad fringe of thatched or slate-roofed dwellings. Even the monastery for which Curthose's mother had paid, had had to be placed outside.

The fringe of suburbs broke at the south-east corner, where the ducal towers overlooked a swamp. But as if in compensation, they spread rampantly on the far bank of the Seine, which guarded Rouen from the south.

On this grey November day, there were mists on the swampland. They were parodied, in ghastly fashion, by the haze of smoke over the suburbs to the south and west. And on the bridge which carried the south road over the Seine, antlike figures swarmed, dragging a treetrunk mounted on wheels.

The streets within the walls were also swarming, as rioting factions, Rufus' adherents versus the duke's, surged back and forth, fighting. Several houses were on fire. Those who did not care who ruled in Rouen, or Normandy, if only life could go on there in peace, huddled in cellars if they could find them. Some, astute enough to recognise the danger signs and prudent enough to act on them quickly, had fled in time.

The conflict was hottest round the south and west gates, which were both under assault from outside. But the two sets of besiegers were not allies. Rufus' standard waved above the mob of mailed figures attacking from the west, though Rufus himself remained in England and this army

163

was led by Norman barons who wished to present him with Normandy. At the south gate, however, the ram whose onslaught was sending its vibrations into the very walls of the castle represented reinforcements for Duke Curthose.

Conan the Burgher, who had started all the uproar by spearheading the demand that Rouen should declare Rufus its duke, was leading an obstinate resistance from within, holding off the attack from the south, unable to spare any men to help his friends to the west, and praying that the west gate would soon give way.

Curthose's forces were not yet in the fray. His men, in the castle bailey, were awaiting the order to sortie. The duke himself, up on the flat roof of one of the towers, had been intending to hasten down and give it. But his brother Count Henry, who had come to his aid accompanied by his own armed followers, had just demonstrated a new type of fraternal solidarity by knocking his elder brother unconscious.

'It was the only way,' he said across Curthose's slumped body, to three of Curthose's knights, who were regarding him and his own two companions with outrage and suspicion. 'If he were to sortie now, he'd have as much chance as an icicle in a furnace. We're outnumbered four to one down there, till Belleme gets in through that south gate.' Under their feet, the tower shuddered again in answer to the crash of the ram. 'Dear God, he wasn't even wearing a bloody helmet! Wanted his own men to recognise him! The first enemy who recognised him would have swiped his head off. If he'd had his helmet on,' Henry added thoughtfully, taking a moment to lick the knuckles of his right hand, 'I couldn't have hit him on the jaw like that.'

One of the duke's knights, still regarding Henry doubtfully, eyes hard and wary on either side of his steel nosepiece, said: 'What do we do with him now? What happens next?'

'I'll tell you what won't happen,' said Henry. 'I'm not, whatever you may think, taking a quick way to make myself duke. I'm merely taking a quick way to make sure my brother doesn't kill himself instead of living to *be*

164

duke. I propose to take command and save his duchy for him and hand it back on a plate. I suggest that you take your lord to a place of safety. He keeps a boat at the river postern. Get him over the river to our mother's monastery. No harm can come to him there, from me *or* Conan.'

One of the knights, as he bent to lift Curthose's limp shoulders, said: 'He wanted the pleasure of killing Conan himself.'

'It's beneath the Duke of Normandy to kill the likes of Conan personally. Leave that to me,' said Henry evenly. 'You can trust me to see to it.'

Something unexpected, something chill, in Henry's voice made all the five knights, his own and Curthose's, look at him sharply. 'He's more than Rufus' creature,' Henry said. 'He's an outrage. He's a *merchant*. It isn't for him and his kind to decide who the Duke of Normandy is. No, I didn't come here out of pure brotherly love, any more than I came here to grab my brother's title. I came here to deal with Conan. And I will.'

There were townships in his own leased province and burghers in his towns, and if one set of merchants got the idea that they could choose their masters for themselves, the next ex-overlord might well be himself. As would undoubtedly be the case if Rufus won the contest. He, for sure, would have Henry sprawling in the gutter the very next morning. On both counts, it had seemed to Henry desirable that he should support Duke Curthose. And if necessary, snatch the command of the battle from him. Below, the sounds of fighting had grown louder and the air was pungent with smoke. But there could be no question of a sortie until the army at the south gate was in. The noise dragged at him but he must resist. He had waited all day, leashing his brother's impatience along with his own, until he was lightheaded with frustration. How much longer?

But even as the thought shaped itself, the thudding of the ram at the south gate ceased and a further surge of noise arose from that quarter.

'The gate's gone or I'm the archangel Gabriel,' said Henry, and ran for the battlements, hoisting himself on to a crenellation for a better view. The squabbling human

165

ants, the miniature roofs and vein-like streets reeled sickeningly below and he grasped at a flagpole for support. But he had seen what he wanted. He jumped down. 'Belleme's in! That's reinforcements for us in the town and the west gate's still holding. Things have evened up.' He jerked his head at Curthose's knights, who had lifted their lord but were standing irresolute. Curthose, with a red lump now rising on his jaw, was beginning to groan and stir. 'Get him away across the river. Hurry! You're doing nothing wrong. You're saving your lord's life. You –' he turned to his own men ' – follow me.'

He left Curthose's men, muttering, suspicious but perforce obedient, to see to their leader and clattered down the tower stairs with his two knights behind him. The men waiting in the courtyard cheered as he appeared. The duke's brother was evidently as good as the duke to them, which was heartwarming. Henry made a trumpet of his hands and bawled: 'Open the gate!'

He meant to make the sortie an orderly business, with a strong drive to the south gate to meet Belleme's relief force. But even as he sped down to the bailey, the situation had changed. The west gate had broken. Before the sortie was fifty yards from the castle, the enemy was bearing down on them from the west. Confusion closed in. Smoke blew everywhere, making eyes and throat smart, blurring vision. The streets were choked with conflict and strewn with the fallen. The injured tried to crawl to shelter, non-combatants scuttled. Henry fought warily, with the respect for his own person which Curthose would certainly not have shown, and with his helmet firmly clamped on to his head, which was as well, for his sword was bloodied instantly. Thereafter, the pace only grew hotter.

He slipped in the blood trail of a dying man and came near being killed himself. Someone hurled a stone from a rooftop; he dodged and by sheer chance came face to face with Belleme. In partnership they began to marshal their joint forces. Shortly after that, it began to appear that despite the enemy incursion from the west, their own side was now numerically superior. Encouraged, they set about improving the odds still further.

It is possible to become drunk on slaying. Henry and Belleme were both extremely intoxicated before that day was over.

Belleme was older and had a big personal following, but the ducal house was the ducal house. When it was finished and the leaders had withdrawn to the castle hall to receive their captains' reports and examine prisoners, it was Henry who seated himself on Curthose's throne, and Henry to whom Conan the Burgher was brought.

Henry was still in his blood-smeared armour. He had removed his helmet and sweat-soaked hair was stuck to his forehead. War-fever, something akin to the berserker madness which his Viking ancestors had cultivated to make them strong in battle, still raced through his veins. He had never fought on foot and hand to hand like that before, never before been in command like that. And he knew he had done far better than feckless Curthose would have done, for all his courage. He regretted that he had not managed to come hand to hand with Conan in the struggle but perhaps this was better. There were things he wished Conan to know before he died.

The presumptuous Conan was in his thirties, sandy and too well fed but with an underlying toughness of mind. He had been marched to the hall through streets littered with bloodstained bundles; he had heard the castle gate slam shut behind him and here in front of him was Henry, enthroned and dangerous. But he kept his nerve, looked straight into Henry's bright-brown, inimical eyes, and said: 'Where is Duke Robert?'

'Not here and if he were it would be beneath his dignity to deal with you himself,' said Henry. 'Who are you?'

'I am Conan, son of Pilatus and . . .'

'I know your name. I said, who are you?'

Conan said steadily: 'A burgher of Rouen and like my fellow burghers here and elsewhere in this duchy of Normandy, I have for years been losing money because I must hire soldiers to protect my consignments from robbers. My – our – lawful complaints have been ignored by the duke and . . .'

'I heard that Rufus bought you.'

'He offered silver. But the promise that he would bring

167

back law and order meant more,' said Conan with dignity. 'I refused the silver.'

'Oh, did you now? Then your losses through robbery can't have been so serious.' There was laughter from those who were standing by. From outside came a shocking wave of noise. Belleme had turned his men loose to pillage. Belleme himself, lounging rather than sitting on one of Curthose's divans, said to Henry: 'I know what we ought to do with him,' and offered three suggestions, each more appalling than the last. Conan stood still but the sweat sprang out on his skin and his face, at last, turned ashen.

'No,' said Henry, but not reassuringly, 'I think not.'

The most infuriating thing about Conan's defence was that it contained much truth. Curthose had let Normandy fall into anarchy and this was the result. But it was not Conan's business to depose him. Henry stood up. 'Come with me. I've something to show you,' he said.

Conan obeyed, because a couple of men-at-arms pushed him. On Henry's heels he climbed a long spiral staircase until they emerged on to the tower from which Henry had gazed out earlier. Henry walked to the battlements and leaned on them. Without turning to look at Conan, he beckoned.

The men-at-arms pushed him to Henry's side. 'Look there,' Henry said. 'No, not into the city, not yet. Beyond. What do you see?'

'Beyond Rouen?' Conan was puzzled, taut with doubt. His tongue seemed reluctant to move in his mouth. 'Beyond the Seine? Well, farmland. Then forest.'

'Yes. Rich farms. Forests full of game,' said Henry dreamily. 'Rolling on for leagues till the blue distance swallows them.' Conan winced away from him. The words were gentle and poetic but the tone would have been appropriate if Henry had been listing the denizens of a snakepit. 'The Seine itself,' said Henry, 'is full of fish and it's the highway for the ships that bring goods to Rouen from all the world. *Now* look down into the city. It's strewn with dead men just now. Women too. Tragic, isn't it?' Conan shuddered again, recoiling from the unholy juxtaposition of the humane, the imaginative, with the

168

murderous in Henry's voice. 'It looks quite different on an ordinary day,' Henry observed. 'Then it's full of people going about their business, buying and selling, gossiping, working. A wedding party here, a man up a ladder mending a roof somewhere else. Bells ringing from the churches. This is the heart of Normandy. But it beats for no one but its lawful lord.'

'My lord, you are gifted with words,' said Conan, much as Rufus had once done. He tried to smile.

'And now,' said Henry, his hand on Conan's elbow, 'look straight down. No, don't draw back. What do you see?'

'The . . . the courtyard.'

'Yes, the courtyard.' Over Conan's head, Henry glanced towards the men-at-arms and they came nearer. 'It's paved with flagstones. Can you see the separate stones?'

'N . . . not very well.'

'Why is that?'

'We're too high! No, in the name of our common Maker . . .!'

Henry's grip had shifted, forcing Conan's arm up his back and thrusting his upper body half over the wall between two battlements. Conan's muscles were soft compared to Henry's sword-toughened arms. He was helpless. It was said afterwards that Henry let him draw back when he cried out. It was said that he waited until the last of Conan's nerve and pride were gone, let him offer gold and land and lifelong service, let him plead for a priest, let him kneel clutching at Henry's feet. Let him weep and claw the stone as Henry dragged him up again and once more thrust him between the battlements.

It was said that he vomited as he hung there in the moment before he went. And it was said that if one went to Conan's Leap at dusk (especially in November) one might still hear the shriek, less a man's scream than the agonised wail of a hurt and terrified child, as Henry grasped him by belt and shoulder and, needing no help, heaved him over.

Back in the hall, Henry was aglow, his body at ease with

169

itself, satisfied as though he had spent the day in lovemaking. Rouen was subdued, her ruler restored. Normandy went where Rouen led. He could send for Curthose now and hand him his property, as a loyal brother and henchman should. From Curthose, surely, he could expect reward.

Henry was still only twenty-two, young enough to be in some respects naive. He had underestimated the resentment inspired by a hearty punch on the jaw and the theft of kudos.

Others also saw the matter differently.

'It must have been a temptation,' drawled Belleme, 'to let your ducal brother get his brains knocked out today. I congratulate you on your sense of family.'

'One can disagree with a brother without wishing to commit fratricide,' said Henry shortly. 'Conan was one thing. Curthose is another.'

'Indeed?' said Belleme, blue and yellow eyes staring flatly.

Robert of Belleme, as Henry was already quite aware, was an evil man. But he was not a fool. He was a gifted military engineer; castles designed by Belleme were usually impregnable and castles attacked by him were usually not. Now he said: 'I wish I'd seen Conan go over the edge,' and added perceptively: 'If you ask me, you threw him over as a substitute for Curthose.'

With Sybil's departure, the Fallowdene household settled into a state of calm, preserved by tacit yet perfectly clearcut arrangements.

When Richard was absent from home, Alice might sit in the lady of the manor's place on the dais when the regular meetings were held to settle villagers' disputes and decide which crops should be planted in which fields at the next sowing. But Wulfhild sat beside her and although Alice gave the decisions, Wulfhild told her what they ought to be.

She might do half the weaving but it was understood that she would share her skills at weaving and stitchery with Gunnor or anyone else who sought instruction, and also that she should have nothing to do with making or

170

mending the tapestries, which were the province of Wulfhild and Editha.

The brewing of mead and elderberry wine was Wulfhild's task alone and no one, least of all Alice, ever touched it. Nor did she ever intrude now on Editha's breadmaking.

She was, however, free to milk cows and work in the dairy. Wulfhild herself had decreed that she should, and those already engaged on these tasks were glad of help. The ageing widow who had hitherto looked after the dairy was called Crooked Elfrida because one shoulder was higher than the other. Elfrida was often tired and as long as Alice remembered her subordinate place, she was welcome, while young Bebbe, who had the job of milking, had always considered eight cows too many. In any case, Bebbe had formed a semi-alliance with Alice because, being pretty, she was interested in her appearance and Alice had many recipes for hair washes and skin lotions.

The hall was crosshatched like a chequerboard with demarcation lines, 'but I suppose it's peaceful,' Richard said philosophically when the cheese ran out because Crooked Elfrida and Alice had both been ill and no one would intrude on the tasks of either of them.

He was keenly aware of his mother's eyes continually watching his wife for shortcomings. But Alice was carefully polite and for the time being, undisturbed by constant reminders of Wulfhild's superior fertility in the shape of Sybil, the quiet held.

At the time when the bishops of Normandy were pleading for Rufus' help, Gunnor, who also looked after most of the linen at Fallowdene, went whispering to Editha, Editha in turn spoke privily to Wulfhild, and for a while there were even smiles in Alice's direction. Wulfhild issued orders that Alice was to have extra meat and must not carry the milk pails any more.

Father Bruno, who approved of Alice's piety and deplored Wulfhild's lack of it with all a new broom's energy, suggested that Wulfhild should light candles in the church, for the fulfilment of their hopes, and Wulfhild actually did so. Richard lit candles too, and said: 'She's not being sick this time as she was before. Is that a good sign?'

171

In June Alice miscarried again and between one hour and the next, all the ground she had gained was lost. Richard was obliged to forbid his mother the sick-chamber. He ordered Gunnor to do the nursing instead. But Wulfhild's smouldering rage still pervaded the air and Alice became tearful if she even heard the tapping of her mother-in-law's stick pass by outside. 'I didn't make it happen!' she wept in Richard's arms. 'I was careful. I did everything she told me! She called me *nithing* – I couldn't help it, Richard, it just happened, I couldn't help it!'

It had certainly been no pleasure for her. Lying with her feet propped higher than her head, white with exhaustion and loss of blood, Alice was a frightening sight. But when he remonstrated with her, Wulfhild was unrepentant.

'If there's no child and something happens to you, where am I? That's what I want to know.'

'Here where you've always been. You would always have the right to live at Fallowdene.'

'Yes, as a pensioner, with a right to bed and food and a seat by the fire! Like that man of your father's, Goscelin – remember him? – who got ill and couldn't work but was looked after till he died. I *made* this place, my son. I've given my heart and my body for it. I want something better than that. Under the laws we had before the Normans came,' said Wulfhild, 'your land would revert to me for my lifetime if you died childless, but these Normans do as they please. Young de Warenne will treat Fallowdene as *hers* if he feels like it. Then it'll go to her next husband and his kin. I'll be *here*, oh yes, but what as? An old woman by the fire, that people talk across and push out of the way!'

'It might go to Blanche and Sybil.'

'And the land be divided, half to Withysham, and half to Sybil's husband? To young Brian of Little Dene? *No!*' said Wulfhild with passion. She banged her stick on the floor. 'I want to see a child of *you*, my son.'

'I'll call Bruno and make a will in your favour,' snapped Richard. 'Will that content you? Fallowdene to you unless I have issue. And now, please, will you leave Alice alone? You've always put the manor where you ought to put God,' he added. Wulfhild went away grumbling.

He made the will. Calm descended once more. Wulfhild

172

at least desisted from open unpleasantness. Alice was ill for many weeks and for a long time after that, because he was afraid of what another pregnancy might do to her, he did not venture to approach her. When the deprivation at last became too much for either of them, he remembered a piece of advice his mother had given him in her outspoken fashion, in the days before Alice came – in fact as soon as he reached an age to profit from it. For a further length of time, therefore, he defended them both from frustration and danger by withdrawing himself at the crucial moment.

He did not expect that the Christmas feast of 1090 would overturn his good resolutions. It was a very modest affair.

There had been another poor harvest and an outbreak of milk fever among the cows. They had lost three of their eight milch cows, just when the sales of Alice's excellent cheese at the markets in Chichester and the nearer community of Beechtrees was beginning to bring in a useful contribution to their finances.

But if the manor was short of cheese, the bees still made honey and Wulfhild had been able to brew plenty of mead. There were ample supplies at the feast. It promoted sensuality. Unfortunately, it promoted woolly-mindedness, too.

'I wasn't quick enough,' he said apologetically afterwards, his head against Alice's breasts. 'I'm sorry. I wasn't quick enough.'

'Don't mind so much. It was only once. I don't expect anything will happen,' said Alice kindly, caressing his head. Alice *was* kind. The very first time he had walked into her father's hall and seen her, he had known that. With Alice there was no mockery, no leading on, no eleventh-hour evasions. If he gave his heart to this girl, he had known instantly, she would treat it gently. He wished his mother did not dislike her so.

Three weeks later, when it became clear that Alice's optimism was misplaced, she was terrified. 'Not for myself, Richard, don't think that. But if it all goes wrong again, what will your mother say to me? I'm frightened of *her*.'

The summons from de Warenne, calling Richard to arms because King Rufus and Duke Curthose had made a treaty in which each was the other's heir, and Count Henry was going to war about it, could not have been more malevolently timed.

Wulfhild, brushing Alice aside – 'I'll see to it, I'm used to it' – took over the packing of Richard's gear, conveying the task to her own room, where he found her methodically filling his leather sack, with the items still to be stowed laid out in a row along a bench: spare cloak, some shirts, cleaning things for armour and saddlery.

'Alice should be doing that,' he said sharply. 'She's upset because she's not, as a matter of fact.'

'Better she doesn't lift and bend just now,' said Wulfhild. Her shawled head bobbed up and down as she put away sandbox and oilpot. 'I must leave Alice in your care,' Richard said. 'And it may be a long business. But if when I come home I hear that you've said one, just one, harsh word to her for any reason – even if she loses this baby too – I'll tear up that will and bundle you on a pony and take you to Withysham to be boarded with the nuns and keep Sybil company.'

'You can't,' said Wulfhild. 'I've my rights, by law, even these days. You've said it yourself. I've a right to a place in this house.'

'If there's no other way to protect Alice, I'll override your rights. Don't go to law about them. The king sells his justice these days and you haven't got the wherewithal. You've nothing to complain about. If I'm killed, Fallowdene's yours and Alice goes home to her father, with her dowry.'

'And that on its own'd make a tidy hole in our coffers!' Wulfhild snapped.

Richard looked at her. The intense blue of her eyes was fading now and the eyes themselves had sunk a little; one needed to look hard to read them. But now that he did, he saw misery there as well as anger.

'Don't talk of dying, my son,' said Wulfhild. 'You're all the world to me, for all you've got so hard with your mother and your little sister since you married.'

The money isn't the point, he thought. Even

174

Fallowdene's only half the point. The rest of the point is me. She doesn't want to share either Fallowdene or me with Alice.

She would have to. 'Take care of Alice,' he said again, 'or else. Remember this. Fallowdene won't fall apart without you.'

Wulfhild compressed her mouth and went back to her packing. Richard, shrugging, left the resthouse. It was a blessing that Sybil was out of the way, he decided. He had done right there. That was one weapon, at least, knocked out of his mother's hand.

PART III

IN WHICH AN ARCHBISHOP UNSUCCESSFULLY ATTEMPTS TO START A FOREST FIRE
1090–1094 AD

One

Private Crosses
1090–1

The monk who had answered Abbot Anselm's jangling handbell had to flatten himself against the wall as the abbot's departing guest strode out of his host's office. The guest was a well-dressed young man with fiercely rowelled spurs on his boots, and a fiercely set expression on his face. He didn't even see the cowled figure which effaced itself so hurriedly from his path.

The monk, having let him go by, tapped at the door, received the Deo Gratias, and went in. Anselm was sitting pensively at his desk. 'Ah, Brother Bernhard. Did you see him?'

'Benedicite, Father. The man who has just gone? Yes.'

'You could hardly have missed him, I daresay. You may have noticed, Brother Bernhard, that it's very difficult to be a Christian. One falls short often enough oneself and when it comes to preaching perfection to other men – how does one *not* sound patronising? Or hypocritical? I wanted to help that young man but the only advice I could possibly give him merely made him angry.'

Brother Bernhard refrained from committing the sin of curiosity verbally and hoped the abbot wouldn't see that he was committing it with his eyes. He looked at the desk top, as a precaution.

Anselm however took pity on him. 'He's a devout youth, of a devout family. He and his sister recently made a pilgrimage to the Holy Land. On the way, his sister was kidnapped. Her brother and the friends who were in the party found that she had been sold into slavery and managed to learn to whom – a Moorish noble in Spain. He refused to sell her back to them and her brother wants me to make representations to the Moorish authorities, or try to intercede with her buyer myself. He overestimates my influence, poor fellow. It really can't be done. I tried to offer him comfort by pointing out that there are other

179

aspects to these things. It has long been agreed within the church that Christians should not repine too much if they suffer enslavement for where better can a Christian soul cultivate humility? It is a way of taking up one's cross. But he resented it.'

Brother Bernhard wanted to say: 'I'm not surprised!' but restrained himself.

'He said some harsh things,' Anselm admitted. His face, worn thin by abstemiousness and continual sentry-duty against his own human faults, rarely showed colour but there were two crimson spots on it now. They were already fading, however. Anselm had convicted himself of clumsiness but not of giving bad advice. 'But I didn't call you in simply to break off an unpleasant interview. I have a letter to dictate. It's to that English earl who has invited me to England.' Bernhard at once went over to the writing desk, which was always in readiness. 'The usual salutations,' said Anselm.

When the dictation was finished, Anselm glanced at his scribe, now putting the stopper back in his ink bottle, and rising, moved to the window. Beyond it were the hills which bordered this lonely Norman valley of Bec, far away from Normandy's raucous and competitive heart in Rouen. 'One of the disadvantages of knowing you all so well, my son, is that I can hear you thinking. Say it.'

'My lord, I . . . we . . .'

'We. You discuss such matters among yourselves, I know. You shouldn't, but you do. You, plural, think . . .?'

'My lord, if this English earl wants your help so much in founding this monastery he speaks of, would it not be, well . . .?'

'Courteous at the least to go?' Anselm turned his back on the window. 'Is that it? My son, there are plenty of prelates, even in England where the king seems determined to reduce their numbers, who can advise this ageing nobleman with the bloodthirsty past and the desire for repentance, on how to save his soul. He does not need me. One of the king's friends, Robert FitzHamon, is at this moment planning to found a monastery too and has asked my advice, but found an exchange of letters sufficient. No. It is the English bishops who want me in

180

England, for their own reasons. It is they who have urged this invitation. Listen to me, Brother Bernhard, and report what I say back to your brethren. The fact is that certain good but misguided people in England and, I fear, here in Bec, are campaigning to have me nominated as . . . I find it difficult even to put this into words . . . as the new Archbishop of Canterbury.' Colour reappeared in Anselm's face. 'It is improper even to admit that I know of the suggestion. But the time has come to stop these attempts to manoeuvre me into position, as it were. You know, Brother Bernhard – because you've taken the dictation – that I have written repeatedly to King Rufus telling him that it is his duty to appoint a new Archbishop. But you also know that I didn't volunteer myself. I should be a disastrous choice. Archbishop of Canterbury? Archbishop of Catastrophe would be more accurate. It would be my duty to instruct the king in his moral obligations. I should shortly be even more unpopular with him than I was with that unhappy young man. King Rufus' character being what it is, it wouldn't be long, I feel sure, before he disliked me so much that I wouldn't be able to function at all.

'I could have worked with his father. Old King William committed many terrible deeds, but he knew they were terrible; he desired virtue even if he couldn't attain it. But King Rufus, from all accounts, enjoys his sins. There is this about the practice of humility, Brother Bernhard. It is difficult but it can save you from still graver difficulties. It stops your eyes from ever getting bigger than your stomach.'

When Brother Bernhard had gone, Anselm turned back to the window. It was summer and above the window arch was the busy flicker of wings as the house martins came and went from their nestholes under the monastery's eaves. Across the valley were the dense green woods full of shy wild creatures, living lives that were hard and dangerous but innocent, Anselm thought, untroubled by mankind's dreadful privilege of the knowledge of good and evil. Untroubled by guilt.

He hadn't told Bernhard everything about the interview with the angry youth. He should not, he castigated himself

181

now, no, really he should not have said to that poor boy, who would certainly never see his sister again, that she was to be envied in one respect, since she had seen the land where the feet of Christ had trodden.

'Envied?' the boy had said scornfully. 'She's beautiful. She's trodden land herself by now. Trodden as in cock and hen and an infidel's doing the treading. And please don't offer me any more pious cant about taking up crosses,' he added viciously. That was the point at which Anselm, shaking his head sadly, had rung for his scribe, whereupon the youth had spun round, with a swish of his cloak, and marched out.

And the boy had been right. For who was Anselm to talk of crosses, who had never been asked to carry one? He had entered his monastery in the hope of following his lord to Calvary but where had he found himself instead? Here in this serene valley, this orderly house of prayer and study and the mind-cleansing singing of the Office. It offered all that he desired. Where, in all this, was his cross? Did he want to refuse Canterbury truly out of humility, or because for him it would be the end of his life in Bec?

Watching the busy house martins, it seemed to him that their innocent domesticity and that of all creatures like them, birds, beasts or people, could only be defended by huge and secret sacrifices. Christ had shown the way and those who chose to follow Him must expect at His bidding to make their own.

What if this unwanted honour were His bidding to His servant, Anselm?

The first time that Ralph des Aix, lying in the darkness on his crackly straw pallet, saw a shaded taper move across the hall towards him and felt the furred, thickset body invade the privacy of his rugs, he was terrified.

He lay with pounding heart, conscious of the heat of the human furnace beside him, and wondered why he had been so blind, so naive. He should have expected this. Now that it was too late, he thought that some part of him had expected it. But Rufus' extraordinary court with its mix of hardheaded political giants and decorative

182

hangers-on had both bemused and excited him. So too had the unlooked for favour of a king. His instincts had warned him but he hadn't listened.

Confusingly, he liked Rufus. Quite apart from the fact that of all men, a king was the one with the most land in his gift, Rufus was fun. De Warenne had been amiably dull. Helias was stimulating but he was pious, prone to preface remarks with phrases like: 'With God's help.' On his first day as Rufus' employee, Ralph had heard the king tell an abbot: 'Leave God's will out of it. Our will is the one that matters here.' It was exhilarating.

Rufus' gruff whisper spoke in his ear. 'Don't be afraid. I mean you no harm.' The very words, thought Ralph wildly, that he himself had used when coaxing a nervous girl at La Fleche to leave her haymaking and let him repeat the delightful experience he had had for the first time just before he left home. Had he not been nearly paralysed between the dread of what was about to happen and the equal dread of what would happen instead if he sat up and shouted for help, he could have laughed. Then Rufus' hand was on him. 'Don't be alarmed. Give me your hand. Ah. That's nice. Is this nice too? Are these three moles that I can feel on your chest? They're in a straight line, on a slant, like the belt of Orion. Oh my dear boy, you're so finely made . . .'

In the event, there was less to fear that he had thought. If he could once accustom himself to the sheer unnaturalness of it all, he could manage. Discomfort could be borne, caresses made a technical skill. He could learn to receive them in turn, to throw his head back, close his eyes and shudder with pretended delight. Could learn to shut out of his mind the fact that the enquiring hand belonged to a man. Could learn to whisper answers to the lovetalk.

Could construct in his mind a barrier between the day and the night. Again and again, when morning came, he would look back on the events of the night with amazement and disbelief that the young man who figured in those amorous passages with King Rufus was himself. At the beginning, the amazement and disbelief were compounded by shame. On the very first morning, when they were all breaking their fast in the hall, Rufus having left him and gone to join his nobles, Ralph found himself scarcely able to meet the eyes of his fellows.

De Warenne was still at the court then and with him, among his knights, was Richard. They had been glad to meet again when Richard came to de Warenne's household for his annual knight service, and had formed the habit of talking together during the informal breakfast hour. At dinner, Richard, as a knight, was always higher up the table but in the morning, people ate standing up, wandered about and spoke to whom they would.

On that first morning after Rufus had come to him, he observed Richard approaching, made believe not to have seen him, and went out of the hall. In the end, he supposed, if Rufus persisted with his attentions, it would become known and Richard would find out. But he wanted to conceal the truth from his friend as long as he could. Richard was too straightforward, too normal, surely, to understand this and Ralph had no words with which to explain. He was afraid of losing the friendship.

But as the days and nights passed, he grew hardened to his curious new position and could conduct himself by day as if nothing had happened. Before Richard went home, they were on easy terms again. Gossip there certainly was; Ralph could tell that by the remarkable degree of politeness with which even men of rank now addressed him. But if Richard had heard it, he gave no sign, and behaved as though Ralph's new post on the royal hunt staff were the only change in Ralph's life.

It was no honorary position. He worked by day with the king's personal huntsman Croc, who was perfectly well aware of Ralph's real function in the court; was, like everyone else, polite to the king's new friend, but seemed to feel it his duty to keep this latest addition to his staff well occupied.

Croc was not a knight huntsman, most of whom lived in the districts where they had land, lending hounds and harbourers to the king when he visited the area. Croc was a plain man, half-English, well on in life, small and wiry with veins and muscles knotted round his bones like ivy round a tree. He spoke Anglo-French patois most of the time, and crudely, scattering misplaced aspirates with abandon, although he was quite capable of speaking correct French and in the king's hearing, did so. He had been using the rough accent for so long that he had forgotten why he took to it but Ralph suspected that it was simply a means of refusing to lick the arses, in Croc's own inelegant phrase, of the numerous noblemen with whom he spent so much time. The only one of them he actually admired was Rufus himself.

The king in turn seemed to like Croc and occasionally called him in to add his name when charters were being witnessed. Anyone who could write his name was eligible for that and Croc, surprisingly, was literate. He was in fact a failed monastic novice. 'They chucked me out and I was thankful. Stuck inside they walls all day – bah!' said Croc.

His business was to organise hunting for Rufus wherever the king chanced to be. 'If we're in a royal forest where there's a Keeper of the Walk, or anywhere where there's a Knight Huntsman handy, it's easy,' he told Ralph. 'We just hand the job to them and make sure they do it right, which they don't. Not ever. Always miles to go to find a stag or else they've let the chases get overgrown. You'll see.'

But when Rufus' vast and continually mobile court had made one of its landslide descents on a place outside forest jurisdiction and possessed of neither Knight Huntsman nor Keeper, Croc and his staff must themselves search for sign and question or bribe the locals to find the whereabouts of game. These occasions had their side benefits. Rufus' court was bigger than his father's and still growing. Feeding and housing it on its travels was a massive task usually achieved simply by commandeering what was needed along the way.

Local populations, therefore, on getting wind of its approach, were apt to remove portable goods and all edibles, including those on the hoof, into the nearest cellar, wood or similar hiding place. Royal gratuities could be earned, said Croc, by discovering such missing items and sequestering them for the king.

Ralph's life became a strange, compartmental affair, divided between the forest glades where he and Croc searched for deer tracks, the descents on villages where as a king's officer he searched out provisions, and the feverish hours with Rufus on Ralph's pallet or, sometimes, in the king's down bed.

It was in the forest, he knew, that he was truly at home. Forests had a thousand moods. A wood on a summer morning, bright with dew and haunted by birdsong, was a different world from the same wood in early November where the leaves were dying in the colours of flame and an immense dignity like the funeral pyre of a pagan king. Different again, as night from day or Heaven from Valhalla, was the winter forest, with the bare branches outlined black against the snow, and a cold orange sun slanting through. He was aware, in the forest, that what he felt was love, or near to it.

With Rufus, he did not know what he felt. Fear, excitement, admiration were all there, mingled with distaste, which was not only for the histrionics in Rufus' bed. He made useful tips from, but found he loathed, the harrying of the villages. Too many of the houses reminded him of Aix. Yet when he was with Rufus, tenderness was also present. In some secret fashion which was not just physical, Rufus appeared to need comfort and Ralph found in himself an instinct to provide it.

It was a restless life. Rufus was for ever on the move and Ralph and Croc went with him. When he crossed the Channel to make peace with Curthose and sign the Treaty of Rouen which was to seal it, they went too. They were with him when war broke out again.

'So we're off to battle,' Croc said as they loaded their belongings on to their shared pack mule. 'Curt'ose and Rufus are settin' off together in a state of brotherly love – first time in years – to put young 'Enry out on the street, pore little sod.' He used the same tone of gloomy commiseration he would have employed when preparing to put down a deformed pup. In Croc's eyes, the luckless Henry had no prospects, now or ever. 'It's rotten, when you think about it. They've cut him right out of the succession and carved up the lands he thought he'd got a life lease on, and no one paid the pore little bleeder back for that lease, neither. Just, "oh, it's only young 'Enry; if I want to give Rufus some land in Normandy to buy him off leading any more of my burghers astray like Conan, I'll give him 'Enry's and hang on to mine." That's how Curt'ose thinks.'

Ralph had heard all the details already but not couched in Croc's colourful language. Amused, he said: 'Go on.'

'They told him he can go to Brittany if he wants, or Italy, or the 'Oly Land or 'Ell. So he's dug hisself into the toughest fortress on what he still reckons is his land. Mont St. Michel, it's called. Ever 'eard of it, young Ralph?'

'It's where the Brittany coast and the Norman coast meet,' said Ralph, 'I think it's a monastery. Funny place to conduct a war.'

'Got a warlike abbot, though,' said Croc thoughtfully. 'I mind a bit about it now. You saying it's a monastery brought it back. Been there once. It's right in the middle of a ruddy great quicksand. Can't blame him, 'Enry, I mean. He got Rouen back for the duke, bloody ungrateful it is if you arst me, treating him like that, even if he did shove old Curt'ose out of the way and grab all the glory. Reckon Curt'ose is jealous. Well, not for us to 'ave opinions, young Ralph.' He tightened a girth and patted the mule. 'We go where Rufus goes. That's the way 'e is. Got to be fighting someone. If it's not 'is uncle it's 'is brother and if it's not one brother then it's t'other. Let's 'ope it don't take long. I'd sooner be after game than pushed into archers' lines or sitting down round a castle. What do you do with it when you've taken it?' asked Croc logically. 'Can't eat it.'

It took a very long time indeed.

Mont St. Michel was indeed surrounded by a ruddy great quicksand. It stood, a lonely semi-island, in the midst of a wide estuary into which not one but several rivers flowed. At high tide it was ringed by sea; at ebbtide the sands appeared, segmented by the rivers and passable only on paths invisible to the uninformed eye. Informed eyes were few and local and Henry had prudently herded most of them into the Mont with him. The place was certainly well designed by nature to hold off a siege and perhaps because

187

of this, its abbot had for years had fantasies about doing just that and had kept the Mont well-victualled.

Since it was impossible to camp close to it, Curthose and Rufus contented themselves by placing camps at strategic points round the perimeter of the bay, occupying the town of Avranches to the north, and putting a blockade fleet at sea. 'I'd let him stew in the Mont and not bother to besiege it,' said Curthose, 'only he'd be in Helias of Maine's pocket before we could turn round. He's tried to raise men from Maine already, only luckily we caught the messenger. We'll just have to sit down outside St. Michel until he gives in.'

'You can write this letter for me,' said King Malcolm of Scotland to his wife. 'You can be my secretary. That way it'll come from both of us. You'd best write that it does. That sister o' yourn will tak more notice, likely, of you than of me. Your sister,' he added thoughtfully, 'hates men.'

'Oh, Malcolm. I'm sure that isn't true. Christina was called to the life of religion and has taken a nun's vows of celibacy but I am certain it wasn't that she hated anyone. She loved Christ more, that's all.'

'I'm maybe sharper ower these matters than you are, lass. But never mind. As long as she doesna teach our Edith to hate men.' He glanced down the hall, to where his ten-year-old daughter was trying to teach a young dog to jump through a hoop. Malcolm doted on Edith and did not care who knew it. He was not afraid of being laughed at because few people dared to laugh at Malcolm. To laugh at someone was to underestimate them, and of those who in the past had underestimated Malcolm, few remained alive.

'Edith's for a prince's bed and board, one of these days,' he said now to Margaret. 'So write this. To Christina, Abbess of Romsey Abbey in the county of Hampshire in England, from Malcolm King of Scotland, Greeting. Then tell her that we're pleased to know that she's willing to tak charge of our Edith, and educate her in reading and writing and Latin and account-keeping and stitchery and all the things a royal lady should know, and that we're

188

sending Edith to her with the bearer of this letter.' At the end of the hall, Edith broke off her game with the dog in order to sneeze. 'Ye're maybe right to want to send her south,' Malcolm observed. 'This climate's ower sair on her. Be milder down there. *But* . . . now, mark ye put this in and put it clearly. There's to be no misunderstandings. The girl is going to Romsey for her education only. She's destined for marriage. She's no' to become a nun nor to wear a veil. She's to keep that in mind and so's your sister Christina. Make it very plain, my lass.'

The siege was boring. The besiegers spent much time literally sitting down outside Mont St. Michel, on folding camp furniture, burnishing helmets for lack of livelier occupation. Patrols were organised from time to time, which played a game of tag with the foraging parties Henry regularly despatched across the safe paths, in an attempt to dodge away inland to raid farms for fresh provisions.

As the boredom intensified, the antagonists developed a species of bond. Henry took to sending out little bands of knights who cantered up and down in front of the besiegers' camps until someone rode out to fight them. The resultant trials of arms were half serious and half sporting, 'and a nice distraction while that young bugger gets his foraging expeditions past us,' said FitzHamon angrily. 'There's supposed to be a war on!' In FitzHamon's large, craggy face his mouth looked smaller than it really was, as though his facial muscles were not mobile enough to let it open wide. But now he managed it, and from the square dark aperture there issued a rumble of exasperated laughter. 'All the king says is: "Charge the onlookers to watch, it'll help with the siege expenses!" He's ridden out to joust with the enemy himself, more than once!' FitzHamon threw up his hands and made an indescribable noise. 'Aaargh! The crosses I have to bear!'

Two

Secret Terrors
1091

The presence of a horde of more or less unoccupied men round the Mont had its natural effect on the locality's inhabitants. Anyone with anything to sell, from dried fruit to destriers, arrived forthwith, 'like bluebottles round a nice 'igh carcase,' said Croc cynically.

It broke the monotony. Too well, at times.

Rufus had marshals in abundance whose business was to see to his horses but Ralph's skill with them had been noted. The morning a vendor brought a spectacular piebald stallion for the king to inspect, it was Ralph who was called to look it over, because Ralph would do it well, and he was there.

He approached the task nervously. He knew Rufus well enough by now to know that the king would expect sound judgement and clever bargaining. Before an audience, too. In this bored camp, the transaction was attracting notice and a small crowd had already gathered.

It was a dull day. The ebbtide sands of the bay were dun-coloured and veiled in a grey haze. Droplets of water clung to the stallion's parti-coloured mane. Ralph went over him bit by bit, teeth, feet, legs. It was a fine horse, no doubt about it. 'What are you asking?' he said to the vendor.

Rufus had visibly taken a fancy to the animal. He had been about to lead a patrol in search of Henry's foragers when the dealer arrived and his usual black horse had been saddled. He kept glancing from one to the other and the black was clearly coming off worst in the comparison. The dealer had noticed. 'Twenty silver marks.'

'*Twenty*? There's never been a horse foaled that was worth that much,' said Ralph with irritation. 'He's worth fourteen at the outside.' He wished Rufus would move away. His eager gaze was only encouraging the dealer in exorbitant demands. He stepped back, examined the

190

piebald with narrowed eyes and seized on a borderline imperfection. 'His hocks are too high.'

'Perhaps my lord king would like to try him out,' suggested the dealer, shifting his full blue gaze to Rufus.

Rufus came forward. 'All right. Tighten that girth. I'm getting on him.'

He put a hand on the pommel and mounted without using the stirrups. The bystanders, who included several of the prospective patrol members, holding their mounts' bridles, murmured approvingly. Rufus thrust his feet into the stirrups and made the horse arch its thick neck and fret against the heavy bit. Then he gathered it as though he were winding a crossbow and let it go, departing across the thin sandy grass at a gallop. One of the bystanders led his horse over to Ralph. 'Shouldn't you have tried it out first?' Ralph did not answer. He did not like Gilbert Clare, who was inclined to make double-edged remarks, and had been pointed out by Croc as an example of unwise generosity on Rufus' part.

'Tried for treachery after Odo's rising, but Rufus forgave him. He's still Earl of Tonbridge, even. *I* wouldn't have forgiven him. Reminds me of a 'ound I had once. Offer 'im a titbit and 'e'd have your fingers off.' Not prepared to be gibed at by Clare, Ralph edged away.

In the distance, Rufus had pulled up. He put the horse into a gallop again from a standstill, stopped once more, backed and spun the stallion on its hocks. The dealer smiled. Ralph sat down on a folding stool. Clare's remark had stung because it had substance. He *should* have tested the horse before Rufus spoke. He had been shown up as inexperienced. He dug the point of his dagger into the sandy soil in front of his feet and concentrated fiercely if distractedly on drawing a figure like an X joined across the top.

Quietly, not speaking, the dealer sat down on a spare stool beside him, reached out with his riding whip and across Ralph's design drew another V-shaped figure, converting the figure into a five-pointed star. He glanced up at Ralph and they exchanged a long stare. Ralph nodded.

The dealer said: 'Your king wants the horse but he

191

wants you to get it for him cheap and he gives you no help. Sixteen marks?'

'It's still too much.'

'It's a good horse. Tell him you beat me down.'

'Very well. If he consents.'

'Oh, he will,' said the dealer, glancing with satisfaction to where Rufus was still cavorting. 'It's barely April,' he said, 'but if May Eve finds you still here, come up the River See, on this bank, at sunset. A mile beyond Avranches there's a dead tree standing alone. I'll meet you there.'

'Gladly, if we're still here.' He had not celebrated Beltane as Elise had taught him it should be celebrated, since he was fourteen. To think of honouring it properly again was like going home. The dealer said casually: 'Look as if we're talking business. The king's coming back. What's wrong with him?'

Rufus had wheeled the piebald and spurred him towards them. He shouted, waving his right arm towards the north-east corner of the bay. At that point, a deep arm of the sands ran into the land, making a secondary estuary round the mouth of a river. There, just visible through the mist, something was moving. Rufus slid the stallion onto its hocks in front of them.

'You cretins! Are you all blind? Gaping at me instead of keeping an eye on the enemy? Look, damn you, look!' He pointed again. What could be seen of his face behind the nosepiece of his helm was crimson.

They could see now. The fugitive movement was a party of horsemen, undoubtedly from the Mont, one of Henry's foraging expeditions, for sure. 'You oafs!' Rufus bawled at his patrol members, as helms came out from under arms and were rammed on to heads, and feet reached up for stirrups. 'Do you think they'll wait for you?' A ferocious gesture pushed them back out of the saddles into which they were scrambling. '*I* saw them first! They're my meat. Ralph, close the deal, I'm taking this horse. Don't you dare follow me, any of you. I can manage without such fools at my side!' He whirled the stallion again and with a war yell which set the held horses dancing, spurred away, sword out, straight towards the foe.

192

'Christ almighty!' gasped Gilbert Clare. 'He usually rides the black with the blaze! He's got a helmet on! They won't know who he is on that patchwork thing!' He stood as if paralysed. 'He ordered us not to follow!'

In the distance, Henry's sortie had seen the oncoming rider and wheeled to meet him, galloping across a river ford. A groom was still holding Rufus' saddled black destrier. They were only feet away from Ralph. He ran and leapt, snatching the reins, groping for the stirrups, hoping the girths were firm, trying to forget that he wore no helmet himself. It was six to one out there and that was a raiding party, not a bunch of sporting challengers and Ralph wasn't leaving his king alone with them.

The others could obey Rufus if they liked. They weren't his lovers. Ralph was.

From the corner of his eye he saw that Gilbert Clare had mounted after all and was following. But the black was fast and outstripped him. Coarse grass flowed back beneath. Rufus had changed course to avoid a dangerous patch of soft sand and had lost some of his lead but he was still far ahead and one of the enemy knights had broken away from the rest, was charging him, spear levelled . . .

In the frame between the black horse's ears, Ralph saw them meet, evade each other's spears, circle and charge again. The girth on which he had taken a chance was loose after all. The saddle was slipping. Rufus and his adversary met again, leaning from their horses to strike at each other. The piebald reared. Ralph was closing up. He was near enough to see the great blood-poppy flower on the piebald flank before his own stupid saddle slithered under the black's belly and dumped him on the ground.

He fell rolling, got to his feet. Rufus had been thrown as well and one foot was caught in the stirrup. He was being dragged like a felon, behind a bucketing, wounded stallion. Henry's knights were closing in to kill. Ralph ran. Clare had come face to face with the same sucking sandbar which had made Rufus swerve and his horse had balked. Rufus' horse had collapsed. A blade flashed in the air above the king. 'No, no!' Ralph heard himself sobbing. Rufus was shouting, on a hoarse and urgent note Ralph had never heard him use before. He tried to shout too:

193

'Hold back, he's the king!' and hoped to God they could hear him.

Panting, stumbling, spurs and boots nothing but hindrances. Ralph caught up just as the threatening sword was lowered. Rufus, still attached to the dead horse, was wrenching at the stirrup iron. His foot had slipped right through it. He was covered with dirt and swearing horribly. The erstwhile foe had all jumped off their mounts and one of them was helping him.

'Get back!' said Rufus, catching sight of Ralph and responding ungratefully. 'I said don't follow me!' He shook his released foot to make sure it was unhurt and got up. One of Henry's men offered his horse and Rufus mounted. Henry's knight glanced towards Ralph. 'We heard him shout out who he was before we heard you. We wouldn't dare harm the king. We don't want to end up on a gibbet with Count Henry and Duke Curthose shaking hands in front of it!'

'Ralph, go away!' Rufus barked. Ralph retreated to catch the black horse, which was grazing. He busied himself with adjusting the saddle. A gust of laughter made him glance back. Rufus was clapping an enemy knight on the shoulder. Gilbert Clare rode up and remarked: 'We might as well have let him be. Well, that's one mouth fewer for Henry to feed.' The knight whom Rufus had amiably buffeted was kneeling with his hands between the king's.

'I thought it was water they were short of in the Mont,' said Ralph acidly but Gilbert had already ridden out of earshot. He mounted and walked the black back towards the camp. Rufus thundered past, his new liegeman behind him. 'Damned nursemaid!' he shouted.

In the camp, the dealer was waiting, with a crowd round him. One face seemed to spring from the rest. Ralph pulled up, half-glad to see Richard and half-doubtful. He had known that Richard was here, part of a contingent sent by de Warenne. But he had had a return of embarrassment and had kept their encounters to salutations exchanged at a distance. Richard's face, however, was friendly as he said: 'That was a near thing. You don't have an enviable job.'

That could have had more than one meaning. Was Richard far enough away from the royal circle not to have heard the gossip, or was he obliquely referring to it? Richard's grey eyes however were tranquil. Ralph wished that Richard could know, and yet not to reject him. But he could not think how to approach the subject and did not try.

'He's still got to pay for that piebald horse,' he said. Everyone, including Richard and the dealer, laughed.

In the pavilion where dinner was communally eaten, Ralph still had only a modest place. Rufus did not mix business with pleasure. To be the companion of his nights did not change one's place in the political hierarchy. Ralph did not mind this for it fended off jealousy. Gilbert Clare might make the occasional barbed remark; the Count of Meulan, who resented anyone close to the king (he only tolerated FitzHamon because of a quirk of personal liking for him), might pointedly take precedence in doorways. But the rest treated him with the casual courtesy he had noticed at once and they respected his prowess at shooting and horsemanship. Occasionally, people even asked him to put in a word with Rufus about this or that. He helped if he could, but with caution. He was afraid of being presumptuous. He had never dared yet, much as he would have liked to, to ask for anything for himself.

Therefore it was not until dinner was over that the king caught his eye and gave him the tiny nod which was a signal between them. After dark, Ralph took a lantern and went to the royal tent. The guard outside and the chamberlains in the outer compartment as usual behaved as if he were invisible. He shed his clothes and slipped quietly under Rufus' rugs. The king had drunk heavily at dinner and the wine-smell at once enveloped him. Hot, powerful arms closed round him. But when Ralph ('like a well-trained whore,' he thought to himself at times) attempted to arouse the king, the response failed.

'I'm sorry,' Ralph whispered. In interactions between king and subject, if the king ran the subject through by mistake, the subject would still be the one who had to apologise.

But no. 'N . . . not your fault,' Rufus muttered gruffly. 'I'm pleased with you. You're a dear good boy. Beating that dealer down by four marks. Wonderful.' The matter of paying for the deceased piebald had been the only conversation they had had since morning. 'I've something to say to you,' Rufus whispered.

That could mean anything from 'I'm making you Archbishop of Canterbury' to 'You're under arrest.' Ralph waited.

'I'm in your debt,' Rufus said at last. 'I owe you my thanks.'

'Your thanks, my lord?'

'You came to save my life today. I didn't thank you then. Couldn't. Had to pretend I was angry with you, in front of Henry's boys. But . . . sweet Christ,' said Rufus, pressing a heavy arm down across Ralph's chest, 'I wouldn't say this except that the wine's talking, but I've never been so bloody glad to see anyone in my life.'

'But, my lord, when you called out who you were, they put their weapons up at once. You saved yourself. I did nothing.'

'You were there and you had a sword. They were excited. When that blade was up in the sky over me, I thought it was the last thing I'd ever see, till I heard you shouting. However much I bellowed that I was the king. I was frightened. I'm ashamed.'

He rolled over, burying his face in his arms. Ralph, not knowing what to say, did his best. 'Anyone would be afraid at such a time.'

'Not a knight, Ralph. And not a king.' Rufus' voice was muffled. 'We must be able to stand face to face with death and look him straight in the eye. We're told that when we're children. And I *can't*!'

'My lord!' Ralph was alarmed now. Tomorrow, if Rufus remembered this conversation at all, he might well regret it. But he was sorry for Rufus. He tried again. 'Most men have secret fears. I'm afraid of . . .' He didn't quite know what he was most afraid of. Dying still landless was a thought that appalled him. But to say that was like asking for favours and much as he desired land, he had never dared to say so to Rufus. His voice died away. Rufus, who had hardly been listening, plunged on.

'I've wanted to say this for years. Never could get drunk

enough at the right moment. I'm afraid of death. Understand? Not all the time; it's mostly all right till the last moment. I can go into battle first, cross swords, all that. But then when I'm close to it, suddenly – I see what might happen and . . . first time was years ago. I was just a boy. Henry and I got into a fight with Curthose and his friends, and someone pulled a knife on me. I snatched it off him. My father praised my speed. But I was only so quick because I was *frightened*, Ralph! I saw that knife and I saw the sword today and I knew how it would feel if it went into me and I knew that behind it was nothing but a great darkness . . . or else hell, I don't know which. They're the same, maybe. Can you imagine not existing? Could you bear not to be alive? To be cast away into blackness? I hate darkness. I sleep without a lamp on principle, did you know that? To defy the fear. But it never leaves me.'

'My *lord*!' Ralph made the king hear him this time. Rufus stopped. 'Everyone feels the same,' said Ralph firmly. 'We all feel queasy at some point in a battle. With most men it's when they're waiting to begin. With you, perhaps it strikes later. My lord, in the morning you'll wish you hadn't told me. But I shall have forgotten it by then.'

'You're a good friend, Ralph. I trust you. You've got loyalty and good sense. Let's talk of something else, then. I'm being nagged right and left to put a new Archbishop into Canterbury. Suppose I made Ranulf Flambard Archbishop?'

'Risky,' said Ralph, recognising that he was being required to play up to a joke. 'He might set fire to the cathedral.'

A chuckle rewarded him. 'You've heard his newest nickname, have you? Not just Flambard, the Cresset, now. People call him Passe-Flamme because he sets other men ablaze with his ideas. I wouldn't have got this army mustered and over here as fast as I did without him. He had everyone working twenty-five hours in the day. No, perhaps not Canterbury for our Ranulf. I couldn't spare him, anyhow. Come to that, I can't spare Canterbury! It's valuable. But it was a glorious thought.'

197

Rufus laughed out loud. Ralph laughed too and beside him, Rufus' desire awoke at last.

'Your brains have gone begging, Curthose,' said Rufus coldly.

He sat in Curthose's tent, feet planted squarely on the floor, knees apart and hands planted squarely on knees. Curthose gazed serenely back at him, a lazy arm stretched along the back of his settle. He glanced at the tent's open flap as a ship under oars went past on the high tide, probably bound for the mouth of the River See beside which Rufus' camp lay. Beyond the ship, far away cross the sparkling water which now hid the sands, was the dark and battlemented cone of the Mont.

'It's not a matter of brains. It's a matter of feeling,' he said. 'How could I refuse an appeal like that? It wouldn't be chivalrous.'

'This is a siege. The idea is to bring young Henry to heel! We get him to the edge of surrender and what do you do? *Send in water*!' Rufus thundered. Meulan, sitting near him, nodded vigorously.

'Only water, not food,' said Curthose pacifically. 'He won't last long without food. The patrols are properly organised now and he can't forage any more. But we can't let our own brother die of thirst.'

'He wouldn't die of thirst, you wantwit! He'd surrender. That's the p . . . point! That's what we're bloody here for!'

There was a curious imaginative strand in the characters of all three brothers. 'There's something symbolic about the place he chose for his final stand,' Curthose said.

'Symbolic of what?' snorted Rufus. His imagination worked differently.

'Well, look at it. Go on, look. What do you see?'

'I see what looks like a distant molehill with a lot of water all round it. At low tide, it's sand. Well?'

'I'll tell you what I see. I see isolation. I see dignity. We've taken everything from him, Rufus. And to fight back, he's picked not only the strongest fortress he can find, but the loneliest. I think he's feeling lonely. And I'm beginning to feel conscience-stricken.'

'You mean you're sorry for the little brute. I'm not. You forget what we're thrusting him out for, aren't you? I sent him off with short shrift because he only came to me when he was dissatisfied with you. I don't like faithlessness. Then he went back to you and you locked him up for a while and we thought he'd learned his lesson. He came to you when Rouen was in danger . . .'

'Well,' said Curthose, although his hand caressed his jaw as he spoke, 'he *did*.'

'Yes, in his own way! He knocked you unconscious, had you rowed out of the city and led your troops himself! If he'd stood on a pile of boxes in the m . . . marketplace and said: "Good citizens of Rouen, how about me for duke instead?" he couldn't have made himself plainer. *You* said as much, if I remember! And now you're s . . . sorry for him?'

'Yes, I am. He *did* save Rouen. Sometimes I imagine him riding away with just a handful of friends and a pack mule for company and I don't like to think what's churning on in his mind.'

'Bah! He's got money hidden away still. He'll make himself a life in France, or Brittany, out of our way. That's what you wanted, isn't it, when you withdrew his lease and gave the lands to me? The sooner he goes, the better. We've other things to do, or you have. What about Maine? Weren't you going to bring Helias to heel as well as Henry? I'm supposed to help you by the terms of our agreement but if I'm kept waiting about much longer . . .'

From where Meulan was sitting, he could see Rufus' tents, pitched on the higher ground near the north-east corner of the bay. The ship had indeed been going there; it was already drawn up from the water. And above Rufus' great white tent, a flag was being hoisted. 'My lord,' said Meulan, 'they're signalling for you.'

'Scotland!' said Richard of Fallowdene disgustedly to Ralph. 'I was hoping to get home. I left my wife expecting. I suppose the Scottish king invaded because he thought King Rufus was out of the way. And what's to happen to Count Henry?'

'He's surrendered,' said Ralph. 'The envoy's with the king now. They ran out of food.'

Firmly, he pushed aside the sudden vision of the mosaic floor at Aix, which Richard's casual reference to going home had inspired. It had gone through him like a swordthrust. He wished he had a home, even if he did have to go there via Scotland. Would he ever, he wondered, win or earn one?

He might justly say that he'd earned one already. But on that subject, Rufus was silent.

The shutters of Abbot Anselm's windows were open and the summer world outside poured in; the scent of green things growing, the bleating of the abbey's sheep, the brightness of the sun. It looked like a promising season, for once.

But in some minds, the prospect of a reasonable harvest meant only an invitation to new extortions, and that before the corn was even ripe.

His old friend the Conqueror, that remarkable mixture of the bloodthirsty and the pious, had given Bec lands in England. Bec had appointed an English agent to look after them. The report now lying on Anselm's desk was liberally strewn with words in extra thick ink and large lettering. *Extortion. Intolerable burden. Insatiable rapacity . . .*

The English agent, in fact, was in hysterics.

A final phrase, in the blackest ink of all, glared at Anselm from the page. *Only your personal intervention . . .*

He doubted whether that would have much effect either, from all he had heard of Rufus and his grasping financial adviser Ranulf Flambard. There was a war on, too. Wars always meant more taxes. But if anyone could have influence at all on this outrageous new demand, he supposed it was himself. He at least had the authority to agree terms on the spot.

He could refuse a plea from a frantic nobleman wanting to save his smirched soul by founding a monastery, because others could advise him just as ably. But this time, if anything at all could be done, he was the one who could best do it.

200

Only it would take him straight into the arms of those who wished to keep him in England as harness-mate to a truculent, irreverent, sodomite king.

Well, no one could actually force him to accept Canterbury, he reminded himself. He could go to England purely to attend to his abbey's financial affairs. He could visit that penitent old killer of a nobleman and give him the advice he desired, which could include a few swingeing penances. He could then ignore all other blandishments and come home.

Rufus' irreverence and avarice might even turn out a blessing. Rufus wasn't going to allocate Canterbury unless somebody made him, and who in the world was capable of doing that?

This was a disgraceful way to think. Rebuking himself, Anselm went to kneel at the priedieu which stood against his office wall. He looked up at the Rood which hung above. If he went to England, he must not cling to Rufus' scandalous faults for protection, but strive to mitigate them, for the sake of Rufus' own soul, whatever might result. He need not decide to go immediately – no, surely not that. That too was a kind of vainglory, to think that nothing could possibly be done about these shocking demands unless he did it in person. He might, with propriety, make one more attempt to settle the matter through an intermediary. But if that failed . . .

He closed his eyes and let his spirit go, out of the flesh and into the heart of the Mystery which was the Trinity, which was sacrifice and despair and redemption, which was the blazing light at the heart of all darkness, and from which he could not be alienated.

Wherever he went and whatever he was, or did, or was made to do, the Mystery would be with him still and it would sustain him.

Three

Female Children
1091

'Mother, it's too early, the baby'll die!'

'Three weeks. Richard was earlier than that. The baby will *not* die,' Wulfhild contradicted her, rolling up her sleeves. 'We're into September.' And a fair, silver-gilt September at that, the mists clearing every morning before a sun which within fourteen days would bring the wheat to perfection if only it held. They'd have a saleable surplus this year, with luck. It wasn't going to be spoilt by the loss of this child. 'Gunnor, take her arm and keep her walking till I say she can lie down. Alice, you've been a good girl all summer and done what I told you. Just keep it up a few hours more and you'll get your reward. Stoke the brazier, Editha, and get that water hot . . .'

'. . . it's a girl. And healthy. Sweet Mary, what a voice.'

'A girl?' Alice moaned.

'Nothing wrong with girls. I was one myself,' said Wulfhild, flintily good-humoured now the struggle was over. There had been a bad few minutes when she thought the baby's head wouldn't pass the pelvis. Alice *was* too narrow. If Richard had left the choice of a bride to his mother, she'd have chosen better. But: 'Where there's a sound girl, a sound boy may follow. And even a girl can inherit a manor.'

Romsey Abbey in the county of Hampshire, where Edith of Scotland had come for her education, in the care of her aunt, the Abbess Christina, was bigger than humble Withysham where Sybil of Fallowdene, also in the care of an aunt abbess, was reluctantly enduring hers.

Romsey was wealthy too, which Withysham certainly was not. Lying amid gracious rolling country, it too was gracious, the work of the finest Norman masons grafted on to the fabric of the old English abbey, but so tastefully that one could hardly detect the join.

202

And nowhere was the abbey lovelier than at its heart, where a cloistered walk encircled a garden in which grassy walks wound among beds of cultivated roses, and trellis tunnels, twined with climbing roses and starred, in June, with pale pink blooms, lay across the square garden in the sacred shape of the cross, thus consecrating, said Abbess Christina, these most beautiful of flowers to their creator.

The roses were of several varieties. Beginning with the hedgerow dogrose and a few variants bred by her predecessors, Abbess Christina had coaxed a dozen more colours and patterns of bloom into being. Her flowers were famous; even King Rufus had heard of them and sent for plants. He liked flowers to adorn his halls, apparently.

Edith loved the roses and the cloister walk and the warmth and gentleness of Hampshire after Scotland. Her health was better here; she caught fewer colds and shook them off more easily. She would have been ready to love the abbey altogether but it did have one serious drawback. Aunt Christina.

She walked in the cloister on a blustery autumn day, watching the wind shake the rose bushes, feeling it stir her brown hair. She was in the company of several other girls, of ages from nine to sixteen, all of them destined to be nuns. Edith was not destined to be a nun, by order of her father, a state of affairs for which she regularly thanked God on her knees. She was not yet quite eleven but she was already physically mature. Christina, on learning this, had been overcome with horror and had ordered her niece into a three-day retreat, fasting, and insisted on praying with her for the blessing of a pure mind and for freedom from the lusts of the flesh.

But Edith, in the rose-haunted days of the previous summer, with doves and cuckoos in the surrounding woods filling the air with a sound like a soft grey-blue cloud, had felt the first awakening within her of a yearning at once thrilling and slumberous, and knew that the thing which her aunt condemned as lust could have another name, and was her proper destiny.

Even if her father had not forbidden it, she would never be a nun. Whatever Aunt Christina said or did.

But her father was far away and her aunt was here.

203

Because the day was cold, she and the other girls were all wrapped in thick mantles, but unlike the others, Edith wore no black veil over her head. The veil had a significance.

And only yesterday, her aunt – since Edith had ignored several hints – had commanded her to wear one. Walking bareheaded, she was defying the abbess and though she walked boldly and openly as the daughter of the King of Scotland should, holding her head high, within herself, Edith was afraid.

Christina sat in her office, going through the month's accounts. They would soon be salting down meat for the winter and the annual consignment of salt for the purpose had arrived. But why on earth was it so much larger than last year's? The quantity of meat would be the same. She must speak to the sister responsible.

The order for vellum, on the other hand, erred in the opposite direction. They always needed more than they could make and to have enough was vital. Without it, the work of translating books of devotion and learning between English, French and Latin, and putting the result into exquisite illuminated volumes, would be hampered.

It must not be hampered, since the preservation and perpetuation of learning was one of the things that abbeys were for. In a world racked with wars and struggles for power, the abbeys, the monasteries, were like fortresses housing between them a great treasure. Only within their walls could anyone hope to have the resources of time and energy to devote to scholarship – or even the space, come to that, to make a rose garden. In any house out in the world, it would have been dug up to grow cabbages, or turned into an enclosure for breaking colts.

And only within monastic walls, too, could women find time or freedom to expand their minds or think about their souls. In the world, they were for ever doomed to household cares and an endless cycle of pregnancies at the behest of men who not only wouldn't give them time to think but would for the most part bitterly resent it if they tried.

Christina most heartily pitied her sister Margaret,

forced into marriage with the Scottish king to please their brother Edgar. The three of them, Christina, Margaret and Edgar, were all that remained of the old English royal house. There had never been any real question of Edgar challenging the Norman house for the throne. He was far too ineffectual ('Now, if only *I'd* been a man!' Christina sometimes thought fiercely) and although the English didn't like the Normans, they weren't foolish enough to want Edgar in exchange. He had still needed asylum from the Normans, and had sought it from Malcolm, taking his sisters with him. And Malcolm had taken one look at Margaret and made her the price of his friendship, and the fact that Margaret, like Christina, greatly desired to become a nun meant nothing to him whatever, the unregenerate heathen! Christina, thinking of her sister's fate, was apt to begin muttering to herself.

So poor Margaret had been handed over, a living sacrifice, to be defiled and invaded by that northern savage.

Christina sincerely believed that she herself regarded Malcolm with loathing. She would not have admitted, even in the face of death, that once the sweat and leather smell of Malcolm's solid body had made her dizzy and that the glimpse of hair at the open neck of his tunic had set her imagining what he would look like naked and what that hard furred chest would feel like if one were pressed against it. She would have died by fire before she would have confessed, even to herself, that she hated him only because he had never looked at her, or that her present driving need to waken a sense of vocation in his daughter Edith, and win her for a nun against his wishes, was her ancient anger seeking revenge.

The sound of young voices made her look up. The small arched window on her right overlooked the cloister and the rose garden. Edith was out there, with the other girls, just cutting across a corner of the garden. The shining brown plaits of her niece gleamed shamelessly amid the demure veiled heads of Edith's companions. With an outraged exclamation, Christina flung down her quill pen, and gathering her dark skirts clear of her feet, swept out.

She bore down on her quarry, striding across the grass

by the quickest route, mouth and brow in straight lines across her face, hard-edged as a sword. Edith, seeing her, stopped short. Her knees felt shaky but she kept her back straight. Her father King Malcolm was afraid of nothing and she must be the same or she would not be worthy of him.

'*Where is your veil?*'

'I can't wear a veil, Mother Abbess.' Edith always used the correct form of address. It was deliberate, Christina knew. Correct or not, it was a rejection of their relationship and it only made her angrier. 'My father forbade it,' said Edith, 'in view of its meaning. It is only for nuns or novices.'

'This is England. Your father is not king here and if he were, he would still not give the orders inside my abbey. You are a woman now, Edith, and therefore subject to the temptations which beset womankind. It is time to armour yourself against them and to give grace a chance to enter your heart. To accept the veil and the state of mind that comes with it, is one way of doing so. Did I or did I not, yesterday, order you to put on the veil?'

Mutinous silence.

'Did I?' said Christina dangerously.

'Yes. Mother Abbess,' Edith muttered. Under Christina's hard blue stare, her own eyes – which were grey-green, the colour of the sea, *Scottish* eyes, thought Christina, detesting them – fell.

'And what did I say would happen to you if you persisted in arguing with me?'

Edith made herself look up again. 'It will make no difference. I can't wear the veil. Because of what my father said.'

'Because you are hard of heart, impious, unable to recognise a magnificent opportunity when it is put before you. I will give you one more chance, Edith. Go to your dorter and fetch the veil I gave you. Put it on. Then we will say no more about this foolish fit of defiance.'

Edith stared at her feet again and neither moved nor answered.

'Very well,' said Christina, and shot out a hand to grasp Edith's arm. She was only in her forties, but her fingers

206

looked as if they belonged to a woman much older. They were, however, extremely strong. 'Come with me,' said Christina.

The other girls, who had drawn back, sorry for Edith but too frightened to speak in her defence, followed slowly, in an awed cluster, exchanging a few whispers. In the abbey building, they gathered at the foot of the steps to the dorter, up which Christina had dragged her victim.

They could hear it all. The most heartrending part was that they heard the whistle of Christina's cane for so long before Edith shrieked. They turned to scatter as their abbess stormed down again but she saw them and spoke sharply, calling them back. 'None of you are to go to the dorter or speak to her. She will come to the refectory, I hope, in a chastened state of mind and wearing her veil. You may speak to her then but not to express sympathy. And those of you who are crying had better dry your tears. They're wasted. She brought her troubles on herself.'

Edith came into the refectory at the end of the afternoon last of all, and all heads turned to see her enter. She was walking stiffly, her eyes red. But she was still holding her head high, and on it there was no veil.

There were gasps, quickly checked, and furtive glances towards Christina.

Abbess Christina, who was standing up, awaiting the last arrival before pronouncing grace, went rigid, from head to heels, a shuddering rigidity of anger which could be felt throughout the silent refectory.

But she was a strategist. In thinking that had she been a man she could not have put up a better challenge to Norman William than her brother, she was quite right. She also knew a good deal about the ability of human beings to withstand agony once, twice, or three times and then break down at the fourth.

'Still obstinate, I see,' she said coolly. 'Perhaps we need time to think, do we, Edith? We will let the matter rest for seven days. This time next week, Edith, I hope to see you wearing your veil in obedience to my orders, like all the others. If not – well, you will have the week in which to consider whether you wish your experience this afternoon to be repeated.'

In the November of that year, 1091, after Rufus and Curthose in partnership had driven Malcolm back from England's northern borders, the Scottish king arrived home in a bad temper and forthwith quarrelled with his wife.

The subject of the quarrel was Edith.

It was rare for Malcolm and Margaret to fall out. For one thing, he reverenced her. Malcolm had been reared to think that reading and writing and quoting from the Scriptures were all so difficult that only the most dedicated intellects could master them.

Margaret could do them all and weave and bake and nurse sick children too. She was also the only person Malcolm had ever met, male or female, who actually lived according to Christ's precepts, who really would whisk off an expensive beaver mantle and give it to a poor woman in the street on a cold day.

On her side, Margaret somehow managed to include within her saintly standards of behaviour an apparently endless tenderness towards the crude, stocky warrior who had insisted on marrying her in the face of her longing for a nunnery. There were times, certainly, when she found marriage to Malcolm rather like walking a tightrope but mostly, by some miracle, she kept her balance.

On this occasion, however, as she afterwards said to her confessor, she had been sufficiently weak, or sufficiently human, to fall off.

'That's enough,' said Malcolm, interrupting her attempts to reason with him. 'That's more than enough. A pity that clacketty-tongued sister o' yourn never learned to mind on her own business. I said she could have the lassie to educate. I said I wanted her accomplished, like her mother. It's an ornament in a wife, I said. But I also mind I said that a wife she should be and nothing else. One more letter from your sister in her southron abbey, bleating about vocations, and the girl comes home!'

The Inverness fortress was stoutly built and furnished with gloomy magnificence, in which thick furs and velvet hangings in dark shades of red and green predominated. But at the moment it was wrapped in wind and nothing stopped the hearthsmoke from swirling out into the hall. Margaret coughed and strengthened her determination that Edith should not be recalled from her Hampshire Abbey and the milder climate of England. Besides, if Christina were right, it would be a grave sin to recall her. Somehow she must make Malcolm understand. She studied him gravely, her hands at rest in her lap. Margaret never stitched or spun while talking to her husband but gave him, always, her entire attention.

'Malcolm, if Christina thinks that Edith may have a true calling, should we not listen? At least, will you not do as Christina asks and withdraw your objection to the wearing of the veil? So as to leave the child free to decide? My sister is a most learned and devout woman . . .'

'Your sister is a dried-up old virgin who'd be the better of a good . . .'

'Malcolm!'

'All this talk of Edith having a calling; it's nothing but notions in your sister's mind. Sooner be like her than wed to me, eh, lassie? Envy her, do you? Wish your bonny bairns had never seen the light? Want to keep Edith from having any? Balls!' said Malcolm. 'Now tak heed. I've more to say and I'd have said it sooner but you got in first with your yammering about vocations. I got another letter yesterday. You were at your Mass for All Souls so I got a clerk to read it to me. Well? Ye don't ask who it's from?'

'Anselm, the Abbot of Bec. I saw his courier in the hall when I came back yesterday and asked who it was. In fact I spoke to him to make sure his lodgings were as they should be.'

'Ye still think I'm a heathen who'll lodge churchmen in the byre if ye don't watch me? Instead o' fussing over the messenger's lodgings, why didn't ye ask me what the message was?'

'I knew that if it concerned me, you would tell me.'

'Och, have ye no human curiosity, woman? Anselm had an idea to offer me. I've looked at many a lord for Edith but I hadna thocht of this. Anselm was gey sorry I'd been fighting with the English again though not as sorry as I am that I lost . . .' Malcolm almost went off at a tangent but pulled himself back '. . . and he's got a sense of responsibility towards that English bugger's soul and his succession. Funny,' said Malcolm, off at another tangent, 'how all you saintly folk spend so much time worrying over the state of other folks' souls. He's thinking to come to England next year and nae doot he'll hae a try at converting their heathen king. He suggested . . .'

'Edith and Rufus?' said Margaret, and sat up very straight.

'Ye're sharp,' said Malcolm admiringly. 'Aye. Edith and Rufus.'

'*No*, Malcolm!'

'God in heaven, woman, why not? She'd be Queen of England!'

'But Rufus is . . .you said the word yourself, just now.' Margaret's pale skin had turned deep rose. Malcolm's expression became still more admiring.

'Ye mean, he likes men more than women? Och, it happens. But as often or not the man can manage with a woman when he's got a good reason, like getting an heir.'

'Malcolm, Edith is only a child. And delicately reared. To a young girl, even when the man is . . .is like other men, marriage can be . . .'

'Was it so dreadful, then?' enquired Malcolm. 'Were my rough old embraces so little to your taste, my pretty violet? You came,' said Malcolm lyrically, 'the very first time, like the Hammer of Thor beating a swordblade.'

'We're talking of Edith, not me. And we're talking of Rufus, not you. You can't seriously . . .'

'We can give her time to grow up. It needn't happen tomorrow,' said Malcolm easily. After this, Margaret would avoid his company for the rest of the day but he'd put it right in a quarter of an hour, come nightfall. 'Once she's grown,' he said, 'I've no fears for her, with Rufus or any other man. She's my daughter, my lady. And what's more, she's yours.'

In Withysham Abbey, Sybil's aunt, the calm and dedicated Abbess Edgiva, neither desired nor recoiled from the estate of matrimony but was on the contrary quite content to train her niece as somebody's future wife. Sybil, however, unaware of her good fortune (she had never heard of Romsey or Edith), escaped from Withysham on a cold autumn day, timing her departure with care. About midday, she decided, after their noon meal. She must begin her five-mile journey with something in her stomach and the heavier main meal would be too late. She did not want darkness to overtake her in the forest. She must go through the woods because once she was missed, people might look for her on the road. So, midday it must be, at about the time for singing the office of Sext.

They always rested after the noon meal, and filed from the dorter to the church for Sext, under the eye of the nun in charge of the children, Sister Ermengarde, who was thin and sharp and convinced that baptism did a poor job of ejecting original sin from her charges. Christina would have found a kindred spirit in her.

Halfway across the courtyard on her chosen day, Sybil left her place and said: 'Sister Ermengarde, I'm sorry, I've got to go to the privy.'

'Nonsense. You went before you got into line, like the others.'

'I know, I'm sorry, but I *couldn't* go then. I tried.'

'Well, you must wait.' Sister Ermengarde rather enjoyed this kind of thing. They had to learn, these children. A few years of her training and the wildest of them became decent, devout girls who knew how to subdue the flesh.

'Sister, I can't!' Sybil's brilliant blue eyes brimmed with frightened tears. 'There'll be an accident. Oooh!' She gripped her stomach hard and half-crouched, knees pressed together.

'If I let you go, there'll be a penance.'

'Yes, Sister Ermengarde. Oooh!'

There won't be a penance, you silly old cow, because I shan't be here.

'Very well. Be quick and be very quiet when you come into the church. See me afterwards.'

'Yes, Sister Ermengarde. Thank you, Sister Ermengarde,' said Sybil and ran for the dorter. She went straight through, ignoring the privy stair on her left. Passing her bed, she snatched up the mantle she had left there in readiness. There was another way out, the one they used at playtime. She darted through, arriving in the open safely out of sight of the church and made for the place in the outer wall where the stonework was broken. She had been industriously working bits of stone loose over a period of months, seizing opportunities whenever she could, usually during recreation. She had made sufficient footholds now.

In the church, the singing of the Office had begun. Everyone must be inside. She clambered up the wall, hoisted herself astride the top of it and sat there, panting. Then, suddenly sick with terror that Sister Ermengarde would come in search of her, even so soon, and catch her, she dropped down on the other side, to land in a crackling drift of leaves. She lay, massaging a scraped ankle. She was committed now. The drop was further on this side and there was no broken stonework. She couldn't get back even if she wanted to.

Moving as quietly as possible, she stood up and began working her way round the wall to find the track that led towards home. She must use it as a guide, she thought, keeping it in sight while she walked through the trees to one side of it. She must not get lost.

That was vital. She was in the Forest of Andred and once lost in Andred, she would stay lost for ever.

Andred was older than legend. It swept like a green ocean up to the northern march of the downs, where the soil grew chalky and too thin for trees. The woods of Fallowdene were an outpost of Andred, where the trees had flowed like water into a trough of earth deep enough to sustain them. Andred was twenty miles deep from north to south and fifty miles broad from east to west and the Conqueror's New Forest of Hampshire was only its western extremity. It was crossed by roads here and there and a few patches of farmland had been carved out of it but these interruptions were few. The trees and the heathland reigned for the greater part unchallenged and there were wild creatures deep within it which scarcely knew the scent of man.

Most of them feared him and all were shy, even the wolf

212

and the wild boar. Sybil, flitting cautiously among the trees with the homeward path on her left, knew she was unlikely to meet either so near to a path, and if she did, it would probably run away. Anyway, she told herself stoutly, she was agile enough to climb a tree at speed if necessary.

The going was slower than she had imagined and much noisier. Dead leaves were everywhere and even her light feet sounded to her like a marching army. There were also patches of undergrowth through which she couldn't push her way and she frightened herself several times, thinking that in avoiding them she had gone too far from the track and lost it. Once, after a particularly bad fright, she sobbed with relief to see it again and risked walking on it for a time. But presently she heard hoofbeats behind her, coming from Withysham. She ran back to the trees and crouched behind a wide-girthed oak, heart pounding, until the rider, whoever it was, had gone past. After that, she went back to her cautious route among the woods. Presently, after what seemed to her like a very long time, she began to grow tired.

Her feet felt heavy. Roots and brambles began to seem like snares deliberately laid, and trees appeared to move into her path on purpose. She had no idea how far she had come. But the November afternoon was darkening; dusk was near. A gust of wind, getting up suddenly, ripped through the boughs and brown leaves whirled past her face. A mournful whining began in the branches overhead. She began to hurry.

The ground was too rough and the brush too tangled for running. Stopping to nurse a stitch, she glanced longingly towards the track. But there were more hoofbeats, coming the other way this time, more than one horse by the sound of it. Presently she crept out from the bush which had sheltered her while they went by, and went on through the wood, trying another way to make haste; walking and running alternately. Walk ten steps, run ten steps, walk ten, run ten, trip on something she couldn't see in the olive-tinged twilight and fall sprawling. She lay face down, trying not to cry, her ankle throbbing where it had now been hit twice on the same place. She sat up to rub it and found herself listening.

213

Not for hoofbeats or even the howl of a wolf but to the wail of the wind and to the nearer, smaller rustlings in the dark undergrowth. To the voice of the forest itself.

In Withysham, she had prayed to Herne. She had also made a game of him. Her best friend, an orphan girl of peasant stock, had given her new information and she had used it, whispering to the others that she knew secrets about the demons of the Wood, and threatening to call up Herne, the master demon, to snatch them away if they annoyed her or reported her to Sister Ermengarde. She had gained a fair amount of ascendancy over some of the more nervous.

But the thought of Herne was different here. Rain had begun to splash through the trees and it was almost night. She was by herself in the moaning, pattering gloom and yet not by herself for she was in the midst of Andred and Andred was alive. There was an inhuman anger in the tossing branches and mingled with it, an elemental glee. The forest was aware of her and her fear and her smallness. She was an intruder in Herne's kingdom, and she had not respected Herne.

She scrambled up and stood uneasily under a chestnut tree, looking up. High overhead, outlined against a dim patch of scurrying greyness, which was all she could see of the sky, a spray of still-surviving leaves was like the shape of a giant hand, waiting to strike her down. Even as she stared, the wind wrenched at it, bent its fingers back and tore them off one by one. Panic gripped her. She ran, limping, stumbling, bolting headlong through brambles and leaves to reach the path and safety. She had feared wolves and human pursuers but they were only flesh and blood, as she was. The trees and the wind, which were not, were the foe.

Back on the track, she found herself stumbling head down into a wall of wind. It blew her hood back and her hair, coming unbraided, was turned into soaking rats' tails. Rain drenched her and leaves snowed round her. When the forest began to hurl missiles at her, her whimpers were of fear but not surprise. Something crashed and broke at her feet; something else smashed to the ground behind her. She flung up her arms to shield her

214

head and then screamed as a dark looming shape stepped into her path and fingers like steel talons bit into her shoulder.

Although, even in her terror, it did occur to her that she would not have expected Herne to carry a lantern.

You wicked girl. You wicked girl. She was at home but her mother's greeting had been a slap and even as she changed Sybil's clothes and roughly dried her soaking hair and sent Editha for hot broth, she went on scolding. 'You could have been lost in the forest for ever. You could have been eaten. Ufi and Gurth are out in the weather now, searching for you. Withysham sent word you'd run off. You wicked girl!'

Editha said it too, in the very act of handing her the broth. Alice said it most fiercely of all, thrusting her small white face at Sybil. 'What will they think at Little Dene when they hear of this? Do you think they'll want you now? Running away from an abbey of God, indeed! What a wicked thing to do. How did you find her, Father Bruno?'

The priest was holding his drenched mantle to the fire to steam. 'I heard slates coming off the church roof, in the wind. I took a lantern and went out to see how bad it was. She ran straight into me, out of the trees behind the church. She must have come on foot all the way from Withysham. Ufi and Gurth missed her somehow.'

'Why did you do it?' Alice demanded, rounding on Sybil.

Tears dripping into her broth, Sybil tried to explain. 'I'm not wicked, I'm not! Withysham's horrible, cruel, all rules, rules about this and rules about that and if you don't keep every last little rule you don't get enough to eat and the church is so cold and we're in it for hours every day. I couldn't bear it. I prayed to come home.' No need to go into details about the deity to whom she had addressed those prayers. 'But nothing happened so I ran away. I wanted to come home, so much . . .!'

'Eat your broth while it's hot,' said Wulfhild.

Sybil spooned and swallowed and snuffled. She had dreamed day and night of coming home but now she was

215

here, it was all dreadfully wrong. It was different. It looked the same; the wallhangings were as usual, the swords on their hooks by the door. But *something* was strange . . .

On the other side of the fire trench down the centre of the hall, a baby started to cry.

Sybil looked up in astonishment as Alice hurried to the child. 'Yes, you have a niece now,' Wulfhild said. 'Her name is Maud.'

Her mother sounded pleased. Maud was a favourite, evidently. While she had been immured in Withysham, remembering home every hour of the day and most of the night, had everyone at Fallowdene been forgetting Sybil, giving their love to this Maud instead? 'Mother, don't send me back again! Don't send me back to that place!'

'We'll talk about that later,' said Wulfhild. Sybil put down her empty bowl and shivered. Her mother was different too, older and *further off*, in some way. Wulfhild picked up her damp, discarded clothes and began to mutter over the tears the brambles had made. Father Bruno was studiously not looking at Sybil and the other women were ignoring her as well. Inquisitively, she left her stool and went round the fire to peer into the cradle which held the unknown Maud.

Alice was leaning over it, crooning. Very little could be seen of Maud herself; she was all swaddled up. But at the foot of the cradle, lying on top of the rug which was its outermost layer, was Sybil's old stuffed toy, the one her mother had made for her, which looked slightly like a fox, Woollypaws.

'Put that down!' cried Alice. She snatched the toy away as Sybil picked it up. 'Leave it alone!'

'But it's Woollypaws! It's mine!'

'No, it isn't. It belongs to Maud now.'

'It's *not* Maud's, it's mine!' Sybil held on to the other end of Woollypaws. 'Anyway she's too small to play with it!'

'She'll grow and it'll be there when she's ready for it . . .let go, you wicked girl, let go!' Alice slapped at her and Sybil released the toy with a cry.

216

'*Now* what's going on?' Wulfhild came hurrying round the fire trench, as fast as her stick would aid her.

'This naughty child is trying to steal Maud's toy . . .!'

'It isn't Maud's, it's mine, it's *Woollypaws*!' Sybil stamped her foot at Alice and burst into renewed tears.

Alice seized her shoulders and shook her. 'Be quiet, be quiet at once! Stop it! You bring nothing but trouble . . .!'

'Leave her alone, Alice. The toy used to be hers, that's true enough . . .'

'She's almost eleven. She's too old for toys. She's got to get ready for marriage. She's got a lot to learn. Back you go to your abbey, my girl, first light tomorrow . . .'

'I won't, I won't! You only want me to go to make room for her!' Sybil howled, pointing at Maud. 'You all love her now and not me. You've let her take my place. You've given her my *Woollypaws*! I hate her!' The method by which, in the abbey, she had bent her contemporaries to her will came back to her. She knew by instinct that some of their fears, on which she had played, were shared by Alice. 'I'll curse her,' she said, and stopped crying in order to rearrange her features in the expression of menacing knowingness which had had such an electrifying effect on several girls who were bigger than herself. 'I'll wish for Herne to come and take her away and leave a changeling in her place and then she'll have to go and live with him for ever in the cold, wet forest . . .'

Running frightened through the forest she had known that Herne was not something to play with. In the warm hall, although she was afraid of the anger of the people round her, she had forgotten the anger of the trees. Now it was as if it had followed her inside. Father Bruno's voice was booming above her with a note of wrath she had never heard in it hitherto, even when he had been angry with her before. Alice, her hands clapped over her ears, was staring at Sybil aghast as though she had suddenly sprouted horns. Editha was making the sign against the Evil Eye. The very air quivered with outrage and fury. The only person who was not angry was her mother, who had burst out laughing, or cackling. It implied that her mother was now on her side but it was not reassuring since it seemed to be enraging everyone else still further.

217

'She's bad luck, that's what she is. A witch!' Alice lowered her hands and got between Sybil and the cradle. 'I wonder I never saw it before. The harvests have been better since she's been gone . . .'

'Nonsense!' snapped Wulfhild.

'Oh, *is* it? And the very evening she comes home, the gale tears the new church roof to pieces, that I paid for? That's nonsense too, I suppose? She brought the gale with her, I tell you!'

'If Richard were here, my girl, instead of in Scotland, he'd tell *you* . . .'

'You like to think he's an unbeliever like you but I tell you he isn't!'

'You think you know more about him than I do, his mother?'

'I am of the opinion,' interposed Father Bruno calmly, 'that what we have to deal with here is no more than an exceptionally ill-behaved child, but I agree that we have that. There have been gales all through this autumn,' he said, turning to Alice. 'The minstrel who visited us at All Souls told us that timber churches had been blown down in London in a storm and that people had been killed, if you remember. We cannot hold the child responsible because there is a gale tonight. But we can hold her responsible for her own disgraceful actions in running away. We . . .'

'I'm not sending her back,' said Wulfhild flatly. Sybil, trembling in the midst of them, looked at her mother with hope.

'You must,' said Father Bruno quietly. 'She must learn manners and self-restraint. She will be married within three or four years. She must be prepared for that. She must not be allowed to think that defiance and . . . and blasphemy . . . will gain her anything. It was very very wrong to run away, Sybil. Two men are still out looking for you! As for this nonsense about pretending to curse people, and calling on demons . . .'

'She's just a child. She doesn't know . . .' Wulfhild began.

'You always defend her because she's *just a child*. You won't see that she's growing up and what is she growing up

218

into?' cried Alice. She looked at Sybil as though she were a giant spider. Sybil whimpered.

'She's desperate because she's miserable. You heard what she said. They're starving her.'

'She looks adequately fed to me,' said Bruno dryly. 'Children exaggerate, you know. I'll take her back myself, tomorrow.'

'You will not.'

'He will,' said Alice. 'I'm speaking for Richard. If he were here, that's what he'd say.'

'Oh, would he indeed?'

'If he has his sister's interests truly at heart, *yes*.'

'I can't go back!' Sybil burst out in terror. 'Sister Ermengarde will birch me! I can't, I can't!'

'You'll have to put up with it,' Bruno informed her. 'You should have thought of that before.'

'I say *no*!' Wulfhild moved towards her daughter.

'And I say yes and I have the right to say it!' Alice's head was up and her voice breathless. 'I'm Richard's wife. Yes, and the mother of his child! When Maud was born, Mother, I had from you the first trace of approval since I came into this house. Good. But it was long overdue; I'm entitled to more. *Entitled*. I have the right to speak for Richard when he's away from home and it's time that right was recognised. Whether you like it or not, I believe that Richard would send Sybil back and I say on his behalf that back she goes!'

'I'm going to saddle my mare. I must go out and see if I can meet Ufi and Gurth. I ask you both to consider carefully and resolve this quarrel before I return,' said Bruno. 'I have no wish to take sides. But quite apart from her own best interests, Sybil is clearly causing so much trouble under this roof that I would say it's best that she goes elsewhere.'

'You and Bruno,' said Wulfhild, turning on Alice as the priest went out, 'you think you run Fallowdene between you. You're always together, hatching plots, about church roofs and harvesting Richard's plants. It was for him to say, I'd have thought, whether we try the stuff out this year or next. Editha doesn't like being given queer spices she doesn't know and told to put them in the food, not by

219

you. The time you and Bruno spend together, I sometimes wonder what Richard would say to *that*"

'Mother!' Alice flushed with indignation and embarrassment. 'Father Bruno is a most devout and honest priest.'

'And not a day over thirty, and he's a man, my girl.'

'Say what you like.' Alice shrugged and turned back to the cradle to tidy the coverings. The baby, as though the raised voices had been a lullaby, had fallen asleep. 'Sybil still goes back to Withysham tomorrow.'

'When Richard comes home, we'll hear what he really has to say about it.'

'He'll say I did right,' said Alice coldly.

Sybil, weeping silently now, stomach roiling in fear of tomorrow and Sister Ermengarde, said nothing. She had already grasped that in a sense they had both lost interest in her, that she was no more than a symbol of a territory over which they were fighting, the territory of her brother Richard's soul.

And that this time Alice had won.

Four

Admitted Fear
1091–3

Ralph des Aix was made a knight on a Scottish hillside, one week before Malcolm decided to go home and fight with his wife instead. 'I called you a nursemaid once for trying to rescue me but I'm glad you didn't let that stop you today,' Rufus said, grinning. 'All right, you can rise. You're Sir Ralph now. Hear that?' he boomed at the witnesses, who stood round clad in stained armour and dishevelled surcoats. Duke Curthose, who had campaigned on the Scottish border in his father's day and was here to give Rufus the benefit of his local knowledge, was among them. So, smiling broadly, was Richard of Fallowdene. Ralph returned the smile. He was a knight like Richard now. A land grant, the traditional knight's fee, must surely follow.

Around them, the heather-grown hillside was littered with dead Scotsmen whose idea of where precisely the border lay differed from Rufus' opinion. Two lay transfixed by the same shaft, like two chunks of meat on a skewer.

In the evening, Rufus came, as he sometimes did, in search of Ralph instead of sending for him and said, gruffly and shyly: 'Today was like the first time I saw you. You came riding down that hill, guiding your horse with your knees and using both hands for the bow. Those two Scots devils would have killed me but you got them both with one shaft. You were like a young god. Is that a new bow you're making?'

'Yes. I like doing it. I've had this length of yew by me since last winter.' Ralph, sitting on the heather outside his tent, was still polishing the white sapwood back of the bow with steady, even strokes of an oiled cloth.

'And always will, I expect, even though you're now a knight. Still the same Ralph, eh? With still the same income, or lack of it. You'll want your knight's fee, won't you? A bit of land you can let out or live on when you need a rest from my wandering court.' Ralph nodded, lowering his eyes to hide the flash of joy he knew was in them. Rufus mustn't think he was loved only for the sake of gain. That would harm Ralph, hurt Rufus and anyway wasn't true. Or hurting Rufus would not matter, and it did.

'I'll see to it,' said Rufus easily, 'as soon as we've cleared Malcolm and his barbarians out of the way.'

In seven days they had achieved that. Rufus and Curthose then fell out, in a quarrel which drove all other matters out of the fuming Rufus' head.

'Rufus says 'e ain't done with Scotland.' Croc had a knack of hearing the news even before Ralph, for all his privy conversations in the royal tent, did. 'The border still ain't where 'e thinks it ought to be. But Curthose, 'e wants to start on Maine. And Rufus won't go with 'im yet. Oh well, if they didn't fall out over one thing, it'd be another. Put those two together and they're like a cat and a dog in one basket.'

By the time Malcolm was back in Inverness, Curthose was ill-temperedly en route for Normandy alone, and Rufus was on his way, sullenly, to celebrate Christmas in the south. And in Ralph's mind, a gloomy suspicion had solidified into certainty.

Rufus had made him a knight but he had completely forgotten the knight's fee. Ralph was still landless.

He could have reminded the king but he did not. He was deeper into Rufus' court by now and he had learned who among the barons and the other knights shared Rufus' tastes, and which of the squires and pages and hangers-on supplied them. With Rufus, he had attended some unrestrained parties. And he had heard lovers who thought themselves ill done by, nagging their partners. He did not want to hear his own voice raised in those aggrieved, shrill accents.

He was a knight, a member now of a privileged brotherhood, occupying a more honourable place on the battlefield and riding a destrier. The latter was in itself an expense. His old Blue was both too aged and too lightly built for the task. He bought an unschooled horse with the

222

proceeds of selling a couple of swords looted from Scottish corpses, and devoted the winter to training it. Supporting his new estate was a worry but for the time being, the honour must suffice him.

But he would keep alert for opportunity. Richard had gone home and invited Ralph to visit him there. Rufus would have granted him a short leave, but he declined. He said to Richard that he did not think the lady Wulfhild liked him, and shook his head smilingly when Richard retorted that Fallowdene was his and he would invite whom he liked to stay there. But at heart he was afraid that the sight of Richard's manor would rub his own homeless condition in too painfully, and also, he wished to stay close to the king. At any moment, a chance might come to serve his lord in such a way that the thought of reward would again occur to Rufus.

All through the long second Scottish campaign of the following summer, it never happened. Rufus indeed was short-tempered and preoccupied. Couriers arrived, some from Anselm of Bec, who was said to be definitely coming to England that year, and one from Malcolm of Scotland. Ralph did not know what news or enquiries they brought, but he did know that they all made Rufus irritable for days afterwards. Like a good wife, Ralph comforted his lord and did not harass him with questions.

The second campaign ended, more or less satisfactorily this time. Christmas came again. The spring followed, or so the calendar alleged, although the wet and stormy weather scarcely bore it out. Curthose sent renewed pleas for Rufus to help him against Maine and also against Henry who with a handful of friends was now trekking from castle to castle round the Franco-Norman border, staying in them as a cross between guests and auxiliary garrison, and making forays into Normandy to annoy its duke.

Rufus hesitated, began to muster, heard of disturbances on the Welsh border and set off westwards instead.

"'E's like an old stag pacing round and round 'is 'inds,' said Croc, who was bored by campaigning and would sooner have been crouching in a thicket to watch his graceful, wary, beloved deer step across the path so that he could mark their daytime covert as they faded into it. 'First Scotland, now Wales. 'E won't leave England till they're both quiet. It'll be messy fighting in Wales. More ambushes and night raids than open battle.'

Rufus, beckoning Ralph to ride with him as they started on the last few miles to the Bristol Channel, confirmed this. 'It's horrible terrain, Ralph. Armies can hide in those ravines. You can have a thousand men within bowshot and not know it. Aargh!' He suddenly made a face and an angry noise and pulled up. 'Holy Face, not again! Hold my horse.' He threw the reins to Ralph, dismounted and plunged out of sight behind a clump of bushes.

He was a long time. Ralph was debating whether to send or go after him, when Rufus finally reappeared. He looked angry. 'Are you unwell, sir?' Ralph asked. The king had kept them waiting before they set off that morning, he remembered.

'I'm never unwell. I had the gripes this morning before we started and it's just happened again, that's all. If my cook's been hanging the venison too long again, I'll hang *him*,' said Rufus. 'Oh *Christ*.' He bolted back into the bushes. Ralph in turn threw the reins in his charge to somebody else, got down and followed. He found the king crouched, hands to belly, shivering.

'I d . . . don't know what's wrong with me. I was quite well last night. I . . . urgh . . . eugggh . . .!'

Ralph held him as bowels and stomach alike emptied themselves. Against his fingers, Rufus' skin was hot. Others were coming up, concerned. Someone had called for the royal physician and he arrived at a run. 'You're ill, my lord?'

'I'm never ill!' said Rufus defiantly. He was very ill indeed and knew it. The terror in his eyes confessed as much.

'You are not going to die,' Ralph said, over and over during the week or century he spent at the king's bedside. They had got him to shelter. St. Peter's Abbey at Gloucester had a good reputation for healing skills. '*You are not going die*. You've eaten something that didn't agree with you, that's all. Drink this. Let me sponge you.

Let me steady you. Here's the basin. Yes, I'm here. I won't leave you. Hold on to me. You're *not going to die.*'

Day and night blurred into one. He dozed occasionally on a truckle bed beside the king's couch. Most of the time he kept vigil on a stool. Afterwards, whenever he recalled that week, memory always insisted on presenting him with a midnight picture: himself at the bedside gripping Rufus' hot, dry hand; candlelight playing on the king's sunken features, on the limewashed walls of the chamber, on the fingers of the monks who shared the vigil, telling beads; throwing into relief the deep lines on the face of Serlo, Abbot of Gloucester, who visited the king often, day or night, so deeply did he feel his responsibility.

Rufus, drifting between flaccid rationality and semidelirium, said the same things over and over. 'Oh, God, I'm dying. Where am I going? I know I'm dying.' And then, as his illness worsened: 'Fetch Anselm. He's in England. I know he is, I kept him here. I want Anselm. Fetch him.'

'I've sent for Abbot Anselm,' Serlo said. 'He's coming.'

'I said *fetch* him! He won't come otherwise. He'd have come for my father, not for me. No churchman'd come for me. Wouldn't myself, in their place. Fetch Anselm! I'm dying, I tell you, it's no good sending for him . . . fetch him, fetch him, I say . . .!'

Ralph, who understood better than Serlo did the dark and ultimate horror of oblivion which hung before Rufus' eyes, gripped his lord's burning hand again, trying to transmit strength from himself, and for the thousandth time repeated: '*You are not going to die!*'

The Council members rode in. They came and went, speaking in hushed voices, anxious. On the eighth day, Anselm arrived.

Serlo brought him in. Ralph, who had been half-drowsing on the stool which had become his home, roused himself. So this was Anselm, the Conqueror's friend, who somehow or other in Rufus's confused mind represented salvation. Why? Listening to the king's reiterated demands that Anselm should be brought to him, Ralph had been puzzled by that. Guilt over Canterbury, perhaps? It was still empty and there had been pressure on Rufus to appoint someone to it. And Anselm had been named.

The Abbot of Bec was outwardly frail, his silver tonsure thin as silk, his skin papery. But his blue eyes were sharp. He looked competent. He might know what to do. Ralph rose to greet him. 'My lord of Bec. I am glad to see you.'

Anselm nodded, acknowledging Ralph's dedication without approving of Ralph whose identity, his cool glance made clear, he knew. He turned to Serlo. 'What has been done for him? What precisely are his symptoms?'

'High fever, loose bowels, nausea. He's thirsty all the time. We give him water. It's all he can hold, anyway. We've tried purges and ginger to cleanse his system, bleeding and feverfew brews to cool him but nothing works.' Serlo's face, habitually careworn, also now looked aggrieved. He was a man of medicine as much as a man of God and disliked being defeated. 'We have a chain of prayer continuously in this room. I fear he harmed himself when he insisted on being brought here. It was twenty-five miles from where he first fell ill and he travelled the last ten in an ox-cart, delirious.'

'He knows your abbey's reputation. I can understand his wish to reach you,' said Anselm.

'We'd have gone to him! He had only to send for us. But he believes that every churchman in the land must wish him dead. I don't know why he believes that, and it isn't true. He maintains law and order in this realm and no one wants him harmed. We only wish for his own soul's sake . . .'

'Anselm,' said the king's voice from the bed, 'is that Anselm?'

The Abbot of Bec went quicky to his side. Rufus had been provided only an hour ago with clean sheets and a scoured basin, but the whole room smelt, of sickness and, unmistakably, of terror. Anselm knelt by the bed, murmured a short prayer, rose, crossed himself and looked down at the king. Rufus's pupils were dilated so that his normally light eyes appeared dark. 'I'm dying,' he said, in a voice so near a moan that Ralph's own guts twisted.

'You've had no practice at being ill,' said Anselm

226

calmly. 'You may not be as bad as you think. But if you're right – death comes to us all and there's nothing to fear. Have you confessed?'

'No. Wanted to confess to you.'

'By all means. But shouldn't your regular spiritual advisor . . .?'

'Flambard's not here. Don't want him now anyway.' He was too weak to think out complex sentences. 'Took his advice,' Rufus explained. 'Bad advice.'

'He advised you badly? You did something you now regret?' Anselm frowned at the bystanders. 'Leave us.'

'Let them stay. They know about it anyway,' Rufus whispered. And then, confirming Ralph's guess: 'I'm talking about Canterbury.'

It had been Rufus' worst night yet. Anselm looked at the exhausted faces of the Council members, who had fetched him back to the king's bedside in this predawn hour. Half a dozen times, said the physician, they had thought the king to be sinking into his last coma. The king thought it himself. His eyes were pleading with Anselm.

Once, thought Anselm wretchedly, he had hoped cravenly that Rufus' own unwillingness to appoint him to Canterbury might be his protection. Now Rufus himself was begging him to take up the cross, to be the ransom, for the sake of Rufus' own soul.

He had brought monks with him from Bec. It was one of these who now said: 'My lord, if this is God's will for you . . .'

'It isn't. It's the will of these men here.' Anselm regarded the haggard Council members sternly. 'I am aware, my lords, that you have been working on the king since before Christmas – or I would have been allowed to leave England when I asked, and not kept here all through the winter. I have said it before and I say it again: indeed, as the king now says, it is wrong that Canterbury should have been kept vacant for the sake of its revenues. But I am not the man it needs. I was a friend to the king's parents and will gladly be a friend to the king himself but not in this manner. Certainly the See should be filled. But there are many worthy bishops in England . . .'

'The king will hear of no one but you,' said one of the worthy bishops, a Council member. He drew Anselm aside. 'And unless you relieve his mind by agreeing,' he said in a low voice, 'the doctors think there is no chance at all that he will live. If he dies, the whole land will be torn to pieces between his brothers. You are our one chance. He is too ill to reason with.'

'It's true.' FitzHamon had moved aside with them and was nodding over the bishop's shoulder. Anselm looked at him thoughtfully. FitzHamon was a man he respected. He might have a face like the aftermath of a landslide, but he was honest and was in the process of founding what would one day be a magnificent abbey in the west country, at a place called Tewkesbury.

'Anselm!' Rufus called fretfully.

Anselm walked slowly back to him. 'I heard you call yourself my friend,' Rufus whispered. He put out a hand and hot fingers closed weakly round the abbot's wrist. 'If you're my friend, then what do you think you're doing? If I die now, holding C . . . Canterbury, I'll be damned, won't I? So take it away from me, take it *away*!' He tried excitedly to sit up. A physician came quickly to press him gently down again. 'Take it away!' Rufus cried, and thrust at the physician as if the man somehow represented the loathed Archbishopric. '*Make* him agree!' Rufus, with his spare hand, made a feeble, but imperious gesture at the Council members 'Kneel. I order you to kneel and b . . . beg him. Kneel, Serlo! And you, FitzHamon. Kneel, damn you all!'

FitzHamon, taking control, nodded brusquely to the rest. 'No!' said Anselm in alarm, freeing himself and backing away. But already, bishops and barons were on their knees in a semicircle round him. The sickroom, lit red and yellow from brazier and candle, might have been a painting of purgatory with himself as a saint hearing the pleas of supplicants. His face was hot. One of the bishops said: 'Please listen to the will of God.' Another, more practical, muttered that it was harassing a dying man to go on arguing.

'I *can't*,' said Anselm desperately.

Back in Bec, while he was still hesitating over whether

or not to leave for England, he had tried to face the thought that this might be required of him, had tried to say *Thy will be done*.

But now that the moment was here, it was unbearable. If he let these men thrust him into Canterbury, he might never see his quiet room in Bec again. There would be no more contemplative peace, no more untroubled hours of study. The Archbishop of Canterbury lived in a political arena and for Rufus' Archbishop it would be worse even than that, not merely political but gladiatorial. He preferred not to imagine what it would be like if Rufus died anyway and Curthose and Henry fought over England.

He should not have left Bec. St. Benedict had said that monks should not travel out of their monasteries, that it was not to the advantage of their vocations. How wise St. Benedict had been. The eyes in the upturned circle of faces were driving him towards the unthinkable. They were like wolves closing in on a lamb. Unable to bear standing up in their midst any longer, he knelt down himself. 'No, please. Really . . .'

'Enough of this nonesense.' FitzHamon's craggy face and ox-like build were not wholly misleading. 'The king gives the orders here.' The wolves got to their feet, and pounced. Anselm was hauled up and dragged towards the bed. Someone had produced a pastoral crook – had they had the thing hidden in the bed curtains in readiness? – and was placing Rufus' fingers round it. Someone else was making Anselm put out his own hand for it. He clenched his fist against it but FitzHamon, with an exasperated snort, seized his little finger and bent it back. Anselm cried out and his hand opened. The crook was thrust against his palm and his fingers were forcibly closed on it. A number of voices began to sing an impromtu Te Deum and he found himself being bodily picked up and lifted onto a set of shoulders which he recognised indignantly as belonging to his own monks. 'Put me down! Where are you taking me?'

'To the monastery church,' said somebody. 'You have to be invested.'

He came back within the hour, on his two feet. He swept into the sick chamber with various prelates, monks and barons trailing after him. His mild eyes were as near to flashing with anger as it was possible for them to be. He marched to the bedside. Ralph was in his place. 'He's sleeping,' Ralph said.

'No, I'm not.' Rufus opened his eyes. 'Is it done? Has he been made Archbishop?'

'I've been invested,' said Anselm, 'invalidly and improperly. I wish to say that . . .'

He stopped. It was full daylight now and opened shutters were letting it into the room. It showed him something. He reached a finger to Rufus' forehead. Across the bed, Ralph nodded. 'Yes, it's sweat. The first natural sweat since this illness started.'

'I was going to say,' said Anselm, 'that if you recovered, I would regard you as free to undo this unwise appointment. But now I say, *when* you are well, I shall regard you as free to dethrone me. I don't think you'll die this time. And if you refuse to dethrone me,' he added sternly, 'then I shall begin at once to advise you for the health of your soul and your kingdom. And this will be my first piece of advice.' He gave Ralph one cold look and then concentrated on the king. 'If you had died of this illness, just what do you imagine would have happened to your kingdom? Marry,' said Anselm, 'and get a son. You should have done it years ago.'

'I made a fool of myself,' said Rufus grimly.

'My lord, you were very ill,' Ralph said.

'I know. I remember it all, even the dreams I had when I was out of my head. I know what I said and what I've done. I'm saddled with Anselm now and he's saddled with me. The bishops won't let either of us back out. I hate bishops,' said Rufus glumly.

They were in the garden of Gloucester Abbey. There was no more talk of expeditions to Wales. The muster was disbanded and Rufus himself was convalescent. He liked the garden. In his otherwise unpoetic personality was one poetic quirk; he liked flowers. At Gloucester, the garden was cheerful with primrose and daffodil. They pleased him, unlike the bishops.

'Bishops,' said Rufus, 'always behave as if they thought

they ran the country instead of me. Anselm's making the best of it in his own way. He hasn't as much as been confirmed by the Pope yet – though that worries him more than it does me – and he's already demanding *all* of Canterbury's lands. He knows them by heart. Amazing how these unworldly men always know things like that. They say it's their duty to make an honest accounting to God.'

'As though He were a celestial Ranulf Flambard?'

Rufus let out a yelp of laughter. And then looked embarrassed. 'Ralph. I thought of other things besides Canterbury while I was ill. In some ways I've not been a good lord to you. Have you never been tempted to go back to de Warenne, or Helias of La Fleche?'

'No, my lord.'

'What *is* he like, this Helias?' Rufus asked curiously. 'He's a nuisance to my brother Curthose, so he must have his virtues.'

'He has. He's handsome, generous . . . knightly,' said Ralph laughing. 'But pious.'

'No one's perfect. But he can't be far off it. Why in the world did you leave him?'

'I wanted to seek out some of my father's friends in England. Also – I was no one much at La Fleche. Here it's different. You've made me a knight.' He wondered if he had disappointed Rufus with that, if he should have protested love instead. But Rufus said: 'You regard yourself as *someone*? My friendship and Sir on the front of your name are enough for that though you haven't a f . . . foot of land to call your own? I promised you a holding, didn't I, Ralph? And I forgot. Forgot a promise to a knight. I'm sorry. I didn't quite forget, to tell you the truth. But I thought, if I give him land, he won't be so much mine any more. He'll want to go and see it, perhaps live there. Anselm's been at me again to marry but I feel married already and I want you to think only of me, as a wife would. You should have reminded me. I owe you an apology, Ralph, and what's more, I owe you a holding. Promises must be kept.' He grinned. 'Well, I've got somewhere for you.'

231

Five

Chenna's Tun
Spring 1093

It wasn't a big holding, Ralph gathered. It lay in the New Forest, where it would often be easy for him to call on it even when on duty. It was not in a part that he knew well. It was vacant because its former tenant, a man called Chenna, had died without heirs. It was a little bigger now than the mere fifteen acres to which it had shrunk when the Domesday survey was made, said the clerk who gave him its history. There had been representations from Minstead, to which it technically belonged, and permission had been granted for lapsed land to come back under the plough, though as the land was within the Forest, it could not be fenced.

But it still amounted to only thirty acres, and probably they were none too productive. The soil of the district was known to be thin, and Lord Roger, who owned Minstead, had been suspiciously willing to sell his rights over it to the king in order that it might be passed on to Ralph. Rufus, even when rewarding a lover, never could resist the temptation to drive a hard bargain. Years later, on hearing that Ranulf Flambard had been made Bishop of Durham but had had to pay for the privilege, Ralph commented dryly: 'What else did Flambard expect?'

But small or not, poor or not, Chenna's Tun was land. Rufus gave him leave to go and take possession. He rode away, to claim it.

It was 30th April, a cool, overcast day, when Ralph turned off the main road from Winchester to the coast, and took the track for the Tun. He was riding Blue and leading his bay destrier Arrow. He wore his armour because he was alone. He could not afford a servant. But although it was now twenty-seven years since the Conquest, accidents still sometimes befell Norman appointees who arrived on remote manors without the backing of at least one sword-carrying companion, or a suit of chain mail.

He knew that his tenants numbered between eighteen and twenty souls, dispersed between four households. As he neared his destination, his thoughts became much occupied with wondering how they would receive him. He was jogging along a forest track, following a sketch map provided by the clerk, but it was crude and not to scale, and he came on the Tun before he expected to. He trotted suddenly out of the trees, to see it spread before him. It came on him like a revelation, like the great light in the sky which had once startled some shepherds on watch near Bethlehem, that this cluster of thatched dwellings, that curving glint of stream, those fields, those tethered goats, those beehives, were his.

He who had been homeless since the day he left Aix had a home at last and this was it.

He jerked the destrier's halter and rode closer. The horses both shied as a dog on a long leash sprang from behind the first cottage and barked at them furiously, neck stretched at the end of its chain and forefeet solidly planted. Ralph halted again, waiting for someone to come out and see what had upset the dog. Nothing happened. Looking round, be observed that the fields seemed as devoid of human life as the cottages. The dog's challenge subsided into a low growling. Apart from that, Chenna's Tun was still.

He rode round the cottages. They were thatch and daub, walls made of rubble and plastered with cowdung, looking as if they had grown where they stood rather than been built. Every door was shut. But the place hadn't been abandoned; the dog was there, and the goats, and he found a byre with four oxen in it. Puzzled and uneasy, he followed the track to the stream. It brought him to a ford and continued on the far side towards another house, which stood alone with a patch of trodden earth in front and a lean-to byre of its own at the side. It resembled the other dwellings but was a little bigger. Two more goats were tethered to it.

Goats had to be tethered under Forest Law, since they were destructive of the young foliage if allowed to roam.

233

These would be his own personal goats, he supposed, since this was certainly his house, according to the clerk's description.

He splashed across the ford and up to the house. This too was closed and when he dismounted to examine the door, it was locked.

At a loss, he gazed round. He had a vegetable patch, he observed, and it had been weeded. There were signs of sprouting crops in the fields. But where the devil was everyone? The skin of his back prickled as though someone were watching him from hiding and he spun round. Across the stream, the dog barked again and suddenly he saw that from one of the cottage roofs, a thin smoke was trickling. He mounted, quickly, and rode back.

He jumped down at the door of the cottage and pounded on it. He was rewarded presently by a shuffling noise. The door opened a little. A face peered out. It was brown, seamed and whiskery of chin, and framed in grey wispy hair. Despite the whiskers, the owner of the face was apparently female though not, thought Ralph, eyeing the grime in the wrinkles, over-fond of washing. At Rufus' court and at La Fleche, even with de Warenne, although his household was less cultured than the others, Ralph had grown used to reasonably good standards of cleanliness. The deepset grey-blue eyes, though, were surprisingly alert and clear. They stared at him.

'My name is Ralph des Aix and I'm your new landlord. I've come to take possession.'

He hoped she understood him. He had polished his English in the last few years but accents could be extraordinary in these remote places. The eyes, however, showed comprehension and an intelligible answer resulted. 'They're all over to Minstead. Be back later. They'm setting up the Maypole for termorrer. Can't be bothered with all they silly japes myself. I stop here.'

'I see. Well, I want to get into my house. It's locked. Who has the key? What's your name?'

'Elfgiva, I am. Key's over to Minstead too. Father Ilger, he'll have it. He took charge, after he buried Old Chenna.'

234

'How far is Minstead?'

'Two mile or so. Back to the coast road and acrost it. Then take the right fork after you get past the old hunting lodge.' Ralph nodded. He knew the old lodge, which was in any case marked on his map. It was a small place like a miniature fortified castle but not at the moment in use. Rufus said it was damp and had closed it.

There seemed to be nothing else to do but go to Minstead. He would have liked something to eat or drink but the crone hadn't offered him anything and anyway, it would have had to be prepared by her filthy hands. He mounted and rode off. He glanced back once. One bright eye was watching his departure round the edge of the door and in it was a somewhat disconcerting expression.

Rufus' *bel ami* was not supposed to be interested in girls but Ralph did notice them sometimes and knew that they noticed him too. The expression in that bright old eye was distinctly appreciative. One could almost say salacious.

The deserted hunting lodge stood on a mound and Minstead was on lower ground to the south of it. It was much bigger than the Tun, a modestly thriving place surrounded by fields, with a few slate roofed buildings and its own church, a modern Norman-style affair.

At first, however, it seemed as empty of human life as the Tun. Then he heard the music, and changed course to meet it.

It was a procession, winding its way among the dwellings in the general direction of the church. It was led by two young lads, one playing a pipe and the other tapping a small hand drum. They were setting a rhythm for a slow dance and behind them, weaving a measured step in and out and around each other, were a man dressed in green, with some roughly carved wooden antlers fixed to his cap, another man prancing astride a hobby horse draped in green cloth and with a realistic piebald-painted head, and a third individual clad in red and yellow and flourishing a wand. Behind them again came a long, creaking cart pulled by an ox and carrying what seemed to be a long pole all wrapped round in colourful strips of cloth. A girl sat on top of it. She had an

235

ivy crown and she too wore green, a tight-fitting garment which revealed a juicy plumpness. She had a soft, pliant mouth and she was giggling. Behind the cart, also intricately dancing, came what the marvelling Ralph concluded was virtually the whole population of Minstead and, presumably, Chenna's Tun. Even those who could not dance were following as best they could; a girl heavy with child was giving an arm to an old man; a man and a woman led a blind man between them, holding his elbows since his wrists ended in stumps. Some children were trying to pick up the steps and last came three young women carrying tiny babies, walking together and chattering.

Ralph, holding his two horses to the necessary slow pace, joined the tail of the procession which followed a convoluted route but eventually fetched up on a patch of green in front of the church. Here the music continued but the dance stopped and all hands were put to unloading the maypole and setting it up in a ready-dug hole. Ralph saw what must be the priest, whom old Elfgiva had mentioned, standing in front of the church. He rode round the edge of the green to join him. 'Father Ilger?'

'The same.' The priest looked up at him. 'I saw you arrive. I was wondering who you were but I can guess. Ralph des Aix? I've been expecting you.'

'I think you've got the key of my house. What's going on?'

The priest sighed. He was a thin, nervy man, taut as a lyre string from what was probably a lifelong struggle against a wayward flock. 'You may well ask. I do my best,' he said gloomily. He waved a lean hand at the activity round the maypole. 'Are you going to live here? You'll get to know it all if so. I'll be glad of your support. I allow them this. They put the maypole up today and dance round it tomorrow. I bless it once it's up and after the dance I'll lead them in prayer for a good harvest and give them some ale and pasties and so on in the church. Lord Roger of Minstead comes along and says a few words. But . . .' He made a helpless gesture. 'There're pockets of it, you know. No one knows what we priests in these benighted places have to put up with. I go on hoping that one day I'll be able to teach them to think of their May Day revels as part of the Christian year. Lord Roger says I talk nonsense, that *he* doesn't know anything about the goings on – well, he wouldn't, he keeps himself remote most of the time – and even the bishop doesn't really believe me when I complain. But I worry about it. I worry about *them*.'

'Do you mean,' said Ralph, 'that this is a sort of . . . of heathen celebration? And that they know it is – I mean, it's not just an old custom, something they do for fun, out of habit?'

'Quite. I see you've met such things before.'

'The man with the antlers – he's acting the part of some kind of forest god?'

'Yes. Yes, you *do* know! The one with the hobby horse is being some other forest demon, a divine huntsman or something . . . when Old Chenna died, I thought it might all fade away because he always used to be the one with the antlers. But no, this young fellow from the Tun, Oswin, he's taking the part this year. He's a steady sort as a rule and a wonder with his hands. He made that ox-cart and he carved the pipe that boy's playing, over there. But over this – none of them are steady. I fear for their souls,' said Father Ilger simply. 'They believe in the forest demons, you see.'

A wild question was shaping itself in Ralph's mind. 'I've heard of this sort of thing before, as you say. In some places there are secret meetings at night. God alone knows for what reason,' he added piously. 'Is that what you meant by goings on?'

'I'm afraid so. They'll dance here tomorrow and they've danced already today. You'd think they'd want a night's sleep in between, but do they?' said Ilger bitterly. 'Not that I've ever followed them . . . but I've seen them slipping off at dusk on May Eve and by the end of tomorrow they'll be dazed, *dazed* with exhaustion. And at other times too. But if they had a good-living landlord setting an example . . .' he regarded Ralph doubtfully, as if recalling that the new landlord came from Rufus' court, which did not precisely have a good-living reputation. 'I have my successes,' said the priest, brightening. 'There's a

237

boy at the Tun wants to join a monastery. I've made enquiries and St. Peter's at Gloucester will accept him, if you're willing to let him go. I hope you will be. I went to some trouble to find a monastery which won't just use him as a servant because of his peasant birth. Abbot Serlo will see he has a proper chance to rise. He's an intelligent lad. And I wouldn't want anything to stand in the way of his salvation. He'll be one soul saved in this place, at least.'

'I won't stand in his way,' said Ralph gently. It was his first essay in overlordship. 'You have a hard furrow to plough, here,' he said. Father Ilger looked grateful for even this small piece of understanding. 'I'd like to meet some of my people,' Ralph said. 'And there's still the matter of the key.'

The maypole was up. 'I must do the blessing now but I'll fetch the key afterwards and present some of them to you. They go home for their suppers before they get up to – well, whatever it is they do get up to later. I shall pray for rain tonight,' said Father Ilger, 'but I shan't get it. The cloud's lifting. You might care to go back to the Tun in their company?'

'. . . hardhearted, obstinate and now deceitful. Trying to bribe a carpenter to carry a letter! He most properly brought it straight to me. Shameful!'

'I thought it was time my father knew how I was being treated,' said Edith, and made herself meet Christina's eyes, although her body shrank within itself, crying *no*!

In the past eighteen months, the matter of the veil had become a long drawn-out war, conducted by intermittent battles, with pauses in between. Edith, reduced at last by pain and the fear of it, would adopt the veil. After a week or two, hating herself, feeling unworthy of her father, she would begin to leave it off. Christina, as often as not, would affect not to notice, perhaps for several days, sometimes longer, once for as much as a month. Then without warning or any apparent extra provocation, she would pounce and the whole hideous cycle would begin again.

Christina had experimented with various forms of attack. She had tried incarceration, hunger, and lengthy sessions of praying with or at Edith, that God should soften her niece's uncompromising heart. These had no effect at all and lately she had resorted again to simple violence.

Edith, sick to the stomach and aware that her head was now bare and had been for ten days, saw that she was about to resort to it now.

And prayed secretly, within herself, for strength, not to be quite broken, not to plead. Or make promises which she could not, would not, keep. Or bring on to her Aunt Christina's face that look, that taut, narrow-eyed, bright-eyed, wet-lipped look of atrocious satisfaction.

She prayed. She tried her best. She failed. It was July before she summoned the courage to cross her Aunt Christina again.

'. . . this is Oswin,' said Father Ilger. Oswin, his antlered cap removed, was flaxen and weatherbeaten, with good teeth. He was quite young. Ralph thought he had seen him somewhere before. 'And here's his brother Osmund.'

'Oswin can make almost anything,' said Osmund, 'and whatever he can make, I can break. They call me Osmund the Clumsy.' He laughed heartily and so did all his companions. He was heavier in build than his brother and looked less intelligent.

'But he's got a good eye for throwing stones to scare rooks off the seed,' said an older man, lean, grey-haired, wary. Though they were all wary of their new lord. 'I'm Hunta,' the older man said. 'This is my son, Penna Cowherd . . .'

Penna had small features and bulging grey eyes but a general facial resemblance to his fellows. The next to be presented, however, a boy of no more than thirteen was quite unlike anyone else in the group. His name was Cild and he was not flaxen like most of them but ash fair, almost silver, and his eyes were a strong, cold, blue-green, almond shaped, in no way reminiscent of the round grey or blue eyes of the rest. His fine skin was lightly bronzed with no trace of ruddiness and where did that chiselled, patrician bone structure come from?

'And this lad is my youngest brother, Ketel,' said Oswin, yanking another lad forward.

239

'He's the one who wants to enter St. Peter's,' said Father Ilger in Ralph's ear.

The introductions continued, bewilderingly. He could absorb only a little. He shifted so that the horses he still held were between him and Ilger. He leant on Blue's accommodating shoulder and as if idly, the Norman landlord bored by his peasantry, he scored the ground with the spur on his left heel. He drew an X. The ground was trodden bare and wet; the mark showed plainly. He looked fixedly at Oswin and then glanced down, drawing his spur across the earth, joining the top points of the figure.

'This is Blind Edric and here's Cild's brother Uffa . . .' but Oswin's voice had become mechanical. He had seen. So had the others and a stillness had fallen on them. The lightening sky grew lighter still and showed Ralph the mingled surprise and caution passing across their faces before, peasantlike, they smoothed it into a careful blankness. Several, he thought, were holding their breath.

'Blind Edric's from Minstead, not Chenna's,' Oswin said. 'He's what happens when the Forest Law gets broken. He always has to be . . . shown off, so to speak. Lord Roger's orders.' He stared down, as if awkward or sullen. The toe of his boot, on top of Ralph's spurmarks, traced a V-shape over Ralph's figure. The five-pointed star lay between Ralph and his tenants for a count of ten before Ralph's bootsole casually wiped it out.

'I'm sorry for what was done to Edric,' said Ralph. 'Will someone lead my horses? I'll walk back with you to the Tun.'

He knew what he had implied by that. On the way back, he spoke to them openly of the plans for the night and Oswin startled him by holding out the antlered cap to him. 'It was allus whoever lived in Chenna's house as wore these,' he said. 'I was only standing in, like. Tonight I was going to fight a man from Truham for the antlers – the proper ones, not these daft things. These're just to keep Ilger happy, make him think we're just playing games. Truham's allus had an eye to upsetting the custom,' he added, 'but no one ought to challenge you. You're entitled.'

240

He might have been one of them all his life. He had drawn a figure in the soil at their feet and suspicion had become acceptance, just like that. He turned the antlered cap over in his hands and on impulse put it on. And then looked at them, shaken, as the folk of Chenna's Tun dropped to their knees amid the mud and last year's leafmould. He thought it was the cowherd, Penna, who whispered: 'Lord.'

'Daft things, are they?' he said, and took the cap quickly off. 'Get up. Not here. In the forest at the right time, keep it for that. Let's get on. I want to unlock my house and eat.' Speaking of his house brought a picture of it to mind and he remembered something. 'I saw that I had a byre, but no oxen. Where are they?'

'Dead,' said Hunta. 'We've had cattle sickness and yours were unlucky. We've had a lot of bad luck here over the last few years. But there *are* oxen you can borrow.'

'Maybe the luck'll change now,' Penna said.

'I learned my ritual in Normandy,' Ralph said as they walked on. 'You'd best tell me how you do it here. I want to do it as I should, as it's always been done at Chenna's Tun.'

Oswin nodded. And Ralph, with a surging in his blood, thought of the ripe-fruit breasts and the sleepy eyes of the girl in the green dress, who had ridden on the maypole. She was not here: evidently she did not come from the Tun. But she would surely be in the Wood tonight. Surely, she would be the Maiden.

The cult of the Wood, as Elise had told him long ago, was never a unity, not even in the days when it was open, before Christianity and the condemnation of the priests drove it underground. From place to place, she said, the names of god and goddess varied, rituals varied, and so did some of the beliefs.

But north to south, from the fjord country to the shores of the Mediterranean, and east to west 'from what they call Russia to the coast of Wales and maybe beyond but that I don't know', certain elements were the same. There was a god who was lord of sky and forest, who was

241

represented by a man in the rituals, who wore horns for a crown. In southern England, it appeared, he was Herne and he had antlers. In Normandy, as Ralph had said, he was also antlered, but was simply called The Horned One. In the south of Europe he was Pan and horned like a goat; far to the north he was Odin, or Woden, and horned like a bull. He was Skyfather and Huntsman of Souls and if times were hard he was the Sacrifice and his earthly representative might well be put to death, though it was a long time now since that had happened.

His consort was the Goddess of Earth and Harvest and sometimes of the Moon, for she was Mother and Maiden alike. It had occurred to Ralph quite soon that to the Lady of the Wood, who was called Freya or Eostre or Diana, the Virgin that most people venerated owed more than they knew, or would care to admit if they did know.

'When the Christian priests began to campaign against the Worship,' Elise had said, 'it took to the woods or – in some places – hilltops or heathland.' Devotees had taken to recognising each other by means of signs. 'We use the five-pointed star. Some places they use a cross with a loop for its topmost arm. And there's others,' Elise said.

The sense of being under threat had drawn the Worship closer, eventually, than it had been when it was open. Lodges became more secret and then, to offset the sense of isolation and the fear of dwindling, sent out travellers to carry greetings to other Lodges and learn how the Worship fared elsewhere. 'Frail as spider thread and no more visible to the outside work, but strong in their own fashion, we formed our links. That's how I know so much,' his stepmother told him. 'We're tighter-knit now than ever before. Not a unity, no. But still a . . .'

'Still a federation,' said Ralph, understanding.

That night in the firelit clearing, seated on the log throne and feeling the weight of the genuine antlers on his head, Ralph was far away from Aix where Elise had initiated him, yet was utterly at home. He had not been able to accept the horse dealer's invitation at Mont St. Michel, for Rufus' army had left too soon. He had therefore not attended a Beltane since he was fourteen. But the ritual came back to him as if it had been yesterday.

242

At Chenna's Tun, it did not differ much from that at Aix. He had only to put the words into English and use the title of Herne.

As if he had been doing it for years, he asked the ceremonious question: 'Does anyone challenge the right of the King?' He was less surprised than Oswin when the challenge was answered ('Yes, it was the fellow I was to fight,' Oswin said afterwards). In Normandy, there was always a fight when the kingship fell vacant for no one at Aix ever simply inherited it; in this respect the customs did diverge.

Winning the contest was easy, however. He had been trained for battle and that meant more than learning how to handle a sword. They took off their masks and went to it with knives. In five minutes, he had his opponent, the Truham man, face down on the ground, left arm locked behind him, right arm pinned under Ralph's knee, and Ralph's own blade at his throat. The man yielded and was allowed to rise and swear his fealty to his conqueror. Oswin and Hunta between them then replaced the antlered mask upon Ralph's head.

Enthroned once more, with the thrill of conflict singing through him, he asked for declarations and a figure rose and asked permission to leave the Worship and enter a Christian Monastery, and to take the Oath of Quittance.

This must be Ketel. No one wanted to hold people in the Worship who did not want to stay there: they were unlucky. Provided they swore never to speak of its doings to those outside, they were free to depart. Ralph gave his consent and administered the oath. Ketel, kneeling before the log throne, promised never by word or deed or look to reveal knowledge of the Worship to anyone who was not part of it, or even to admit to its existence, and was set free of it. He left at once, before the dancing began.

Presently, Ralph lay with the Maiden.

As he had supposed, she was the girl he had seen riding on the maypole. He learned later that she belonged to Minstead. She was not genuinely a maiden (far from it, he suspected) but perhaps because of this, she made him very welcome. She was all smooth soft curves and moist warm crevices and though she smelt rank and he concluded from

243

the few words that they exchanged that she was stupid, she was unarguably female and she released him from a secret fear which he had harboured for some time now, that he could no longer respond to a woman. Afterwards, it was the thought of Rufus' embraces which were repulsive, and when he caught himself, un-thinkingly, making one of the feminine gestures he had picked up at court, he checked himself with loathing.

Thinking of his return to court, he was pulled two ways. He had land now, not very much of it and not very good land but his, and in need of looking after, and for that very reason extraordinarily satisfactory to him. He had seen within two days how much the Tun needed him to bully and reorganise it. There was a field that needed draining; he must invent a system and chivvy people into digging it. It would be worth the expense to the community to buy two piglets from Minstead instead of one, and rear one for the Christmas feast as usual but kill the other in November and salt it down. To think about these plans, and realise that they depended on him, created a warmth within him.

But there was still a part of him which wanted Rufus' company and the privilege of being in the inner circle. He wanted these things enough to be prepared, still, to make love with a man though not enough to be able to pretend to himself that the idea did not repel him. Well, he had leave of absence till the end of August. He need not face the question yet.

Meanwhile, he set about learning the ins and outs of his new home. He learned the names and boundaries of the surrounding woods, Brook Wood and the Hoar Woods.

He made friends with the dogs of the Tun and grew used to the pungent body odour of their owners. He learned who belonged to the Cult of the Wood and which were the few – very few in the district as a whole and none in the Tun – who did not. He discovered that his own Lodge was not the only Cult Lodge within the New Forest, and that the charcoal burners who sometimes used his Lodge's clearing belonged to another.

They were a semi-itinerant family or tribe and no one knew for sure how many of them there were, for the smoke-seamed faces in which the whites of the eyes always seemed so luminous all looked alike to outsiders and the women wore hose and jerkin like the men. They all answered to the name of Purkiss.

The identities of his own Tun people were easier to sort out. The strange, ash-fair Cild turned out on his mother's side to be the son – incredibly – of the crone Elfgiva, who was not quite as ancient as she looked. But Ralph learned without surprise that on his father's side, the boy was foreign. He was a Child of the Wood and was believed to be the offspring of a Norwegian visitor who had shared one of their feasts fourteen years before.

He found that Oswin was indeed exceptionally gifted at all manual skills, and made beautiful arrows of distinctive craftsmanship. He used birchwood, with flight feathers of goose pinions, and wickedly barbed arrowheads which he got made to his own pattern at the Minstead forge.

He had a trade at Brockenhurst where he sold his wares when the court was there, which explained why Ralph had thought he had seen Oswin before. He was a recognised local bowmaker and the presence of such goods in his house was accepted by the Foresters. The people of the Tun were reticent about this matter, but Ralph gradually gathered that at times this had come in useful and that Old Chenna had once been foolish in allowing a bow ('and other things,' said Penna darkly) to be kept in his own house.

He learned too that Oswin's brother Osmund, though an excellent shot with stone or arrow, was in other respects more than deserving of the name Clumsy. He learned that the pop-eyed Penna was given to seeing signs, to an extent which amused even his superstitious fellow-villagers. 'If he sees a magpie in the morning, he looks over his shoulder for bad luck all day,' said Elfgiva caustically. 'And mostly gets it. You do, if you keep glancing behind you while you walk straight towards a tree.'

Elfgiva had baked Old Chenna's bread and washed his clothes and she now took over these tasks for Ralph. He saw to the rest himself. Of such fripperies as wallhangings and cushions he had no need. After the court luxury he even found timber walls and a swept earthen floor a refreshing change, and recognised the leather curtains which created rough rooms inside the barnlike house for what they were; a minor pretension on Old Chenna's part. The other houses had no dividing curtains.

He was not indoors much, anyway. There was work and to spare outside and jobs like mending horse-tackle or making arrows were best done outside for the sake of the daylight. He was fashioning an arrow, sitting outside his door in the July sun, hoping that the spell of good weather would hold till the corn began to ripen, when Ranulf Flambard rode up, alone.

'My lord!' Ralph shot to his feet. 'I didn't expect . . .'

'I bet you didn't,' Flambard grinned. Then he said sharply: 'Go indoors. I'll see you there,' and rode his horse straight into the byre. He entered the house a few moments later, ducking under the low door. He was dressed more quietly than usual but in Old Chenna's house amid bare walls and plain benches, he still looked as out of place as a popinjay in a sparrow's nest. He had a hawk on his arm, which Ralph bemusedly took from him and established on a low beam. He looked round for refreshments to offer this improbable visitor, found nothing but earthenware goblets and thin ale, and a very commonplace stew bubbling in its cauldron, and did not know what to say.

Flambard, not in the least disconcerted, sat down on a bench. 'Can I have something to drink? I'm hot. I've ridden miles, very fast. Oh, come on, Ralph, what are you all in a dither for? Anything will do, milk or well water if there's nothing else.'

'There's ale, sir, but it's not fit for you. This place isn't fit for you.'

'Rubbish. I was born in a hovel far worse than this and grew up in it, too. Did you suppose I was wrapped in velvet and fed from a silver spoon from infancy? Good God, I believe you did! Well, I wasn't. That's why I appreciate the velvet and the silver now. But I can do without them if I must. I'm here on business and I'm in a hurry and it's secret. I was hawking and I got separated from my companions, that's to be my story. I had to see you in private. I've an errand for you. It would be as well if it isn't traced to either of us but it's to our mutual advantage. Which is why I picked on you, though I'll pay you for your trouble. What's in the cauldron? It smells good whatever it is.' Flambard leaned forward, picked up the poker and expertly livened up the fire. Ralph, still bewildered, handed him a beaker of ale. 'Now then, Ralph, as I said I'm in a hurry. So listen.'

'. . . I've heard about this before,' Ralph said. 'I was there at Gloucester when Anselm walked up to the king's bedside and told him to get married. In fact, I think it was raised even before that and in respect of the same lady. Anselm and King Malcolm both wrote to Rufus last year if I remember aright. Was that to do with this? Because whatever it was, it made Rufus angry.'

'You're right. It was to do with this. And . . .'

'It could be necessary,' said Ralph slowly. 'If there's no heir . . .'

'What's the matter with you, Ralph? You've as much to lose as anyone. What do you mean, no heir? He's got two brothers. All he has to do is make a definite will in favour of one of them and make his barons swear to uphold his choice. We'd all be better off that way than if he were to die leaving a baby to inherit. That's always trouble. Children take time to grow, remember, and this girl herself is only twelve. It could be years before she has a baby. All this chatter about heirs is only Anselm's excuse. What he really means is, if the king insists on going to bed with somebody, it ought to be a woman and preferably his wife. Anselm wants to save Rufus' soul, not his kingdom. He'd let the whole kingdom slide into the sea without a second thought if he imagined he could preserve the king from damnation thereby. I'd like a mouthful of that stew.'

'It's only chicken and herbs.'

'My mother used to make stews like that. Thank you.' Flambard watched Ralph spoon stew into a bowl, and then sat with it steaming on his knees, eating with the wooden spoon Ralph had handed him and intermittently gesticulating with the spoon. 'See here, Ralph. If the king goes through with this it means disaster. Don't you realise that? For you, for me, for him and for *her*.'

'I don't think I understand.'

Flambard gulped hot stew and waved the spoon. 'You can't be that simple. Take you, first. She'll push you aside. The king might want to keep your friendship going but you don't suppose she'd allow it, do you? You'll be in the outer darkness before you know it. No more being courted by the court, Ralph. No more people entertaining you to dinner and slipping you little presents to say a word in the king's ear.' Flambard's hot, bright eyes observed Ralph's shocked discomfort with amusement. 'I know all about it. You manage very well. You know exactly how much influence you've got and you never forget your place. But that place gives you a certain importance and you like that, don't you? Well, why not? I like mine too. And you pay for yours. You provide services that go against your nature. But you won't ever have the option of purchasing importance that way once Edith of Scotland is queen in Rufus' court, believe me.'

'But if she's only twelve . . .'

'Her father is Malcolm of Scotland, as tough and canny a warrior as ever swung an axe, and her mother is the much-revered Margaret who must have a lot more to her than piety and good works or she couldn't run her virtuous spirit in double harness with Malcolm without catastrophe and there hasn't been any catastrophe. Added to which, Edith, through her mother, is descended from the same house as the Old English ruling family. If she becomes queen, she'll have a huge, invisible weight of support behind her, from every soul in the land who secretly hankers for the days before the Normans came. And on top of that, you don't imagine, do you, that she'd be handed over to Rufus without being given a vast, influential entourage of her own, handpicked by her parents and most unlikely to be sympathetic either to you or to me? The first thing,' said Flambard, 'that that vast and influential entourage will do, will be to clean up the court.' He took a final mouthful and scraped the spoon round the bowl in an engagingly thorough search for the final drops. 'They'll get rid of the immoral elements like you and the irreverent ones like me. I make money out of the church, remember? The saintly Margaret's handpicked party will join instant forces with Anselm to put a stop to both of us.'

Ralph was silent. Flambard, watching his face, put the empty bowl aside. 'I'm not asking if you love him, Ralph. But I can tell you this: he loves you. He's the king and he'd put his royal dignity first if it came to a clash between it and you, but still, he loves you. Oh yes,' said Flambard, observing Ralph's startled expression, 'everyone thinks I have an abacus where other men have hearts.' Laughter suddenly lit up his features and for the first time Ralph truly appreciated how he had acquired those nicknames, Flambard and Passe-Flamme. That amusement was strong and illuminating and more: it was infectious. 'But if I use other men's feelings to my advantage,' Flambard said, 'I don't deny the feelings are there. One reason why Rufus cares for you is that you are always careful never to embarrass him. He appreciates that. Do you want to see him embarrassed?'

'Embarrassed?'

'*Yes*! All this talk of heirs. I don't know what makes Anselm so sure there'd be any child of the marriage at all. Just what do you think is going to happen after the wedding when Rufus is left alone with a pure-minded, piously-reared, nobly-born girl scarcely into maidenhood and certainly not yet released from it? Well, what?'

'Well, I . . .he . . .he has been known to have girls.'

'Professionals, hired to attend drunken parties where hardly anyone knows what they're doing or with whom anyway. Even at that, they have to help him. I don't attend those parties – as a prelate I have to conduct myself with some degree of propriety. Not much,' said Flambard, 'but some.' His amusement shone out again. 'But I hear things. Do you think this modest little Edith of Scotland will be able to help him? And what will it be like for either of them? I'm not completely callous about her plight either. If you care for the king at all, Ralph, if he is anything, *anything*, more to you than a cow to be milked

249

for station or land – though he's short-changed you shockingly with this place, I must say – and if you are capable of feeling the smallest compassion for a young girl faced with a nightmare marriage, then you'll do as I ask and save them both.'

Six

Interview in a Rose Garden
July 1093

On that July morning, getting out of bed at sunrise, into a world echoing with blackbird and song-thrush, looking from the dorter window at a dawn sky of blazing gold, like a fanfare of trumpets transmuted into vision, Edith had found the courage, or the anger, to pick up the hated black veil, tear it in half, fling it down and tread it underfoot.

But now, once more confronted in the rose garden by her Aunt Christina, she had lost her nerve. 'I'm . . . I'm sorry, Mother Abbess. I was late this morning, I came out in a hurry, I forgot. I'm sorry, I forgot the veil.' I can't go through that again, after all. I can't bear it. I'd rather die. I will die, if she does that to me again. No, no, please . . .

She'd put the torn veil into her personal chest and locked it. Her aunt couldn't have found it there. Or could she? Christina did not approve of her charges having any privacy. She almost certainly had a key to that chest, which was abbey property.

But the veil which Christina was now holding out was not the damaged one; it was a new one, intact, and her voice was calm as she said: 'There is a particular reason why you must wear this today. I don't want to hear that you refuse to wear it because it's halfway to being a nun. That is exactly how you must appear. And you would please your father by doing so. Your father would not want you to be molested. The king is coming here to see you.'

'The king?'

'Yes, King William Rufus. And whatever excuse he gives, his intentions will be bad. He has heard you are pretty. Some decent man, afraid to give his name, has sent me a warning. The king is on his way, now. He's young and wild and does whatever comes into his head and . . .'

'But will molesting me come into his head?' asked

251

Edith, quite seriously, startling her aunt by the maturity of her tone. 'I believe,' said Edith, 'that he doesn't like women.'

There were a few timid giggles from the other girls, who, once again, had hung back at the sight of the abbess. They had been weeding the roses. Christina withered the amusement with a sharp glance. 'You are not old enough to know anything of such things or such men. The king respects nothing and no one. Well, hardly anyone. It is possible that even he would not actually insult a vowed nun, so . . .'

'But I'm not a vowed nun.'

'And you want to be insulted, is that it? Perhaps you do! Nothing would surprise me, with you, Edith. But I hardly think the prospect would please your father. If the king sees you wearing a veil, he may think you are a nun and in this instance, your father would approve. Now put this on at once.'

It was such a glorious day, thought Edith rebelliously. The garden lay flooded with July sunshine and the scent of late roses. And in the midst of all this loveliness, there stood Aunt Christina, draped in black, gaunt as a scarecrow, spoiling it. The disapproving lines of her face, thought Edith furiously, would turn fresh milk to curds on the instant if her aunt as much as glanced at a milk pail.

A nun hurried from the abbey building at an unmonastic speed, wimple awry. 'Mother Abbess, he's here, the king is here!'

'Put it on!' Christina deposited the veil on Edith's head willy nilly, with shaking hands. 'And keep it on! And stay here! He may not come so far. I must meet him.'

She and the nun hastened away. Edith stuck out her tongue and half raised her hands to her head but let them drop. One of the other girls said: 'Old sourpuss! I bet she wishes the king would molest *her*!' Another said soberly: 'I can hear a man's voice. I think he's coming out here after all.'

From within the cloister, there were indeed voices. A masculine one, undoubtedly accustomed to making itself heard, and coming nearer while it was talking, was declaring jovially that in Winchester a previous batch of

Romsey's rose plants was thriving. 'We want to inspect your latest ones! Ah,' said Rufus, stumping out into the sunlight, 'so this is the famous garden where you cultivate them?'

'Back,' muttered Edith, and with the others withdrew into one of the trellised walks, out of sight. She found a place however where she could look through the trellis unseen and the others crowded round to peer inquisitively with her. That was King Rufus, was it? He was a funny looking man, with that red face and barrel-shaped body and that long light ginger hair that didn't go with the rest of him. But oddly enough, Edith rather liked his resonant voice.

Christina was looking bemused. From what Edith could hear of the conversation, it seemed that although a message had come to say that the king was making for Romsey in order to see the King of Scotland's daughter, now that he was here, he only wanted to talk about Romsey's famous roses. He had gone unhesitatingly to one of the newest varieties and clearly he knew something of the subject for he was asking how it was propogated and when would be the best time to take plants to Winchester.

Then, in mid-sentence, he stopped.

Watching, Edith saw him raise his head from the flower he was examining. It was precisely the movement of a deer that scents danger. He had sensed the watching eyes. His gaze swept over the trellis. Instinctively, Edith drew back, pushing the others away as well. But he must have glimpsed the movement for at once, with Abbess Christina trailing after him and attempting to draw his attention to some crimson roses in the opposite direction, he came round to the entrance of the walk. He looked along it to where the girls stood clustered. 'More pretty blossoms!'

Behind him, Aunt Christina made frantic signs. Edith, recollecting herself, knelt. The others did the same. 'King Malcolm's girl's here, isn't she?' Rufus turned to Christina. 'Is she one of these? If so, p . . .present her.' He had a slight stammer, Edith noticed.

Seeing that her aunt was going to hesitate and would probably annoy him, she called: 'I am the lady Edith.' He

253

extended a hand and, rising, she went towards him. A breeze caught the veil as she stepped from the shelter of the trellis. She caught it back and Rufus, his attention drawn to it, suddenly blushed. 'I see . . . I didn't know. You're well, Lady? They take care of you here?'

'Excellent care, sir.'

'Good. That's good.' He appeared to grope for something more to say and Edith thought: 'Poor man, he's shy. This isn't his world. Girls in a rose garden, clothes that mean dedication to the eternal – he doesn't know where he is with any of them. He'd never have molested me. What a fool Aunt Christina is.'

'I hope to see your father soon,' said Rufus. 'I expect him sh . . .shortly at my c . . .court.' He was so nervous that he was actually sweating. 'Have you any m . . .message for him?'

It was as if a dungeon door had opened.

'Please give him my respectful love, sir, and say that if while he is in England he has opportunity to visit me, I should be overjoyed to see him. And please, would you say to him that . . . that you found me in good health, and veiled as a nun. He would want to know those things.' She did not look towards Christina.

Rufus, she thought, had sensed the ulterior motives behind this daughterly message, but he was too shy to question her. He said: 'Of course. Pleasure. Well.' He then stared at them all for a few seconds more, made a noise that sounded like 'Harrumph!' nodded to them and went. Christina accompanied him. She returned alone, walking rapidly, in wrath.

'If you imagine that that naughty, deliberately insulting message you gave the king will save you from what I have waiting for you, you are mistaken. You don't imagine he will pass the message on, do you?'

'He may,' said Edith. She looked her aunt in the face. 'I wouldn't gamble on him *not* giving it, Mother Abbess. But,' she added softly, and with dishonourable intentions, 'meanwhile, I will wear the veil.'

Rufus kept his word. Within a week, her father Malcolm was in Romsey as though a strong wind were blowing him, demanding to see his daughter and when

Edith came to the guest chamber, he took one furious look at her, let out a roar of rage, and tore the black veil off her head. 'My lord!' expostulated Christina, who had come with her. 'When a young girl is considering whether she has a vocation . . .'

'My girls have vocations when I say so and not before, and I'm no more likely to say so than the sun's like to set in the east. Is that what you meant King Rufus to think? That she'd got a vocation? I come all the way from Scotland to talk marriage with him; *marriage*, woman, and he'll not even see me! But he sends me a lackey with a message saying my daughter in Romsey is dressed up like a nun and wants me to visit her! He came here, didn't he? Well, he came here to propose and if he never got the words out, it's your fault, woman, or I'm an infidel. Pack her things! She comes home with me to Scotland, this very day!'

'Thank God you're back, Ralph. You were gone too long. I wouldn't have given you as much as a chicken run if I'd known you'd go and spend all summer there and forget me. I know I *said* you could have four months but I didn't think you'd take me at my word. Oh Ralph, Ralph!'

In the dim summer night, Ralph could hardly see his king but Rufus' voice and now the urgent buttings and burrowings of his heavy body told him that the king was in distress and that Ralph, as a dutiful and affectionate lover, must enquire into it.

'I'm sorry I was gone so long. There was much to do. My lord, is something wrong?'

'No. What should be wrong? You're back, that's all that matters.'

'Were you afraid I wouldn't come back?' He stroked and petted, made his voice teasing.

'I was terrified I wouldn't be able to let you come back! The moment you were out of sight, Anselm was at me again about marriage – no, it's all right, it's all over, it won't happen and I never want to hear the word marriage again as long as I live! A man like me is cut off from all that and Anselm had better realise it.'

Carefully, but asking because it was natural to do so,

Ralph said: 'I'm relieved. Did he have a particular lady in mind?'

'Oh yes. I even . . . I went to Romsey Abbey,' Rufus muttered. 'To see Edith. Malcolm's girl. You know.'

'Yes. She's being educated there, isn't she? Is she nice?'

'Of course she's bloody nice!' The hot, chunky body beside him was suddenly taut with anger. 'Pretty, milky-skinned, bright eyed little thing, she was, all among the roses. Delicate as a rose. I could see me, t . . .tearing all her petals off and destroying her. I said, I'm cut off from all that. No family life for me, Ralph. A monk I knew as a boy in Caen put a stop to that. I'd have wanted to run away anyhow, when I saw her, even if she hadn't been wearing that d . . .damnable veil.'

'Veil? Has she taken vows, then? I'd heard that King Malcolm forbade it.' Cunning Christina, Ralph thought. So that was how she'd fenced Edith from the king.

'He did. He's had her out of Romsey and away to Scotland now. But she looked like a nun. That veil finished me. These religious people, Ralph, they think you can buy your way out of death by giving up life but you can't. Buy your way out, I mean. I tried that when I was ill but it was only fear t . . .talking, not hope, I thought I was t . . .trying to escape damnation but the truth is, I was trying to escape death and I can't. Whatever I do or don't d . . .do, I'll have to die one day and then . . .'

Ralph began to say something, unconvincing even to himself, about salvation and was roughly grabbed and shaken like a badly-behaved child. 'Don't give me those old stories. Don't . . . give . . . me . . . those . . . tales! Do you hear? Damnation, salvation, they're neither of them real. Death means darkness, night without end and the worms. The priests dress it up with prayers but what it comes to in the end is you're nailed up in a box and buried because if you were left in the open you'd stink and look disgusting and who wants to see in advance what they're going to be themselves when the maggots get them? You die, you turn into n . . .nasty rubbish that's got to be got rid of. And if I m . . .married Edith, one day I'd turn on her and shout all that at her, smash that pretty dream she and Anselm and people like them live in. I can't l . . .live

256

with all that piety and all those lies, all that p . . .protection payment!'

'Protection . . .?'

'Yes, all the pleasures of life, given up to a God who isn't there, to buy a salvation that d . . .doesn't exist. Danegeld, Ralph. But the Danes always came back for more and so do the maggots.'

Ralph sought for comforting words and found none. He said the king's name, *Rufus*, half a dozen times, and held him firmly.

'She'll die too, one day,' Rufus whispered. 'Think of that. Fresh, sweet thing, she is, used to being cared for. Used to sleeping in a clean bed, wearing clean clothes – imagine her, shovelled into the ground. If there's a God, He's a brute and the only way to live is to be a bigger one. Come here, Ralph.'

He went to sleep afterwards, his blunt sun-reddened nose squashed against Ralph's arm. Ralph watched the dawn lighten slowly, and wished he too could sleep.

He could not. At the Tun, he had begun to forget how protective Rufus made him feel. It had taken Flambard to remind him. He had come back, prepared to resume his duties, as much because he knew Rufus needed him as because he himself wanted the exhilaration of the court.

But he had changed. His body remembered the warm soft flesh of the Maiden at Beltane, and the supple felineness of the other one, the Mother, the Truham woman who had partnered him at Lammas.

At the Tun, he had remembered Rufus' needs as burdensome. Only now did he understand how heavy that burden truly was.

Seven

Stormclouds and Nightingales
1093–4

The great storm came in from the west that October, exacting payment in a single night for all the pleasant summer weather. A wind came ahead of it, whipping up the treetops of Andred like a sea, tearing at thatch, bringing down fences, loosening the roots of a pine tree behind Withysham Abbey so that it leaned and threatened the church window.

Then came the rain, in sheets. The low-lying swampland near Gloucester was flooded in an hour. The Thames, rising, spread itself over the land east of London, swallowing field and cottage, destroying the lives of man and animal alike through drowning and exposure.

In Chenna's Tun, the stream overflowed and washed two feet deep through the cottages. Only Ralph's house, on slightly higher ground, stayed dry. He was visiting his holding at the time and called his folk under his roof for shelter till the floods went down.

In Fallowdene too the river overran its banks and swept away two cornstacks which had been placed there, handy for the watermill. Richard lay long awake the following night, talking to Alice.

'We shall manage. I've stores laid by. But there won't be any surplus. I spent the last of your dowry replacing the cattle when the milk fever came and my plants aren't ready for the market yet. The yield's too low. Thank God the ground they're growing in isn't too low! They're safe, at least.'

'Yes, they increase very slowly. Tch,' said Alice. 'My father would help if I asked. But . . .'

'No need. When that ship I have a share in comes back, there'll be something coming in. It's a pity Hammerfoot's dead. I might have got stud fees for him. But I'll have three more saleable, trained young horses ready next spring.' He did not add that his mother would resent help from Alice's father but Alice heard the unsaid words, and sighed.

She had not been forgiven for sending Sybil back to Withysham. Richard had upheld the decision but this had only sent Wulfhild's rage into more devious channels.

Alice dealt with their frequent and often petty domestic arguments by basing all her opinions on what was best for Fallowdene, or for Richard, but never on any preference of her own.

'Would it matter if we gave so and so permission to marry away from the manor? The goodwill of such and such a neighbour is useful to Fallowdene.' 'We ought to have cornflower garlands at the harvest feast. Richard likes the colour of them.'

At times she yearned to stand in the middle of the hall and announce that she wanted cornflower garlands 'because *I* like them and who's mistress here now, I'd like to know?'

But for Richard's sake, she restrained herself. Life was not unpleasant in other respects. She was on good terms now with both Gunnor and Bebbe, who were both by this time married but still helped in the hall. Maud was thriving and Alice herself felt well most of the time because Richard had been careful not to tax her strength with another baby yet. Wulfhild, unaware that this was deliberate, complained at times about Alice's failure to conceive, and then Alice dropped her eyes and said sadly: 'No doubt it's the will of God,' and enjoyed a secret sense of power.

Secret. It was a pleasure best concealed from Wulfhild who was easier to live with if not provoked. 'What else could we do?' she said to Richard.

'The year we married, my mother thought of cutting some timber. I wouldn't agree, then. But I think now's the time. We have some drying sheds. I'll get them repaired and the trees down and into them before the winter. They can be sold off for shipbuilding later. There's quite a bit of timber that could go. It'll represent money in hand and we'll be on the way to some nearly cleared land. My flowers will soon want more than the border of one field.'

He was glad he had ordered the trees to be cut, when

259

two weeks later the news came that the storm had wrecked the ship in which he had shares. There would be no dividends from that last voyage, or ever again.

'Oh, Richard, I'm so sorry! You were relying on that ship.'

'Fallowdene will manage. It's always possible to think of something, if one tries hard enough.'

'And the crew were all lost. That's dreadful too. If you had been aboard . . .'

'Well, I wasn't. I'm here. As you may be noticing.'

'Oh, no, Richard, not now, I couldn't, not just after hearing about the crew being drowned . . . no, we oughtn't . . . *Richard*! I said no! I'll bite!'

'Oh, would you?' said Richard with interest and commenced a struggle for supremacy. Alice, half-seriously, fought and twisted and carried out her threat to bite. Hot wet skin slid on hot wet skin, fermenting, blurring the distinctions of the two bodies. Then it seemed to Richard that a great engulfing pit had opened and swallowed him; as if he had been trying to dig a well and had accidentally penetrated a volcano.

He had begun to love Alice because she was kind. But now he knew that he loved her because below the kindness there was this, this seething, molten potential, and he desired to melt in it and be thus mysteriously forged anew.

Wulfhild, getting up in the night as she was often forced to do as she grew older, heard them laughing and in the morning saw them come late from their chamber with expressions, despite yesterday's bad news, of the most idiotic content.

Chagrined, she grumbled the whole day long at everything the other women did.

Soon after this, at Withysham, Sybil achieved the first signs of womanhood and certain hitherto formless longings and excitements began to take shape for her.

When the abbess decided that the tree which now threatened to break the church windows must be removed, and imported a young woodsman into the grounds to see to it, Sybil found him interesting. She was discovered sitting on the convent handcart (provided so that he could convert the doomed tree to firewood and take it to the woodpile), chin in hands, asking him artless questions about how he proposed to make the tree fall this way instead of that.

'She's doing no harm,' said the young man soothingly to the scandalised Sister Ermengarde.

'She should be at her lessons,' retorted Sister Ermengarde, and dragged Sybil away.

To the abbess, she said that she hoped Sybil would soon be sent for to marry her betrothed. 'She's a responsibility. Not to mention a liability to the abbey.'

'The child's still only twelve,' said Abbess Edgiva. 'Her family – *my* family, let me remind you – wish her to be fifteen before the marriage takes place. I've no quarrel with that. It's wise. We have three years to wait.'

'And so has she,' said Sister Ermengarde, with meaning.

'My lords,' said Anselm patiently, giving a nod of acknowledgement along the Council table to the Norman envoys, 'I fully recognise that there is an agreement between my Lord King and the Duke of Normandy, under which the king owes his brother help against the insurgents of Maine and the depredations of Count Henry. I see all this very well. But . . .'

Rufus rolled his eyes upwards and shot a *brace yourselves* glance at the envoys. Particularly, Anselm noticed miserably, at the one called Walter Tirel. Tirel was French, not Norman, but he was among the envoys because he was one of Curthose's friends, and had English connections. He had married the sister of Gilbert Clare of Tonbridge. He was a soberly-dressed, strongly-made man, level of voice and balding early. Such hair as he had was short and the effect of the round head and hard, gleaming scalp was a curiously virile contrast to the moderation of his speech and dress.

But virile or not, married or not, he had what Anselm now privately called *propensities*. A few months in Rufus' court had taught him to recognise men with propensities instantly, as though they went round with brands on their

261

foreheads. And Rufus, he saw wearily, had identified Tirel's potential too.

But he must keep to the business in hand. He let the silence last a moment or two before delivering his punchline. '*But*,' he said at length, 'such an expedition must be financed. Where is the money to come from?'

'Flambard?' said the king.

Flambard, back in favour nowadays, was seated close to the king. 'The king's honour is involved,' he said, 'and with it, the honour of his vassals. A tax is to be raised from all those holding land directly of the king.'

'Who will recoup by dunning their own tenants for money,' said Anselm sharply. 'How much more taxation can this land bear? Look out of the window if you don't know what I mean.'

No one accepted the invitation. They knew quite well what was outside. The Christmas Council was being held at Gloucester Abbey and the abbey now stood amid fields which had been first flooded and then frozen. Out there were sheets of ice which had been meadows, and woods where leafless trees were apparently rooted in opaque grey glass.

Even in the council chamber, the cold was savage. The fire made little impression on the stone walls and the high ceiling. The king and Flambard were swathed in great velvet cloaks and the Count of Meulan in a quilted blue affair edged with fur. FitzHamon had gone for fur all the way; his enormous robe was made of beaverskins and in it he resembled some vast, sleek forest denizen. Tirel seemed to be wearing a blanket. They could see each other's breath.

'My lord Archbishop is right.' Abbot Serlo was simply wearing three woollen mantles, one on top of the other. ' Whole square miles of Somerset are under ice and will still be waterlogged at the spring sowing time unless a miracle happens. The winter wheat was never planted at all. It's worse in the east. People are starving *now*.'

'I am willing,' said Anselm, 'to donate five hundred pounds' weight of silver from my own coffers. If other clergy follow my example . . .'

'Five hundred pounds?' Flambard's dark, alive face was

262

full of mischief. 'Your resources would bear two thousand with ease, my lord Archbishop. Why stop at five hundred?'

'Careful, Flambard,' said Rufus, 'he'll bargain with you. He looks innocent but he's been an abbot and we never knew an abbot that wouldn't make a good merchant.'

'My resources would only bear two thousand with ease, my lord Flambard, if I had taken advantage of your recent revaluation of the hide. But I have been raising my Canterbury revenues at the old rate. I dislike sharp practice.'

'Sharp practice? Come now, Archbishop,' said Flambard easily. 'The revaluation was overdue. The work was too hastily done in the Great Survey of 1086 and needed revision.'

'The work was done quite adequately in 1086 and you did not revise it, Messire Flambard, you merely reduced the number of acres to a hide so that landowners found themselves with more hides than before. Then you taxed the hides at the same rate as before. I call that sharp practice.'

'All right, we'll settle for one thousand,' said Flambard cheerfully. FitzHamon let out a snort of laughter and Meulan softly applauded. Anselm looked away.

He had failed. He hadn't wanted to try in the first place but Canterbury had been forced on him, so he had tried to act as an archbishop should. But it meant laying claim to authority, even over Rufus and Rufus would not acknowledge any man's authority. He would not even acknowledge God's.

Edith would have been God's best advocate but the king had run away from her and it was unlikely that he would ever be brought so near the point of marriage again. And in any case . . . Edith was in England again, poor child. Her father had died in an abortive invasion of the north last November and her mother, who had been ailing for a year, had simply given up on hearing the news, and died also. Strange, thought Anselm in parenthesis; Margaret had never wanted to marry Malcolm in the first place but his going had left her as stricken as though her

263

world had ended. Scotland was now in turmoil as Malcolm's brother and his sons from two marriages fought over the succession and Edith had been sent south for safety. She was at the moment staying on a manor belonging to the Bishop of Salisbury. It wouldn't do. She ought to go back to Romsey. It had been reported that she had become a nun at Romsey earlier, and in that case she should not be out in the world; nor was she eligible as a wife for Rufus. Rufus ought to marry but it would have to be someone else . . .

At the moment, it was the projected campaign which was under consideration. Anselm looked at Flambard. 'I shall donate my five hundred pounds, which you apparently don't want, to the relief of the poor. As God is my witness, there are plenty in need in these terrible days. Not one silver penny of mine will go to the Norman expedition. How you finance the campaign in Normandy, Messire, is now your business entirely.'

The amusement was at the expense of Rufus and Flambard this time, which was something. But the campaign would still be at the expense of the cold and hungry peasants, Anselm thought.

'I see,' said Rufus. 'Well, Ralph, if that's what you want. You've done your share in the field these last few years, and a good many of my vassals have offered me men for Normandy this time; we can manage with one man less. You can have home leave.'

'Well . . . I need it.' There was the Candlemas meeting in the Wood, for one thing. And other, practical matters. He had set work in hand to deepen the river channel at the Tun, to prevent future flooding, for instance. He wanted to see that it had been properly done. The place must yield a good living next year. He had been faced with the levy on the king's direct tenants and paid it from his own meagre savings, protecting the Tun as best he could because he was the King of their Wood and they had knelt at his feet and one could not accept such homage and give nothing.

But he had not thought it would be so hard to say to Rufus that he did not want to come to Normandy. There was an excitement, almost a wind, that one could smell and feel, about campaign preparations. He had the right to step aside but it was difficult. And besides . . .

The nights with Rufus had become hateful. They pushed as much as Chenna's Tun pulled. But for Rufus himself he still felt that protective friendship. It was a muddle.

He had chosen to speak to the king while they were on a deer shoot. It was cold, with frost crisping the old leaves underfoot and rimed twigs silver against a white winter sky. Rufus seemed very concerned with flexing chilled fingers and adjusting his bow. He showed no anger but there was a withdrawal in him, as if his personality had retreated from the inside of his skin. He had fallen silent.

Ralph made himself break that silence. 'Will I have a chance to . . . say goodbye before you go, sir?'

Better the worst of those nights than to part estranged. God's love, he didn't want to hurt Rufus or to lose his own place at court, either. But he needed, badly, to rest from the king's demands and concentrate for a while on the Tun. The Tun needed him, too. He *had* earned the right not to go on this expedition. It was the truth.

Rufus was watching the other hunters in the line strung out along the edge of the wood, as Ralph and Croc had placed them, after going out early in the morning to search for deer slots. The hounds and beaters were in the thicket opposite; a deer could break at any moment. Fifty yards off, the envoy Walter Tirel, who would be travelling to Normandy with the king, was drawing his bow. 'Tirel's a remarkably fine archer,' Rufus remarked. 'As good as you are, Ralph. Say goodbye? You've already said it, haven't you?' He turned his head and his pale eyes regarded Ralph dispassionately, as if from a distance. 'You've been drifting away from me for a long time. Ever since you went to your holding. I suppose a bit of land was all you wanted, all the time. In fact, I suspected it. I was afraid to give you too much. But even a place like the Tun seems to have been enough. Well, it's your choice. I shan't try to hold you. I'll be very much occupied from now on. You want to get away to the Tun, don't you? You may set out tomorrow. You have our leave.'

Ralph, panic jabbing through him, thought: I should have known.

He should have known that Rufus would take it hard. It

was difficult to believe that it could happen like this between one moment and the next, as if a boulder which looked fixed for ever should topple at a push. But it had. It was over. He was out.

Panic was suddenly replaced by rage.

If he had never felt a love of the body for Rufus, he had loved him nonetheless and not only for what the king could give, and hadn't he shown it? Hadn't he comforted Rufus when the fear of death was on him at Mont St. Michel and again at St. Peter's in Gloucester? At Gloucester, hadn't he sat up with Rufus night after night, held basins for him, sponged him clean, held back the shadows? Did Rufus think a man did all that to buy a piece of land or even a position? Did Rufus really think he'd never been more than on the make?

He had nothing left now but dignity.

'Thank you, my lord. I'll be off in the morning, then. But I wish you every good fortune in Normandy. I will rejoin my duty in three months.'

'Oh, take all the time you like,' said Rufus.

'Mother Abbess, the Bishop of Salisbury is here, in person. He's brought Edith back!'

'Edith?'

'Of Scotland, Mother. King Malcolm's daughter. I've asked them to wait in the guest chamber.'

'I'll come,' said Christina.

In the plain but beautifully proportioned stone room, Edith and the bishop were taking refreshment, Edith without appetite. They stood up at Christina's entrance. Edith had grown since last August but paradoxically, in her dark travelling mantle, she looked somehow smaller than Christina remembered her, and very slight. Her face was pale.

Since last August, she had lost both parents and one brother, seen her family at each other's throats and her country torn by war. 'My poor girl,' said Christina, with genuine compassion, 'welcome home.'

'I thought, and my superior of Canterbury thought, she should return to you,' said the bishop. 'She has been living under my care but I am not related to her and she should properly be with kinsfolk. Also, I understand that she may

266

be under vows as a nun. She herself says this is not so. But since a doubt exists, I feel, and Archbishop Anselm feels, that she should not be out in the world.'

Christina glanced at her niece, half-expecting an outburst. But Edith only said: 'It isn't true. I have never been a nun and never will be,' in a tired, flat voice as though she had repeated the words so often that they had ceased to have any meaning.

Christina smiled, folding her hands within her sleeves. Because she was truly sorry for the girl, she would not at this moment have attempted to put pressure on her, but in any case, she judged it unnecessary. 'We are glad to see you safe, Edith. We will look after you. And no one will force you to do anything against your will.'

Why get out the oars and exhaust yourself by rowing, when the current is already carrying the ship effortlessly towards its destination?

'I may as well give in,' said Edith to herself, taking her place with the others for the singing of Vespers, aware that she stood out from the rest because, in church, her hair was covered only by the linen headdress that women wore in the world. 'Who is there to marry me now? I should only be an embarrassment to any lord who took me on. The poor man wouldn't know which of my squabbling male relatives to support and they'd all expect him to help them, as though he were a bone, and they a pack of dogs.'

To the Norman ruler of England she might still have value. Through her, he could unite his upstart house with the old ruling family of England. But Rufus had rejected her. He had other preferences.

Yes, she might as well surrender. Christina's present mood of patience and forbearance was unlikely to last. Edith knew her aunt too well. She would be subjected to force once more, this time with no father to come to her rescue. She had been defeated once already since his death. The Bishop of Salisbury had had the consideration not to say so to Christina, but he had brought Edith here virtually by force. Her goods had been packed on her behalf, and when she attempted to sit down in the hall and refuse to move, two of the bishop's men had simply picked her up and carried her out to her horse, telling her to behave or they'd tie her feet to the stirrups.

Vespers had begun. Edith, dispiritedly, opened and shut her mouth without actually singing, which was just now beyond her. It was chilly in the chapel but not yet devoid of daylight. The evenings were lengthening. Soon it would be spring again and then summer, with the roses bursting fragrantly out of bud, and the doves and cuckoos calling. Last year, at dusk, there had been nightingales. Did no one here except herself understand the language which the throbbing birdsong and the roses spoke or long for the wonderful, hidden thing at which they hinted?

She glanced left and right and saw on the faces of the other nuns and novices no trace of the yearning and despair which filled her own heart and must, surely, be reflected on her countenance. Most were serious, a few anxious, some exalted. Those few faces which showed yearning were all turned towards the Rood which hung at the end of the chapel. They were content, it seemed, to have Him for a bridegroom and to desire only the inner certainty of His love.

An earthy, practical voice, Malcolm's legacy speaking in her blood, observed that life with Rufus would have been unlikely to contain much in the way of roses or nightingales.

No, but it would have been life! Journeys, clothes, new people! Reality, not dreams. Action, not inaction. Conflict, not boredom! Rufus, who had been so shy, who had stammered when he spoke to her, and passed her message so faithfully on to her father, would not, she thought, have been wilfully unkind. Whatever marriage to him would have been like, it couldn't have been worse than being in the power of Aunt Christina.

And surely, somewhere in it all would have been, at least, the *possibility* of an occasional nightingale?

Would have been. Would have been. It wouldn't happen now. She would live and die, trapped here. She might as well save herself the pain of resistance, and give in. Perhaps, if she made up her mind to try, she too could turn the passions of the body into a desire of the spirit. If she tried very hard . . .

But how, cried Edith to herself, can I shut out the song of the nightingale?

268

PART IV

IN WHICH A DOE IS BROUGHT TO BAY
1094–1096 AD

One

Contagion
1094

'Not far now,' said Richard's voice close beside him. 'Over the top of the hill and we'll be able to see it. Just hold on. Swithin . . .'

'I've got him,' said the man-at-arms from Ralph's other side. There were just the two of them with Ralph now. Brian of Little Dene and some other Fallowdene men had been there but they had ridden on ahead. Ralph, however, could ride no faster than a walk. He nodded but did not speak because of the raw, dark-red pain in his throat and chest. Only willpower kept his aching body in the saddle. He supposed he would survive the rest of the journey. He had survived so long already that there seemed no particular reason to stop. The world had shrunk to the pain which he carried like an extra saddlebag, the sweats and shivers which ran through him like waves, the desire to drift . . . he felt the movement of his horse, the steadying pressure of Swithin's arm, the supporting thrust of pommel and cantle against his back and belly, as if they were being reported to him rather than experienced.

He was drowsing again, when Richard exclaimed: 'Hearthsmoke!' He raised his heavy eyes and saw a white chalk track winding down into a valley. His swimming senses took in the fields that spread up the hillsides under a rolling grey sky, the habitations further down where there were trees, and he saw the hearthsmoke for himself, blowing about in an irritable, unsummery wind. It was many years since his first and hitherto his only visit to Fallowdene, but he recognised the place. A thought occurred to him. He whispered with difficulty: 'Put me in the barn. I'll bring the infection. Shouldn't be near people.'

Richard said grimly: 'I think it's a bit late to worry, in spite of the hearthsmoke. The hay should have been cut. I

271

can only think of one reason why it hasn't been. Come on!'

The horses moved forward. For what seemed a new eternity, he rolled with his mount's stride and the huddle of roofs below did not noticeably come nearer. But at last they were passing through the palisade gate, and the hall, its thatched eaves sweeping to the ground, was in front of them. The horses, blessedly, halted.

Then Alice was there, running out with her sleeves rolled up and her hands covered in flour, crying Richard's name and then simply crying, standing there and weeping as though something had given way inside her.

Richard was down, embracing her. Swithin's hands were reaching up. Ralph slid, or sagged, out of the saddle into them and was steadied to the ground. Richard had turned to help. He was being carried indoors. There was a pallet. He was lying down, still, quiet, no more jolting horse-movements. His clothes were being eased off. He was being given water to drink; someone was supporting his head. He was being allowed to lie back. He slept.

Of old Dame Editha, who had been at Fallowdene since before Wulfhild came, all that could be seen was a shrivelled chalky face and a hump, oddly small, under the squirrel-skin rug. At rare intervals, she drew a grating breath. 'It's hard to believe,' said Richard. Still unwashed after his journey, without as much as a mouthful of food inside him, he had come straight to the bedside. Alice stood beside him. He had left her pregnant. He hadn't asked the outcome because he could see for himself that there was no child in this thin, pale woman whose grubby clothes hung on her so slackly. She should have been six months on by now. '*Editha*,' he said. 'It's like the end of an era.'

Wulfhild was sitting by the bed. 'She's had the last rites. I heard you come into the yard but I couldn't leave her, not Editha. But she's not the only one.'

'I know. Alice has told me.' He had scarcely taken it in. 'All Swithin's family?' he said questioningly. 'Gerda and Rollo and Swithin's half-brothers? Asa and Crooked Elfrida?'

'Yes. But not Maud, God be praised. I lit so many candles and prayed so hard, and I was heard,' said Alice. 'And Ufi's all right. His wife's gone but his son is pulling through. So is Oger Shepherd. Gunnor and Harold have got it but we think they may come through as well. They're in the hall. I got over it. But I lost . . .'

'Twins,' said Wulfhild harshly. 'It was twins.'

'I had the plague,' said Alice sharply. 'It's a miracle I survived *both*!'

Wulfhild turned away her head with a movement which said *pity you did* but she did not speak. Richard looked at his wife in horror. He was not an imaginative man but once in a while some incident or phrase would find its way to some sensitive place inside him. He knew, from seeing Ralph, how painful this disease was. Alice, miscarrying in that condition, must have been drowned in agony. But at the sight of his appalled face, she gave him her familiar, self-contained little smile and with a dispassionate courage that staggered him said: 'Now you're home, we can try again. I'd like to.'

He said: 'Alice!' on a gasp of admiration and love and stood there looking at her through a long moment of silence and reaffirmation. Into that silence, tersely, Wulfhild said: 'She's gone.'

They turned to Editha. The rough, intermittent breathing had ceased. The silence now had a new quality, the stillness which emanates from a habitation no longer tenanted.

'Father Bruno's over at Withysham. Their chaplain died. Bruno's replacing him till a new man comes,' said Alice. 'He'll be back tomorrow, though. He comes and goes between here and there. He can . . . can bury Editha. Thanks be to God, he's stayed healthy himself.'

'So've I. You don't thank God for that, I notice,' Wulfhild muttered.

'Mother, you always were as tough as an old soldier,' said Richard hastily. 'Is the sickness at Withysham, then? How are Blanche and Sybil? Dear God, are they . . .?'

'Blanche had it lightly and recovered,' said Alice. 'Tch. Sybil as far as I know is perfectly well and according to Father Bruno, all the little girls who aren't ill either have

273

been running wild with Sybil as their leader.' She could not keep the disapproval out of her voice.

Richard let out a sigh of relief. 'We're a strong family. We get that from you, Mother. Abbess Edgiva, your sister, is well too, I take it?' Wulfhild nodded. 'Good. Good. It's bad enough but it could have been . . . they're all dead over at Beechtrees; we came that way. They're our nearest neighbour and when I found what I did find there, I thought . . . what about Little Dene? Brian came back ahead of us but we bypassed it ourselves. Have you seen him, or anyone from there?'

Wulfhild was closing Editha's eyes. Her own were dry but distant. He knew she was remembering times long past, before he was born. 'It's there as well, what do you expect? Bruno told us. He goes everywhere. I'll say this for him, he's tireless in his work even if he is a busybody. But we've no recent news. Brian hasn't been here. All gone at Beechtrees, eh?' Her face remembered the past again. The lord of Beechtrees had once tried to get possession of Fallowdene. 'I won't go so far as to say I'm sorry about that,' said Wulfhild.

Alice, who had tightened her mouth at the word *busybody*, said: 'That was your friend Ralph des Aix you brought back with you, wasn't it? He's very ill, too.'

'Ralph des Aix?' Wulfhild turned from drawing the rug over Editha's face. 'You brought *him* back with you? How is it you're here, anyway? Thought you were bound for Normandy. Time was you wouldn't have had to go to wars overseas, but all that seems to be forgotten nowadays.'

'I had to bring Ralph,' Richard said. 'It's bringing you more trouble and I'm sorry, but it was that or leave him on the beach at Hastings. As to why I'm here, we didn't sail. The old custom was upheld after all. Nobody sailed. The whole undertaking just dissolved into the air. There was a big muster at Hastings, reinforcements for Normandy. That man Flambard was there, the one who revalued all the land . . .'

'Someone'll kill him for that one day,' said Wulfhild, forgot about impressing Alice, and spat.

'Well, they haven't killed him yet. He was getting us all checked off on a great tally list, and collecting our forty

274

days' subsistence money into the common coffer, in the usual way. Then when all the money was in, he announced that the embarkation was off and we could all go home. Without the subsistence money.'

'Clever,' remarked Wulfhild sourly.

'We didn't think so. Ralph hadn't a penny left. He couldn't even find a lodging. There's an odd thing,' Richard said. 'When we got to Hastings, there wasn't a ship to be seen. I don't think we were ever meant to sail. It was a revenue-raising trick from the start. Ralph said, before he got too ill to talk, that it was the sort of thing to expect from Flambard. He knows Flambard personally, as it happens.'

'And the king too,' said Wulfhild with a sniff. 'We hear the gossip, even here. Ufi goes to Chichester to the Shire Court and gets news in plenty, and there were some minstrels round once, while you were away, singing the latest tales from London and Winchester and very interesting they were too. Knows the king very well indeed, your Sir Ralph des Aix, or so we gather. A regular close friend to King Rufus, isn't he?' It was hardly a question, and her disapproval of the answer came across to Richard like a blow.

'He's also a friend of mine,' he said repressively. 'I hope to God we can pull him through. And I expect him to be made welcome,' he added, meeting his mother's eyes warningly.

'If we're to pull any of them through, there's work to do,' said Alice. She turned towards the shape on the bed, crossed herself and stood a moment in silent prayer before moving to the door. 'I was making bread. The ones who are getting better are very hungry.'

'Mighty quick you were to seize Editha's job, the minute she took to her bed,' said Wulfhild.

'Tch. The bread's got to *be* made,' said Alice shortly, and went out.

Ralph tossed and coughed for three days and nights. But his slender olive-skinned body was strong. He was delirious only once. Then, certain gossip he had heard at Hastings, and the newly brusque attitude towards him of

275

men who had once been carefully polite, came together with the last sermon he had heard preached by Father Ilger at Minstead. Lately, Ilger had taken to prophesying the end of the world, attributing this threatened disaster to the unregenerate sinfulness of mankind at large, with the superstitions of his own flock, and the latest news from the Holy Land about the heathen's unchecked rampagings ('Infidel prayers on the very site of Christ's birth, and pilgrims kidnapped for slaves!') in particular.

He dreamed, improbably, that he and Rufus were fighting the infidel in a desert, only the sun was so hot and their throats so choked with sand that they could barely breathe or lift their swords. Then Rufus turned into an infidel himself and Walter Tirel, another infidel, joined him and Ralph was fighting them both. A sandstorm – he had never seen either a desert or a sandstorm but Father Ilger apparently had and had described them in one of his sermons – rose and he was lost in a hot, strangling darkness. He woke to find a priest with pale blue eyes and a high polished forehead tipping goats' milk into his mouth and saying: 'No, the world is not about to end. Drink this.' He drank and slept again and this time did not dream.

The next day his skin was cool and his throat and chest were easing. He managed to stagger groggily to the communal chamber pot and to take in what was happening around him.

He was one of several ill people who occupied pallets at one end of the hall. Its normal life continued at the other. Food was brought by Richard's wife Alice. She looked as frail as a dandelion seed, much more so than when he had first met her, but she worked all day and after dark too, tending the sick, feeding the poultry, baking and sewing. Her mother-in-law still bullied her, as Ralph remembered from the past, but these days Alice turned the edge of the older woman's tongue by a calm courtesy and at times, Ralph thought with weak amusement, a deliberately deaf ear.

On the third day, after sleeping late, he woke to find a household squabble in progress.

'You and your stupid plants!' Wulfhild was banging her stick on the floor to emphasise her words and there were

276

angry tears in her remarkable, almond-shaped blue eyes. They gave her face, and her anger, considerable potency. They had been the first thing about her that Ralph noticed when he came alone to Fallowdene and introduced himself. He had been admiring them, in fact, on the occasion only two days after that when he had suddenly seen from their expression that she did not like him. Their wrath, however, was this time directed at Richard. 'Why did you not put that ground down to rye as I told you? Then this wouldn't have happened. I told you, but no, you must leave it open because you'll want it in the autumn for those silly crocuses and now what have we got? Hemlock, that's what we've got! Five cows lost and their calves and haven't we had trouble enough what with bad harvests and disease? Must you make more? This is your fault!' She rounded on Alice. 'You brought those daft plants here. Bad luck, that's what you are, you useless mewling thing . . .'

'Useless, am I? Dear saints, what would you call use*ful*, I wonder? I work and work but *nothing's* ever enough for you: what would be enough I can't imagine! And I didn't bring those plants here. It was arranged between my father and Richard and they knew what they were doing, I've no doubt.'

'I certainly know what I'm doing. Let Alice alone, Mother. My daft plants as you call them will prove their worth one day.'

'Like *her*? Five years and more, and just one girl child to show for it. Those plants should be dug up and burned.'

'I had the choice originally between those plants and a mark of gold and I picked the plants because in the end they'll be worth it, wait and see.'

'A mark of gold!' Wulfhild screeched. Ralph thought that Richard looked slightly shamefaced, as though wishing he hadn't said that. It had clearly come as news to his mother. 'You passed up a mark of gold for those . . . those . . . !'

'Yes, I did, and I do know what I'm doing.' Richard stopped, eyes focused on distance, visibly thinking. 'We'll have to buy more cattle, of course . . .'

'What with?' enquired Wulfhild. 'All the coin we've got is for tax money.'

277

'We've the mares we used Hammerfoot with, and two batches of colts, two- and three-year-olds. We can sell them off. The trees we felled last year can be sold now. I'd meant to let them season a little longer but again, never mind. Ufi can ride to Chichester and look for buyers for both horses and timber. He can try shipyards for the timber. We'll dispose of half of it and hold the rest. What a good thing, Mother,' said Richard with a grin, 'that I didn't let you cut it at the time of my marriage. It's there to rescue us now.'

'You throw that in my face?' Wulfhild shouted. She had lost a number of teeth and spittle appeared at the corners of her mouth when she was upset. It appeared now.

'I'm not throwing it at you,' said Richard serenely. 'Just pointing out that it's worth trusting my judgement on occasion.' Wulfhild scowled. On his pallet, Ralph found himself inclined to laugh. Alice was gazing at her husband in admiration. 'You're so resourceful,' she said. And then put it into French and for the first time gave Richard the name that in years to come was always to be his. 'Débrouillard!'

The dispute passed although Wulfhild remained sullen for two days. Ralph, the onlooker, watched with interest. He had sensed very quickly that Wulfhild was a dragon because she had a treasure to guard and that its name was Fallowdene, and he understood that, for the Tun was a treasure to him, in the same way. Wulfhild quite evidently still disliked him, but he did not reciprocate this. He admired her.

He graduated to joining the household at table and took to observing his surroundings, more keenly than he had on his previous visit. Chenna's Tun was a poor place compared with this, he knew, but in time he might improve it and if so Fallowdene would be his standard. But much better harvests would have to come before he could buy tapestries or carved furniture like Richard's.

Presently, with Richard, he went shakily out into the sun to look at the weed-grown place where the hemlock had sprung up to kill the cattle. The weedy stretch occupied about half of a patch fifty yards wide and a

278

hundred yards long, along the lower edge and round the corner of the ryefield. The other half contained the strange crocus-like growths of which Wulfhild had spoken so disparagingly. 'What are they, Richard?'

Richard told him. Ralph shook a puzzled head, 'We had it in food sometimes at court when I first came there. At La Fleche too. But I believe it can't be got now. If you're looking for markets, I can tell you who to contact at Westminster.'

'Can you? That would be useful.'

'Anything I can do to repay what you've done for me! I wouldn't have lived through this but for you. You'll be getting that hay in any day, won't you? I'll give you a hand there too.'

'You're not strong enough yet.'

'I can try.'

Richard said: 'We actually did very little for you. We kept you warm and gave you things to drink. You did the rest. It was more than just the illness, wasn't it?'

'What do you mean?' He heard his voice turn defensive.

Richard heard it too. 'I don't mean to pry,' he said pacifically. 'Forgive me. But . . .'

'Me and the king? That's what you meant, isn't it? You've known all along, I suppose. Well, of course. Everyone did. When did you first find out?'

'Very shortly after you joined the hunt staff. There was gossip, you know. I was still at court with de Warenne's men and we didn't keep apart; we mixed with the household knights attached to the king. But I've never commented, have I? I've never felt entitled to. I always assumed that you hadn't much choice, not with Rufus. And it would all have got mixed up with the kind of admiration that most men feel for him anyway.' Ralph, recognising the perceptiveness of this, blinked and the angry blood subsided from his face. 'Only now,' said Richard, '. . . am I wrong? . . . I think you've been grieving.'

Ralph let out his breath in a long sigh. 'I'm sorry too. I had no right to use that tone to you, after all you've done. But the whole court knows how things are now, the whole bloody army knows and now there's you as well and can

279

you imagine how it feels to stand here and . . . and *talk* about it? It's over. He's got someone else – that Frenchman who was with the envoys from Normandy. Tirel. They were all laughing at me at Hastings.'

'I'm not laughing. I said, I think you've been grieving. But you're coming out of it now, aren't you? Making the crossing?'

Ralph stared at him, astonished and relieved by the quality of this friendship he had formed. He was not aware that it closely resembled the friendship which had been between his father and Richard's grandfather. They had neither of them been overly critical of other men's behaviour. As a result, Brand of Fallowdene had found himself in exile, and Peter Longshanks had unhesitatingly followed him.

'How did you know?' he asked Richard now. 'It *is* like that. I have to change from Ralph des Aix the king's friend, into Ralph of Chenna's Tun. Change *back* in a way. I'm not by nature . . . I mean, I don't dislike girls. I hope in due course to marry and have children for the Tun. Only Rufus is such a man that . . .' he lost his thread and started again. 'The illness – yes, it's as though it's burned something out of me. Did I babble when I was feverish?'

'Only once and it wouldn't have meant much except to someone who knew already, like me.'

'About the haymaking . . .' said Ralph.

The malady had attacked the throat and chest and those who died had mostly choked through lung congestion. Physical effort, forcing one to draw air deep into the lungs, found whatever phlegm still lingered, and induced coughing. It was good to be using one's muscles again, and to feel the sun on one's back. But at his first attempt, half an hour was enough to make Ralph pause from scything in order to cough, and Richard said: 'I told you so. Forget the hay. Go back to the hall.'

He shouldered his scythe and made his way slowly down the hill, marvelling at the way in which short distances grew longer when you were unwell. The hay meadow was all at once as big as a sea, the downs a mighty wave of chalk and grass about to break over him. Suddenly, fields and downs and the palisade ahead began to whirl and he sat down heavily on the grass beside the path.

He rested his forehead on his knees and closed his eyes. When he opened them again it was because something was snuffling at his hair. The something was an amiable-looking skewbald horse and standing beside it, holding the bridle, was the priest, Bruno, who was looking down at Ralph with an anxious air. Behind Bruno, someone else was dismounting from the back of a pony. 'We saw you stop and sit down,' Bruno said. 'You've been trying to scythe hay, I suppose. It's too soon. We've had others relapse through trying to work before they're ready.'

'Is he ill?' The priest's companion came forward. It was a girl, wrapped in a light cloak and hood. 'Oh, it's someone I don't know. Are you one of Richard's friends?' Her questions were inquisitive but her voice was kind and the small hand she laid on his arm was gentle. Bruno, with astonishing violence, struck it aside.

'Let him alone. The abbey was full of ailing nuns and did you trouble yourself with them? Take the horses to the stable!'

The child's face quivered. She was little more than a child, Ralph saw. She was studying him with a candid curiosity and her eyes were amazing, set on a trace of a slant like those of a hawk but in colour an intense azure blue. They reminded him of something. He searched his memory for it and then realised that they were like Wulfhild's eyes. This was how Wulfhild had looked, perhaps, when she was young. Only this child surely had a beauty that old Wulfhild had never had. Those fine brows, the delicacy of the cheekbone and nose and that taut bud of a mouth had never been hers. Then who . . .?

Then he knew. 'You don't think you've ever seen me before but I believe you have,' he said. 'You're Sybil, aren't you? Sir Richard's sister. You were here the last time I came.' And had been whisked away shortly afterwards, sent to Withysham Abbey for misbehaviour. He had been sorry for her, he recalled.

'I've just fetched her back from Withysham,' said Bruno shortly. 'There's sickness there and no one's capable of looking after her. She's been getting into mis-

281

chief. Did you hear me, Sybil? Take the horses. Messire
Ralph, take my arm.'

He could walk only slowly and by the time Bruno had
steered him into the hall, Sybil was already there. She was
being simultaneously folded in Wulfhild's arms
(astounding, that the ageing Wulfhild could be this young
thing's mother), and berated by Alice who in shrill tones
was demanding to know what Sybil was doing back in
Fallowdene. Quite clearly, neither Bruno nor Alice was
pleased to see her.

He let Bruno guide him to his pallet and lay down,
closing his eyes. There was, however, no hope of falling
asleep. For the second time since he came here, family
dispute sizzled through the air around him like forked
lightning. Bruno, having seen his patient comfortable, had
plunged headfirst into the storm and was now declaring
loudly that Sybil was a naughty and mischievous child and
that the Withysham nuns had begged him to remove her
because she did nothing but 'lead the others into trouble
and even out of the abbey grounds. Instead of caring for
the sick as you should, Sybil. Old enough to marry and as
thoughtless as when you were seven. It's disgraceful!'

'You and Alice are always against the child. Not a good
word to say for her but what harm's she ever done? She
likes to play and what's wrong with that?' That was
Wulfhild, bristling in defence of her lastborn.

Alice and Bruno, in duet, cut across her.

'. . . irreverent and irresponsible . . .'

'. . . Withysham's no place for her any longer; they've
no idea how to manage her . . .'

'. . . a changeling, in my opinion. She just isn't like
other children . . .'

'. . . and she's a bad influence on other children, the
nuns say . . .'

'I'm not, I'm not!' That was Sybil herself, raising her
voice in a wail. 'I'm not a changeling, I'm not a bad
influence, it isn't fair! Why are you so unkind?' The last
phrase was directed at Bruno. Ralph, opening his eyes,
saw Sybil, sobbing within the curve of her mother's arm,
make a gesture of appeal towards Bruno. It was rewarded
with an expression of extreme disgust. What in the world

had the poor child done at Withysham to warrant that, Ralph wondered?

Someone must have sent for Richard, for he now strode in, still carrying his scythe. 'What's this? Sybil back again? Why, may I ask, Bruno?'

Bruno once more launched into a recital of Sybil's misdoings, the nuns' inability to control her, and her lamentable failure to make herself useful when useful hands were needed.

'Well, there's one thing,' said Wulfhild, with a glance of mingled spite and triumph at Alice, 'they won't have her back from what Father Bruno says, so she'll have to stop here, where she ought to have been all the time. You can't live happily away from Fallowdene, can you, poppet? Nor could I, and I couldn't put up with being shut in an abbey, either. If she'd been allowed to stay here in the first place, under my eye . . .'

'She'd have run even wilder than she has already,' said Alice, 'and all this talk about she can't live happily away from home is utter nonsense. You encourage her in it just to annoy me, Mother, but you never think what harm you might do to her, making her believe such a thing. Tch. What if one day she *has* to live somewhere else? What if young Brian gets on in the world? He may want to take her anywhere! You never know. If he marries her at all, considering how ill-behaved she is,' Alice added grimly.

'Alice is right,' said Richard firmly. 'Sybil is still in need of training. She must be better prepared for marriage than she is now, that's certain.'

'If I may offer an opinion . . .?' said Bruno.

'By all means,' said Richard.

'I think you should get that marriage made,' said Bruno. 'She will then be the responsibility of Little Dene instead of Fallowdene and I think marriage could steady her. Sir Brian and his son have both recovered from the sickness; it would be possible to proceed.'

'I agree,' said Alice with vigour.

'She's very young,' said Richard doubtfully.

His mother, unexpectedly, supported Bruno and Alice. 'No, it might be best. She's grown-up enough. So was I at her age. It would get her away from you two,' she added venomously to Bruno and Alice, 'and without sending her out of the valley.'

'Very well,' Richard nodded. 'So be it. Meanwhile, she's to be kept busy. Alice, set Sybil to baking this minute. Mother, if I find Sybil anywhere but in this hall and occupied when I come back from the hayfield, she'll be sorry. And it's to be the same, all day and every day, till the wedding. You hear, Sybil? And now I'm getting back to the hay.'

'I'll help,' said Bruno, and picking up Ralph's discarded scythe, went out with Richard. Clamour immediately broke out again.

'Richard's her brother and even he won't stand up for her. And I know who is to blame for that, my lady, oh yes!'

'He has her interests at heart if only you'd see it,' retorted Alice, and pulling Sybil away from her mother, hustled her towards the kitchen.

'Much you care about her one way or another. You just want to prove you can make my son dance to your music!' Wulfhild shrieked after her.

'I could say the same of you, only he doesn't dance to yours,' replied Alice over her shoulder.

It was a great pity, Ralph thought. That lovely child could not possibly be as bad as Alice and Bruno appeared to think. The recital of her misdeeds at Withysham sounded as trivial as the peccadilloes which had sent her there in the first place. Some nonsense about telling tales of Herne Huntsman, to other children in the church, wasn't it? Repeating a tale that he himself had told her, in fact. She had been a taking little girl, then as now, and he had enjoyed, one lazy summer afternoon, sitting beside her while they watched sheep being sheared, and telling her stories to amuse her.

He thought that it was true, that Wulfhild and Alice were using her now in a private feud, turning her into a symbol of domination like a sceptre or a chain of office. Whoever controlled Sybil's treatment, controlled this hall.

Poor little thing. Better for her if she were married soon and out of this house.

It took him by surprise, when his stomach suddenly twisted in tenderness and rage on her behalf and an unspeakable spasm of jealousy for the boy who would be her husband.

Two

The Lammas Marriage
1094

It was not a betrothal feast, precisely, for Sybil had been promised to Brian the Younger for years. But the marriage date was set and dowry details finally settled to the accompaniment of a whole roasted sheep, herb-stuffed capons, river trout, elderberry wine and some exotically-flavoured yellow cakes, in a hall draped with flowery garlands.

It was indeed something other than a feast for Sybil. The pestilence had passed and the survivors, almost formally, were giving thanks, and even grief for the dead did not stop them. Most of Fallowdene was there. 'Sybil embroidered her gown herself,' Alice informed Sybil's future husband and father-in-law as Sybil came slowly and ceremoniously up the hall, a cup between her palms, towards the two solid russet-clad figures to pledge them. 'She has been well-taught with the needle and she made the bread you're eating, too. She learned a great deal at Withysham. We're so proud of her,' said Alice mendaciously.

The mendacity lay in the allegation of pride, not in the statement that Sybil was skilled in household arts, for this was true enough although she needed energetic chivvying to make her demonstrate her knowledge. Her manners too were irreproachable as she offered the cup graciously to the two Brians, the elder first. He, as the cup passed to his son, turned politely to say to Ralph, the outsider guest: 'Will you be here for the nuptials? September the first is only four weeks off.'

'No reason why you shouldn't stay, is there?' Richard asked. 'After all, you'd expected to be in Normandy now.'

'I want to be home for the harvest, but I can wait till the start of September if you wish,' Ralph said. He did not want to stay but it would be discourteous to refuse and worse, might require explaining. He could hardly tell

Richard that he wanted to seize the chance to be home for the Lammas Feast, to sit on the log throne himself and not be represented by Oswin. And he could scarcely say, either, that he could not bear the thought of seeing Sybil allied to a boy who was nothing but a stodgy yokel who would be the better for a few years' training with Helias of La Fleche or Rufus, though even they would be hard put to it to get a polish on him.

When he thought about it, he was amazed at himself. He had recognised his true nature for what it was in the Wood. But that was a physical matter. Devotion, loyalty, the bonding of the heart, these things still pertained to Rufus. To let another person, above all a woman, call them out of him was like a betrayal. He had said to Richard: *I hope to marry*. But he had meant some calm, practical arrangement. Not this unlicensed surge of feeling . . .

After the wedding, when he had done his duty as a guest and drunk to the future happiness of the pair (however improbable this might seem) he would go back to the Tun and in time, to court. Perhaps even now Rufus might forgive him. Perhaps even now their friendship, if nothing more, might be restored. He would find a suitable girl to give him an heir for the Tun – and the log throne too – and he would forget Sybil. He would have to.

Her pledging done, Sybil took her place beside her betrothed. She and young Brian took little notice of each other. There were no sly glances or claspings of hands. Ralph wondered if they had ever spoken to each other at all today beyond the formal words of greeting and pledging. The older Brian was addressing Sybil bluffly, as though not quite at ease with the prospect of this elfin girl-child in his house. 'We hope you'll settle down with us, my girl. You'll not be too far from your home and your mam.'

'Unless I leave Little Dene one day. I hope to increase my holdings in time,' said the young Brian, speaking up for the first time outside the formalities. His voice had partially broken. 'Then my wife will come with me, of course.'

'Just as we've been telling her,' said Alice. 'You do

287

right to remind her.' Had she, Ralph wondered, encouraged him to do so?

Sybil was staring down at her hands. He thought that she hated being talked at in this manner and was longing to escape from the hall and the stiff ceremony. She had been kept in the house continuously since she came back from Withysham, baking, embroidering, making cheese and sweeping floors. He had noticed how miserable this restricted life made her. But Brian's predictions for their future did not, he thought, appeal to her either.

Out of experience, and in the hope of making her look happier, he said: 'Getting a land grant may be harder than you think.'

Alice, lightly, with a smile that turned it all into a joke, said: 'Don't look so grave, Sybil. You're very lucky. Why, you'll be mistress of your own home from the moment you set foot in it. You won't even have a mother-in-law.'

At the lower tables, several faces acquired broad grins. Wulfhild glowered. Richard turned sharply to Alice but she was looking so sweetly at him and Wulfhild that he decided to relax into laughter. Sybil raised her head and her gaze met Ralph's. Her eyes were bright as though there were tears in them but there was a sparkle of pure wicked merriment as well. He wanted to wipe away the tears and share the amusement and did not think that the younger Brian would be any good at all, at either.

The evenings were light. The two Brians rode off after dinner and Alice sent Sybil to change her clothes. 'You've been the centre of attention all day but now there's work to do, clearing up the hall.' Ralph went out.

He was intolerably restless. For once, thinking that he might find serenity in it, he went into the church. But Bruno was there before him, prostrate before the altar, lost in a passion of prayer. Ralph withdrew silently and went instead to the stable, to rub down his horse.

Arrow had been turned out during his master's illness and had grown fat. Frequent hard grooming helped to put back muscle. Ralph set about the task with a twisted hank of hay and was stroking the glossy hide, approving a new hardness under the skin, when the door opened and a small face peered round it. 'Hello. I thought you were hard at work tidying the hall,' Ralph said.

'I escaped. I'm sick of working. Sometimes when I can get away I hide in the stable. I didn't know anyone was here. You won't give me away, will you?'

She came in and sat down on a straw bale. The light was dim but good enough to show him how forlorn her face was. The day had certainly held out no promise of joy to her. 'You can watch me if you like,' he said doubtfully. 'But if you're found . . .'

'You didn't know I wasn't supposed to be here.' Sybil smiled angelically at him. 'You're a guest; no one would expect you to know these things. You're not part of the family; you're just my brother's friend. My mother says your father and her father were once friends.'

'Yes, that's true.'

'And you're better from your illness now? If you'd been one of the family, I don't expect you'd have caught it. I didn't, or Richard or Mother or Aunt Edgiva at Withysham. Mother says we're a strong family. Though Father Bruno didn't get it, and my sister Blanche at Withysham did. Nearly all the nuns were ill as well. It was lovely. We did just as we liked.'

'So I heard.'

'Oh don't. Talk like that, I mean. Everyone talks to me like that.'

'Like what?'

'In that tone. Crushing me.'

Her voice quavered. She looked so pathetic that he wanted to sit down beside her and hug her. He refrained. 'How would you like me to talk instead?'

'As if I were a person instead of a lot of faults that needed correcting. Tell me things!'

'What sort of things?'

'Oh, *all* sorts of things. What's the sea like? I've never seen it but Richard says you and he have crossed it. I can't ask Richard, he's no good at describing things.'

'Well, you've been to the top of the down and seen the land spread out below?'

'Yes. From the north down you can look out over miles of forest.'

289

'Imagine that instead of trees, that was all water, all of it, with huge ripples as big as small hills.'

'Ooh! You do know things. Can you tell me,' said Sybil, 'what this means?' The floor of the stable was of earth, and the soil of Fallowdene was chalk. There were always loose pieces about. She dug one out of the floor with her fingernails. 'You told me a story about Herne once,' she said. 'And this is to do with him, I think, but what is it really?' And on the planks of the stable wall, with an X and a line and a V, she drew the five-pointed figure, the pentagram of the Wood.

'Where did you see this?' Ralph asked quietly.

'A girl at Withysham showed me. One of the orphans they adopt.'

'And what did she say about it?'

'That it was something to do with Herne, the god with horns, that you told me about. And that it was something to do, as well, with people going into a wood and doing *that* . . . you know. I asked Sister Ermengarde at Withysham if *that* was what grown-up people did in church – I thought perhaps when children weren't there – but she was so angry!'

'I'm not surprised!' Ralph was inclined to laugh and also to sweat. Priests, and possibly nuns, knew that the worship of the Wood existed but they were its enemies. It must be hidden from them or they would destroy it. Even the children of the devotees were guarded from knowledge until they were ten years old or so, old enough to understood the meaning of secrecy. He had been stupid even to tell Sybil a story of Herne as though it were just a legend, stupid to as much as mention Herne's name. And someone else had been equally indiscreet within earshot of a little orphan girl with sharp ears. 'Listen to me, Sybil. The Sign is secret. You must never draw it or even speak of it again. Forget it exists. Here, take this cloth and get it off that wall. Use spit. And never think of it again, from this day on, or Herne either.'

'Why not? What does that sign *mean*? Why won't you tell me?'

'Shhh.'

'I won't shhh! I want to know!'

Her voice shot up. Arrow moved restlessly. 'You're upsetting my horse. Behave yourself.'

'I won't behave! I want to know what the sign means. I already know half of it so tell me the rest, tell me the rest!' She was jumping up and down. 'Tell me!' she said, changing to a coaxing note. She flung herself at him and into his arms. Ralph, knocked off balance, almost fell under Arrow's stamping feet. The horse reared and squealed. Ralph rolled himself and Sybil clear just in time. 'Now look what you've done!' He had hold of her arms, thrusting her back to safety. He attempted to shake her. She lurched back and forth in his hands like a straw doll and wailed: 'Don't, don't! Everything's so horrible! Why must you be unkind too?' He desisted and she threw herself against him once more, snuggling.

It was the smell of her that did the damage, the heady warm smell of willing femaleness. The smell that after so many years he had known again in the Wood.

It rose into his brain and it was as though the Wood were all about them, dark and rustling and huge with power. There was power in the Worship; few men faltered at May Eve or Lammas, women climaxed who never did at other times, and now and then the barren quickened.

He shut his eyes as Sybil's mouth met his in a long and astonishingly expert kiss, and on the inside of his eyelids he saw again the leaping flames, the tree limbs lit orange and red, stretched out over the lovers in the attitude of blessing and permission. Drums throbbed. For one moment the power failed and he remembered where he was and who Sybil was. But Sybil whispered: 'It's all right, it doesn't matter, I know what to do,' and her hands were on him, gentle, teasing, shockingly knowledgeable.

There was another moment in which she drew back and he reached for her in agony, and she said: 'But you must let me know what the sign means. I won't let you if you don't.'

He moaned and pleaded but she pulled herself away and stood above him and small as she was, when he was lying in the straw at her feet, she towered like a goddess. Her blue eyes no longer sparkled, nor were they childlike

291

any more, but detached and calm. He told her, all the essentials of the Worship, in a few gabbled sentences. What did it matter, when as she said, she knew half of it already and she was in any case, yes, surely this female creature that was Sybil was in any case born to be Maiden and Mother . . . for tonight . . . yes, it had slipped from his mind but it was true, tonight was Lammas.

Then she stooped to him and his arms, enchanted into vigour out of the last remaining weakness of the pestilence, closed about her.

Three

Flames
August 1094

He knew he should leave Fallowdene at once. He made no excuses for himself. He had gone mad, outraged every tenet of hospitality, behaved in a fashion so unknightly that he could not himself believe it. He had abused his host and his friend and the fact that Sybil had almost certainly not been a virgin made no difference.

He told himself that he was staying because he could not think of an excuse to change his mind and leave before the wedding; because Richard, faced with the task of breaking and training four colts ready for market had quite naturally turned for help to the friend who was such a good horseman, and now that he was fit again, he could not refuse. He also knew that like a man caught with a poached deer over his shoulder, telling the Foresters he'd merely found the carcase, he was lying.

He was staying because he could not leave Sybil. It was not possible that he could be engrossed with the mind, the spirit, of a thirteen-year-old girl as once he had been engrossed with those of Rufus but it was true. This went far beyond her body or her beauty. It was terrifying.

It was real.

For three days he busied himself with Richard's colts, avoiding Sybil and simultaneously inventing complicated excuses to be where he might glimpse her in the distance.

He was breaking his fast on the fourth morning, hurriedly, meaning to get to the stable before Sybil came into the hall, when Alice rushed in, shouting for Wulfhild so urgently that Wulfhild, despite her lameness, came out of the kitchen at something approaching a run. 'What is it, Alice?'

'This!' gasped Alice, and thrust an armful of what appeared to be white linen at her mother-in-law. 'I put these in Sybil's chest when she came back. She didn't bring any with her but when I asked her, she said yes,

293

she'd been needing them for a year now. Mother, she's been here six weeks and she hasn't touched them, they're all stacked and folded just as I left them!'

'So? The child's only thirteen. She's not settled down yet.'

'At the moment,' retorted Alice, 'she's being sick. Very sick. That's why I searched the chest. I know all about *that* kind of sickness.'

'Rubbish,' said Wulfhild and then, as if there were no contradiction, 'find Richard.'

Gunnor had come from the kitchen behind Wulfhild. 'I know where he is,' she said. While she was fetching him, Ralph sat down on a bench in a corner, feeling shaky. His first thought had been: it's mine. This is my fault.

His second thought was: no, it can't be, not if she's been here six weeks and there was nothing . . . she wasn't a virgin, I was right.

His third was: but it could have been. I'm as guilty as though it was.

And his fourth: poor, poor child, what will happen to her now?

No one took any notice of him. He might have been invisible. He was still sitting there when Richard hurried in. 'Gunnor said something terrible had happened, but wouldn't tell me what. Is somebody ill again?'

'Sybil,' said Alice starkly, 'is with child.'

'What did you say?'

'I said, Sybil is pregnant.'

'Don't be absurd. She's only a child herself and she's never been alone with him in her life. '

'Alone with who?'

'Brian the Younger, of course.'

'This has nothing to do with Brian the Younger,' said Alice. 'I fancy it happened before she left Withysham.' She began to explain. Richard also collapsed on to a bench, where he sat staring at her. 'I can't believe this. It's a mistake of some kind.'

Alice shook her head.

'But the marriage date is settled. We can't go back on it.'

'We can't go through with it either. They'd never forgive us *or* her, when they found out.'

294

'But what are we to do?' Richard shouted. 'If it's true, we can't keep her here and where can she go?'

'What a fuss,' remarked Wulfhild. She too had sat down, straight-backed, hands folded on the head of her stick. 'My mother stayed where she was and had me, and no one thought anything of it.'

'Your mother wasn't the daughter of a knightly household,' said Richard, harassed. He looked ten years older than his age.

'No,' Wulfhild agreed. 'She was just a thrall. Thrall folk don't make a to-do over what's just natural.' She cast a malevolent look at Alice. 'She was still my mother and Sybil's my daughter. I lost my virtue, as you'd put it in your pompous way, when I was Sybil's age. Thought nothing of it. There's no need for all these hysterics.'

'I'm not hysterical,' said Alice angrily. '*You* didn't have a baby, anyway.'

'I think I almost did, once,' said Wulfhild with a regrettable chuckle, 'but I brought myself on with a pennyroyal brew. I'll make one for Sybil if you like. Then no one'll be the wiser.'

'The bridegroom'll be the wiser,' said Alice ominously.

'I hope he'll have more sense. Too many good girls have had their reputations spoiled by that beldame's tale. I didn't bleed the first time. Plenty of girls don't, my lass. I'll deal with that, if anything's said.'

'But she's not a good girl!' Richard exploded. 'We'll be foisting a wanton onto them however many brews she drinks and whatever stories you tell, Mother. *If* it's true. See here, Alice, she *is* only thirteen and anyone can eat something that upsets them . . .'

'She tried to run out of the room just before she was sick,' said Alice shortly. 'I called her back. I asked what was the matter. She was trying to hide it. And when I taxed her with the cause, she didn't deny it; she just cried.'

With his head in his hands, Richard said: 'One thing I'd like to know then is, if it isn't Young Brian's, who the devil's is it?'

'Probably the devil's,' said Alice.

He sat up again. 'I doubt that but I think we'd better find out. Fetch Sybil here.'

295

From the doorway, Father Bruno said: 'There's no need.'

He must have been there, unnoticed, for some moments. 'No doubt you'll wish to talk to her but you needn't ask her who the man was,' he said. His face was skull-white. Bewildered, they watched as he came forward into the hall. Gunnor followed. 'Gunnor fetched me. She thought you might need a priest's help. So you do, though not for the reasons she supposed. I am the father of the child.'

Every succeeding revelation weakened another pair of knees, knocking people off their feet like skittles. This time it was Alice who staggered and sat down, on a handy stool. They were all speechless until Richard, staring at Bruno in fascinated horror as though, riding through an ordinary forest, he had come face to face with antlered Herne, said: 'How? And when?'

'Coming back from Withysham.' Bruno's voice was steady but sweat stood out in droplets on his smooth, high forehead. 'On the way I tried to speak to her about her bad behaviour there. She laughed at me at first and then became sulky. She jumped off her pony and ran away from me. I called her but she didn't come back so I tied the horses to a bush and went into the trees after her, on foot. The undergrowth was thick; I couldn't ride through it. She ran away again so I chased her. I caught her and she fell and I went down with her and . . . God forgive me,' said Bruno in a low voice. 'She's a devil's snare, as Eve was to Adam, but I have never exonerated Adam. He did not have to eat the apple. I need not have . . . it just happened. She fought me but as if she only half meant it and then she clung to me and . . .'

Ralph, the unheeded audience, could have said: 'I know.'

'I shall leave Fallowdene, of course,' Bruno said. Ralph, studying his blanched face, thought that Bruno, like himself, could hardly believe in his own misdoing. The only person in the hall who was not registering shock and disbelief, in fact, was old Wulfhild, who kept nodding to herself as though she were saying *I told you so*. Had she sensed this potentiality in Bruno – or in Ralph? She certainly detested them both. 'I shall go to my bishop,' Bruno was saying, 'and tell him everything. What comes then must come. But I am still a priest. I can't offer . . .'

'I should think not,' said Alice. She gave him a long stare of sheer revulsion and turned her head away.

'There's always a way to manage,' declared Wulfhild. 'You're good enough at conjuring up ways to make money for cattle, Richard. Now do some conjuring for your sister. I'll make a brew but if that fails she can go to Withysham and we'll say she's ill and being nursed there. When the baby's born they can look after it for a while till the marriage is made. Later, maybe, we'll give a home to an orphaned relative.'

'When a girl has a child, that leaves signs,' said Alice flatly. 'We might have got away with the other but not that.'

'The Brians may not be as well-informed as all that,' said Wulfhild optimistically. 'If Sybil rubs oil into her skin . . .'

'But it's wrong!' Alice shrieked, jumping up again. 'It's deception! Richard!'

'Alice is right.' Richard turned to Bruno. 'Get out. Be off the manor before noon and don't come into my sight again before you go. Go on!'

'I must say one thing before I leave.'

'And that is?'

'I thought she was just a silly child. But now I think your wife has been right all along. I repeat, she is a devil's snare. Watch her.'

'I agree. Or I might well kill you where you stand, priest or no priest. Now get out before I do that anyway.'

'Devil's snare, bah!' Wulfhild spluttered as Bruno went out. 'A child who doesn't know how lovely she is or what weaklings men can be. Once she's married . . .'

'She isn't going to be married,' said Richard. 'We can't saddle Little Dene with her now. Not even if we can get rid of the child, or if it turns out that there isn't one.'

'There's a child,' Alice assured him.

'I can only offset her perfidy,' Richard said grimly, 'by being strictly honourable myself. The final decision has to be Little Dene's, of course. I must go there at once. What

297

I'm to say to them or how I'm even to look them in the face I don't know but I must. I don't want to see Sybil yet after all. I think I'd strangle her if I did. She's to stay in her chamber. Gunnor, go and bar her in. No one is to speak to her or go near her. I shall be back before noon.'

'I'm going to see her,' said Wulfhild fiercely as soon as Richard, as bleak of face as though he were bound for his own execution, had gone.

'But Richard said . . .' Alice began unwisely.

'I take no orders from my own son or from you either,' snapped Wulfhild and when Alice moved hesitantly into her path, struck out with her stick. Alice fell back, pink with anger and clutching her arm where the stick had landed. Wulfhild made her way out at a rapid hobble.

Alice, as if her strength had once more given out, sat down again. Ralph, still invisible as far as the family were concerned, but troubled by a sense of responsibility for Sybil, slipped unobtrusively out of the hall but occupied himself in tasks close by until Richard, two hours later, came riding slowly in. He handed his horse to Gurth (who was visibly agog with questions but was disappointed of answers) and went indoors without speaking. Ralph quietly followed.

Alice was sitting very upright, sewing. 'Your mother is with Sybil, despite your orders.'

'I expected that. It doesn't matter.' He sat down heavily on a settle.

'What happened?' Alice asked.

'What you might suppose. I've been sympathised with, most courteously – as though I'd suffered a bereavement. I've also been courteously, tactfully and finally rejected as a prospective relative by marriage. I've been patronised by *my own tenants*. And I've had to incline my head and accept it because Sir Brian's within his rights. He can do better for his son than Sybil. Well, Sybil is one person I can deal with as I choose. *Now* I'll see her. Fetch her, Alice, while I find a stick.'

Sybil was brought, clinging to her mother's hand, shivering and green-tinged with nausea and fear. Even Alice said: 'Be careful, Richard. She might miscarry.'

'Would it matter?' Richard asked. He wrenched Sybil

away from Wulfhild. 'Mother, let go. Don't interfere. Gunnor, Bebbe, where are you all? Bring the household, everyone you can find. Fetch Gurth in. I'm going to make it very clear where I stand in this and what standards of behaviour I expect in my house. Stand back, Mother, or I'll order someone to restrain you.'

'*No!*' Sybil screamed. The household was crowding in: Gurth, Ufi, Harold, the women, even little Maud, their faces simultaneously horrified and excited. 'Leave me alone! I didn't mean to do anything wrong! I didn't know what would happen, it was only a game, I was only playing a game . . .!

And so she had been, of course. Ralph, walking quickly towards Richard and his captive, his feet carrying him without any instructions from their owner, found that he understood perfectly. She was childish still and she was playful. She had run away from Bruno's solemn nagging and then she had tried to play with him, hide and seek among the trees, with no idea of how her sparkling eyes and elfin elusiveness, and then the feel of her warm skin and fragile bones under his hands, would work on him. Bruno was a priest, a man whose natural longings must remain unsatisfied, but he was also the breed of man in whom those longings were strong. She had played a game and it had turned into something that was no game at all, and worst of all, it had awakened her own longings, set them pouring bewilderingly through her surprised body in a torrent.

And now the torrent was a mill-race in which she was caught with no hope of escape. With child, disgraced, rejected by that tedious Sir Brian and his mirror image of a son, and now her brother proposed to beat her in public. For what? For being a child, and playful.

Never before had it occurred to Ralph to thank God for having been Rufus' lover but he did so now. It had taught him not to judge. He did not even blame Sybil for the interlude in the stable. It had happened and because of it he had the right to protect her and he was glad because he wanted to protect her. All his instincts for taking care of things, frustrated at Aix, channelled makeshift fashion into looking after his horses and calming Rufus' secret fears, and at last lavished on Chenna's Tun, now changed course smoothly once more and raced towards Sybil as if she had been their destination from the beginning. Chenna's Tun should be *for* her, as a realm of her own. (He had temporarily forgotten what it was really like.) He reached Richard and his hand closed on Richard's upraised arm. 'Stop!'

'Get away from me, Ralph! This isn't your business.'

'I want to make it my business. You need a future for Sybil, don't you?'

'Her future's in Withysham. Once the place is straight again after the sickness, back she goes and there she stays for the rest of her life. If they won't take her, I'll find a nunnery that will. Now will you stand back?'

Sybil shuddered and whimpered. Ralph's grip hardened as Richard tried to pull free. 'Is that really the best outlook for her? Listen to me, Richard! I'm offering you another answer. I'll marry her. I want a wife for Chenna's Tun. I'll take Sybil. She'll be safe with me. But I want her in good health and uninjured. Strike her once and the bargain's off. You won't get a better offer.'

Richard was astonished enough to let go of his sister as he turned in amazement to Ralph. 'But you can't want *Sybil*!'

'Yes, I do.' Sybil was looking at him in what seemed to be terror. He thought she supposed he was about to reveal the events of Lammas. He gave her a reassuring smile. 'Put that stick down, Richard. We should talk this over calmly.'

Richard tossed the stick onto a table, but his face remained incredulous. 'The child. She's with child.'

'It's proof she can have children. She'll have mine, later. I'll give houseroom to this one. I don't mind.' At the Tun, people frequently gave houseroom to children of unconventional parentage. And he would be bringing a wife who was already almost a Worshipper! It was as though Herne had arranged it. Perhaps He had.

'You'll take her to Hampshire?'

'Yes. When you like. Would you like that, Sybil? Would you like to come and live with me?'

He was completely unprepared for her reply although

300

he realised afterwards that in this he had been foolish. He had saved her from Richard and from a future of disgrace, but he had forgotten how her mother had encouraged her to think that she could not live away from the valley.

She drew away from him, looking at him not as though he were a saviour but more as though he were Grendel the Monster in person. 'Hampshire?' said Sybil in a high voice. 'I can't! I can't leave Fallowdene. I can't! I can't!'

Suddenly everyone seemed to be shouting at once. 'Don't be a fool!' Richard thundered. 'You're lucky to have the chance. What's all this nonsense? Every girl leaves home in the end. Mother, this is your doing . . .!'

'It isn't nonsense. I know what she means. You don't but I do. I couldn't leave the valley either, it's part of me. She's my daughter and she's like me and I say that if she wants to stay, she stays. She doesn't go to Withysham either. We'll rear the baby here and . . .'

'No! I won't have her devil's spawn here *or* her!' cried Alice. She seized Richard's arm and shook it.

'*You* say you won't have them here? I've had enough of this, my lady.' Wulfhild's stick banged ominously on the floor. 'I'm weary to the bone of you saying how *my* daughter's to be treated!'

'Richard, tell her! I'm your wife and I'm mistress here and . . .'

'I was mistress here before you were born. I sold myself to keep this manor safe – yes, my lady, sold myself in marriage to Richard's father so that I could stay and take care of Fallowdene!' Wulfhild pounded the floor in fury. 'I was lucky, I got a good man, but I'd have taken Satan if I had to. I've worked and sweated and made sacrifices you never dreamt of *and* given the place a son which is more than you have, and now you tell me *you're* the mistress here and it's for *you* to say if my daughter stays or goes . . .?'

'I can't go, I won't!' howled Sybil. She wasn't beautiful now. Her face was slimy with tears and she clutched at Richard with hands like small claws. 'I went nearly mad at Withysham and that's only five miles. *I can't go to Hampshire!*'

'You shan't, darling, you shan't. It's all right. Richard,

if you let this happen I won't forgive you, I warn you. This man –' Wulfhild raised her stick and pointed it angrily at Ralph '– he's one of the king's doxies, didn't you *know*? Friend of the king! I know what that means these days, if you don't.'

'He's good enough for her. She goes,' said Alice savagely, 'or I go, back to my father. I won't share a roof with a blaspheming wanton. It's Withysham or Hampshire for you, my girl, and since you seem to think Hampshire's the worst, Hampshire I think it should be.'

'Go home to your father? You see how much she loves you,' said Wulfhild mockingly to Richard.

'I do love you!' Alice clung to Richard, her face upturned, and with her spare hand she tore Sybil's fingers away from the sleeve they were clutching. 'But I can't live like this any longer, disparaged in my own house . . .'

'*My* house,' corrected Wulfhild.

'You see?' Alice released her husband and turned, on her dignity, to face her foe. '*Your* house, you call it. And *your* son, that's the only way you think of him. You forget that he's *my* husband.' She controlled her voice, putting on affronted good breeding like armour. 'Tch. I've never had my rightful place here and . . .'

'Tch! Tch! Tch! Stop it! Stop that righteous little noise!' The depth of loathing which Wulfhild suddenly revealed took them all aback. 'Never had your rightful place, mistress Pious Airs? You get your own way left and right. Who had Sybil sent away to start with? You, my lady, never mind what I thought of it. I was only her mother! You come in here with your mincing ways and set yourself up to show us all how to make a loaf or stitch a seam . . .'

'You're out of your mind, you old . . .!' Alice choked and bit back what was probably an unsuitably ill-bred epithet. 'A wife is *supposed* . . .ohhh!' She shook her fists in the air in frustration. 'You make my very virtues into faults! What would you have said if I couldn't bake, or mend clothes, tell me that? That would be wrong, too, wouldn't it?'

It was trivial, absurd, pathetic and, to the combatants, agonisingly real. Ralph, aghast at what he had unleashed, and reduced once more to invisibility, listened as the old,

302

silly grudges were dragged out, and saw that once more, Sybil herself had ceased to matter in her own right, was only a counter in the contest. She was sobbing now in fright over the prospect of marrying him but surely, homesickness would pass and she couldn't really pine for long for a home like this. She'd be better off with him.

The invective still flew. '. . . if I even want a feast-day garland made of a certain flower, I have to pretend it's the flower I want least; then you'll insist on it out of spite!' Alice was unconscious of sounding ridiculous. 'You undermine all my authority . . .'

'*Your* authority, prissy-mouth!' Wulfhild thrust her head forward, pursed her lips into a parody of aristocratic distaste, gibbered: 'Tch-tch-tch!' into Alice's face, raised her stick and struck. Alice sprang back with a scream. Wulfhild followed, striking again, knocking Richard aside with her elbow as he made to interfere, driving her victim round the hearth and backing her against the wall. Sybil chose this moment to fling herself once more on Richard, crying: 'Don't send me away, please don't!' Entangled with her, he could not reach Alice who, cringing away from her mother-in-law, clutched at the tapestry behind her, tore it loose and threw it at Wulfhild to muffle the flailing arm.

Wulfhild flung it off and a trailing corner fell on the fire. It blazed up instantly. The floor rushes caught. The fire ran along the floor to the wall and suddenly the wallhangings were made of flame. Three dogs which had been sitting by the hearth ran yelping. People, shouting and jostling, made for the door, tripping over the dogs.

'Get everyone out! Where's Maud? Water, fetch water!' Richard's voice rose above the uproar. He threw Sybil at Ralph, who caught her and ran outside. Alice stood still, terrified, knuckles jammed against her mouth. Richard dragged her and Maud to the door and thrust them through it, dashing back at once to help Harold and Ufi, who had rushed to fetch water from the kitchen barrel and were trying to fight the flames. A moment later they gave up and ran to save themselves. Coughing, smoke-grimed, they joined the rest outside and huddled with them, the dogs cowering against their legs, as the smoke streaming through the thatch turned to flame, pale and dancing in the summer noon.

'It was my home! Thirty years I've lived here and now see what you've done!' Wulfhild would have attacked Alice again except that Richard put himself between them. Burning thatch and timber were whirling up now into the breeze and in their stalls the horses, frightened by the smell and crackle of fire, had begun to whinney. Ralph and Gurth, seeing rags of flame blowing towards the stable thatch, ran. 'Get them out and drive them through the gate!' Ralph gasped.

It was harder than it sounded. Arrow was too frightened to move. Trembling and wide-eyed, he stood rigid until Ralph stripped off his jerkin and bound it round the horse's eyes. Then he consented to be led and the rest, released by Gurth, followed, snorting and shying, out into air filled with smoke and dancing sparks. 'Open the gate! Open the gate!' Ralph yelled. Gurth reached the gate and wrenched it back. Ralph released Arrow's eyes and waved his arms, superfluously, since all the horses were already stampeding for the open and safety. He spun round at the sound of screams and saw Alice tearing off her headshawl and apparently fighting Ufi. Then he saw that a burning ember had fallen on Ufi's sleeve and that Alice was smothering it with the shawl. Richard, shouting for water to soak the thatch of the outbuildings, was at the well, dragging up a bucket, shielding his face from the heat with one hand. The hall roof was ablaze, shedding fire like a deadly rain. Gunnor was dragging Wulfhild out of danger. The gable timbers were glowing. Before Ralph's eyes, they burst into flame. The whole roof sank inwards. The walls buckled. Wulfhild, in Gunnor's arms, was keening as though for a thousand dead. People had run from the village and bucketfuls of water were being hurled protectively on to the outbuildings. Alice, her singed hands wrapped in the remains of her shawl, was wielding a bucket, side by side with Harold. Ufi, dead-white behind his grime, leaning against the palisade and holding his burned arm away from his body, said through clenched teeth: 'Might save some of the other buildings. But the hall's done for.'

*

304

'We'll rebuild it, Mother,' Richard said. They stood, all of them, in a little, awed crowd, looking at the blackened and smouldering heap which that morning had been for most of them home. 'We've logs cut and ready. It's a mercy we have. We've caught the horses again and we're all alive . . .'

'Ufi's hurt.'

'I hope he'll recover. Alice was very quick. She got hurt herself, saving him.'

'Her! This is all her fault.' Wulfhild jabbed a gnarled finger at her daughter-in-law. 'She's destroyed my home. She doesn't destroy my daughter too, understand that. Sybil stays.'

'Sybil goes.' Ralph had never heard his friend use that tone before. Wulfhild's mouth half-opened and then she gasped as if cold water had been thrown over her. 'Keep her here after this?' said Richard. 'It's Ralph or a nunnery for her. Are you still mad enough to take her, Ralph? Sybil, stop that whining.'

'I'm mad enough. I'll take her.' He did not add *poor child*. He was thinking it, angrily.

'You!' Wulfhild rounded on him. He admired and now greatly pitied his future mother-in-law but the feeling would clearly never be reciprocated. 'Then you'll take her with what she stands up in, no more!' Wulfhild said venomously. 'All we've got, we need, after losing our cattle. There's nothing left for a portion.'

'I don't want a portion,' said Ralph stiffly.

'There'll be something,' said Richard. 'My sister will have a dowry of some kind, naturally. It's all right.' He smiled at Alice, who had made a worried exclamation. 'The taxes will be paid and we shall put our home together again. Everything will be done.' He drew his wife to him and put an arm round her.

'Yes, you'd see your home burn before you'd let go of her, wouldn't you?' Wulfhild's shawl was spattered with black flakes. The hard lines of her mouth wavered. 'You'll see your sister sold to a catamite and I don't doubt you'd see your own mother sold into slavery among the infidels, for *her* sake.'

'Just at the moment,' snapped Richard over Alice's head, 'yes, the infidels would be welcome to you!'

Wulfhild stared at them, seeing, as Ralph too could see, the magnetism that held them together, which had pulled them together in the first place and had never changed and never would. She said: 'I feel old . . .'

Four

The End of Childhood
1094

Sybil could not believe it was happening.

In a moment she would wake and be back in the familiar world where she was still a child and games were for playing. She said, or sobbed, over and over: 'It was only a game. I was only playing,' as though the words were a spell and enough repetition would work a miracle.

But the unbelievable continued to happen. The hall burned down before her eyes. The resthouses survived, and she was shut into one of them for two days. Gunnor brought her food from the village where the rest of the household had taken shelter, but would not look at her or speak to her. At the end of the two days, Alice came with a pitcher of cold water and a basin and the embroidered gown Sybil had worn at her betrothal feast, and ordered her to wash and dress. Then she was fetched, by a frigid and uncommunicative Richard, and taken to the church, where a priest she did not know, but whom she gathered was the new chaplain from Withysham, borrowed for this occasion, married her to the young man Ralph.

Ralph spoke to her kindly but she was too numb to respond. When the time came to say *I will* she wanted to say *I won't* but Richard was watching and she dared not. Her mother was not there. She did not see her mother until, after she had been given some food and had forced it down against a surge of queasiness, she was taken to a village cottage where Wulfhild was in bed.

'I don't want to go, don't make me go!' Sybil pleaded, clutching at her mother's hand. But Wulfhild only shook her head helplessly from side to side and Richard dragged her away.

A few minutes later, she was on her pony. Ralph was already mounted, with a pack mule on a leading rein. There was no awakening. She was to be cast out of her home, for ever. At the last moment Richard, a hand on

307

her pony's bridle, murmured a few words of wellwishing but she hardly took them in.

With the stranger Ralph des Aix, who was now her husband, she rode north on the London Road which slashed through Andred Forest. When they reached the town of Guildford, Ralph, who had all the while been trying to talk encouragingly to her, said that although it was called Guildford now, it had once been known as Gildenford, because the River Wey just there ran through meadows gilded in summer with kingcups. A famous massacre had taken place there, long ago, when her grandfather was a boy. Forlorn, she remembered that she must please this man because if she did not, she would be utterly friendless. So she tried to smile and even asked a question or two. But there was no heart in the attempt, which only made the misery within her grow deeper.

From Guildford, they turned west on the Winchester Road. The forest lay on their left, in alternate stretches of deep wood and wild gorse-grown heath. More open land, with farms and pastures, lay to the north. They lodged at abbeys on the way and at one were separated for the night. She was sorry, because Ralph, stranger though he was, was nevertheless familiar compared to the rest of what seemed an increasingly huge and frightening world. He had made no connubial demands on her yet and the warmth of his body at night was some kind of comfort.

On the third day they passed Winchester and now took a southward road, which Ralph said would bring them to his home, Chenna's Tun, that day.

Their destination. Where she was doomed to stay, for ever.

She could not even try to smile now. Seeing this, he told her rather shortly to lead the mule – 'it will give you something to do' – and rode ahead, his shoulders hunched in depression.

They rode for three hours or more on a wide road where the trees were cut well back on either side to make ambush by robbers less likely. Then they turned off to the right on a track which was broad and quiet but closely edged with trees. It was a little damp, dappled with sunlight through a roof of leaves, crossed here and there by the slots of deer or the padmarks of fox and weasel. Birds called. The trees were huge old oaks, with trunks as wide as church doors, and shadowed aisles led away between them into the deep woods.

It was beautiful. But with every stride her pony took, she could feel the miles lengthen behind her. She was in a stupor of wretchedness when they rode round a corner, at a walk, with the horses making little noise on the moist ground, and found themselves confronting three guilt-stricken men, who were in the act of crossing the track, with a deer's carcase carried between two of them.

'In hell's name!' said Ralph.

One of the men, through whom relief could be seen running as if through a conduit, said: 'It's you, sir!'

The three were roughly clad and even to Sybil's inexperienced eyes, looked underfed. The one who was not helping with the carcase, the one who had spoken, carried two bows and two quivers. Ralph said with fury: 'Are you all out of your wits? Walking about with a deer's carcase, on the track, in broad daylight? What do you think you're *doing*?'

'We were just getting home with it,' one of the men holding the deer said sullenly. He was flaxen-haired and squarely built despite his lack of spare flesh. Sybil could follow his speech though the accent was thick and different from that of Sussex. 'We didn't expect you to come round the corner. Foresters b'ain't here. They're all over to Lyndhurst. Damned old Forest Court's sitting. Forest Justice is round, passing judgement on some poor bastards.' He spat.

'Yes, poor bastards who've been as careless as you!' Sybil, listening in astonishment, realised that in the face of all probability, her husband Ralph, knight and Norman, was on the side of the poaching peasantry. Fallowdene was not under Forest Law but even there it was a crime to take a deer and Richard certainly accepted it as criminal. 'The Foresters have set traps before this,' Ralph was saying. 'They put it about that they'll be out of the district and then they turn up where they're not expected and that's the end of you. Do you think I want to come home and find my people mutilated?'

The man holding the other end of the deer was taller than his companions, and remarkable to look at, his hair so fair it was almost silver, and his eyes ice-green and narrow, in a high-cheekboned face as coldly refined as that of some Arctic god. He was young, with a cleanly male beauty beneath his grimy clothing but to Sybil he did not look quite human. He had glanced at her once, and the ice-coloured eyes had flashed appreciation, but she shrank from them. If one touched him, she thought, he would be cold and smooth, like marble.

He said, calmly: 'We've reasons. It's hunt now or starve in the winter. If you ride on to the fields, sir, you'll understand.'

Sybil expected Ralph to pursue the matter then and there, but he seemed at that moment to realise that the three pairs of eyes were continually flicking towards his companion. He turned instead to Sybil. 'I've brought my wife home. This is Sybil. She understands the business of Herne Huntsman. Sybil, these three are from the Tun. This is Osmund.' He pointed to the squarely built man. 'And this is Oswin, carrying all those illegal bows and arrows. And this –' he nodded towards the palehaired youth '– is Cild.' All three gravely bowed to her. Sybil inclined her head in acknowledgement. Cild's eyes made her uneasy again. She swallowed hard to quell the nausea which rose in her so easily, with this unfamiliar state called pregnancy. 'And now,' said Ralph, gathering up his reins, 'we will indeed ride on, and you can come with us, and we shall see what this mystery is all about. At a trot, if you please. Because the sooner your booty's out of sight, the better!'

When the path rounded a clump of barberry and emerged from the forest to the edge of a field, Sybil thought at first that the crop had been burnt. But there was no charred smell, no ash stirring in the faint wind; nor were the surrounding grass or forest touched. Ralph leant from the saddle and plucked a blackened stem. 'Wheat rust,' he said.

310

'Aye. We know about it. See it afore. Afore you come,' Oswin said.

Ralph's face was bleak. Abruptly, he said: 'We've come from Sussex. There's plague there. Have you had that too?'

'Aye. It's been an unlucky season,' Osmund said. 'Hunta's gone and his wife, and that sickly girl of theirs, and Blind Edric. And others.'

Cild, though burdened with the deer, shrugged. 'Means fewer mouths to feed.'

'Plague,' said Ralph bitterly. 'And bad weather two years out of three, and now this.'

'Father Ilger at Minstead's still on about sin and repentance,' said Osmund with derision. 'And about the heathen and the Holy Sepulchre. Says he's sure the world will end with the century if the world don't mend its ways.' His voice acquired a mocking note. ' "What more can we expect, my friends, when the king hisself is no better a Christian than the blackest-souled infidel?" Why we have to pay for what kings do, he don't explain, and the heathen have been around for a good while – what makes them such an outrage all of a sudden? We'd take it more kindly if he'd tell us how to feed ourselves this winter. Since he hasn't, we've thought it out for ourselves. If there's deermeat in the barrels, we can sell the calfmeat to pay the taxes and buy grain, and pay the smith over at Minstead. I broke my ploughshare, trying to sneak a bit of extra land ready for next season. But we can get by, if we poach a bit.'

'But do it so that you don't get caught,' said Ralph. 'All right. Get that deer indoors, cut up, and the head and hoofs and skin buried. Off with you, now.' He watched them go and said to Sybil: 'We call Osmund, Osmund the Clumsy. He would break his ploughshare. Of course.'

Sybil managed a smile this time, but misery had engulfed her once more. She had been wretched all the way here because she had lost her home. She had given little thought to what her new one might actually be like. Neither at Fallowdene nor Withysham had she ever actually been hungry. Was she, then, to be hungry here? There were habitations in the distance but even the largest

311

of them looked like a hovel. Would she have to live in such a place? Even as she was thinking that, Ralph pointed to the bigger dwelling, which stood apart from the rest. 'That's our home,' he said cheerfully.

A few minutes later she stood, clutching her saddlebag, inside the dwelling and misery became despair. Even at Withysham, there had been plaster and murals on some of the stone walls. At Fallowdene and even in Little Dene which should have been her married home, there had been cheerful hangings. She looked about her, at the bare earthen floor, the grimy leather curtains, a pile of droppings which made it plain that goats sometimes shared this roof. She took in Ralph's spartan, soldierly bedstead, at the moment not even graced with a pallet. Her eyes found the shelf with its few earthenware pots, the one dented iron cauldron, the disused loom in a corner, the cobwebs under the thatch.

She sat down on the floor and the tears she had held back since she parted from her mother burst uncontrollably out of her. 'I want to go home!' wept Sybil.

Ralph was kind, although with impatience only just below the surface. He found rugs and a pallet somewhere and settled her on the bed, saying she would feel better when she had rested.

He went out, and came back with some firewood. He laid and lit the fire, deftly, and presently an old woman from one of the other houses came in with some food. Ralph said her name was Elfgiva and that she was Cild's mother. She studied Sybil curiously. She heated broth and they all ate some, accompanied by chunks of bread. Sybil went back to the pallet and tried to sleep. Later, Ralph joined her and with urgent caresses made it plain that he wished to exercise his conjugal rights.

This was not as it had been in the woods with Bruno or in the stable with Ralph himself. There was no playfulness, no excitement, it had nothing to do with her own wishes. This was an uninvited demand by one who had the right to demand. She lay passive, accepting him without pleasure, unable in her pit of wretchedness to make the least response. She could not see his face in the darkness but she knew that he was trying to shake her out of her inertia, that there was anger in his thrusts. But eventually it was over. He shifted off her and lay still with his back to her. He said nothing at all. After a time, she fell into an exhausted sleep.

She woke at daybreak to a dull, clenching pain in the lower abdomen and a warm wetness oozing between her thighs. She prodded Ralph, who woke with a questioning grunt. Mutely she pushed back the rugs.

'Hell!' shouted Ralph, on a note equally of alarm and aversion as he saw the scarlet stain. He leapt off the bed and began scrambling into his clothes. 'Put a cloth pad on and lie still till I get back!'

'Where are you going?'

'To fetch Elfgiva. She'll know what to do.'

'There'll be others. She's young yet. It happens, you know. Happened to me a time or two. Had a long ride, hasn't she? That didn't do no good,' Elfgiva said reprovingly to Ralph. Sybil was asleep, lulled by a herbal brew Elfgiva had made. 'It came away quick. Let her lie up a few days and there'll be no harm done. She ought to have summat hot when she wakes. That stew, in that pot?'

Ralph sat by the fire, hands hanging betwen his knees. 'Yes, I killed a hen. No good worrying yet how we're going to get through the winter . . . I should never have brought her here. It was more than the journey, Elfgiva. She's homesick, ill with it. I can't do anything with her. I meant well. I . . . I fell in love with her. She put a spell on me, almost. And if I hadn't married her, I'd have left her to . . .' He stopped and stared at the floor.

'You've told us she knows about Herne. So Cild says. That right?' Elfgiva picked up a spoon and stirred the stew.

'More or less. She's still to be initiated but . . .'

'That child she's lost, was it yours or a Child of the Wood?'

'Neither, really.' Ralph put his head in his hands and pummelled his skull. Father Ilger at Minstead might raise his hands in horror at the lax goings on of his flock – he knew little for sure concerning the Wood but guessed

313

plenty – but the truth was that the people of the Tun were strict in their everyday behaviour. The Wood was a rite, and separate. He raised his head and found Elfgiva regarding him with an all too knowing expression.

'Slipped up, did she? And her family threw her out?'

'She's barely more than a child and a priest took advantage of her. See here, Elfgiva, I want no one at the Tun pointing fingers at the past. Gossip about this, say one word of this to the other women when you're all chattering round the well, and I'll silence you myself, for good.'

'I shan't talk, what do you take me for?' Elfgiva was offended. 'Seen a thing or two in my time, I have. It's the young who have stiff ideas, not us old ones. We know too much. But I'll tell you one thing. I've never seen anyone die of homesickness. You're worried about her, ain't you? Don't be. She'll be all right. I'll try to get her out of it. Shame about the baby,' she added. 'That would have given her somewhere to put herself, if you follow me. The sooner she has another, the better.' She chuckled and stirred the stew again. 'You ought to have some of this. Keep your strength up.'

Spent and defenceless, like an archer who on the battlefield has used up all his shafts, Sybil lay on the pallet. It was as though in thrusting the child out of her body, she had made her last attempt to thrust away the horrible reality of Chenna's Tun. Now she had nothing left to fight with. She looked at the cobwebby rafters and the dirty leather curtain and tried to believe that they were dimming, fading, that she was slipping away through her weakness, into death.

Unfortunately, nothing of the kind was happening. She felt better than she had yesterday. Apparently, one couldn't die to order.

The curtain was swept back and Elfgiva came through with a bowl. 'Got some nice hot stew here with a little bit of venison in it but don't mention that if the Foresters come round. Now, you're going to eat this, my girl.' Elfgiva winked at her, put an arm under her shoulders and sat her up. If she refused to eat as she had yesterday, Sybil thought, she would certainly achieve a step in the direction of death. But the smell of the food was enticing. Elfgiva thrust a spoon into her hand. She sat doubtfully clutching it, staring at the bowl beside her.

'Eat. Make more blood. You may as well,' said Elfgiva. 'You will in the end. I know what's wrong with you, girl. You want to go home. Well, you can't. But you're going to go on living, whether you like it or not. Now eat!'

Sybil slowly took a spoonful. With luck, she'd just throw it all up later. Her body would take the decision for her and starve itself to death, she thought hopefully.

But the tendency to nausea had vanished with the pregnancy. Her stomach, exasperatingly, wrapped itself round the offering and growled for more. Elfgiva watched with approval while Sybil slowly and dismally consumed the entire bowlful. Then she said: 'I know. I can guess, anyhow. I've lived all my life at the Tun and wouldn't be anywhere else. An' my husband – he got killed at Hastings or leastways he never came back – he was born here too. When the fyrd was called out and all the men as could bear weapons had to go to help King Harold, I can mind on my husband, just settin' off to the muster at Minstead, saying: "It ain't the fighting, I'll fight same as the next man but I wish I could fight for my home here *at* home; I don't want to die in some strange place." But he had to all the same, and there's times, in the night, I feel sick with thinking about him dying far away, maybe not as quick as he'd have liked, wanting his home and me. I never knew just what happened to him, you see. A few men got back of those from hereabouts but they'd no news of him . . . well, there it is, don't think no one knows how it is with you but don't go thinking anyone can make magic for you either. You're here and here you'll stay. So what're you going to do about it?'

Sybil stared at her, spoon in mid-air. Until now, Elfgiva had been merely an old villein woman of no status, a grimy crone, a shawl-wrapped bundle smelling of sweat and onions, with hands like bundles of sticks in bags of wrinkled skin, knotted together with veins. Now, Sybil looked at her and saw a person, separate from all others, capable of grief and loss.

315

And capable of surviving them. The possibility of survival existed, then. The feeling that ahead of her lay a blank wall into which she was running headlong, very slightly subsided.

'Take it one day at a time,' said Elfgiva. 'When you wake in the morning, don't look beyond nightfall. You could do with company too. All the women are wild to see you. Soon as you're up, you'll be with us. It won't be so bad, you'll see. I don't say life won't be hard. You saw the wheat. We're in for a rough winter. But . . .'

'Oh!' Sybil shoved the bowl at her and tried to get out of bed. 'I forgot!'

Elfgiva pushed her back. 'Keep your feet up. I don't want you bleeding again. What did you forget?'

'It's in my saddlebag, on the floor. Where's . . . my husband?'

'Here.' Ralph ducked through the curtain. 'I've just got back from Minstead. I've been trying to buy grain. Did you call me?'

'My saddlebag!' Sybil insisted. He brought it and she scrabbled in it, bringing out a leather pouch. 'Richard gave me this, just as we were leaving.' She glanced up at Ralph. *Those eyes go through me,* he thought. *If only she were older, or the Tun were different . . .*

'. . . just as we were leaving,' Sybil said, 'he whispered goodbye and said you'd refused to take any dowry with me beyond the pony I rode here on and the pack mule, but that he didn't think . . . don't be angry, please, I couldn't say no, could I? . . . he pushed this into my saddlebag and said there was silver in it . . .'

Ralph and Elfgiva both grabbed for the pouch together. 'Hands off, it's mine,' said Ralph, knocking her hand away but grinning at Elfgiva as though she were his sister. He undid the drawstring and the contents fell out on to the floor. All three of them stared at the result, slowly taking in its implications. 'There's enough there,' said Ralph in a hushed voice at last, 'to buy grain for half a year, for every soul in the Tun. I couldn't get any for love nor money in Minstead – they've lost half theirs as well – but I can try other places, maybe even get some to help Minstead out too. Angry! No, Sybil, of course not. You . . . you've

316

saved us, don't you understand? We won't be hungry here this winter, now.'

'Reckon *that* needn't be secret,' Elfgiva remarked. She picked up the empty bowl and spoon and went out. Ralph came to the bed and put his hands on Sybil's shoulders. 'My love. It's strange and hard and lonely here, I know. But it will get better. I'll look after you. It's all I want to do, don't you know that? Try to grow up, my darling, and then you'll see. Only, you must grow up.' His fingers hardened. 'You'll have to come with us to the Wood, and the Wood's not what you think. This is important, I may as well choose now for saying it. It's not a game for children. We go to the Wood to buy Herne's favour and the dear knows, in times like these, we need it. What we do in the Wood is real; we dare not withhold one single thing which may win the goodwill of the Huntsman. We can afford not even one reluctant or self-regarding thought. I'd save you from all the pains in the world, my sweet, and I love you so much that it's torment for me to think of another man with you. But although the thought agonises me, and although I am very much afraid that the Worship will agonise you, that you will detest it, I cannot protect either you or myself when we go to the Wood. Sybil, dear heart, your childhood is over.'

'Worth that much?' Wulfhild stared from the box of orange-yellow stigmas in Richard's hand, to Richard himself and then to Alice and her father Roland. 'This stuff – saffron – is worth *that much*? Fifteen shillings the ounce, like gold?'

'I told Richard at the start that it was worth its weight in gold,' said Roland. 'He didn't realise I meant it literally.'

'It doesn't matter that we've used the last of our timber for the new hall,' said Richard gently. 'We're still well off. You'll be under your own roof again by Christmas, Mother, with new furnishings, and silver in the coffer for next year's taxes, and no anxieties at all. As if the fire had never been.'

'Except for Ufi!' Wulfhild glowered at Alice. 'Very touching how you wept and turned sick when we had to take his arm off. But for you, he'd still have it. You'll

317

never sell this saffron stuff, Richard. Who'll buy, at that price?'

'The court,' said Roland, 'and some of the great lords. Richard knows who to get in touch with at Westminster and I can give him other names. I haven't been able to get supplies for three years now so he'll have no competition from me. Not that I'd have given him any, over this. I want him to do well from this, for Alice's sake.'

'The fire was Sybil's fault. And yours,' said Alice to her mother-in-law.

They were in Swithin's farmstead at Westwater. Camping in Fallowdene village and in their resthouses had proved extremely cramped, and Swithin had welcomed their company, since the pestilence had taken his family. It was he who now saw that this latest news, good though it was, had seriously shaken Wulfhild, who had come to Westwater in a state of collapse to begin with. He steered her to a stool. Richard, only meaning well, anxious to persuade his mother to put her worries aside and to see Alice in a kindlier light, rubbed it in. 'We owe it all to my marriage, Mother. There's eleven ounces there and next year we'll double that at least. We'll do very well. Isn't it wonderful?'

'I think our luck's changed,' Alice agreed.

She did not actually say *because Sybil's gone*. But the words hung in the air. It was at that moment that Wulfhild began to die.

At All Hallows, Sybil went with Ralph to the Wood for the first time. Man and woman did not come together at this festival, for this was the celebration of the dying year.

At All Hallows, instead of the dance and the lovemaking, they sacrificed a goat, giving its blood to the earth to make the next spring fruitful. Sybil sat on the log throne beside her husband, naked, shuddering, in the autumn cold, despite the fire. It was a good one. Cutting wood was normally forbidden in the forest but the charcoal burners had a dispensation – or the king's hunting lodges would have gone short of kitchen fuel – and the Purkisses always placed good firewood in the

318

right clearings at the right time. But even their best efforts left Sybil trembling. Though not only with cold.

She watched Ralph step forward to slaughter the goat and saw the firelight gleam on the polished tips of his antler crown. She smelt the blood and heard the half-man, half-beast, with her husband's voice, pray aloud to Herne Huntsman to defend them from disease and famine, to avert the end of the world which she had heard the Minstead priest declare was imminent. 'Herne who this year has hunted so many souls to oblivion, do not hunt ours . . .'

She saw him come back to the throne, the bloody knife still in his hand, the blood crusted under his nails and splashed over the moles on his chest. He sat down beside her, knife laid across his knees, as alien, as dangerous, as though the antlers were truly growing out of his brow, as though Herne Huntsman to whom he had prayed had indeed come down and entered him.

At Candlemas it was worse, for at Candlemas she was initiated.

She had found her place in the Tun by then. Living as Elfgiva had said, one day at a time, she had managed, and the folk of the Tun themselves had tried to help. Normally clannish and distant with outsiders, they had nevertheless recognised her as their King's choice and besides, her dowry was getting them through this winter. She was good luck. And she had no airs, she didn't swank because she was pretty. She was a poor, homesick, woebegone thing and only young, so they tried to amuse her with talk of their private jokes and quarrels. She on her side, trying to let herself be distracted, had duly clicked her tongue over the way Leoba Huntasdaughter nagged her husband Oswin, had laughed at pop-eyed Penna's earnestness, made fun with the rest of Clumsy Osmund's eternal state of war with the world of inanimate objects.

But masked and animal-headed in the Wood, they lost all appearance of familiarity; their presence could not comfort her. And in the shadows away from the fire, by the command of her husband, of all people, she must let an unknown animal-man possess her.

As King, Ralph had the right to claim her on her initiation night but he had waived it, a sacrifice to Herne, he said, because of the hard times. She was sick afterwards, there in the clearing, and the women gathered round full of jocular remarks. They thought she was with child again.

Sybil knew otherwise. It was because she was sure, almost sure, that the man in the shadows had been Cild, who had so often stared at her, and whom she loathed – with good reason, she now knew.

As a child at Withysham, she had prayed to Herne. And now Herne had come for her.

Five

Warnings
1094–6

Rufus came home in the winter and Ralph was summoned to the court at Southampton but not to meet the king. He saw Rufus only occasionally while he was there, at a distance, going about his royal business in a cloud of splendidly dressed dignitaries. They came close enough to speak only once. 'Ah, Ralph, back again? Keeping well? I hear you've got married,' said Rufus, *en passant* in a doorway, and that was all.

Nobles who had once passed the time of day with him, ignored him or else made pointed observations. Meulan, who had always been jealous, said: 'So you've reappeared. You must notice a lot of changes since you were last at court.'

But the man he had been summoned to see was Croc.

'There's a job for you. There's a disused 'unting lodge a mile from your 'olding. A place called Malwood.'

'Yes, Ru . . . the king used to say it was a dirty, cramped hole, no good, *mal*. That's how it got its name. What about it?'

''E wants it cleaned and made fit to use again. Refurnished, stables and kennels repaired, staff 'ired, arrowsmiths and blacksmiths prepared to serve. You've a free 'and within reason and there's money ready for the work.'

'Very well.' Ralph paused. 'The king – how is he?'

Croc's glance was half shrewd, half commiserating. 'Lively as a flea. Came back with a trophy, did you know?'

'Helias of Maine's head? Helias is running Maine now, isn't he?'

'Rufus never got to Maine. Fell out with Curt'ose as soon as 'e landed. I was there, waiting to witness a charter. Curt'ose accused Rufus of being tardy and Rufus got so wild he tore up their treaty. *Really* tore it up,' said Croc with enjoyment. 'Sent for 'is copy of it and slashed

321

the parchment up then and there. Next thing we knew, we were fighting Curt'ose instead of Maine, though it come to nothing, just fizzled. But none of that's important. I was talking about 'is trophy. Count 'Enry.'

'Henry's made peace?'

'Bought it. Money talks, with Rufus. You ought to know that,' said Croc. ''Enry seems to 'ave been quite a success as a robber baron. 'E 'ad enough to settle accounts with Rufus, anyhow. 'E's here now. They're going about arm in arm and loving as twins or more or less. Don't know that I 'aven't seen a funny considering look on 'Enry's face once or twice but . . .'

'Why did he want to make peace?'

Once he wouldn't have had to ask Croc. Once, Rufus would have told him, in the deeps of the night, and Ralph would have admired the bargain he had struck and they would have laughed over it. He did not want to share Rufus' bed again. He had Sybil now, still childish and prone to fits of grief for her home but coming round. Yet still . . . he dragged his mind back to Croc, who was answering him.

'You 'eard Belleme's father died?'

'Yes.'

'Well, 'is sons didn't waste much time on filial mourning, not that lot. Belleme started fighting one of 'is brothers for their daddy's possessions in Normandy and 'Enry found 'imself kind of pig-in-the-middle. Belleme and 'is brother were each saying, "Join me!" and threatening to carve 'im up for dinner if 'e didn't. They were both bigger than 'e was. So 'e sold out to Rufus.'

'Why not to Curthose?'

'Probably reckoned Rufus is more reliable. Or less likely to marry and get 'imself an heir. If you ask me, 'Enry's got 'is eye on that position. That's what I meant by a considerin' look . . . 'eard about Flambard?' Croc added, with a sudden change of subject.

'No, what about him?'

'Well, 'e escaped all right, trust 'im. But 'e got kidnapped, and bloody nearly murdered.'

'I told you so,' said Flambard's mother grimly to her son. 'There's danger abroad, I said. Next time maybe you'll heed.'

322

'I wasn't hurt, Mother.'

'No, talked your way out of trouble as usual. You scared 'em green, saying what the king would do to 'em if they killed you and he caught them. That ain't the point. What is the point is that what I saw in the scrying bowl come true. Well, I saw danger to you, and there's *more danger about* and this time it's not to you, it's to the king. You could see the signs yourself if you'd look . . .'

'What signs?'

'*I* don't know, you're the one what knows about the things that go on in the court and round it. But signs there must be if you'll only search for 'em. Just little, maybe, like tiny islands sticking out of smiling water. But under the surface the slopes go down, son, down to where it's dark and cold as death and there's monsters with shapes no one knows . . .'

'I wish I knew what you were talking about, Mother.'

'And I wish you'd get it through your head that what I'm saying is, I was right this time and I might be right next time too. I say there's danger to the king and you're near enough to do something, maybe. That's what I'm saying.'

Flambard sighed. He never forgot his mother's struggle to rear and educate himself and his brothers against the wind, but at the moment such deplorable phrases as *superstitious old hag* kept forming themselves in his mind.

His mother eyed him knowingly. He had an uncomfortable feeling that she had somehow heard the unsaid words.

'Pity you didn't let him marry,' she said.

When in Winchester, Rufus had a wide choice of places in which to stay, but the choice nearly always fell on the new palace which his father had built in the centre, just south of the main street. It was roomier than the functional fortress in the south-west corner, and with its stone walls and touch of Byzantine in the architecture, it was more dignified to the Norman mind than the timber English palace on the north side of the city.

It possessed a lesser hall, for less formal audiences. Occasions such as the meeting held privately between Rufus and his Archbishop of Canterbury, in the May of 1095.

323

'You wanted a private talk, you said. Do you mean you want to preach at me again?' asked Rufus.

'No, my lord, there would be no point,' said Anselm. 'Although I wish you understood that when I preach as you call it, I do it only out of my care for your well-being. Once, you cried out to me for help. If only you know how glad I would be to help you again.'

'Get to the point.'

The Archbishop sighed. 'You hardly make that easy, my lord. You invent quarrels with me. We quarrel over which of two contending Popes to recognise, over the details of how I am to have papal confirmation of my position. I find these things distracting and I suspect that you intend them to be . . .'

'We did an excellent deal with your pet candidate.' Rufus was wearing his naughty-boy expression. 'He paid up like a lamb for the privilege of confirming you as Archbishop. I imagine he thinks that means I've recognised him. I haven't. I nearly levered you out over that,' he added thoughtfully, 'but it was more profitable to let you stay.'

'Your baronage wouldn't let you throw me out, when it came to it.' Anselm regarded him quietly out of eyes in which mildness and implacability were curiously blended. Rufus glowered at him but did not speak. 'You like to pretend,' said Anselm, 'that nothing matters to you but money. You used that pretence to save your face on that occasion. You did a deal with Urban, as you put it, and claimed that you preferred the proceeds to the relief of getting rid of me. No, it isn't easy for me to talk to you and when you hear what I have to say, you will very likely wish to rid yourself of me even more than you do now. But it is my business as Archbishop of Canterbury to safeguard both the health of the king's soul and the spiritual health of the realm and I say to you that both are in danger. Will you let me advise you?'

'What are you talking about?'

'I am trying to warn you, as a matter of urgency, that there is trouble brewing in your realm.'

'What kind of trouble?'

'The land has been for too long tormented by bad

weather and worse crops, and by sickness and also, my lord, by extreme taxation. In such circumstances, people look for somewhere to place the blame.'

'It shouldn't be a long search,' said Rufus. 'These things are in God's hands, as you priests are for ever telling us.'

'Taxation isn't in God's hands,' said Anselm grimly. 'As for the others, to most men, God is invisible, remote. Men look for a scapegoat they can see.'

'Are you trying,' said Rufus after a pause, 'to warn me of a rising?'

'Yes. A court that ravages the land like an invading army wherever it goes is liable to breed insurrection even without storms and plagues. The barons themselves are complaining. Damage done to their peasantry echoes back to them. With the disastrous harvests and the sickness added, I should say the outcome is almost inevitable. And the signs are there,' said Anselm with emphasis. 'Your adviser Ranulf Flambard was almost murdered recently because he is seen as your right hand and the author of much misery.'

'Poor old Flambard.' Rufus chuckled. 'Kidnapped, taken out to sea and told he was going over the side with weights on his feet. But he told them what I'd do to them when they were caught and they put him ashore all in one piece. There are still a good many men too afraid of me to rise against me, Anselm.'

'Are there enough, I wonder? My lord, will you hear my advice?'

'I have a feeling that I'm going to hear it anyway. It may as well be now. Proceed.'

'It isn't new advice,' said Anselm. 'But it's urgent now, a matter of the realm's safety as well as your own salvation. Reduce taxes. Regulate the behaviour of your court – all aspects of it. And reconsider the matter of marriage so that a secure future can be assured for us all by the birth in due course of an unquestionable successor. I don't suggest Edith of Scotland this time. She is in England still but as it is possible that she has worn the veil, she can't now be considered suitable. However, there are other ladies . . .'

'What lady in her right mind would have me? And what father in his senses would commit his daughter to me?'

'You undervalue yourself,' said Anselm, suddenly compassionate. 'And for all your self-mockery and your apparent pride in your wrongdoing, I think at heart you are lonely and feel cut off from other men, and from women. A wife might heal you.'

'I might be the ruin of her.'

'You bewilder me.' Anselm shook his head wearily. 'That a man can prefer other men . . . if you graze two stallions in a field together they don't mount each other. A stallion only becomes excited when he sees a mare. This thing is unnatural, my lord. If you could only tear it out of yourself . . .'

'Well, I can't.'

'Then God preserve you.' Anselm rose, shaking his head. 'Have I your leave to go?'

'You have indeed.' Compassion had been a mistake; Rufus had flushed in resentment. He sat in his chair with his knees apart, palms resting upon them. 'Understand this, Anselm. I rule here, no one else. Not you, not any of my barons. Anyone who starts an insurrection will be very s . . .sorry. Now stop prophesying doom and trying to save my s . . . soul. It's beyond redemption,' said Rufus with a grin.

Anselm sighed, folding his hands into the sleeves of the embroidered Archbishop's robe which was much too ornate for his taste, and went out, down a flight of steps, and out of doors, into the open air. He wanted the freshness of air and wind to blow away the cloud of hopelessness which had settled on him, and the sick spiritual smell of corruption.

But he was careful of his Archbishop's panoply, even though he disliked it, and he did not linger outside, for once again, it was pouring with rain.

It was in the November of the next year, just as Rufus was putting down the revolt among his barons which Anselm had foretold, that Pope Urban, after a long and truly sorrowful contemplation of a Europe racked by bitter winters and soaking summers and the misery of hunger and disease which these things inevitably bred, climbed into the pulpit of Clermont-Ferrand cathedral, looked down at the distinguished congregation afforded by a full-scale Papal Council, and then, repeating with authority what many priests were already saying without it, announced that the sins of men had now piled so high that the end of the century would surely mean the end of the world unless they bestirred themselves to set things right.

Let them repent, he said, and go forth to right the greatest wrong of all and pray that God in His mercy would allow them in so doing to ransom themselves from the consequences of all other sins.

Let them go forth to the Holy Land and set free the Holy Sepulchre from the hands of the infidel.

The response was immediate and huge, like the waves rolling outwards from a submarine earthquake.

They deposited Normandy, like a piece of gigantic and valuable flotsam, on King Rufus' personal beach.

And then, as though the earthquake had been accompanied by storms, both Rufus and his brother Henry were smitten, lightning-blasted, into love.

PART V

IN WHICH LIGHTNING STRIKES TWICE
1096–1098 AD

One

Count and Lady
1096

Archbishop Anselm, not one of those who believed in the imminent end of the world, and strongly of the opinion that a land still shuddering from a barely-crushed baronial revolt needed to retain all the spiritual guides it could, not to mention the lawkeeping abilities of its most honest magnates and their knights, had already, and passionately, made his views clear.

But the news of the crusade was nevertheless humming round England as the appalling winter of 1095 and 1096 crawled miserably towards an overdue spring. In Romsey, it caught the Abbess Christina's imagination.

'As it chances, we have nearly completed a beautiful illuminated copy of Bede's Ecclesiastical History,' she informed her nuns. 'It was meant for our own library but now we shall sell it. We shall also turn to at once and make a new copy of Asser's Life of King Alfred, also to be illuminated, and penned in our most elegant Carolingian book-hand. Our abbey is not poor and we shall of course send a straightforward donation as well – but would it not be wonderful, my daughters, if through the work of our own hands, we could contribute a little band of knights, with their horses and armour and mounted squires? They would carry our badge into battle. We must go about it so that toil and devotion take the place of expenditure on raw materials wherever possible. We have ample vellum in stock, but what we use, we must replace this year from the skins of calves reared on the abbey estates. We must mix all our own ink and gather as many of the ingredients for ourselves as we can, not take the easy way and buy them in. We must . . .'

Winters in Romsey were not as bad as those in Inverness, but this one, thought Edith, was bad enough. There was a heavy snowfall in March. Mixing ink, therefore, though messy and apt to smell peculiar, was a task

331

with compensations. The black ink was made with bark and galls gathered from trees in the nearby woods and crushed with a pestle, while the red ink needed beaten egg. Crushing and beating were energetic and kept one warm. In addition, before being finally mixed with iron salts, gum arabic and some sour wine condemned as unfit for drinking, the crushed bark and gall had to be thoroughly boiled. The little stone workroom with the vaulted ceiling and the narrow windows filled with green-tinged glass had a fire. Edith and the two nuns assigned with her to the work, pounded, whisked, boiled and strained in an atmosphere cheerful with steam and firelight.

'It's fortunate that we have sufficient galls and things in hand,' young Sister Lucy remarked, stoking the fire, while Edith's pestle steadily thudded. 'I wouldn't care to be out in the woods just now. I heard a wolf last night.' She shivered. 'It was a long way off, but still . . .'

Edith had heard it too, a distant howl like grey smoke wreathing upwards to the frosty moon. Unlike Sister Lucy, she had not been afraid. The sound had excited her with its wildness and its desire. A cuckoo, a nightingale, a wolf . . . strange, even wondrous, that they could all call the selfsame echo out of her soul.

Because of that echo, her brown hair was still unveiled and uncut, in swinging braids. Her aunt had not yet renewed her campaign to make a nun of Edith. Edith had felt Christina's eyes on her many times; the campaign was not ended. As yet, nothing had happened, but she was still vulnerable, only fifteen. And Christina, she suspected, to use a warriorlike turn of phrase such as might have appealed to King Malcolm, was waiting for a good opening. There were times when Edith secretly quailed after catching her aunt's eye and wondered, as she had at Vespers just after her return to Romsey, whether she would not do best simply to give in.

But she hadn't quite come to it yet. Not yet. It was as though she, too, were waiting . . .

'This lot is ready to strain now,' said the elderly Sister Winefred, peering into the pan. She set the iron mesh strainer over an earthenware bowl. 'Bring it here, Sister

332

Lucy. Sister Lucy, why are you cocking your head to one side like that? Have you heard another wolf?'

'No, Sister. I thought I heard a man's voice,' said Sister Lucy.

'Is there much difference?' Sister Winefred never hesitated to tell anyone who would listen that she had entered religion because she preferred to take orders from an abbess who had earned the right to give them, rather from some man who imagined that authority came with masculinity like the mane on a horse, no matter how stupid or ignorant he might be. 'Bring that pan here, I said. And Edith, would you . . . Edith, where are you going?'

'We need some more firewood and some more of that sour wine,' said Edith breathlessly, and also cunningly providing herself with a double errand by way of ensuring that she had at least a single one.

'We've enough wine, what are you talking about? Firewood . . . well, presently perhaps, but . . .'

'Now,' said Edith decisively, and was gone.

The workroom door opened onto a paved courtyard round which various functional buildings stood. The kitchen and buttery were nearby. Edith ran into the kitchen, waved away the noisesome steam from her face – one of the Lenten meals of salt fish was being cooked – and found the Sister in charge. 'We need another jug of that bad red wine and some wood . . . oh, Sister, I am so very sorry to bother you when you're so busy.'

She was in luck.

When visitors came, refreshments were usually served and a tray was being assembled now, and with the best silver cups and dishes at that. 'Is that for the guest room? Can I take it in for you? To make up for being a nuisance?' She gave the Sister a most winning smile and received one back; most of the nuns liked Edith.

'That's thoughtful of you. Someone'll run along to the workroom with your firewood and that while you're seeing to this. Mind your manners, now. The guest's someone important.'

'I can see that,' said Edith, indicating the silver, and with thumping heart took up the tray.

She went out of the door on the far side of the kitchen, not into the courtyard but into the snow-covered grassy space in front of the guest house. The workroom had windows looking that way, too. It was through these that that resonant male voice, so startlingly familiar although she had only heard it once, had come. She bore the tray across the snow, indifferent to the chill of it through her soft shoes, knocked and went in.

And stood for a moment transfixed, because she had been completely mistaken. The man talking to Abbess Christina was not Rufus. She would have laid her hand on a pile of saints' bones and sworn that the voice had been his, but this was someone much younger, still surely in his twenties, with black hair, cut short although a lock of it was tumbling into his brown eyes, and a strong, square, tanned face.

He smiled at her appreciatively, however, as ignoring her aunt's what-on-earth-are-you-doing-here? eyebrows, she poured wine and handed him cakes. He was certainly important, even if he wasn't Rufus. Edith's eye, practised in these matters as the eye of a princess was bound to be, took in the extreme fineness of his mulberry-coloured wool tunic and the fact that the clasp of his fashionably short blue cloak was solid gold set with amethysts and garnets. She wanted to know who he was. She therefore curtsied gracefully as she gave him his goblet and said boldly: 'Edith of Scotland at your service, sir.'

'My God, I wish you were,' said the young man sincerely, and with the freedom of one who is used to speaking his mind.

In tones of steel, Abbess Christina said: 'This is Count Henry, brother of the king.' That explained it. Brothers, with different faces but the same voice. 'You will be interested in his purpose here.' The steel now had an edge on it. 'He comes from Normandy with the news that Robert Duke of Normandy will take part in the crusade and will gladly accept our abbey's contribution. The ink you should at this moment be making is for the books which will provide part of that contribution.'

'I'm a double courier as it were,' said Count Henry. 'I bear letters both to Mother Abbess and to my brother the

334

king. I am delighted to meet you, Lady Edith. I am rewarded for humbling myself to be a messenger. Please take some wine with me.'

Abbess Christina's expression verged on the murderous. There might well be retribution after Count Henry had gone. Nevertheless Edith was obliged to repress a giggle before saying gravely: 'But my lord, there are only two goblets.'

'Share mine,' said Henry gallantly, holding it out to her. His brown eyes danced. With a surge of wonder, for the first time Edith became aware of possessing power. She could almost see herself reflected in those eyes; a little flushed from her run to the kitchen and her cold walk across the snow with the tray, her brown hair smooth and shining (how fortunate that she had washed it only two days ago). She took the cup and sipped, and smiled back at Henry.

She recognised his breed. There were hard lines already in his face; he had had to fight for survival and he had learned how to be ruthless. But her father had been like that; it was something she understood. Her father had loved and protected her mother all the more for his ability to fight mercilessly against other men. And she was her father's daughter. She was attracted, not repelled.

But Aunt Christina was glowering at her and Count Henry wouldn't stay long. He couldn't protect her once he was out of sight. She gave the cup back to him and shook her head gently. 'I must go back to my work now, my lord. I am happy to have met you. The work goes well, Mother Abbess. The scribes won't be delayed for lack of ink.' She curtsied and smiled again and her eyes said to Henry: come back if you can. Gracefully, she left.

'I'm so sorry,' she said meekly to Abbess Christina later, standing with downcast eyes in order that her aunt should not see the wild dancing in them. 'But what could I do? I went to the kitchen for some things we needed and offered to carry the tray to help Sister. And then . . .' Planning her defence, while pounding bark, she had been visited by inspiration. '. . . he seemed a very bold man. I was a little afraid of what he might say. I thought it best just to tell him who I was. I had to drink from his cup

335

when he gave it to me. It wouldn't have been polite to refuse. I am sorry if I did wrong.'

'No,' said Abbess Christina unwillingly, eyeing her niece with extreme suspicion. 'I can't say that you did wrong.' If the child were truly as innocent as she appeared, it would be a mistake to say anything which might disturb that innocence. If only one could be sure that it existed to start with. 'We'll say no more about it,' said the abbess, cautiously.

In seven days, Henry was back.

'He wishes to talk to you privately. He has a message for you from some member of your family, I understand,' said Christina. 'I shall of course be in the room though not within hearing. Count Henry has never been reported as misbehaving himself with ladies in public. But I will be there.'

'A message from my family?' Edith asked when she was face to face with Henry, the obligatory tray of refreshments between them, this time officially for her to share. Joyously she studied his face, filling in the details of the image which she had held in her mind throughout all the intervening week.

'No,' said Henry. 'I just wanted to see you again. We'll have to invent a message. Your brother King Edgar of Scotland is well, recognised by my brother King William, and on excellent terms with him, but I suppose you know all that. You could say that although your brother does not yet summon you home, he wants you to know you're not forgotten and he hopes to see you in Scotland one day. I expect he would send you a message like that if he'd happened to think of it.'

'Yes, I'll say that. It might be a good thing. Aunt Christina would like me to become a proper nun. It might be as well if she thinks my brother is against it, as my father was. You say you came only because . . .'

'I have to go back to Normandy soon, with the king's answer to Duke Robert. But I had to come here first. I think when I came before, the abbess was angry with you. I wanted to make sure you were all right.'

'She told me I was forward,' said Edith candidly. 'But that's nothing, with her.'

'Oh? And what, with Mother Abbess, amounts to *something*? Tell me.'

She found herself answering, telling him of the old struggle between herself and her aunt over the veil. Henry, listening, was gripped with an astonishing mixture of indignation, pity, and sheer admiration. He had been, a week ago, extraordinarily moved by the sight of this vivacious Scottish princess, so completely unsuited to her surroundings. He had gone away with the memory of her shining in his brain and found, that same night, that as though Edith were a flame and himself a taper, he had urgent need of a woman. A serving girl had obliged him. But he had recognised the origin of the symptoms. Only, with a princess of Scotland, there could be no easy taking and leaving. If he loved Edith, it could only be as a husband. And finding himself not averse to the idea, he had come back to talk to her a second time.

To discover that she was not only a young and delightfully pretty princess of Scotland; she was also the victim of ill-usage and a valiant fighter into the bargain. It would take a valiant fighter, he thought, to stand up to Abbess Christina, especially when hampered by the twin disadvantages of youth and a good upbringing.

'I wish you were not in the Abbess's power,' he said. 'Something must be done about that, I think.'

'I think she dislikes me,' said Edith. 'She thinks I'm silly.'

'I can't believe that you're ever silly. In what way?'

'We hear wolves sometimes in the forest, especially in winter. I said once that a wolf's howl sounded like smoke rising to the sky and she told me not to be absurd, that you can't talk about a noise as though it were something you could see. But it did sound like that, to me!'

'It sounds like it to me as well and of course you can use words to do with seeing, to describe a noise. The nuns have to sing the Office, don't they? I wonder how many times Mother Abbess has said that this nun or that has a silvery voice, or a golden voice? Sunlight,' said Henry, 'always sounds to me like a clash of cymbals. Especially very bright sunlight, on a July morning in a heatwave.'

337

'Cymbals? I've always thought it was like trumpets. But there isn't much difference, is there? But only in the morning. In the afternoon when it's become sleepy and hazy, it's like a bee humming, an enormous golden bumble bee.'

'Or a vast ginger cat purring. What does a blackbird's song look like?'

'Streaks and dapples of white light! And cuckoos and wood doves are a soft grey-blue . . .'

'Why, there we are again. It isn't just sight and sound that can be mixed up. Things feel soft, but you've just said a colour can be soft. As though it were something you could touch, that had a texture . . .'

They began to laugh, sea-coloured eyes and brown eyes locked on to each other, hands, arms, bodies, tingling with a yearning to be similarly locked, frustrated by Christina's presence. Henry suddenly caught himself up. 'Edith, I must tell you that I am my brother King William Rufus' liegeman, and can take no important step in life without his consent. I must also tell you that I am not in some ways a good man. I have had love affairs and I have shed blood. But . . .'

'I know. In Romsey we seem to live retired from the world but we hear most of what there is to hear. One does not expect a man to behave like a . . . a wall painting of a saint, motionless for ever and always holy. My father and brothers aren't and weren't like that.'

'So that if one day – as yet I can only say one day – I were to be in a position to ask you to be my wife . . .?'

'If Aunt Christina hasn't driven me into taking the veil at knifepoint . . . no, she shan't, she won't! I won't let her! She can kill me first.'

'I'd rather you were neither dead nor a nun. Is your answer yes?'

'Yes, it is. Yes!'

'Then,' said Henry, pitching his voice so that Christina could now hear, 'your brother asks me to give you this, from him.' It was not a long kiss, with the abbess watching, but it was a real one, his tongue probing into her mouth to find hers, as though they were tasting each other, and their arms, at last, around each other's bodies. 'Only,' said Henry under his breath as they parted, 'it isn't from Edgar at all. It's from me, my love.'

'I had intended,' said Abbess Christina, 'to speak to you soon, Edith, about your future. You are old enough now to understand the true nature of the religious life and to appreciate the immense privilege it is to be offered it. But I have been subjected to interference. I have received a letter from King William Rufus stating that he understands that you are not yet a full nun, and instructing me that you are not to take vows without his consent. I have no idea what this means. I very much regret it. Do you know anything about this?'

'Nothing, Mother Abbess.'

'Indeed?' Christina looked with distaste at the vellum roll on her desk, with the royal seal attached, and then gestured to Edith to join her on the straight-backed settle which stood at one end of the abbess's room. It was used for informal talks with her nuns and novices, for the seeking and giving of advice. There were nuns in Romsey, biddable women who did not provoke Christina as Edith did, who thought of her as their mother and whom she called her good, dutiful daughters.

'Listen carefully, my dear,' she said when they were seated, 'for this is important. If you yourself were to seek permission to take the veil, to state that you are unwilling for any earthly marriage but desire to become a Bride of Christ, I think that Archbishop Anselm would support you. I can't imagine that the king would then persist in this extraordinary prohibition. No, wait.' She lifted a hand before Edith could speak. 'Edith, I want you to think very carefully indeed about the things that life here has to give you, compared with life in the world. There are so many perils to beset women out in the world. I don't mean only the violent attentions of men. I mean the exhaustion, the danger, of constant childbearing, and the being squabbled over for the sake of your high birth or inheritance, as happens often to widows of good standing. Women often become widows. There are so many wars. You're safe in here from the wars as well. Here we have peace and order, and above all, my dear, here in Romsey we have freedom to live the life of the mind and the spirit. There is endless joy in the pursuit of learning. And there is the certainty of salvation, the delight of union through prayer, with God. But only in such a place as this can we give ourselves fully to such things. Consider these things, Edith. I implore you to consider them well.'

Edith looked at her aunt gravely. She found that she understood Christina better than her aunt knew. She knew that the careful, reasoned phrases were a strategic mask above a fierce will. She also knew that some of the arguments had validity, that the life Christina described had virtue, that it had once attracted her mother and was even attractive to some part of herself.

But she had seen Henry now and the thought of him, the male smell of him, the aura of desire, filled her, reducing Christina's life of the mind, the spirit, to a thin, pale insubstantial thing like watered milk. 'Mother Abbess,' said Edith seriously, 'I could not go against the wishes of the king. How could I?'

Her aunt looked back at her, inimically.

Two

Count and King
1096

'The last time we were all together was at Mont St. Michel,' Curthose said. 'It's been only two at a time since then.'

'Even then we were quarrelling, two versus one,' said Henry dryly. 'I can't remember when we were last all in one place, in peace.'

The Council of Rouen, convened to arrange the government of Normandy while its duke was on crusade, was over for the day. In the airy upper hall of the castle, the trio were private together. All three had changed since they were last in each other's company like this, and knew it.

Curthose, the host, was no less exotic but much less indolent. He had taken the Cross and knew himself to be on the eve of holy adventure. It had given him a channel where the fantasy of his nature could flow, conferring on him a new gravity and purpose.

Henry, a man of status now in England and nursing greater if as yet unspoken hopes, appeared to have grown bigger, as though he filled his excellent clothes more thoroughly. There was however something watchful about him; he stood apart from the others as though he did not quite trust them. Even through the euphoria of imminent departure, Curthose had particularly noticed that his youngest brother's eyes, when they rested on Rufus, had a curiously considering and wary expression.

Rufus was still fresh from quelling his barons' revolt. He had made examples of the worst perpetrators, not many of them, but terrible ones, awaking memories of his father's savage vengeances. He had neither rejoiced in the business, nor shrunk from it. He was intensified, the barrel-shaped body more solid, the bright pale eyes truculent enough now to pin a man to the wall or flatten argument with a glance, like a bootsole on an ant.

341

The graceful hall was the quiet centre of a maelstrom. The castle seethed, full of squires and pages packing their masters' goods, sewing maids stitching appliqué crosses to mantles, and lordly entourages wrangling over precedence. Hooves clattered in the courtyard where the horses for the expedition were being inspected. The harsh voice of a marshal could be heard criticising someone's grooming. The sun, just losing power as September got under way, glowed on the rose and azure of the carpet-hung walls. Curthose, at ease on a couch, said, picking the idea out of the air: 'Have you thought that we may never be all together again? If I don't die on a paynim sword, I could die of a paynim disease. Our grandfather died that way on a pilgrimage. This journey of mine is a solemn undertaking.'

'Our grandfather,' remarked Henry, 'shod his pack mules with gold when he entered Byzantium and had the nails made short so that the shoes would be lost. It was his way of distributing largesse to the population. Are you going to do that, Curthose? That would be a gesture to remember you by!'

'He couldn't afford it. Ten thousand silver marks won't finance a campaign the size of his and golden horseshoes too,' said Rufus. Like Henry, he was on his feet. He prowled to the window. 'And ten thousand is my limit,' he added over his shoulder. 'Not one silver penny more. Couldn't get it out of my tightpurse subjects if I wanted to.'

'All right, you've hammered me down by two thousand marks already,' said Curthose calmly. 'What a fine living you could make as a pawnbroker! Ten thousand silver marks for a whole duchy! Still, it'll be that much cheaper to redeem if I do come back. Will you be praying for my safety, Rufus? In your place, I'd have very mixed feelings about me.'

'Rufus doesn't go in for prayer,' Henry said.

'I don't believe it works.' Rufus turned his back to the window and considered Curthose with interest. 'Do you believe it works, Curthose? Is there a God and does He listen? Are you really going to Palestine to save the Holy Sepulchre and buy us all out of bad summers and rotten harvests? Or just for the thrill of it?'

Curthose smiled and shook his head. 'It's an adventure,

but it's a good one. It might achieve something miraculous, I think. Look, if there's nothing but the here and now, no other world than this, then *this* world makes no sense. It's too full of queer echoes.'

'Echoes?' asked Henry.

'Yes, things that seem to mean more than they do on the surface.' He waved a slender brown hand, impatient at the limitations of words. 'Like music, or comradeship. What it feels like to swear an oath of fealty and keep it even though you risk your life for it. What it feels like when they come and tell you you're a father.' A new uproar broke out below, with stamping and whinnying, the barking of a dog and a chorus of indignant shouts. 'Talking of being a father,' said Curthose, coming back to earth, 'that's my son's voice, isn't it?' He joined Rufus at the window.

Below, horses reared and danced while grooms clung to their heads and swore. A tiny brown thing, a rat, was zig-zagging across the flagstones with a dog and a boy in pursuit. Curthose pushed his head out of the window, which was just wide enough to let it through. 'Richie, get out of the courtyard and take that dog with you!' He withdrew his head. 'I gave him a pup as a parting gift,' he said. 'He likes to hunt. Rats will do when deer aren't available. You ought to get on with Richie, Rufus. Look after him for me while I'm gone.' He paused and then added: 'There's something I must mention. Our father was born out of wedlock and still inherited Normandy. But times have changed. The bishops wouldn't have it now. Richie is not and never will be my heir. Biota was never more than my concubine. I want to make this clear for Richie's sake. I'm leaving him in your hands. You're my heir, Rufus, and I'm yours. We've signed the agreement and I meant it, just as you did.'

'He'll be all right with me,' said Rufus easily. 'I'll look after him. Get some practice. You may not be my heir for ever, Curthose. I may have a son of my own, one day.'

He tossed it out as casually as though he were saying it might rain tomorrow. 'What did you say?' said Curthose disbelievingly.

'I'm considering marriage,' said Rufus. With an elbow propped on a window ledge, he enjoyed their shocked faces. 'I've even sent Walter Tirel home.'

'Who are you going to marry?' demanded Curthose.

'Probably Edith of Scotland.'

Henry opened his mouth but checked himself before he spoke. Then he said: 'I thought that had all fallen through,' in a neutral voice.

'Anselm talks sense now and then,' said Rufus. 'He warned me I had a rebellion coming and he was right. Took me all last summer to deal with it. He says I need a son. Perhaps he's right there too.' The naughty royal grin appeared. 'But he doesn't recommend Edith, not now. She's had a square of black woollen cloth on her head at some time or other and to Anselm, that puts her out of reach. But she's taken no vows. I checked with the bishop of the diocese, and Henry here's seen her still wearing her hair long. So I sent orders that she wasn't to take any vows without my consent and when I get back to England, I'll visit her. I'll enjoy taking Anselm's advice in one way and f . . . flouting it in another, both at once . . .'

Oh, my God, I knew it! Inside Henry's skull, trapped words tumbled and whirled. I knew it! I was afraid of this when, before I could ask you, you casually told me you'd taken steps to keep Edith from becoming a nun. I was right! Oh, God! Oh, Edith!

They had been planning their journey to Normandy. He had known that nothing would happen until after Rufus had his hands on the duchy. If Rufus had intended otherwise, he would have said so then and there. So there had been time in hand. Best, Henry had thought, to wait. With a little luck, Normandy would distract his brother, drive Edith out of his head. He'd had this idea before and changed his mind, so it was said. But now . . .

Edith! She had come into that room like a vision, like an annunciation of his destiny. And he had thought she would be safe there, while he picked his moment to speak to Rufus. Safe! Where a pervert like Rufus could stretch out his hand and pick her up. Oh dear God, Rufus, haven't you done enough? Made me your man without an inch of land to call my own. Made Curthose your heir for

344

England instead of me, who was born there, the son of its king. Now you want to take Edith from me. What am I to do? What can I do . . .?

'She'll make an admirable queen,' said Rufus. 'Don't suppose I'll be a very admirable husband but she'll cope with me.'

Doubtless she will, my dear, sodomite brother. Edith is magnificent. She's the daughter of tough, earthy old Malcolm and Margaret the saint. She's valiant and honest. If she's forced to it, she'll cope with you. She'll hold up her head, keep her eyes averted from me whom she loves, saturate the astonished court with good works and give you an heir if it kills her, or you. She'll learn what to do to make you give her a baby and she'll do it no matter how revolting. Why should she have to? Yes, she's fit to be a queen. My queen. I'd make a better king one day than Curthose. Oh may you die tomorrow of one of the plagues that keep sweeping the world. Why didn't you die years ago, at Gloucester?

He was so angry that in another moment he would have burst out with every unforgivable word, had not God or Providence not blessedly intervened. God or Providence in fact hedged its bets, providing two interruptions in rapid succession. The first was another uproar below, this time the trumpets of a lordly visitor arriving. Curthose stuck his head out of the window again and said: 'Good God, that's the banner of Maine. I think it's Helias in person! What's *he* doing here?'

He was then cut short by the second interruption, as a gawky, tan-coated, half-grown hound with enormous feet came pell mell up the stairs into the room. He had one ear turned inside out and carried a rat in his mouth. A boy bounded up the stairs after him. The dog ran to Curthose and dropped the rat at his feet. It was dead. The boy skidded to a halt behind the dog and panted: 'I'm sorry, Father, he still thinks he's your dog when he gets excited. He only wants you to see how clever he is.'

The boy was about twelve, wiry and healthy and the image, in reduced size, of his uncle Rufus: pale red hair, sturdy build and all. He was apologetic but not abject. He was proud of his dog.

345

'He can't bring rats in here,' said Curthose. 'If the sewing women see it we'll have screaming females all over the place.' The dog wagged an ingratiating tail. 'You stupid animal,' said Curthose, but the words were a caress and his hands were gentle as they took the animal's head between them. 'You've got to control him better, Richie. He was out of hand down there in the courtyard and . . .'

A new set of feet rang on the stairs. An usher appeared. 'My lords! Count Helias of Maine!' A dark, athletic man strode in, with a tall white wolfhound at his side. Its claws clicked on the gleaming floor. Richie's young dog saw it, twisted out of Curthose's grasp, bristled, snarled and sprang. The wolfhound met it halfway. The centre of the hall became a whirligig of white and tan, yelps, growls and glistening bared teeth and then, in an instant, of scarlet blood.

'Stagbane!' yelled Richie in panic, trying to grab his pet and failing.

'Leloup!' roared Count Helias with a baritone resonance which made the room vibrate, and attempted with a similar lack of success to collar his. Richie sprang back with a shout, shaking a bitten hand. 'Throw water over them!' advised Henry at the top of his voice.

'There isn't any damned water!' bellowed Helias, and then, inventively, snatched up a wine jug from the refreshment tray and hurled the contents of that over the dogs instead. They leapt apart, sneezing and shaking themselves, streaked with dark fluid. Their respective owners pounced.

'I'm sorry, I'm sorry!' gabbled Richie. It was his hound which had been wounded. Boy and dog bled in unison as Richie sat on the floor with his arms round Stagbane. The white wolfhound showed signs of wishing to continue the combat but Helias' sinewy fingers wound into its collar prevented it.

'I'm the one who should apologise. I should have had Leloup on a leash, in a strange place. He'd give his life for me but he obeys me only when it suits him. One wrong look from another dog and he's away, and if he sees a hare, or a gamebird . . .! He burst into the middle of a cockfight once and ran off with the cock that was winning

346

and ate it. I had to grovel to the owner and pay compensation to him *and* the men who'd lost their bets.'

He did not look like a man in the habit of grovelling. His voice rang with self-assurance. If Helias of Maine paid anyone compensation for anything, it was because he thought it was due, and he would be the one to decide it was due, no one else. The whole room knew it.

'Richie!' snapped Curthose. 'Get out! We don't want you bleeding all over the floor!' Richie scrambled up, picked up his pet and bore him away, tawny legs dangling from the boy's arms. Helias brushed a dog hair or two off his violet cloak. For the first time they noticed the white cross stitched to it. When Helias drew the mantle round him, the cross would rest on his breast.

'My lord of Maine,' said Curthose formally, 'I am Duke Robert of Normandy and I can only apologise for your reception.'

Helias had a broad smile full of good humour and good teeth. 'No need. Dogs will fight. When I said the fault was partly mine, I meant it. May I know your companions?'

'Of course.' The occasion returned to conventional lines. 'My brother, William of England . . .'

'I am delighted to meet you at last, my lord.'

'. . . our younger brother, Count Henry . . .'

Henry, exchanging greetings, noticed that Rufus was standing very still, and glanced sideways at him. Rufus was standing not just still, but rigid, blanched, as if a thunderbolt had struck him. His eyes were fixed on the Count of Maine as though he had lost the power to withdraw them and the pupils of his eyes had expanded so that they seemed pale no longer, but dark as midnight as he looked at the man whom he had last seen blithely mounting a horse beside Fulk of Anjou, in the courtyard of St. Gervais Abbey near Rouen, while from his father's death chamber, Rufus watched.

347

Three

Desperation
1096

In the great hall of Rouen, Rufus sat enthroned in the chair which had originally been made for his father (walnut, with carvings inlaid with walrus ivory). Henry stood beside him. The barons were assembled. Curthose had ridden away and his nobles now looked to Rufus as their duke. This should have been the mightiest moment of Rufus' life. He could have wept.

Last night, in the privacy of his chamber, he had.

Helias of Maine was kneeling before him, making a request. He had made it first to Curthose but Curthose had said: 'Rufus is acting duke. Speak to him when I've left.' Now, in his vigorous baritone and with his courtly turns of phrase, Helias was obeying. He was only seven feet away. It might as well have been seven leagues.

'. . . formally, then, I make this plea. My lord king, I desire to leave my home to fight the infidel. When I am absent, in the Holy Land, I ask for a treaty of peace between us. I know that in your eyes, as in Duke's Robert's, Maine is part of Normandy. When I return, we will settle this dispute by arms or diplomacy as you or the duke decide. But while I am away, I beg that Normandy will respect my frontiers and leave my people in peace.'

There were a few snorts of laughter, principally from Belleme and Meulan, who were nearest to Helias. Their amusement was immediately justified.

'No,' said Rufus.

He knew very well how he appeared to others. It was a poor joke on the part of fate that a barrel-shaped, paunchy, redfaced man with long light hair that didn't go with his pugnacious face, and a gruff voice and a stammer, should suddenly become the inappropriate housing for a passion so pure in its unmixed love, so oceanic in its depths, so searing in its cruelty.

It was three days now.

Three days since he had made Helias a personal gift in the form of a fine bay destrier with gold-studded tackle. Three days since, standing with Helias at the animal's side, he had covertly (he had taken such care to make sure no one else could see) taken Helias' hand and drawn it to him and pressed the lean hard palm against himself, *there*.

Only to have it firmly withdrawn and to hear its owner say quietly: 'My lord, I think you do me honour in your fashion. But it is not my fashion. Forgive me. I should not accept this horse from you. I will do so only if you think it best, to avoid talk.'

'Keep it,' said Rufus, the only words he could force out, and stepped back to let Helias mount.

Helias now was looking up at him with a line between his frank and luminous brown eyes. His lips were pressed tightly together. He was waiting for Rufus to answer.

He was not thinking about Rufus except as a possible obstruction and Rufus knew it. Inside his mind, Helias, cross on breast, was already couching his lance against the heathen. He was already kneeling in wonder and worship on the ground where the Cross had stood. He was welcoming with generosity infidels who had been so moved by the valour and piety of the crusaders that they had abandoned heathenism and embraced the one true faith.

And because of this very thing, even more than when Rufus first laid eyes on him, long ago at St. Gervais, Helias represented a vision.

As a boy, Rufus had seen the world as a golden globe filled with the figures of splendid men whom he must emulate. Now all that golden radiance had gathered itself about one gallant, courtly form, so infinitely desirable, so strong, that to join oneself to it would, surely, mean safety for ever from the darkness outside. This was the reality, of which all other loves, including Ralph des Aix (especially Ralph des Aix who physically resembled Helias) had been only the reflections.

And all Helias wanted was to go to Palestine and fight for God.

Rufus wanted to kill him where he stood. Or else to put his arms round that magnificent body and hold it still. If Helias went out of his reach . . .

He had just one weapon.

'You are refusing me?' Helias asked.

'You are free to go to the Holy Land,' said Rufus, wondering what he would do if he were taken at his word. 'Go where you please.' That had the right ring of indifference. He hoped it would deceive his barons. 'But before you go, hand over to us your city of Le Mans and the County of Maine. We shall be a good lord to them. On your return, you may do us homage for the right to govern as our vassal.' He sat back, praying that the sweat on his forehead had not been noticed, to await the result of this.

Helias frowned. Well, what did the fool expect? Rufus thought with a rush of anger, though he knew it to be the reverse side of love. He had said no to the king. Did he look for favours? 'We intend,' said Rufus pompously, since Helias did not answer him, 'to restore as one estate all that our father had. We owe it to his memory.'

'You hear the king,' said Meulan maliciously.

'I think,' said Helias, 'that the argument would be best settled before I go. I ask, my lord, that a court be appointed to decide between us. I will abide by its decision. I can tell you now what my own plea will be. I shall plead that I inherited Maine from my forefathers as you inherited your lands from yours and that I wish to pass it to my children unencumbered by heavy dues of fealty.'

His voice was frank. He had not used the word *children* with any intent to underline the difference between himself and Rufus.

But a dagger jabbed at random may go home by chance.

For a moment, Rufus could not speak or move. His face scorched. He was afraid to stir in case he lost control, ordered Helias' arrest, or snatched out his own dagger and yielded to that terrible, diabolical temptation to kill what he loved so that it should torment him no more.

His barons were watching him. They guessed he was in love. But it would only matter if they thought he couldn't control it.

'There will be no court.' He let the heat sink out of his face and kept his voice level. That first instinctive move to use Maine as a means of controlling Helias' movements,

350

had been sound. 'We offered you friendship,' he said, 'as lord to vassal. But it seems it isn't g . . .good enough. So you will learn instead how it f . . . feels to have us for an enemy. Our plea, Helias of Maine, will be made with swords and lances and a multitude of arrows. What have you to say now?'

Helias studied him. Rufus in return let his eyes travel over the Count's person, almost as blatant a caress as if he had run his hands over Helias' body. Helias understood. This time it was his face that flamed. He sprang to his feet and faced the barons.

'I've this to say. I wanted to fight the infidel but it seems the foes of Christ are everywhere! If I go to Jerusalem now, I throw my county to the wolves. Very well. I stay. But I shan't give up the Cross. On the contrary, I shall place it on every garment I possess. I'll put it on my shield and helm, on my armour and the saddle and bridle of my horse. Whoever attacks me, attacks a soldier of Christ. I bid you all good day.'

He marched out of the hall. Rufus watched, hating to see him go, triumphant because he would not now go far. He would stay in Maine to protect it and while he was there, within reach, there was hope. There was hope.

Henry exchanged glances with Meulan and rubbed a pensive forefinger across his square chin. So Rufus was in love again, and not with Edith of Scotland.

Edith, very likely, was safe, and Rufus would have no son.

'That,' said Henry as one who carefully adds brushwood to a promising young blaze, 'is a remarkable man. I find him most impressive.'

'It's over,' Richard said.

Alice said: 'If only she hadn't disliked me so. I did try.'

'I know. I think she had to live through too many changes. After the Conquest, she fought so hard for the manor I think she felt it was hers by right for ever. It's not your fault.'

It was hard to believe that Wulfhild was gone. To the very end, he had thought she was too tough and too irascible to die.

351

'The new hall is so handsome,' said Alice, 'and she never had a chance to enjoy it.'

The new hall was handsome. Richard, planning it, had decided on sleeping space on an upper floor, with the old resthouses kept as storerooms. There was a stone-built kitchen and dairy at one end of the hall, and pleasing tapestries and furnishings had been bought. On the stretch of wall which had no hangings because tools and weapons hung there, were painted decorations in the latest fashion, with bright-coloured zig-zags. And after all that, there was still silver in the coffers.

But during dinner, two days after they took possession, Wulfhild had collapsed and when she came to, her right side was paralysed. She had never left her bed or spoken clearly again.

A week ago now, Alice had borne a second daughter, Beatrice, and Richard went to break the news to his mother. Whether she was not pleased that the child was a daughter, or whether it was simply that the arrival of new life through the medium of Alice was something she now resented, he did not know. But Wulfhild sat up, mouthing and glaring, and then fell back, senseless once again, this time not to recover consciousness at all, before, forty-eight hours later, slipping into death.

'Poor Mother,' said Alice earnestly and thought she meant it. But even as she spoke, her mind was travelling round the fine new hall, admiring all its delectable detail and rejoicing because (although it had a one-armed steward for whose condition she genuinely sorrowed), her home was now indisputably her own.

Rufus never forgot he was a king. Henry had to give him his due for that. When upheavals on the Welsh March called him home to England, he left Normandy, and Helias, and went.

But he must have felt as though he had left half of himself behind, for when the chance came, even though it meant a November crossing, he returned.

'And I confess defeat,' said Anselm. 'He is on his way to the coast now and ultimately, I fear, to Helias. He's going

352

to make war on him but what the war is a substitute for, I dread to think.'

'As bad as that, my lord?' Abbot Serlo of Gloucester had heard rumours of Anselm's intentions and taken time after a London Council to come to Canterbury and assure himself that gossip lied. Only to make the melancholy discovery that it did not. 'I know he's not amenable to reason but . . .'

'He's not amenable to anything! He only appointed me out of fear. When he was ill at your abbey, he was frightened for his soul. When he got better, the fear went. And now I must go. I need advice. I'm going to Rome. Without Rufus' permission, but he won't grant it, and I can't go on as I am. I'm leaving secretly.'

'If he won't give you permission to go,' suggested Serlo, 'perhaps at heart he knows he needs you?'

'He does need me. That's why I'm going, to ask for help, to find out how best to serve him. I'm coming back. I'd be betraying him if I didn't. Listen, Serlo. Not long ago, when I was travelling with my household, some young men of my escort did some hunting along the way and a hare they were chasing took refuge under the legs of my horse. The poor thing's eyes were bulging with fright and its heart was hammering so that its whole body shook. All it wanted was to live, just to go on having the grass to run on and the sky above. I made them call off the dogs and let it go. You'll find this hard to believe but Rufus reminds me of that hare. He'd burst out laughing if I said so, but it's the truth. He was being hunted down by death at Gloucester and he called to me for help then. Now he thinks the hounds are off his trail, but they're not.'

'I'm sorry. I don't understand.' Serlo's perennially worried face sank into deeper worry lines than ever.

'Nor do I, quite,' Anselm admitted. 'I was anxious for him before the barons started their revolt. I saw that coming and I thought that that was the danger I was afraid of, that I sensed approaching. But he's dealt with that and still I can sense danger.'

Anselm would have been horrified if anyone had suggested that he had powers of scrying; he condemned all such practices as witch-craft. But like many who spent

353

their lives in contemplation of otherworldly matters, he had acquired spiritual vision without knowing it. He tried to make sense of his own instincts. 'No one can live as Rufus does, offending all the laws of God, and avoid a reckoning. But there's something about him that makes me want to save him. Only I don't know how. So I'm going to ask the Pope's assistance. Perhaps His Holiness can tell me what to do.'

'It will be a rough crossing,' said Serlo. The drenching rain and the buffeting wind were bad even for November.

'I know.' Anselm nodded as he heard the weather driving against the walls of the Archbishop's Canterbury palace. 'You have to be desperate to face the Channel in this!'

Four

Love and War
1098

'Letting the horses out of the stable,' said Helias of Maine to his standard bearer as they galloped side by side, with a squadron of knights in close formation behind them, 'was a stroke of genius, Harvey.'

'I like horses. I couldn't set fire to the stable while they were inside it,' said Harvey de Montfort reasonably.

'No. And while they're stampeding all over the countryside they'll keep a lot of people busy, and on foot, rounding them up again. Admirable and decent. I like horses too. But by God I don't like Robert of Belleme. It sticks in my gullet. That was *my* countryside that I've just been into as a raider as if it were enemy territory. And I'd like to know where Belleme is now.'

'So would I,' Harvey agreed. 'That raid was too easy.'

He was right. They had swooped close in to one of the Maine fortresses which Belleme had seized from Helias, in order to deal in exemplary fashion with a smallholder who had been supplying Belleme with victuals 'unpaid, unforced and *unasked*!' as the outraged Helias put it when his intelligence service brought in the report.

And it had been too easy. They had met no patrols, drawn no sortie from the castle. It was a change in an expected pattern and with a man of Belleme's malevolent brilliance, changes were usually for the worse.

Now, riding back to base at Dangeul, the castle he had built north of Le Mans to provide an extra bulwark between the city of Normandy, Helias' nerves were on the stretch.

His eyes continually raked the wide commonland around them. Belleme was campaigning under orders from Rufus and Rufus was in Rouen, awaiting the outcome. Rufus would not desist from hounding Helias and Helias, whose stomach clenched into a ball and shouted for help whenever he thought about it, knew why.

355

And while Rufus' rough parody of a wooing was in progress, with Belleme as marriage broker, it was very strange indeed that Helias should be able to enter what was now Belleme's territory unchallenged, extraordinary that a stretch of commonland in that district should lie so calm and shining under the April sun, with the gorse serenely flowering and the anemones in bloom, as though Belleme were nothing but a legendary ogre invented to scare naughty children.

Belleme was no legend. He was very real. But where the hell was he?

The gorse grew denser and became scattered with birch trees. Another mile and the birch gave way to oak and elm. During the recent tense years, with so many men away from home, under arms for fear of Norman attack, homely matters had often gone overlooked, including the practice of cutting back woodlands for a bowshot on either side of main tracks. Bushes and saplings grew close to the path. Helias did not like this. Those bushes could easily conceal men.

Or, he added grimly to himself during the one and a half seconds it took his horse to turn a somersault, accommodate a trip-wire, coloured to match the dust of the track and strung at the level of a horse's knees.

FitzHamon was over forty and also overweight and was developing a tendency to wheeze. The ash-laden air round Le Mans made him cough at the end of every sentence while he explained to a simmering Meulan that although it was no doubt true that Meulan's Marshal of Horse was a rogue and a liar who ought to be impaled for his habit of regularly swindling his employer, on this occasion he was being more or less honest. 'My feed bills are the same. Oats really are that expensive now.' (*Hack*). 'You can see why,' said FitzHamon (*hack*). 'There hasn't been a harvest left untouched for leagues.'

Helias was a prisoner in Rouen but his removal had not left Le Mans either leaderless or vulnerable. The misanthropic Fulk of Anjou, who for so many years had been gnawing at Maine's southern border, like a surly dog with a very old bone, had seen the chance of fresh meat and

356

pounced on Le Mans with an enthusiastic growl the moment Helias was gone. His resistance was quite as able as anything Helias could have mounted. Rufus, arriving on the field to take charge of it in person, had been driven to somewhat over-desperate expedients.

'It's food for men as well as for horses.' Walter Tirel had been walking at FitzHamon's side when Meulan whizzed out of his tent like an infuriated wasp and waved a tally in their faces. 'There's nothing left in the district for either, so it's all having to be brought in and even so, it's hard to get. The weather's created shortages too.'

'We've burnt every barn and granary and acre of standing corn for miles to starve out Fulk and now we're starving ourselves out instead. I *said* it was stupid,' said FitzHamon and lost what he had to say next in a paroxysm of such violent coughing that Meulan said: 'You need a drink. Come into my tent.'

'What's this rumour that the king may raise the siege?' Meulan said when they were inside with a flagon on the table between them. 'Do you know about it, Tirel?'

'And do I know if it's true?' said Tirel acutely. 'Yes, I heard it but no I don't know if there's anything in it. The siege is going badly. We all know *that*.'

Even within the tent walls, the air still smelled of smoke from the blackened fields and vineyards which ringed the camp. Le Mans had apparently been well-victualled before Belleme, who had had charge of the operation, had set to work on its surroundings.

'Rufus seems distracted these days,' Meulan said. 'There's something on his mind. Or should I say, *someone*?'

They regarded each other thoughtfully. Tirel nodded his balding head. 'You agree?' Meulan asked him. Despite his tendency to be jealous of Rufus' other friends, Meulan tolerated Tirel as he did FitzHamon. Walter Tirel, Count of Poix, brother-in-law to Earl Gilbert Clare of Tonbridge, was for one thing sufficiently well bred to have some sort of claim to the king's notice and for another thing, never presumed on his relationship to Rufus. He had come to the siege, and Meulan knew it, because whatever else Rufus might mean to him, he was also Rufus' friend in the same way that Meulan himself was.

'Helias,' said Tirel, trying the name out on them as if bouncing a stone on water.

'You hate his guts?' said FitzHamon, not sympathetically but as one who really wanted to know.

'No. I think he's a menace,' said Tirel quietly. They studied him as if he were some kind of fabulous beast, such as a unicorn or griffin. 'I call the king my friend,' he said. 'There was a time when that meant doing certain things which I, personally, could take or leave alone. But one doesn't refuse a king. At least, I can't,' he added frankly. 'But when the demands ceased, I didn't resent it. And because of that, I have remained his friend. I feel that that position is threatened now. So are your positions. We're all in the same leaky vessel.'

'What does that mean?' enquired FitzHamon brusquely.

'If Helias yields to the king, I think he'll be taken into Rufus' inner councils. He has as brilliant a mind as you could find anywhere, you know.'

'In what sense do you mean *yield*?' Meulan asked.

Tirel found with amusement that he had them as a riveted audience. It was a new experience. He had not been able to say no to a king because he had not enough confidence in himself. It was the first time in his life he had ever held a company's attention so securely. 'I mean what you think I mean,' he said. 'But I'd go further. Even if Helias were to make a purely political peace with Rufus, with nothing personal in it, I believe they might still draw very close. Excuse me. In this respect I know Rufus very well indeed, as you may imagine. I believe that the king wants Count Helias' friendship, his esteem, so passionately that he'd settle for almost any terms. If Helias refuses to become his lover but agrees to become his liegeman, we shall still find him at Rufus' side for evermore. Something of the sort happened with Ranulf Flambard once. The king told me. Flambard had the hardihood to refuse to be his lover, but he became instead his chief minister in England. Not more, but not less, either.'

358

'Flambard,' said Meulan sharply, 'isn't lord of an exceptionally bloodyminded province with a history of rebellion as long as the Old Testament. It's more than a question of our own positions. It's dangerous to make a confidant of a man who has reason to rebel against you. Confidants know all the things your enemies would *like* to know, such as how much money you have and how many swords you can command. If Helias ever walks out of prison as Rufus' friend, on any terms . . .' The usually dapper Count of Meulan dragged his fingers through his hair. 'I don't understand this. This is Helias' capital city we're encamped round and that stink is the ash from his crops. If Rufus wants to win Helias as a leman, how can he expect . . .?'

'I think,' Tirel said slowly, 'that he's wild to enter Le Mans because he can't release Helias till the place is taken. Well, he can't. What would we all think of him if he let Le Mans go and then freed Helias too? He has his pride. But while Helias is a prisoner, Rufus can't – er – court him.'

'This is disgusting,' FitzHamon declared. He gulped wine angrily. 'He should be getting himself a son, like other men. If anything happens to him, I for one don't want Curthose! Even if Curthose were here. And he hasn't got a lawful heir either.'

'There are some things,' Tirel said, still following his train of thought, 'that one can't ask of a captive. Things it's dishonourable to take by force and are worthless anyway if there's the least suggestion of duress.'

'He's gone mad!' said FitzHamon.

'He has deep feelings,' said Tirel. 'He's never forgiven Ralph des Aix for deserting him. One day I think he may take some kind of revenge on des Aix. Even Helias hasn't made him forget that injury. But Helias is another thing about which he feels deeply, I fear. I'm worried about this rumour that the siege may be raised. If so, it will be because there's no alternative, because in trying to starve out the city by destroying the crops, we've starved ourselves out instead. And then what?'

No one knew, but in all three minds was the same displeasing picture of a Rufus trailing back to Rouen

359

defeated, wound in like a salmon by Helias, who ought to be his humble captive but instead had gained the ascendancy.

FitzHamon yanked his seat nearer the table. Meulan leant forward. So did Tirel. It had begun as a fortuitous gathering. It had become a council of war.

The August night was too hot for closed shutters so the light of the full moon poured into Rufus' chamber and onto his face. Some men thought that this could cause madness and would have had their beds moved. But Rufus liked the moon. Cold and weak though its light was, it mitigated the darkness. And as for the risk of insanity, he was mad already.

Helias of Maine was in the next room.

A mosquito whined and he slapped it angrily. Rouen was rich in the bloodsucking little horrors, for the Seine bred them. But he did not need mosquito bites to keep him awake. Not with Helias in the next room.

Helias was still a captive but honourably so. He had airy, well furnished quarters, a seat at the high table, a tailor to dress him at Rufus' expense, a horse to ride, albeit under escort. It had been a joy, to Rufus, to observe all the laws of knightly behaviour towards Helias.

Belleme had taken Le Mans, making Rufus its lord. Trust Belleme; he was no angel but he was peerless in the field. Rufus had withdrawn his own troops, leaving Robert of Belleme in sole charge of this siege. It had been Meulan's and FitzHamon's idea and it had worked, reducing the siege forces to a number which could – just – be fed. Belleme had done the rest, winning this campaign as he had won others, because he was devoid even of the residual conscience which restrained other men from doing certain things. If a moat had to be crossed and he had nothing but corpses to pile in for a walkway, Belleme would pile in corpses. Probably headless ones since another charming Belleme stratagem was to use heads as slingshot. This time he hadn't needed such extremes, though. A few of Fulk's nobles had carelessly let him capture them and the rest was easy since no one inside Le Mans was foolish enough to disbelieve Belleme's imaginative warnings about the fate of his hostages if surrender were not instantly forthcoming.

Rufus, summoned to the city, had made a triumphal entry, promising peace and good government to all Maine and even extending diplomatic friendship to the defeated Fulk. The people of Le Mans had been so relieved to see him taking over control from Belleme, that they had actually greeted him with trumpets.

Helias ought to think himself lucky that he mattered to Rufus. Belleme had brought him straight to Rouen and handed him over. Where would Helias be now if Belleme hadn't known that his lord wanted him unharmed? Humph, yes, where indeed?

Rufus groaned and turned onto his face. Once, the hosannas of Le Mans were all he desired in the world. Now, Maine was nothing more than a stepping stone on the way to somewhere else. His triumph had been spoilt.

Stepping stone? Bargaining counter!

Helias was in the adjoining chamber.

Rufus had sent his own chamberlains away at nightfall. Helias had none. He lay alone, unattended, because after all, there must be *some* differences between captor and captive. Rufus thought of Helias' unprotected state, rolled over again and sat up in the moonlight.

But lay back. Helias *was* still a prisoner. That was a gulf that could not be crossed. The question could not again be asked, the agonised hope had no chance of fulfilment until Helias was free. And to use Maine for this purpose would be wrong, quite wrong, unknightly . . .

So why had he sent his chamberlains away? What had been in the depths of his mind, when he gave that order? Rufus sat up once more and this time rose, girding on the robe which had lain across the foot of his couch. There was no law which prevented a captor from talking, merely talking, to his prisoner, after all. That was all he wanted to do; just talk. Perhaps just mention . . . he padded out.

The tiny stone landing in the tower where he and Helias were sleeping was empty, dark. Only a faint gleam of torchlight came up from the floor below, where the guards were. He hesitated. But he could feel Helias' whereabouts through the gloom, like a shaft of heat. Blindly, groping, he found his way to Helias' door. It had no inner lock and opened silently.

Helias too lay in the moonlight. Rufus moved noiselessly to the bedside and looked down at his captive's sleeping face. Helias' eyes opened at once. He jerked upright.

'I only want to talk, in private.' Rufus sank onto the end of the couch. 'It's me, Rufus.' He paused, unsure what to say next and then spoke humbly, from the depths of Rufus the man and as though the king had never been. 'I need your help.'

If Helias' faculties were impaired by this small-hours awakening, he didn't show it. He had been trained as Rufus himself had. Both, as boys, had been often roused from a dead sleep by a trumpet or a shout and had learned to be out of bed within seconds, sword in hand and reflexes working, as an alternative to a hiding on the spot.

'Yesterday,' said Helias as though he were in the middle of an established conversation, 'I offered you my service in arms and my fidelity, in the hope that one day you would see fit to give me back my county. It was an honest offer and you appeared to accept it. I will help you in any way that is also honest.'

'It's about that offer. And m . . . my acceptance.'

'Yes?'

The moon shone directly onto Helias. Highlighted in silver, the symmetrical bones of his face, the firm, clean-cut mouth, were very beautiful. His smooth, naked chest was silver-washed too and as he settled his back against the bedhead, his shoulder muscles slid powerful and easy between white light and black shadow.

'Let's n . . . not pretend,' said Rufus roughly. It seemed that after all there was no gentle way into the subject. Stalk his quarry as warily as he might, the end must be the same. The prey's recognition of this danger; the piercing arrow and then the bloody scrimmage. 'We have drawn up a treaty. You helped. It concerns the future of Maine. There's a blank space where the name of my representative, the governor, will be entered. I might put Fulk's name, which is what he expects. But I might put yours.'

362

'I see. You want to buy me.'

'No! By the Face, it's not I . . .like that! Count Robert of Meulan came to see me last night. FitzHamon came with him and Walter Tirel and three or four more. They had something to say to me. They hedged, by God they hedged,' said Rufus fiercely, 'and no w . . . wonder, seeing what the point was when they g . . . got to it. They told me that if I gave you back Maine, or if I made any treaty which offers you as much as the chance of regaining it, or even accept your allegiance on any terms which will keep you near me, they'll withdraw their own fealty. In fact, if I actually gave you control of Maine, I could have another rebellion to deal with, led by my oldest friends. But I'll risk it. I'll see if they dare do it, if only . . .'

He ran out of words. Ever since that miraculous glimpse of this man at St. Gervais, even though he had not then known the name of his dream, he had been haunted by Helias, finding echoes of him in other men, but always, unknowing, searching for the original. Then Helias had walked through a door and into Rufus' life . . . and Helias had said no.

Helias found words, of course. Helias was never at a loss for words in all his life. 'If I break the laws of God and man and share your bed, you'll return Maine to me and chance an uprising? You'll trade a province and the trust of your closest friends to commit buggery with me? Is that it?'

Rufus leant down, resting his hands on either side of Helias' hips, bringing his face close to the other man. 'I can make you, you know. If you called the guards, they'd come but when they see who's with you, do you think they'll interfere? I could order them to hold you. They'd do it.'

'I wouldn't need to call the guards. I can break your neck myself.'

'You forget who you're talking to.'

'You forget who *you're* talking to. I'm your prisoner. I should be safe from some kinds of harassment.'

'You're a petted, pampered prisoner. If I'd been Belleme, you'd be rotting in a dungeon now, wet and starving. Wrists and ankles flayed with gyves. I can still do it. There's such a thing as ing . . . g . . . gratitude.'

'There's such a thing as demanding too much damned gratitude! You took my lands from me. Now you want to turn me into a catamite as you did a fine young man who was incidentally once the best huntsman I ever had. I know about Ralph des Aix. And you expect me to be grateful because in addition to all this you haven't fettered and starved me too?'

It came as if it had been struck out of Rufus by flint. 'You b . . . blind fool! Can't you understand? I l . . . love you!'

The last three words burst out with such force that for a crazy moment Helias had the illusion that the face six inches from his own had briefly glowed with flame. There was a silence.

'I'm sorry,' said Helias at last.

'Think about it!' Rufus was shaking. 'Think what I can do for you and think what I can do to you. I'll ask you again tomorrow. In p . . . public but only you and I will know. I shall d . . . drop something, a cup or a knife, anything, on the floor near you. Pick it up and you've said yes. In the hall, when we meet to discuss the treaty. Leave the thing I drop l . . . lying and l . . . look out! Good night!'

He waited a second longer but Helias neither moved nor spoke and had he stayed in that room, Rufus knew, he would have flung himself on his knees before the Count. Clutching at the very last of his self-respect, he flung himself from the couch and fled, bare feet thudding on the stone floor. In his chamber again, he threw himself on his bed. But he did not sleep.

'It would be unwise to ask him again,' said Henry. With his back to the watchful Christina, and Edith facing him, he could surreptitiously take Edith's hands. 'One refusal is enough. To persist would provoke him. But if we wait . . .'

She was drooping, he could see it, withering like an unwatered flower in this harsh place. It was harder for her to wait than for him. He had campaigns to occupy him, and other women to quench his fires. What had she to help her through? She was meeting his eyes and trying to smile. He wished Rufus could see her now; perhaps he'd take pity on Edith if not Henry. The memory of Rufus' brusque refusal of his plea still burned him. They had been coming back to England to attend to the Welsh disturbances. They had been on board ship. 'No,' Rufus had said. 'For more than one reason and you know what they are. D . . . don't ask me to recite them. And d . . . don't look at me as if you wished I'd fall overboard!'

'Why not? I do,' said Henry angrily.

He had known it was useless to ask again, and that the time was still not ripe even now, two years later. He looked very tenderly at Edith and was anxious. Although she was so brave, and not innocent in the sense of being ignorant, she was completely uncorrupted; it was part of her enchantment. He must be careful what he said next. He could not say outright, to Edith, that he hoped for a brother's death although he did, to the point of prayer. Either brother would do.

'My eldest brother is in the Holy Land. No one knows when or if he will return. There's been no news. Sooner or later, Rufus must see that he needs an heir at home. Many of the barons are telling him so already. Since he clearly doesn't mean to provide one for himself, he must eventually turn to me. Then my position will be very different; he could not refuse to let me marry and I would be expected to marry appropriately. You would be that.'

'I'm afraid,' said Edith. Her eyes glanced past him. 'Of *her*. My aunt. The king hasn't countermanded his order that I'm not to become a nun without his permission. But he only gave that order because he was thinking of marrying me himself, didn't he?' She said it simply, a statement of fact, without coyness. She was a princess and had from birth known her value in the marriage market. She was a princess and would make a queen. 'It wasn't to please you that he gave that order,' Edith said. 'I thought so at first but you yourself have told me the truth. Now that he has . . . another interest . . . well, if his permission was asked, he would probably give it. He might even not care if I took vows without it. He has probably forgotten me, and his order about me, altogether. My aunt has . . . suggested as much. I'm afraid of her, Henry!'

'Oh, my dear darling. Listen.' He grasped her hand and thought urgently, with the rapid resourcefulness of a man who has lived by his wits. 'Is there any way you could put a signal which could be seen from outside, from the road?'

'A signal? But you can't sit outside for ever, watching!'

'I can leave a man of my household nearby with orders to ride past regularly and keep watch for me. What signal could it be?'

'There's ivy under our dorter window.' Edith too was capable of thinking quickly. 'You can see that bit of wall from outside. A white cloth, caught in the ivy?'

'That'll do. If he sees that, he'll get word to me and I'll come even if I have to come from Normandy . . . or Jerusalem! I swear I'll come. You have only to hold out till I arrive. Oh my love, you must, don't slip away from me behind walls and veils. Feign illness, madness, anything! But don't give in!'

Edith, with her fingers tight on his, said: 'Don't go too far away!'

On his way out, he said to Christina: 'Treat her very kindly. Her brother is a close friend of King Rufus, you know.'

Christina looked at him as though she knew exactly what instructions from Count Henry were worth.

They were worth as much as his status in England, as his brother's landless liegeman, was worth.

Nothing. And the knowledge was eating him like acid.

The gathering at which the treaty for the future of Maine was to be settled was ceremonious. Rufus was on the dais, in his Chair of State. Beside him was a table, with the treaty laid out on it together with pen and ink. A wine flagon and a set of goblets had been set there too, for the customary pledging after a document of such importance was signed. Henry and Curthose's son Richie stood behind Rufus. The barons made an avenue leading

366

to the dais. Near it, two on each side, were FitzHamon and Tirel, Meulan and Belleme. The quartet did not resemble each other. FitzHamon towered over Tirel; Meulan's showy gold embroidery on crimson was a startling contrast to the svelte and feline elegance of Belleme's silver and dark blue. But they were all watching the king with the same intensity. On his side, Rufus when he came in ignored them all impartially, greeting only his brother and nephew. He looked as if he had not slept for a fortnight.

When Helias was brought in, nor did he.

He had an escort but they fell back to let him walk alone to the dais. He knelt at its foot, was bidden to rise, and did so. Silence fell.

'Well, sir!' said Rufus, in hearty, encouraging tones, at last. Silence then fell again.

Helias' expression suggested that he wished he knew what he was supposed to say next. He glanced at the table with the treaty on it. Then he took a deep breath and with great formality said that he accepted that Rufus was now lord of Maine, and reminded him that his, Helias', service and fealty were among the terms offered in the agreement now awaiting signature. He wished to serve Rufus in arms in the hope of one day earning the right to hold Maine as his vassal '. . . the liegeman of a king who has bested me in honourable warfare.'

'He hasn't seen the mess round Le Mans yet,' Meulan muttered, cynically and just audibly..

'You have already, unofficially, accepted the terms,' Helias said. 'May we now sign our names to them? And will you strike off my chains?'

It was a courtly, polished speech and deserved a kindlier reception than Rufus' observation that Helias wasn't wearing any chains. There was laughter.

'A man with his turbulent history,' Meulan remarked, ostensibly to Belleme but loudly, 'shouldn't be trusted as a liegeman. He ought to be in fetters now and stay in them for good.'

Helias whitened. He turned his head. 'When I'm a free man, tell me again that I'm untrustworthy. Say it to my face if you dare.'

'That will do!' Rufus crashed his palm onto the table and as he did so, caught the edge of a goblet. It fell onto the floor at Helias' feet. Helias stepped back quickly. He and Rufus stared at each other. Rufus said nothing. Helias glanced at the nearest page with a silent command to him to pick the goblet up.

'Before you make threats under my roof,' said Rufus, 'you might remember that you are s . . . still in my power.'

'Yes. Fortune's on your side there,' Helias agreed. The air was tense. It was as if they all knew that something was happening under the surface, but did not know what. All they had seen was Helias retreating from a harmless fallen goblet as though he were afraid of it, and Rufus apparently waiting for something to be said or done, which had not been said or done. The page who had picked the goblet up, replaced it on the table. The assembly waited.

'If you refuse both my honourable fealty and my freedom,' said Helias, 'if you withdraw now from the terms of the treaty, then I shall only say that I shall escape if I can and that I will then do my utmost to perform all that the Count of Meulan so gratifyingly expects me to perform anyway!'

Again the hall waited. The guards looked at Rufus, as if expecting him to order them to seize Helias. But he did it himself, springing from his chair and off the dais, to grab the Count of Maine by the upper arms and shake him. 'You will, will you? You . . . you . . . oh, you fool, you! G . . . get out of my sight! Out! Out! To hell with the treaty!' He spun Helias to face the door. It was clear that he took pleasure in having his hands on the Count, however briefly. 'Out! Go where you like, do as you like! Do you think it makes any difference to me?' He was shouting at the top of his voice and his final push almost sent Helias onto all fours. Richie laughed. Rufus flung himself away from the Count, back to the table, snatched up the treaty and tore it across, resisted by the strong vellum, but powerful enough in his anger to defeat it. Helias recovered his balance and whirled round.

'Thank you, my lord. I accept my freedom gladly.' He

was shaking, perhaps with rage, perhaps with relief. 'May I have the customary safe conduct to your borders, at the nearest point to my personal estates?'

'Yes! Now go!' Rufus bellowed. He stumped back to his chair. For a moment he stood with his back to the hall, staring at the chair as though he did not know what it was. When at last he resumed his seat and faced the hall again, Helias had gone.

PART VI

IN WHICH WILD HUNTSMEN
ARE ABROAD
1099–1100 AD

One

The Stag King
April 1099

'Where is the Lady Edith? I want to see her.' Henry had
been pacing the quiet guest room when Abbess Christina
came in. When his man arrived with the news that there
was a white cloth in the ivy on the wall of Romsey Abbey,
he had been in the mews of Winchester Palace, consulting
with the falconer about an ailing peregrine. He had come
just as he was, in the old clothes he wore in mews or
stable, patched at the elbows and splashed with mutes. He
had saddled his own horse, shouting for his men, but not
waiting for them; they had had to catch him up on the
way. Striding about the austere chamber with its smell of
cold stone and incense and meditation, he was like a
leopard in a boudoir. The abbess folded her hands inside
her sleeves, largely to conceal the teethmarks in one of
them, and said: 'The Lady Edith is unwell, I regret to say.
You cannot see her today.'

'What's wrong with her?'

Abbess Christina's eyebrows said: is it any of your
business? Aloud, she said: 'A fever of some kind. I will
tell her you called and asked after her.'

'That won't do. I insist on seeing her.'

'I am sorry, Count Henry, but it's impossible. Please sit
down. You've evidently ridden a long way. I will send for
refreshments . . .'

He had five men with him. They stood in a group near
the door. He turned to them. 'Come on.' They
accompanied him as he pushed past Christina and strode
out into the abbey grounds. He looked up at the main
abbey building. 'Edith! Where are you?' There was
silence, although some half-scared, half-excited faces
were peering from various windows and doorways. 'Count
Henry!' The abbess had pursued them. 'This is most improper! You are disturbing my nuns' hour of private
prayer . . .'

'Be quiet,' said Henry. He strode twenty yards along the side of the building, stopped and shouted again.

'Count Henry! I shall complain to the bishop . . .'

Henry held up his hand. But the silence was unbroken. He shook his head and made for the arch through which lay the rose garden and cloister. Christina did not try to stop him, but stood aside, hands once more folded, head up. There was something faintly triumphant in her attitude. He halted in front of her, stared into her face, swung round and made instead for the kitchen block. He was rewarded, as he glanced back at her, by a visible dimming of her assurance. 'This way, lads,' he said. 'We're getting warm.'

He had stood in the kitchen courtyard and shouted only twice when he heard it, faint, and apparently coming from underground, a girl's voice calling, or crying, and a dull thumping as though she hammered on a door.

'Very well.' Christina stepped into his path. Her eyes were hard with anger. 'You think highly of the lady Edith and I had no wish to distress you, or embarrass her. But she has behaved herself very ill. Yes, she is incarcerated, until tomorrow. It is a matter of monastic discipline and . . .'

'Monastic horseshit,' said Henry. *'Where is she?'*

'It's this way, sir,' said one of his men, who had been questing like a hound meanwhile, to establish the direction of the sound. 'Over here – yes, look, there!'

Beside the kitchen was a shallow, stone-lined pit, with steps, giving entrance to a wooden door beneath the building. The door was bolted on the outside. It shook to the pounding of someone within, and Edith's voice, muffled but now intelligible, cried from beyond it: 'Henry!'

He was down the steps, yanking back the bolts, in an instant. He was in, kneeling on a cold flagstoned floor, holding her. She cried out at his touch but as he quickly released her, clutched at him with fingers chilled and quivering, as if afraid he would vanish.

'Edith. Oh my darling. What has she done to you?'

His eyes adjusted to the gloom of the little underground room. It was a cell, he saw, a stone box, with nothing in it

374

but their two selves. And Edith had no clothing beyond a dirty sleeveless shift of white linen, and there were bruises all over her arms, plum-coloured fingerprints of violence amid the gooseflesh. The back of the shift was streaked with her dried blood, and in places had stuck to her body.

'She beat me, and threw me in here. Yesterday. But I knew it was going to happen. I put out the signal. I knew you'd come . . .'

The trust in her voice shook him even more than the exhausted tears into which she now dissolved. One day, please God, she would be his wife, living close to him. And one day, for sure, she would learn what he was, how little to be trusted in so many ways. She would know of his black furies, in which he could kill as easily as treading on a beetle; she would learn that although it was true he loved her, he would never be faithful, never think of a world full of young women as other than a garden full of fruit for picking.

But in certain ways he would be trustworthy. Indeed he would. 'I said I'd come and I kept my word. Let me lift you – gently now. This will never happen to you again, I swear it. Never. Believe me.' He raised her, carefully, not to hurt her, and she clung to him as he carried her outside and up the steps from the sunken area, to where Christina stood, a pillar of black-draped wrath, with his men watchfully beside her.

'What did she do?' he enquired contemptuously of Christina. 'Murder someone? What a shame it wasn't you. Someone give me a cloak. She's freezing.'

'She committed disobedience and then blasphemy,' said Christina. 'You approve of such things, Count Henry?'

'She tried to make me say I'd ask the king's leave to take vows. She tried to make me wear the veil again. She put one on my head. When she'd gone out, I took it off and threw it on the floor but she came back and caught me. She said I could have two days to decide whether to obey her or not.' Edith moved in his arms and put her lips against his ear. 'That's when I put out the sign.' Someone offered Henry a cloak and in response to his nod, laid it carefully over her. 'The two days were up yesterday,' said Edith. 'But I didn't give in.' She spoke loudly now. 'I call you all to bear witness. I didn't give in! I bit her!'

There were admiring murmurs from Henry's men, who would one and all have knocked unconscious any wife or daughter who defied them as Edith had defied Christina, but could pay homage to sheer guts when these were not a personal affront.

'I heard your voice,' Edith said, her face upturned to her rescuer. 'I was half-stupid, lying on that floor. She said I should have no food or water till tonight. I was in a dream . . . or a nightmare. But I heard your voice. It woke me. I made myself kneel up and bang on the door and scream for you to find me.'

She was shivering and the shivers might well be genuine incipient fever. 'The infirmary!' Henry snapped at Christina. 'Take us there. At once!'

He stood over the Infirmarian Sister himself, barking orders, till Edith had been given wine and hot meat broth with some bread soaked in it, a draught to reduce fever and another to ease pain, had had her weals dressed and bound with pads of soft cloth, and was safely in bed, lying on her stomach with a light rug over her and a brazier lit to warm the room.

She was frightened when she realised he was leaving her, but she was growing drowsy and he gave her all the reassurance he could. 'It won't happen again. I'll tell you why.' He whispered. Edith's eyes widened and she gave what might have been a shaky chuckle. He kissed her in farewell.

And then turned to Christina, who had stood in the room, majestic in her resentment, but silent now. 'Madam, come with me.'

He did not leave it to her to decide whether she would do as he said, but grasped her upper arm and walked her out into the open air. She did not resist and he knew that she too was afraid. She might have laws behind her that declared her person sacrosanct; she might have the power of the bishop at her back. But laws were only words on parchment and the bishop wasn't here. Henry and his men, with years of violent lawlessness behind them, were.

Her shoulders were stiff and her profile stony. Edith's phenomenal courage, Henry thought, was possibly drawn from her mother's side of the family as well as her father's. Christina undoubtedly had nerve.

And then, as he reached his men, who were waiting outside, and stopped and jerked Christina round to face him, he knew, out of a long and extensive experience, that she was disturbed by him in another way, that in the grip of his hard male fingers was something of which Abbess Christina had been deprived, and that behind her fear and her affront, was a dreadful unadmitted hunger. And the desire to yield.

Henry, outrageously, grinned into his victim's face, before he looked at his men.

'A moment ago, the Lady Edith called on you all to bear witness to her words. Now I ask you to bear witness to mine. Listen to me, Mother Abbess.' He turned back to Christina, 'I leave Lady Edith in your care but henceforth she is to be treated only with tenderness. If she is mistreated in any way, I shall know. Oh yes, I shall be informed. I have my methods. And if word reaches me that Edith has been hurt in any way while she is here, I shall come and what you did to Edith yesterday, I shall do to you, myself.'

He allowed himself a count of three in which to enjoy the horror and the heat rushing into the abbess's face, before he let go of her, gestured to his men who were grinning just as he was, and strode away with them to the gate. Their horses were tethered outside it. The Abbess Christina, standing rigid with shock in the midst of her own abbey buildings, did not move, until after their hoofbeats had died away.

Rufus was out of Winchester, on a progress in fact to the north-east, to meet Edith's brother King Edgar, who was about to pay a state visit to England. Henry, riding as if possessed, thundering through villages where empty streets and silent houses were clear signs that Rufus' court had been before him, and that those inhabitants who had

377

not hidden away with their goods and livestock were now crouching indoors to nurse the shock of loss and impotent anger, caught up at nightfall. 'At another blasted abbey,' he said aloud, dismounting at its gate.

The king was already in his bedchamber and when Herbert the Chamberlain, in response to Henry's furious insistence, had admitted him, Rufus' reception was grudging.

'What is it, Henry? Even if there's a Viking invasion we can't do much about it until dawn.'

He then sat on the edge of his couch, chunky and fulminating in his blue gown, while Henry, his words punching the air like fists, explained what he had come for.

'You've asked me this before. I told you no,' said Rufus. His pale hard stare reduced Henry from the status of Count to that of younger brother with a tendency to get above himself. 'You've chased after me to ask me that, when you're supposed to be in Winchester representing me? Where there are three separate functions within the next seven days at which you're needed? You've no business here. You may not marry Edith of Scotland. Is that clear?'

'Why not? Her brother's on his way south; it is a perfect moment to ask for his agreement and . . .'

'It's my agreement that's essential. I am King of England and Edith is living in England and both she and you are living here at my expense. I pay Romsey Abbey for her upkeep; I pay you a salary. Your marriages, both of them, are in my gift and I'm not granting it.'

'Why not? Rufus, I've just told you in what state I found her. I don't like leaving her there, even after the threats I made. Have you no pity?'

'I could ask you the same question. Withdraw your suit and she will be in no danger. She can become a nun and probably that would be best. Yes, I said she wasn't to take vows without my consent, didn't I? I must release her from that.'

'But why can't we marry? For the love of God, Rufus! She's the daughter of one king and the sister of another. I'm the son of one king and the brother of another. If Curthose doesn't come back . . .'

'What has that to do with it?'

378

'There's no point in tiptoeing around it. If he doesn't come back, I'm your heir.'

'Curthose isn't dead as far as we know and neither am I. You'll have a long wait. It wouldn't add much to your value as a bridegroom, even if you were my heir, and you're not. You are not in fact of sufficient status to marry a king's daughter, and you know it.'

'You're afraid. That's it, isn't it? You're just plain afraid that with Curthose away and maybe never coming home . . .'

'Have you been melting a wax image of him over a fire, Henry? I wouldn't put it past you.'

'. . . I'll marry and get my own heir and look such a solid proposition that I'll gather a rival party and challenge you! That's it. That's what you were hinting at when I spoke of this on the boat and you said I knew what your reasons were; you need not recite them. No wonder you wouldn't recite them! You're ashamed! You want to keep me down to protect yourself and you're ashamed!'

'No, you fool. I want to keep you away from temptation. Do you remember what happened to the last set of men who challenged my authority? When I'd done with them, they couldn't see and they couldn't fuck. Even Gilbert Clare had more sense than you seem to have; he knew I wasn't safe to play games with. He repented just in time and warned me of the rising and who the ringleaders were.'

'Changed his mind about who to sink his teeth into, the treacherous little rat,' said Henry. 'No one should ever trust that man. I don't want to discuss Gilbert Clare. I'm talking about Edith. I love her. Don't you know what that means?'

'Yes, I know what that m . . . means.' Rufus was seven months and two hundred and fifty miles away from Helias. 'I live without it. So can you.'

'You'll get another rebellion in the end, whatever threats you make!' Henry blazed at him. 'Unless you stop turning every court journey into a looting expedition and wringing out taxes as if you couldn't stand the thought of a man with a penny piece to call his own. The villages I came through on the way here . . .'

'Don't be so righteous. How many villages did you strip when you were living off the land in Normandy?'

'I was feuding with the duke. War's different. This is a time of peace and these are your own people.'

'Quite, and England's my own fief. I've a right to claim subsistence from it.' Rufus' hard stare had not wavered. 'There'll be no rising. Certainly not in your favour. I'm going to bed. You'll go back to Winchester tomorrow. *Winchester*. I forbid you to visit Romsey. Do you hear? I'm keeping you down, as you call it, for your own good,' he added patronisingly. And if he recognised the hatred in his brother's brown eyes, it did not trouble him.

Ordered back to Winchester, forbidden to see Edith though she was within a few miles of him (though if her distress signal appeared again, he would defy even the king and go to her), longing for her, afraid for her, frustration smouldering in him like charcoal, Henry did what his father and brothers would all have done in like circumstances, which was to sally forth and kill something.

Ralph des Aix, the senior huntsman for the area since Croc had suddenly announced that he was getting old and had retired to his holding to raise onions and barley, was absent from court, still engaged on renovating Malwood, said in fact to be tracking down charcoal burners instead of deer, to arrange for fuel supplies in time to come, for Malwood's kitchens. It was not the season for much hunting, for the hinds were carrying their young and the adult stags losing their antlers.

Pricket stags however kept their small single-point crowns longer. The deputy huntsman said he could find some. He had been having reports brought in from the Keepers of the Walk, in preparation for a May Day hunt on the morrow to be arranged for those of the court who had remained at Winchester.

They found the herd (just in time, before Count Henry lost his temper) sixteen miles from Winchester. Henry and the friends who had accompanied him lined up with their bows and the young stags were driven on to them. To a man who had been belittled and deprived, there was great satisfaction in this, in picking a target and seeing the shaft go accurately home, in the arrested leap and the change from life to death.

The fallen quarry were disembowelled and slung on poles, the pack rewarded with the steaming offal. Henry, his ill-humour a little eased, paid the huntsmen and said the sport had satisfied him. 'We'll sleep at Malwood. It's nearest and fit for use now. The weather's going to change.' It had been a dry, grey day, but during the last few hours it had become curiously warm for April, and heavy. Once or twice, there had been distant thunder.

As he mounted his horse, Henry was aware that although the slaughter had partly relieved the tight anger within him, something was still lacking. If Malwood were not far off, he thought, neither was Brockenhurst. In Brockenhurst hamlet there lived a good-natured widow, still quite young, who from time to time had made herself agreeable to Henry. She wasn't Edith. But Edith was on a sickbed, behind convent walls. Bread wasn't venison, but lacking finer fare a man might fill his belly with ryebread and be glad of it. 'I'll join the rest of you at Malwood in the morning,' he said, and left, alone. They knew him well and asked no questions.

He took his own path and in under an hour was tethering his horse on the common close to Saehild's cottage. The air by now was very close and his skin was sticky. Saehild's ale, cooled in the stream behind her house, would be nearly as welcome as her caresses. The usual racket of barking dog and clacking geese started up as he made for her door and it opened before he reached it.

But the person who ducked out of the low entrance and stood hands on hips to receive him was not Saehild. It was a big man who addressed him in the local English accent but without a trace of deference. 'I were expecting you sooner or later. Count Henry, b'ain't it?'

'It is. Who are you?'

'My name's neither here nor there but my title maybe is. I'm Saehild's husband, that's who I am. A woman like her's not going to stay single for ever. Her past's not my business, but from now on's another matter. No offence meant, Count Henry, but you've no place in this house now.'

In Normandy, in a state of feud with its duke, he would have drawn his sword on this impertinent yokel.

But this was not Normandy. Meeting the calm, man-in-possession gaze of Saehild's official husband, he did not remind himself in words that if Curthose never came back, he might one day inherit England and then he might need this man's blade. He thought only that he would after all have to sleep alone that night. But the thought was there under the surface and it restrained him.

Added to which, Saehild wouldn't think the better of him for killing her husband and Henry was not in the habit of committing rape. He had never needed to, for one thing.

'I wish you goodnight and joy of your wife. Give her a kiss from me,' he said with intentional impudence. But as he went back to his horse he found himself trudging.

Disappointment piled on frustration had done what hard riding could not. He was tired. He did not want to lodge nearby. There was a village called Lyndhurst on the way back to Malwood. The Chief Forester's home was there. He would put up there for the night.

The air was very hot and still indeed by now, the daylight drawing off early under a sky that felt as though it pressed upon his head. On either side of the track, the trees were just coming into leaf but the new foliage looked more livid than fresh in this olive-tinged twilight. He rode slowly, but his horse's chestnut neck showed dark patches of sweat. The windless air carried little sound beyond his mount's footfalls. No birds sang. There was a flicker in the sky and thunder rumbled again, faint but threatening, somewhere towards the west.

Then, without warning, there came a sizzling crash and a zig-zag streak of lightning stabbed the path in front of him. His horse reared and he stayed on by a mixture of skill and will, struggling for control. The lightning stabbed again, beside him, and the horse, ears flat to its head, took off. The track poured back beneath its frightened hooves. He ducked to avoid a low branch, hauled on the bit, swore vehemently and then attempted to speak soothingly, but was drowned by an almighty crack of thunder immediately overhead, which acted on his steed as though he had used his spurs instead.

He had thought the animal was already going at its fastest gallop and now discovered that he had been sadly mistaken. A fork in the track rushed towards him. The right-hand one led to Lyndhurst and ultimately to Malwood but even this amount of guidance was beyond him. They hurtled into the left-hand path just as a sheet of rain swept down. Moments later, he saw through the rain that the path was narrowing, turning into nothing more than a tenuous winding way that plunged deep into the woods. Henry crouched, stomach arched over the pommel, head as near his mount's withers as he could get it, to avoid overhanging branches. There were two emergency techniques for dealing with a bolting horse. One was to drag it round in a circle and the other was to let go and fall. In the midst of treetrunks and knobbly roots, neither was feasible. He shut his eyes.

The horse's speed slackened. He opened his eyes and found that the trees had closed in so densely that they had forced the pace down. He sat up and was able to rein in. The horse stopped. It lowered its head and stood shivering. Rain and wind swished above but the leaves at least provided some sort of protection and the trees were not only close, but modest in height. Those likely to draw lightning were the solitary or the towering. He might do well to wait here till the storm had passed.

Presently, the flickering and the rumbling died away eastwards and the rain ceased. The forest rustled with a fitful breeze. Foliage dripped. It was growing genuinely dark.

It was then that he realised that he was lost.

He tried to retrace his steps, leaning down to search for his mount's hoofmarks. But the light was too poor; he lost them. The faint path which had brought them through the forest, seemed to disappear. He pulled up.

This was ridiculous. He knew the forest like the lines on his own palm. Well, he thought he did. The Foresters and the Keepers said that no one ever truly knew it, that it had a capacity for endless surprises and something near to a mind of its own. He sat still, listening for the sound of a dog barking in the distance, or a church bell. He heard the wind and the water drops spattering; some small birds twittered; something rustled jerkily in a hazel brake. His horse sighed, resting a hind hoof. Under the quiet aisles of the trees, the shadows were gathering like a dark mist. Somewhere, eerie and tremulous, like a disbodied spirit calling to another, an owl hooted.

He could try riding in a straight line, for as long as the light still lasted. He urged the horse forward and realised that he was not only tired but also hungry. The horse was tired too. Some time later, it balked on boggy, indiscernible ground, and an invisible branch snatched the cap off Henry's head. He cursed colourfully and dismounted.

For a little while longer, he felt his way on foot, skirting the marshy ground, a hand stretched ahead to feel for obstructions, the horse at his shoulder a warm and breathing entity which he could not see. The owl's eldritch voice startled him again. He stopped.

He might know the forest well but he had never been alone in it before, let alone lost, after dark. It felt enormous, alien and uncomfortably alive. And the darkness, by now, was a black curtain before his eyes.

He would get nowhere till morning. He had better unsaddle the horse, hobble it (rope and a spare cloak lived permanently in any regular campaigner's saddlebag) and sleep as best he might at the foot of a tree to wait for dawn.

The air had cooled after the storm and his wet clothes had been drying on him. He was chilly and also hungry. But thrusting both out of his mind as his campaigning years had taught him to do, he saw to the horse, found a place that felt fairly dry, between the roots of a tree, wrapped the extra cloak round him and after a time, dozed. He woke up an unknown length of time later. He was unpleasantly cold now, and the darkness was still absolute. But somewhere, not far off, there were voices.

He got swiftly to his feet and moved round the tree. About fifty yards beyond it, visible as a faint wavering glow, was red firelight.

That lifetime of war had taught him other things besides

how to get to sleep under a tree when chilled and empty. He knew that the unknown was best approached with caution. He advanced soft-footed, moving from trunk to trunk and keeping them between him and the fire.

The blaze was in a clearing. It crackled and spluttered as the flames licked damp wood, but it was lively and the warmth billowed invitingly towards him. There were people in the clearing. Some were crouched round cooking pots. An iron spoon scraped pleasantly and he smelt meat.

The wobbly light created illusions. He could not properly make out the figures that moved to and fro. Something about their heads seemed odd . . .

He must not lose track of his horse. He marked the tree where he was standing, using his knife to score a cross in the bark just where it forked and noting that it was an oak with a holly bush beside it. Then began working his way round the clearing to find a better vantage point. Then he saw the bleached log and the Being that sat upon it.

His muscles froze. He had been trained to control physical fear but this was not physical; it was spiritual, the terror of the myth made flesh, of that which should not be. The thing occupied its rustic seat with a dignity as great as that of Rufus himself. Its back was straight and its hands lay on its naked thighs. The firelight played on a lean ribcage and a hairless chest. But it was man only up to the throat. Above that it was stag, and it bore a twelve-point crown of antlers and the prong tips shone in the flames like ivory.

Something else was happening. Something was being carried to the log throne. A bowel-melting shaft of horror went through him as he saw the figures close for the first time and understood that they were all animal-headed, with the muzzles and horns of goats. The thing they carried was a real goat, which kicked and bleated. Henry shut his eyes, as he had done on the bolting horse. He was still asleep, he thought, and dreaming. The bleating grew frantic; the animal had smelt danger. He opened his eyes again. The Stag King was on his feet and there was the red flash of firelight on bright steel in his hand. A drum began to tap, to a slow, muted rhythm. The Stag King spoke, his voice strong if muffled.

'To the Lord of this Wood, to Herne the Hunter and the Stag which is His quarry, we dedicate the blood of this sacrifice, that the ground may receive the seed and our mouths be fed.' Through his horror at the blasphemy, Henry's own hunger pangs sharpened and he saw that the bodies of the semi-bestial worshippers were all thin. 'May He relent to us,' said the Stag King. 'May He make our furrows fruitful once more. May He turn from us the knife edge of hunger and sickness. May He turn from all the world the knife edge of destruction that threatens it.' There followed words he could not understand, some kind of incantation. The knife flashed downwards. There was more frantic bleating and convulsive movement, and the head of one of the creatures holding the goat fell off.

Halfway between shock and relief, he saw that it was a mask and that its wearer was actually entirely human. Stories he had heard as a child came back to him, legends that the Church abhorred, a tale of Foresters searching in a barn for evidence of poaching and coming on a sackful of animal masks. He remembered that tomorrow was May Day.

Which meant that this was May Eve. Whose other name was Beltane.

Then he looked at the face which the mask had revealed and his heart almost stopped for quite another reason, for the face was that of a young girl and he had never seen one so beautiful, not even Edith. That this face, lit brightly now as someone fed the fire, was tired and even a little frightened, that there were sunken hollows of privation under the lovely moulding of the cheekbones, did nothing but enhance the beauty. As the sight of Edith on that cell floor had done, this damaged creature instantly called out of him not only desire but tenderness.

She had thrown the ill-fitting mask aside and darted to snatch up another. There seemed to be a pile at the edge of the clearing, a few yards off. Donning it in haste, she ran back to the throne. A libation seemed to be in

386

progress. He glimpsed a cup being tipped towards the ground. There was another incantation. The dead goat was removed. The drumbeat continued.

There was an interruption, comic in its mundaneness. An annoyed voice, high in pitch but male, said: 'It b'aint no good. Feast by feast we've been a'doing of it, every time these days 'stead of only in November or for initiations, and what's the good? That there were my goat and I can't spare no more. We'll go hungrier than ever for losing 'er kids and 'er cheese and what for, I say, what for?'

The drums died. 'Penna says it's not enough,' said the Stag King's hollow voice. 'So. Does anyone volunteer an ox?'

Goats' heads swivelled as people appeared to examine each other's masked faces. No one volunteered an ox.

'Who says an ox'd be enough either?' demanded the high-pitched voice with scorn. 'It's all over the place, ain't it? Priest at Minstead say so. North and south, east and west, here and over the water and next year's *the* year, he says. One thousand and one hundred. The Day of Wrath's coming, the priest says. He'll want more nor goats or oxen, that's for sure. Like in the olden days.'

'Perhaps.' Henry, pressed hard against the wide trunk of a tree, thought there was dry amusement in the Stag King's voice. 'You don't offer yourself, I see.' The voice had some kind of accent, French, Henry thought. 'But talk of *that* offering is only for the one who offers. And that means,' he added, in a tone so inhumanly tranquil that Henry only caught up with the meaning of his words a few seconds after he had spoken them, 'that it's only to be made by me. It's only for the King to do. But we're not there yet. One thousand and one hundred? One thousand one hundred years since what? What has the Christian god to do with Herne?'

'Makes no odds anyhow,' said another voice roundly. 'If it's all over, the whole world that's going, then we can't stop it with any offerings. King o' the Wood here only stands for this Wood. What about the rest?'

There was silence.

Then the King said: 'Let us hope. Perhaps this year

387

we'll have a harvest fit to call one. Let us proceed. Who comes to the Beltane Fire as the Maiden?'

A female figure was led forward. It was not the girl Henry had seen. That girl's new goat mask had a patch of white hair between its small horns and he could still see her. The Stag King rose as the nominated Maiden was brought to him. He took her hand. The swift fire-shadows which patterned the wide oak trunks behind them patterned the couple also, uniting them with their forest background. The king's antlers, springing graciously curved from his brow, were branched like the trees. He raised the Maiden's hand aloft and what had a moment before been frightening and grotesque slipped over an unseen boundary and took on an extraordinary nobility. It was as though the nature of the forest, the aliveness which Henry had sensed when he found himself alone at nightfall, had entered into them.

Henry, pressed behind his tree, was also changed, was no longer a count and the brother of a king, but was an intruder at a stranger's court, less than nobody, with neither the right nor the duty to do other than run from his hiding place and kneel at the Stag King's feet. He dug his fingers into the rough bark and leant his face against it, trying to shut out the compulsion of that terrible, calm, animal mask between the man's body and the ivory-pronged crown. And went on seeing the King inside his closed eyelids, in detail, even to the tiny point of an embryo thirteenth point on one antler and the three moles that made a slanting line across the gleaming chest.

The Stag King's voice came again. 'We have shed blood to make the earth kind. May our union cause the seed to spring. Begin the dance!'

The drums had started up again. A flute joined in. They made an intertwined rhythm as troublesome to the human soul as certain caresses to the human body. The King and the Maiden still stood hand in hand before the throne but the others were forming into a double circle, women on the inside, holding hands and facing out; men outside and facing in. The two circles were moving, dancing, in opposite directions. The tempo quickened.

The dancers released each other's hands, began to whirl and stamp, each now dancing alone.

The clearing was full of danger. Those within it were detached from the daylight world where they were humble and afraid. Ancient violences were barely below the surface. Henry remembered other tales, of Foresters found mysteriously dead, seemingly thrown headfirst against a tree by a plunging horse, a common enough accident (it had almost happened to him a few hours ago), but in the New Forest at least, it was commoner than it ought to be. But he could see the white-patched mask and below it the body of that beautiful, worn girl, swaying from the hips, visible between two spinning, leaping male dancers. Her hipbones jutted and her breasts were like small apples. His palms burned for them.

The drums were beating in his blood and even fear could be an aphrodisiac. He was already wrenching at his clothing. He shed it, haphazard, and ran, crouching. He caught up a mask from the pile and crammed it on. It seemed to fasten at the back. He secured it as he started to dance. The weight of the horns made it feel queer, unbalanced; it restricted vision and he lost his bearings for a moment. But a knight's helm had a similar effect; he adjusted quickly. He mingled with the others, melting easily in among them in the wavering mix of light and shadow, working his way towards the white-patched mask, giving himself up, like the rest, to the insistence of the drums. No one heeded him.

The moment came and he did not know how he knew it. The drums knew, his body knew, all their bodies understood as though they were linked into one mind. Hands outstretched, he made for the girl. Someone almost cut in on him but his aching flesh wouldn't be denied three times in two days; he shouldered the opposition aside. He caught the girl's hands. He found that the masks were designed to allow kissing. She smelt of wildness and fresh herbs and female animal. He was hot and huge, crying for relief. He swept her away from the light, into the blackness at the clearing's edge, and together they slid to the damp soft leafmould. He had thought she would yield at once but although she did not hold him off, he sensed

389

through his own urgency a hesitation in her. He coaxed, crooning and stroking where he knew response should be,, until it began. She softened and drew him to her, guiding him home.

She took time to climb. It was anguish but he held himself back to wait for her, anxious not to disappoint her, as though it would somehow invalidate a rite. Then he heard her gasp: 'Yes! Now!' and he let go. They lay collapsed, the mould clinging to their sweating skin. He felt belatedly how very very thin she was, thinner even than she had seemed in the firelight. Her knees were sharp and her wrists unbearably fragile. He stroked them. Suddenly, she whispered: 'Who are you? You're not one of us! No one said a visitor was with us tonight! How did you get here?'

He clutched her hard because as long as they lay embracing, no one would interrupt them. For the moment, she was his shield. But they were out of the world where earthly titles mattered and he knew that if she shouted her discovery to the meeting, he would be found in the morning with his brains knocked out, against a tree. No doubt someone would think of the theory that lightning had frightened his horse. There might well be little enquiry. 'How do you know?' he whispered back.

'You're not *thin*! And you spoke in French just now when we were near the top. Only the King knows French and you're not him.' Her hands stroked his back but he felt them trembling. 'They'll kill you if they find out. Where did you come from?'

'I missed my way in the woods. I meant to introduce myself to your – er – elders, earlier but I didn't arrive in time.' Henry invented details at a speed born out of the urge to survive. 'Then I saw the light of your fire. I stood and watched and then your mask slipped and I saw you. I couldn't keep aloof after that. Forgive me?' He made his voice sound pleading. 'I *am* one of you, you know,' he said untruthfully, 'though I haven't been officially introduced.'

'But it's forbidden to take part unless you're announced!' He could hear the terror in her voice. 'You must go away, quickly, quickly! Your clothes, where are they?'

'Behind a tree somewhere. Over there.' He hadn't marked that tree and hoped to God he could find it again.

'You're nice. It was . . . there's one who almost always manages to catch me and I hate him, he does little, cruel things. I complained once to my husband but he said that in the Wood, what happens . . . must happen; it's the sacrifice we make to Herne. They'd all be cruel if they caught you. I don't want you to be hurt. Go now, quickly!'

'I know I'm well fed compared to you,' said Henry meekly. 'But I was lost for hours. I'm starving and I can smell food.'

'You're mad, why don't you *go*? You could slip off while they're all still thinking of other things. There won't be much to eat, we can't spare much. These feasts are a burden to us. It'll be a mouthful of goatmeat and a piece of bread all round. Oh, very well!' She yielded, sensing that he would not. People were drifting back into the clearing, their frenzy spent, and food was being handed out. She darted out into the clearing and in a few minutes slipped back with the victuals. The bread was black and coarse, the meat half-burnt and half-raw, but he wolfed it thankfully. 'Which way do I go?' he muttered with his mouth full. 'I was lost; I told you.'

'There's a path. It crosses the road from Winchester to the coast, near a place called Malwood. Hide till it's light enough to see. Then go. We'll be gone before dawn.'

'Blessings on you. What's your name?'

She drew back. 'I can't tell you, you know that! We leave our names behind when we come here. Is that not the custom where you come from?'

He had made an error. He retrieved it quickly. 'Not so strictly, no.' She was still trembling and he stroked her as one might a nervous dog. 'Listen, you hate this business. You must, if someone you detest keeps grabbing you. Why do you do it?'

'Because I must! I have to. I'm the wife of the King.'

'I knew I had good taste. Out of you all, I pick the queen. But your husband makes you go with this man you're afraid of! Come away with me now and I'll see that nothing like that ever happens to you again. I'll protect you.'

'I can't. I'd be afraid. You could be anyone. Anyone could say that. Don't, please.'

391

'All right. But take off your mask again and let me see your face just once more.'

'No, it's forbidden!'

'I've seen your face already tonight, even though it was by chance,' he said, and removed her mask himself, sheltering her with his body so that no one else should see. Her beauty astounded him all over again when he turned her face into the light. She smiled timidly and said: 'Now you.'

He took off his own mask and they looked at each other and kissed once, bareface. 'The path is over there,' she whispered, pointing. 'Hide well away from it till we're gone.'

He did as she said, crawling away from her into the thicket and then prowling warily round the clearing edge until, to his relief, he had found his clothes again. Lying in a bush-fringed hollow, he heard the gathering depart and when they had gone, he found his horse easily in the first light of daybreak. By sheer good luck, it seemed, he and the horse had halted well away from the path and no one had fallen over them as they assembled.

He might have thought it was all a dream, except that when he returned to the clearing to get his bearings in order to find the path, the bleached log throne was there, and the ashes of a fire, still warm.

Two

Orion's Belt
June 1099

Rise at first light. Blow last night's fire to life or wrestle with flint and tinder to start it again. Feed the poultry, milk the one remaining goat. If Ralph was away, feed the oxen and the horses too. Then take a breakfast of sorts; diluted ale and a chunk of bread smeared with honey. Only smeared. They sold most of their honey now.

Then hunt for eggs, bake, spin, weave, make cheese if the goat's milk ran to enough curds. Or weed the vegetables or brew, or make candles or clothes . . . and always, always, with a daily main meal to prepare which brought the same nagging question: how much of our slender food supply dare we eat today?

The silver she had brought from home had long been spent but as a Senior Knight Huntsman, Ralph was not now ill-paid. They should have been reasonably well-found. But one harvest after another had failed, through wheat-rust, or flooding, or storms. At Fallowdene, Richard had rents from his villagers but at the Tun, Ralph considered himself his tenants' leader rather than their lord, and half the time he supported them instead of the reverse. The King of the Wood played more part in his daily life than was ever openly admitted by him or by them.

He was home at present; he'd soon be in from the byre. Sybil poked a sluggish fire irritably, doing it no good, for miserable fingers were clumsy. She tried to be cheerful and not to think of Fallowdene, the Eden which she had lost, for to think of it much was to risk drowning in her own tears. Better to gossip with Elfgiva and laugh at Penna's latest portent. He had foretold disaster from seeing a cloud shaped like a dragon. '*More* disaster?' Cild had enquired caustically.

Better not think of Cild either though he thought of her. She had only to pass within a hundred feet of him and his head would turn. Outside the Wood, she was safe for he kept the Tun's laws. But in the Wood, he had managed to have her again and again. He was a spiteful lover, taking pleasure in secret nastiness, like squeezing a doubled little finger or biting his partner's tongue. Despite the masks, she knew him by these tokens as well as by the way he moved and the chill that seemed to emanate from him. But when she had tried to tell Ralph, he had silenced her with talk of the sacrifices due to Herne . . .

She hated Herne. The demon she had played games about as a child, had been excited and fascinated by, had proved to be a demon in good earnest, and would have been so even without Cild. It always gave her nightmares afterwards, to see her own husband, Ralph, normally kindly and human, turned into a creature half-beast and brandishing a sacrificial knife. The Wood had given her pleasure once and only once, last Beltane, when instead of Cild, the Stranger had come, who was skilled in his loving and had minded how it was for her.

He was gone but perhaps she could evade Cild for a while. She rose to greet Ralph as he came in. And then was overtaken, for the third morning running though for the first time in Ralph's presence, by nausea. She dived past him into the open air.

When she came back, he was sitting meditatively by the fire, whittling yet another yew bow. It was not correct for knights to make money in such a way, but Ralph constructed bows and sent them to market with Oswin's. 'We need the silver,' he said. His hands continued to be busy as he asked: 'When?'

Sybil sank onto her heels beside him. 'Elfgiva thinks near the end of January.'

He was silent, working it out. Then he laid down his work and looked at her. 'Is it a Child of the Wood?'

She had been about to ask if he were glad, and then go on to ask about not going to the Wood. His tone startled her. She drew back. 'It could be, I suppose.'

'It must be. All through April and most of May, I was either at Winchester or at Malwood. I slept at Malwood as a guard, remember? And ran about the countryside looking for the charcoal burners. I saw you only once in all those weeks and that was in the Wood and even then we didn't . . .' He got suddenly to his feet. 'After all this time. I'd almost given up hope. And then it happens in the Wood, with someone else.' Without looking at her again, he went out. Sybil stared after him and then rose and followed. He was standing with his back to the door of the dwelling, gazing towards the forest. 'Are you angry?'

'No. Leave me alone. Leave me *alone*, Sybil. Go inside.'

'You are angry,' said Sybil flatly. 'But why?'

'Get away from me!' He turned and made a half-gesture as if to strike her. She recoiled but only by a step. She was frightened, but the injustice of it gave her courage. 'That's not fair. You took me to the Wood yourself. You gave up your right to lie with me. You said it was a sacrifice to make Herne relent so that our crops would grow . . .'

'Be quiet.'

'I won't be quiet, why should I?' Angry tears sprang into her eyes. 'You told me that the Children of the Wood are a blessing. You told me very sternly how I must be prepared to go with anyone. You . . .'

'Don't throw my words in my face!' This time he did strike out but Sybil dodged and darted back into the house. He came after her and found her facing him with a brand from the fire. 'I won't crawl and cringe and pretend I've done wrong! Hit me and I'll hit you back, with this! You were willing to take in Bruno's child. If this one isn't yours either, whose fault is that?'

'Put that torch down! Are you going to burn another house to the ground?'

'Another house? I didn't burn Fallowdene down! My mother was quarrelling with Alice.' The branch in her hand crackled and sparked.

Ralph ground a clenched fist across his forehead. 'Let me remind you that we came together in the first place, that you came to the Wood in the first place, because you were a wanton!'

'You helped! Anyway, that was then! This is now! This is a Child of the Wood and I won't apologise for it and I won't be made to lose it this time, either!'

'What do you mean? You weren't made to lose the last one.'

'No? Torn from my home, made to ride a pony for three days on end, what do you call that? Don't come a step nearer!'

'I was trying to save you. If I'd left you there, they'd have shut you in a nunnery for life!'

'So you dragged me here instead, to work and starve and be forced to go to the Wood and then blamed for it . . .' The tears spilled. The brand shook wildly in Sybil's hand. She flung it onto the fire, stumbled back to the bed and sank down, crying desperately. 'And now you turn on me. Would I go to that hateful Wood if you didn't make me? I hate you! I wish I was dead. I hope I die when the baby comes so I don't have to live here, hungry all the time and you blaming me, blaming me, for something you make me do!'

'No, Sybil . . .!' He went after her, meaning to pull her to her feet and shake some sense into her but her words dissolved into such weeping that his strength and all his anger were leached away and he found himself kneeling instead, his face in her lap. 'I'm sorry, I'm sorry. In the Wood I endure hell because I so hate giving you up. I can't bear you to go with other people, I never expected it would be like this, it feels as if you choose to go, as if you're deserting me . . .'

'But I'm not! I don't want the others. I don't *want* them!' She knew as she said it that it was the truth, that she would not even want the Stranger, although his must be the seed she carried, if only she could have Ralph and no other.

'I know,' Ralph said. 'But that's how it feels. Oh, why couldn't you have conceived by me, at least, oh why couldn't you?'

'I can't order such things.'

'No, I know, I said, I'm sorry. Sybil, I love you, don't you see, if I didn't love you I wouldn't be hurt like this, I wouldn't be angry. It's having to share you that hurts.'

Very gently, Sybil laid her hand upon his head.

The first time she had ever touched him, on the day he had become faint on the way back from the hayfield, he

396

had noticed the gentleness of her hand. He looked up, moving his head with care so as not to disturb that soft hand, and saw that the gesture had been not only kindly but curiously royal, as though she were truly a queen. A compassionate queen. In the stable at Fallowdene, he had yielded to her, given her power over him, but it had been a power only of the body. Now he had given her power over his spirit and although Sybil of the Fallowdene stable would not have known what to do with such a gift, this Sybil was older, no longer a child, could respond. She did move her hand, but only to take his face between her palms.

'I will never go to the Wood again,' she said. 'All the children I have in time to come will be yours, or there will be no children. I promise.'

'You can't,' he said, on a sob. 'I can't cheat Herne. Even in good times, it was never the custom for the King to claim his wife always. Herne's laws must be kept.'

'Is Herne so real, then?' Sybil asked.

'He's real. When I wear the antlers, He enters into me. I become Him. There is no escape from the Wood.'

'Very well. But it is a sacrifice for me as much as for you. Always remember that, Ralph.' She was crying again, but without violence, the easy-flowing tears of relief which do not distort the face. He rose from his knees and sat beside her. 'The Tun is a hard place for you to be,' he said. 'But it will get better in the end. It must. And one day I will take you back to visit Fallowdene.'

'When we have our own children to show them,' said Sybil.

He wondered if the one she now carried was Cild's. He knew that Cild had paired with her time and again. He had grown to dislike Cild intensely, a sensation which he fought. For he was Cild's King, and hatred for such a reason was a betrayal of Herne.

He wanted to ask Sybil if the man had been Cild. But he knew he never would.

He was expected at the Brockenhurst hunting lodge the next day and he did not want to go, for it meant leaving Sybil. He arrived later than he should, to learn from an impatient Under-Marshal that there was a boarhunt to organise immediately since the king was arriving tomorrow, and that he was to call at Malwood because there was trouble over the slates for the roof of the new kitchen – 'not enough were delivered or some such thing,' said the Under-Marshal disdainfully, bored by such trivialities.

An Under-Marshal. Once he took his orders from the king in person and no Under-Marshal would have used such a tone to him. No one knew what this demotion felt like except those who had experienced it. Only Gilbert Clare of Tonbridge, never quite trusted since he fought on the wrong side in Odo's rising, had ever commiserated with him and even that had been semi-spiteful. 'Beastly, isn't it, des Aix, going down in the world?' He would have taken Sybil and gone, perhaps back to Maine and Helias, were it not for the Tun. The Tun belonged to him but he also belonged to the Tun and while he stayed there he was Rufus' vassal. He also needed his Knight Huntsman's pay.

Next day, the weather turned close and leaden again as it had been at Beltane. He came in from searching the forest for boar sign, with his shirt stuck to his body and his tunic off. The king must have arrived meanwhile; the stable was full and there were people everywhere. But the atmosphere was odd; men stood about in knots with their heads together, excitedly talking. Count Henry and the king's nephew Richie were the centre of a chattering group near the gate. Ralph rubbed his horse down and stabled it, and on emerging from the stable was accosted by a big tan-coloured hound which reared up to put immense paws on his chest and demand a pat.

'Oh, will you never learn manners, Stagbane!' said Richie, hastening up to grab the dog's collar. 'I'm still trying to make him keep to heel unless I say otherwise but he has only to see something that interests him . . .! I've been trying for years! Have you heard the news?'

Ralph had come to know Richie since the boy's arrival at court two and a half years before. Richie loved the hunt, and he and his dog tended to attach themselves to the hunt staff wherever they chanced to be. He was very much Rufus' relative in his passion for sport and in other ways too. In full manhood he would be almost a replica of the king though he was better proportioned, with hazel eyes, and his light ginger hair actually came from his mother's side. He was feeling the heat, for he had taken off his tunic and opened his shirt to the waist.

'I've only just come in,' Ralph said. 'What's afoot?'

'The king's been here and gone. A messenger came in from Belleme, in Maine. Helias has marched back into Le Mans. So the king,' said Richie admiringly, 'ordered a horse, scooped up half a dozen men and rode off to the rescue. Just like that. He said he'd raise men in Normandy. He wouldn't take me with him.' Richie became dejected. 'I'm old enough for war but I never see any action,' he added resentfully.

'The king is responsible to your father for you.' Henry strolled up. 'Good evening, Sir Ralph.'

'Good evening, sir. Is the boarhunt cancelled?' The humid air felt more like a woolly blanket than ever and Ralph opened his own damp shirt. Henry, watching him with a curious intentness, said with a trace of malice: 'Helias beckons and Rufus runs, it seems. It's as well Anselm isn't here. He hasn't managed to see the Pope as yet, I gather. The king has more or less bought Urban. The boarhunt can proceed. I'm still here and so is Messire Richie and a good many others that the king didn't take either.'

Low down in the sky, thunder rolled. 'My uncle's in for a difficult crossing,' Richie said. 'He seems to like them. He travelled in November last time he went across.'

'He has other things on his mind,' said Henry dryly. 'Though this storm may make him notice it. I think it's going to be heavy.'

He spoke cheerfully. It occurred to Ralph to wonder how much Henry would mind if Rufus' ship sank. If it did, Henry would have England and Normandy both in the palm of his hand.

Henry did not however look as though he were brooding on future grandeur. He was in fact eyeing Ralph in a very curious way. It was embarrassing and inexplicable. Ralph took his leave.

*

399

So now he knew. Henry stood in the cramped apartment which at Brockenhurst was his and thought it out. The husband of that bewitching, extraordinary girl of the firelit wood was Ralph des Aix of Chenna's Tun. Ralph was the Stag King. Or was he mistaken?

No. How many men had three moles in a slanting line, like the stars of Orion's Belt, across their chests? And had he not, at the time, detected a French accent in the Stag King's voice?

The rain was falling in sheets now but when it eased he could if he liked go to the Tun and see her. He'd make sure that Ralph was kept busy here. He paced restlessly round the room.

The encounter in the forest had been dreamlike, detached from the real world. If he saw her again it might only be a disastrous anti-climax. Would she still be beautiful or had it all been a spell cast by the firelight and the drums? He might find only an underfed peasant girl with dirt beneath her fingernails and a mind as blank as an unused slate.

Besides, there was Edith.

Where Edith was concerned, Henry had entered a new realm of experience. For the first time in his life he had found a woman who could not simply be replaced by another woman, whose hold on him was not merely that of the body. The girl in the forest had eased him physically but she did not, could not, take Edith's place, any more than Saehild could have done. It was Edith whom he wanted and if he rode anywhere through the hock-deep mud and swollen streams of Hampshire in the next few days (had the climate changed since he was a boy? It seemed like it) it would be to Romsey.

Where Rufus had forbidden him to go and although Rufus was now en route to Maine, he had told Abbess Christina of the prohibition and if Henry broke it she would no doubt let the king know. And he, Henry, was his brother's pensioner, dependent on him for income and status, at risk of being dismissed if he offended, driven overseas again to the hopeless life of a robber lord. He dared not think too much about the power Rufus had over him; it made the black rage rise. Once or twice, in private, he had unwisely let that happen and ended up pounding clenched fists on the wall.

Edith was still safe. He had not depended on the signal they had arranged, in case the abbess had locked her up again without warning. He had in fact sent Saehild to Romsey with orders to represent herself as a grateful recipient of alms from Edith in the past, anxious to thank the almsgiver in person. Saehild, once private with Edith, had found out that the abbess had so far left her niece alone, except for barbed comments. She knew, thought Henry grimly, that if she touched Edith and he got to hear of it, fifty Rufuses brandishing axes wouldn't keep him from carrying out his threat. It wasn't in the best of taste to co-opt one's ex-mistress as a messenger to one's – he hoped – future wife, but Saehild had left him, not the other way about and she was very goodnatured. And she and her husband were hard up, like nearly everyone else these days. Money had talked and it had been worth it. His fear for Edith was relieved.

But not his longing, and he did not want the girl in the wood. He would forget her.

On a quayside in Southampton harbour, Rufus stood beside a moored ship and argued with her owner.

'I'll double the usual passage money. It's only me you've got to carry. I didn't set out alone but I outdistanced the others. One man won't overload you!'

'No, sir. Not for ten times the usual rate. It's too risky. This storm . . .'

'What storm? said Rufus. His cloak was black with rain and flattened to his body by the wind. 'It's passing. Call yourself a mariner? I've urgent business over there and the wind's fair . . .'

'The wind's a gale, sir. And out there beyond the harbour, the sea . . .'

'You think we'll drown? Where's your spirit of adventure? I'm the King of England and whoever heard of a king getting drowned? Treble the usual rate! Oh, come on, man! That vessel of yours is built like a longship. The Vikings could ride out anything.'

'No,' said the captain, but with less conviction and some annoyance.

'Four times the rate!'

Mammon and pride could be seen struggling with natural caution. 'It'ud be at your own risk. If we all end up swimming for it, I'm not to blame.'

'Done!'

Two hours later, at sea, Rufus stood triumphantly beside the mast. He was drenched to the skin with spray and rain but the persistent downpour had flattened out the water and the thunder had gone. The ship rode easily on a slow, rain-pitted swell and the northwesterly wind had slackened to a breeze which merely filled the square sail and drove them forward. 'What did I tell you?' he shouted to the captain.

The dusk was falling but he gazed ahead as though willing the coast of Normandy to appear. He was throwing his heart in front of the ship. He was bound for Normandy and after that for Maine. He was drawing near to Helias. He would see Helias again. Wouldn't he?

Three

I Have Sinned
August–October 1099

Onions, cabbage, some cheese, a piece of bread and a bit of honeycake that Elfgiva, who looked after the bees, had given her, and that, by present standards, would be a lavish supper. The corn was ripening but the crop was thin and if anything went wrong, such as a storm at the wrong moment, they would be desperate.

In June, while on duty, Ralph had come across her brother Richard and she knew that Fallowdene, supported by saffron, was doing well. Richard had found buyers in Cornwall where apparently the stuff had never gone out of use. He had also bought a ship of his own to replace the lost vessel in which he had had a share. The first voyage of the *St. Edith* had been a financial success.

But Ralph would not ask Richard for help and she did not press him, strangely enough, because he might have given in. She knew that she now had power over him and had lately found in her maturing self a fear of abusing that power.

But oh, if they could be at Fallowdene now! Well, if the harvest were enough to feed them next year, and if only, after this baby, she could conceive one by Ralph, then they might visit Fallowdene with pride. She longed to see the soaring downs again, instead of this narrow horizon bounded by the trees which hemmed the Tun round. But she wanted to go back in triumph or not at all, not as a frightened child but as a wife with children, and a husband who appreciated her . . .

If she still had a husband. She had been trying to keep that thought at bay but suddenly it took her by storm and dropping the knife with which she had been prodding the vegetables, she sat down with her hands to her face. And prayed, not to Herne of the hateful Wood, but to the God of Father Ilger and Archbishop Anselm, that the horrible thing which Penna, against all custom, had first in his high

403

excitable voice mentioned at Beltane, and had at Lammas proposed more loudly, would never come to pass.

Then, because whatever happened she must protect the child she carried, which meant eating when possible and trying to sleep at night, she made herself swallow her supper. She hoped that Ralph, who was on duty with the court, was getting better fare. She went to bed.

She was roused at dawn not by a cockerel as usual but by shouts and barking. Someone banged at the door and then ran on. She pulled on some clothes and hurried out. Across the cornfield, where the forest came close to its edge, she glimpsed shadowy animal shapes bounding, fleeing, backs rippling above the grain. In the midst of the field, human figures leapt and waved their arms. She ran clumsily round the edge and they came to meet her: Cild and Oswin, swearing; Penna swearing even louder, shrieking high-pitched imprecations, indeed, and shaking his fist; Elfgiva, long skirts soaked with dew, flourishing a broom; Osmund, red in the face and gesticulating with a hoe. The dogs, which could not run because their fore-claws had been cut in accordance with the Forest Law, trotted about whimpering in frustration.

'Deer!' Elfgiva gasped.

'Like the locust plague of Egypt!' Penna shrilled.

Sybil stared at the swathe of catastrophe in the wheat. 'But . . . there must have been hundreds!'

'Reckon there were,' said Cild grimly.

She couldn't take it in. Last night the corn had been thin but intact. Now there were great flattened patches where full-fed animals . . . like bloated succubi spawned by the Wood . . . had lain down to doze; rank on rank of stalks from which every ear had gone. Eyes distended with earnestness, Penna said: 'Reckon the Horned One's got it in for us proper. Like I said at Lammas.'

'You had no right to say what you did at Lammas, or Beltane either!' said Sybil angrily. 'That was for the King to say. No one else.' She looked at the corn again and tried to brace herself. 'It's not complete ruin. There's a lot left.'

'We've lost a third part,' said Osmund. 'It'll mean hunting again this autumn, never mind the Forest Laws.'

He banged the hoe handle on the ground and the head of it fell off. For once, no one laughed.

'I was only saying what we're all thinking,' Penna said resentfully to Sybil and walked sullenly away.

The great wind came at Martinmas, on the 11th of November, blowing up from the south-west, sweeping torn dark clouds before it. It was stronger even than the gale of 1093 which had wrought such havoc. It whipped up the sea and sent the breakers crashing in spume along the coasts of Cornwall, up the Bristol Channel and along the shores of Wales. It scoured the Devon moorlands. It rushed on across the forests of the south; no hawk was aloft in such weather but if any had been, it would have seen the treetops once more like a sea in turmoil, with blown leaves for spray. Across open ground, it roared; in hollow trees and round the towers of the castle at Winchester, it wailed. It was like a damned and houseless soul crying in despair and fury. After dark, it was terrifying.

Flambard, fetched to the king by the brisk but uncommunicative chamberlain Herbert, said against the banging of the shutters and the undulating howl of the wind: 'I see no difficulty about either paying off the debts of the last campaign or getting in the money for another. There are possibilities still unexplored. The detailed report will be ready in two days.'

'Oh, not now,' said Rufus testily. 'I didn't call you to talk business.' Flambard raised his black eyebrows. 'I simply want,' said Rufus, 'to talk.'

Flambard already knew that. But the king's silence after he entered the tower chamber in Winchester Palace had needed breaking. Rufus pointed to a seat and Flambard, gathering his long robe round him, took it. 'What shall I talk about?'

'What you like as long as it isn't business. They call you Passe-Flamme. Well, pass a flame to me! Interest me! Or discuss the weather, if you can't think of anything better.'

'The gale's getting worse,' said Flambard obediently and also loudly, against a particularly malevolent aerial howl.

405

'If it gets any stronger, it'll blow the tower away,' Rufus agreed. He cocked his head to listen and suddenly began himself to talk. 'It sounds to me like a thousand hounds all baying at once. I can almost see them, can't you? A great pack of black mastiffs pouring through the sky. We had a gale coming back from Normandy – not this bad but bad enough. The noise in the rigging was like crazy laughter. You don't often see experienced captains white with fright but this one thought he'd be feeding the fish before the day was out. But we all survived. Well, we would. I was on board.'

Flambard sat up straighter. He knew the king well but he had now detected a mood he had not seen before, and he didn't like it.

'You've heard the stories, haven't you?' Rufus said.

'Which ones, my lord?'

'How the storm abated to let me cross, when I rushed off from Brockenhurst. How I bullied a captain into taking me and told him that kings never got drowned, and lo and behold, the wind dropped for us. And then I borrowed a priest's mare in Normandy and how she ran like a deer with me on her back, so that I got to my nearest castle before anyone would have thought it possible, and how when the men I'd left plodding after me in England arrived, I already had a muster well under way. Or there's the one about how I chased Helias out of Le Mans and stood between the citizens and Belleme's men and kept Belleme from burning the place right out – the world is full of stories all of a sudden, about what a remarkable king I am.'

'And are the stories true?'

Rufus snorted. 'True enough. Winds do drop sometimes. It didn't damn well drop when I was coming back. It just didn't sink us, that's all. As for the old mare, she went fast because I stuck my spurs into her. She was lazy, nothing more.'

'And Le Mans?'

'There wasn't much left to burn when I got there. I made a gesture that cost nothing and pleased the inhabitants. Though I did it because I hoped . . .'

'What did you hope, my lord?'

'The rumours,' said Rufus, 'are like bad jokes. I can calm the sea and turn a knock-kneed nag into lightning; I can even make the common citizens of Le Mans like me. But I can't damn well conquer Helias, can I? I couldn't get him out of that last stronghold. I hoped that showing mercy towards Le Mans would bring him to me, make him ready to seek terms. Make him . . . give me his fealty. But no. He wouldn't come.'

'It's being said . . .' Flambard stopped in mid-sentence.

'What's being said?'

'I'm afraid of saying the wrong thing,' said Flambard truthfully.

'I don't want you to say the right thing. I w . . . want you to say what you think, what you hear. I have people round me all day saying the right thing. I don't need that from you.'

'They're saying, my lord, that you withdrew because although you could have brought Helias down by force, it would have meant that he was fetched to you in chains and you didn't want that.'

'Really?' Rufus snorted again. 'And do they – whoever *they* are – also say why I have this funny delicacy about Helias?'

'I'd rather not . . .'

'I p . . . pay you to do as you're told. Answer me!'

Flambard had actually paled, a phenomenon which would have amazed most of his acquaintances. 'They say it would give you no pleasure to see Helias in chains because you'd prefer him in your arms.'

Rufus' face darkened. But when his eyes met Flambard's, it was like colliding with a wall. *You made me say it*, said Flambard's gaze.

'They were right,' said Rufus bitterly. 'I wanted a link with Helias that was real – fealty, friendship, if nothing more. Once, my friends threatened to leave me if I gave him Maine. But now that he's seized it, they'd rather see him do me homage than sit behind his castle walls and laugh at me. *And that is what he is doing*. No, I didn't want to bring him down by force. I wanted him to come to me. He would not, and so, like a fool, I backed out of Maine with nothing. And now I've come to understand what I didn't know then, that I'll never forget that. If I were back there now, it would be different. One day, it *will* be different. One day I'll have him in my hands – oh yes, I will! – and then I shan't ask him to be my lover, not now, or even my vassal. I'll ask him instead how he'd like to be torn apart by wild horses. Now what is it?'

Flambard had stiffened, mouth tightening. 'My lord, I'm your confessor.'

'And many a good chuckle we've had over my sins.'

'But if you came to me and confessed that you had done what you suggest – or even that you had made such a threat to Helias when he was in your hands – there's something I'd want to know.'

Rufus had been sitting opposite Flambard. Now he left his settle and threw himself on his knees. 'Give me your blessing, Father, for I have sinned. Confess me now, Ranulf. Yes, I want to see Helias' limbs torn bleeding from their sockets. He has rejected me and made me look foolish. So what's your question?'

In the pale upturned eyes there was laughter. But the upward tilt of the face smoothed the flesh against the bone, making Rufus seem younger, more vulnerable. And below the flippancy there was an appeal for help. 'Even I don't laugh at everything,' said Flambard gravely. 'I should ask you, my son, whether if you carried out your wish, it would give you any joy?'

'Joy?' Rufus let out a yelp of mirth. 'Of course not. It would be revenge, that's all.'

Flambard rarely touched his master but he was impelled now to take Rufus' face between his hands. 'I think,' he said seriously, 'that if you tried to carry out that threat, you would give way at the last and countermand your order. And that if by chance you were too late, you would fling yourself weeping on the corpse and embrace it. And what would that do for your reputation? Pursue your campaign against Maine next year if you must, my son, but not to that end.'

'I must pursue it. I've started this war to get Maine and I can't afford to lose this or any other war.'

'Yes. But treat Helias as just another intransigent vassal.'

408

The shutters rattled violently. Rufus said nothing. 'There are other things in the world besides Helias,' Flambard said.

'I know. But I can't believe it. I try to fill my days. I've sent for Walter Tirel, to keep me company. I think about raising money. I laugh at your cunning schemes for getting it. I plan war to fill the emptiness.'

'Emptiness?'

'If I never see Helias again and sometimes I believe I won't, there's nothing else. Just things to fill the space with, like a starving man eating grass. Sometimes the idea of getting killed on campaign is almost pleasant. I'd be free of him then. Free of wanting, all the time.'

'Unless you turn out to have an immortal soul after all. Then you might find that you were not free but trapped in an eternal tyranny.'

'Tyranny! What a wonderful word for it,' said Rufus. And then, in a whisper: 'But if I have no immortal soul, then there would only be . . . the darkness.'

There was a pause. Then Flambard lifted his hands away and made a rapid sign of blessing. Rufus went back to his settle. Both felt awkward. Flambard was disturbed by this fey mood. Unexpectedly he found himself wishing he had promoted the marriage with Edith after all. He had heard reports of her which suggested that he had underestimated her, that perhaps she could have managed Rufus. Perhaps she could have managed this.

'You're a trustworthy friend,' said Rufus suddenly. 'Sometimes I wish you were a closer friend even than you are.'

Flambard shook his head. 'Friendship can be damaged if it comes too close. And you have Tirel. What you really need, my lord,' he said, with a grin, 'is a nice, all-night orgy.'

Outside, rain had been added to the wind. The air grew suddenly very cold. The gale backed to the north that night and drove a huge tide down the North Sea, surging ashore on the low-lying coasts of East Anglia and up the Thames estuary, wrecking ships, sweeping away the houses which had been so patiently reconstructed after the storms of 1093, carrying away the cattle herds

409

which had been as patiently built up again, drowning crops.

It subsided the next day, as if satisfied with the ruin it had caused, but the cold and wet went on, hunting down more victims, finding them readily among the homeless and hungry, who sickened and died with ease.

Before Christmas, it had started to snow. It was a hard winter.

Four

The Four Horsemen
February 1100

Ralph took shelter in one of the other houses when Sybil's time came but after a day and a night, Elfgiva sent for him, despite his protests that it was no place for a man.

They had been hungry, all winter, and the bitter weather made it harder. With the carefully rationed grain, that part of the harvest which the deer had graciously left them, Ralph's pay and the bowmaking money, and the deer stealthily poached by the men, they could keep alive. But there was not a mouthful to spare. He had watched Sybil grow huge with the greedy child which was none of his, while her arms and legs grew daily more sticklike with privation. 'Save her, but if necessary let the child die,' he told Elfgiva as she dragged him across the threshold.

'You can do as much towards saving both of them as I can. Go on! She's been calling for you.'

Inside the house, although the fire trench was banked as high as possible, the cold was still intense. The room was lit by the firelight and by candles. Sybil crouched on the pallet, rugs cast over her for what little protection they could give. Her face was turned sideways and pressed into the straw pillow. She had no colour and although sometimes she seemed to shiver with cold, the tangled hair at her temples was soaked with sweat as well as tears. Her eyes were shut and she was moaning. 'Take her hand,' Elfgiva ordered him. 'Here he is, Sybil. You'll be all right now.'

He found himself, all snow-spattered as he was, kneeling by the pallet and taking her cold fingers. 'Sybil?' he said. He shouldn't be here. This was women's mystery. The fingers clutched at him as a spasm seized her. 'Good girl, do that again,' encouraged Elfgiva. Sybil tried to speak but the word was ripped apart into a wail.

411

Ralph heard himself saying what he would have said to a wounded comrade who was having a bone set. 'Steady. It won't be long now. Hold on to me. I'm here.'

Sybil was convulsed again but differently, ominously, as though she were a doll shaken by some force outside herself. There was despair in her wail this time. Elfgiva caught Ralph's eye and he saw her lips anxiously compress. 'Fight!' he said. 'Yes, you can, you must! Fight back!' He knew his eyes were showing his horror to Elfgiva and he dropped them. He pressed his forehead to the back of Sybil's hand as though to pass encouragement and pleading directly from his mind to her body. The depth of his horror had startled him, as his jealousy had done last summer.

Kneeling there, he traced in memory the course of his life with Sybil. He had pitied an unhappy child and been seduced by a beautiful one, in whom he had glimpsed a queen for the Tun. He had brought home a girl who was a child again, whose homesick whimperings had annoyed him, yet renewed his pity and certainly demanded so much attention from him that she had done something to keep him from brooding over Rufus and his lost position.

And then had come the knowledge that someone else desired Sybil too, and he had found that the passion which had overtaken him in the stable at Fallowdene was alive and thriving. And in the resultant ugly quarrel, he had again discovered the queen . . . but this time grown to a woman, truly royal, and *kind* . . .

And very human. Sybil who only half-believed in Herne was his crutch, his anchor against those heady, perilous hours in the Wood when it seemed as though Herne were not only real but had possessed him, filling his human body and brain with something they were not shaped to contain. He raised his head and said clearly: 'If you die and leave me, Sybil, I shall break in pieces. Don't die. Don't go away from me!'

There was another contraction, stronger. 'Again!' shouted Elfgiva. 'Aha, we'll win yet, see if we don't! I want more light.' She turned to light another candle.

'And don't you,' panted Sybil, dragging him near with sudden strength, and whispering while Elfgiva's back was turned, 'die and leave me either! Promise!'

412

'Hush, you need your breath.'

'*Promise!*'

'One more thrust and we're there. Come on, my girl!' Elfgiva had set the candle nearby and returned to her task. 'Come on!' Sybil arched, gasped, wailed and faltered. 'Push!' commanded Elfgiva.

'Go *on!*' Ralph gripped her hands, giving her his strength now through his fingers, keeping her in the world with them, in lieu of the promise he dared not make.

The reminder had all but robbed them both of that strength. He shuddered. He had tried, all winter, not to think about that. He had known since his initiation what the Kingship of the Wood could mean. But that final meaning had not been invoked for centuries. He had not thought it would be awakened in his day. Rufus had once confided to him his fear of the ultimate darkness. He knew now what Rufus meant.

Elfgiva exclaimed: 'It's a boy!'

He supposed she knew what she was talking about. The baby looked to Ralph like a mandrake root covered with blood. But Elfgiva seemed to think it was as it should be and would eventually grow up to be a man. If starvation, lung-fever or the end of the world which Father Ilger apparently thought was imminent didn't get in first. When Elfgiva wiped its head, there was a thin dark fuzz to be seen. Dark? It wouldn't resemble Cild, then. Thank Herne for that. He would be able to manage, make some sort of showing as a father to this Wood-hatched cuckoo, to do what the Tun expected, in fact.

Sybil was in the sleep of exhaustion. She had lost too much blood but Cild and Osmund were on a poaching expedition which should mean meat tomorrow. Elfgiva said that if Sybil had some nourishing food soon, it might work miracles.

The light was fading as he went outside. He had been offered supper by Oswin's wife. Underfoot, the slush which had half-melted that day in a weak sunlight was turning crisp again. It would freeze anew tonight. In the dusk, the white-shrouded forest was an army of ghosts. The wind was bitter.

413

Two figures were running towards him from the other cottages, beyond the stream. They halted at the far side of the plank bridge, waiting for him. As he reached them, he recognised Penna and Osmund. 'Osmund, you're back. What luck? Sybil has a son and Elfgiva says . . .'

He saw their faces, and stopped.

'The Foresters,' Osmund said. 'We was running, Cild and me, to pick up a deer we'd shot. He was out in the open before me. I was still back in the thicket. They caught him bloodyhanded, just as he squatted down by the carcase. They've got him. They've got Cild!'

In the five years since Rufus had dismissed him to Chenna's Tun and the life of just another Knight Huntsman, Ralph could count on the fingers of one hand the times he had been as near to the king as he was today and never, in all those years, had he had Rufus' undivided attention as he had it now.

But these privileges had been grudgingly given. It had taken silver he could ill spare to get himself to the foot of Rufus' dais, squeezed in as an unimportant supplicant at the end of a formal audience.

Rufus regarded him with bored and dispassionate eyes, as if they were strangers. As though, thought Ralph with anger, Rufus' stubby fingers had never caressed the moles on his Knight Huntsman's chest, as though they had never fallen asleep in each other's arms. Shocking words took shape in Ralph's mind. 'You didn't look so dignified when you were climbing on my back. I've made you beg for things most men would be ashamed of wanting. Who do you think you are?'

Rufus said coolly: 'You have a request, Messire Ralph des Aix?'

'I have, if it pleases you.' (It wouldn't). 'I have come to ask your royal clemency for a prisoner . . .'

He believed Cild to have fathered Sybil's child and for that, he hated Cild.

And when he knew that the Foresters had taken him, he was riding for the Chief Forester's base at Lyndhurst Manor, in the hope of rescuing the man he loathed, before

414

an hour had passed. He was King of the Wood, of the Tun, and the Tun expected it. He was a knight, with more power than his predecessor Chenna had ever had and must use that advantage if he could.

Forest offenders were usually taken to Lyndhurst first. They would be held there till the Forest Justices came round, if this were to be soon. If not, they would be taken on to Winchester, which was more secure, to wait. As far as Ralph knew, the Justices had just finished with the area. He wanted to get to Cild before Cild vanished into the bowels of Winchester Castle. He rode through an icicle-hung forest where every branch was outlined on its upper edge with an inch of snow. His breath blew away in pale vapour and his feet went numb in his boots. He warmed them, however, kicking his heels for a day at Lyndhurst, waiting to get speech with someone in authority. Only to learn when at last he did, that the Justices were still in Hampshire, still in session at the Sheriff's manor Ringwood, eight miles to the west, and that Cild had been taken straight there. 'Too many of these offences lately,' said the Norman official, who had never had to resort to crime to eat. 'The Justices are staying on. They ought to be on their way to the Midlands by now.'

He rode to Ringwood, head down through a blizzard. On the way it occurred to him to wonder, not why he was taking so much trouble for Cild – by the mores of the Tun he had no choice; the King of the Wood need not love his people but was compelled to defend them – but why it did not after all seem to be against his will. At Lyndhurst, fretting hour after hour, he had found that his anxiety was no dutiful pretence. He was afraid for Cild and truly desired to save him.

The answer came back at him from the air, like the stinging snowflakes. Cild was his benefactor. Cild had not wronged him for he had done only what was customary in the Wood. Outside it, he had done no more than glance admiringly at Sybil. What he had done instead was to hunt deer for her sake and be seized for it. And it was Cild's mother Elfgiva who now watched by Sybil's bed, who had brought her through this far and who depended on him to save her son if he could.

415

When he got to Ringwood, it was mid-morning and the court was sitting.

He had seen Forest Courts before. As a king's man, in the days before the Tun, he had given evidence at one or two. Even then, at the Forest Courts, or when foraging for provisions, commandeering food from villages when the king was on the move, he had never been quite at ease and the Tun had taken from him any belief he had ever had that he was different from the thick-accented, roughly-clad, frightened creatures who owned the snatched provisions, or were accused of stealing deer. Now when he heard them stammer and saw them scan the hall and its implacably well-armed, well-fed officialdom, seeking escape as the blinding iron or the wrist-severing axe came nearer, it was their minds he entered and not those of the officials.

He demanded from the Chief Clerk the names of those whose cases had already been heard and found to his relief that Cild was not among them. He waited at the back of the hall, ready to march out as soon as Cild appeared, to plead for him or if necessary buy him free with the last pieces of silver the Tun could scrape together.

There were fifteen cases still to go and only one day left. The Sheriff and the Justices all wished to get away to other business. Twelve of the fifteen were convicted and taken away, struggling and bellowing, to mutilation. Cild had still not been brought out. The session was being closed. Ralph pushed his way back to where the Chief Clerk sat.

'. . . of Chenna's Tun? I don't recall . . .' the Clerk, in his prim dark official gown, flipped through the contents of his desk and at last discovered a note scrawled on a slate. 'Oh yes, a late arrival. No time for him this session. All today's cases were extras. Quite disgraceful. What are times coming to?'

'According to our local priest,' said Ralph, 'disease, war, famine and death. Most of your disgraceful prisoners were just trying to stay alive.' The Clerk gave him a shocked, pained glance as though he were a dog Ralph had kicked. 'Where is the man Cild now?' demanded Ralph.

'On his way to Winchester with the other overflow

cases. There were a number. They went off this morning to make the best use of the daylight. They'll stay there till the Justices get back, which won't be for two years at the soonest.'

Winchester after all, but at least there was time in hand. He made another cold, difficult ride, using forest trails overhung with trees because here the snow was not so deep. At last he found himself crossing a turnkey's palm with silver and being led down into the underground regions of Winchester Castle. There, housed with half a dozen others in the half-light of a cell under the keep, he found Cild. Cild was not shackled, and walked to meet him, holding himself erect. 'My lord!' he said, and knelt. 'How I hoped you would come.'

'You took a lot of finding. You idiot, what do you mean by getting caught?'

'They were waiting for us. They must have been on the watch for a long time.' Cild's manner was coldly calm but his next words revealed a different state of mind beneath it. 'If they mutilate me I shall kill myself. Can you leave me the means of doing it before they spoil me?'

'You're in no immediate danger. The court won't sit again for at least two years.'

'Two years? Here?' Cild's gesture at the cell, at the low ceiling of vaulted stone, the damp walls and smelly dimness, was full of disbelief and hopelessness. His face was as appalled as though guards had come to drag him to execution that moment.

Even Sybil weighed light, Ralph thought, against this man's danger. He would never like Cild. He knew by instinct the tendency to cruelty that Sybil had experienced. But from this, he would have tried to save even the Devil, if he were of the Tun. 'Take my knife. But don't use it yet. I'm trying to get you released. Give me a chance.'

Cild was still kneeling. In the Wood, Ralph's followers always knelt to him and kissed his feet too. But none of them had ever kissed his hand before.

'With what is the man charged?' Rufus asked from the dais.

417

'He took a deer but . . .'

'Then there's no clemency,' said Rufus, cutting him short. 'That crime's too common. Let men think they can do that and go free and there'll be no end to it.'

It was an official audience and therefore most of the court were present. It was embarrassing to plead in the presence of Meulan and Gilbert Clare, of Count Henry and Richie.

'He and his family were hungry, my lord. I am fed while I'm on duty here. Those I leave at the Tun aren't. Is a deer worth more than a man's life? I mean life. Mutilation can kill.'

On Rufus' face there appeared his wicked, small-boy grin. 'Well, Sir Ralph. How much value do you put on a man's life? In other words, how much are you offering?'

Meulan laughed.

'My lord, I . . .'

'Where shall I start the bidding, Sir Ralph? Three marks of silver?'

'I haven't even one,' said Ralph. 'My Knight Huntsman's pay is eight pence a day. I spend most of what I earn in feeding the people of the Tun and . . .'

'When I gave you the Tun, Sir Ralph, the idea was that it and its villeins should feed you. If you can't manage your affairs better, or insist on turning yourself into a charitable institution, the consequences are your own responsibility.'

'I left home,' said Ralph, 'with all the silver I and the man Cild's friends could put together.' He looked straight at Rufus, for the first time not accepting his dismissal from favour, trying to reach through to the Rufus whose lover he had been. 'Most of it has gone already, on bribes, trying to find out where Cild was . . .'

'You've seen him?'

'Amazing,' observed Meulan audibly. 'We are supposed to take comforts to our villeins when they turn criminal, are we?'

'. . . and to obtain access, my lord, to you. I have nothing left with which to buy Cild's freedom. I am dependent on your mercy and goodwill.'

'You mean you want something for nothing.'

418

'No, my lord.'

'Then what are you offering if you have no money?'

'My gratitude and lifelong loyalty and that of every soul in Chenna's Tun.'

Rufus, and then the entire court, burst out laughing.

Ralph stared at Rufus' feet, understanding the laughter. Ralph and his Tun! Gratitude and loyalty from a pack of rustics! What's that worth? What next?

'The answer,' said Rufus, still shaking with mirth, 'is no. We would advise you, Sir Ralph, if you care so much for your villeins, to warn them away from my deer henceforth.' He made himself become grave again. 'If this Cild becomes an example, it could benefit the rest. By the Face, if we let our deer be taken and did nothing, soon there'd be none left. The court's adjourned. Well, Sir Ralph? You want to say something else?'

'Yes, my lord.'

'All right, get on with it.'

'I have a responsibility towards this man. He was taken at Candlemas. At that time, my wife was near death in process of bearing a son. I believe that Cild went out that day to bring a gift of meat to his lord's wife, to help her to live. I have never known you condemn a man for speaking his mind honestly. I ask leave now to speak freely, without danger.'

'I have an odd feeling, Sir Ralph, that you intend to speak your mind even without safe conduct, as it were.' He wasn't stammering, Ralph noticed. Which meant that he felt nothing. All this amused him, nothing more. There was a tale that Rufus had once, with an outrageousness that was extreme even for him, taken a bribe from the father of a Jewish-born convert to Christianity and attempted to persuade the boy to return to the faith of his ancestors. It had failed, and the youth had indignantly condemned Rufus' own lack of Christianity. And got away with it. Rufus had chosen to find him funny. 'Regard yourself as having leave.'

He should be made to care.

'My wife would have been in less peril if she had had enough to eat during the winter. I am sorry that I have no power to imprison you and keep you hungry till you understand why it is that men take deer.'

419

Into the silence which followed this, while Rufus slowly turned an alarming shade of purple, Henry said enquiringly: 'Your wife had a son at Candlemas, Sir Ralph? Did she come through safely in the end?'

'She was still alive when I left the Tun, my lord. But that was the very day the child was born.'

Rufus had himself under control now though he was still angry, his eyes small and hard. 'We gave you licence to speak, and a promise made between knights is sacrosanct. We will keep our word. Go freely, Sir Ralph. But go. Don't let us see or hear you for seven days at least. In other words, get out.'

As he left the hall he was to his surprise accosted by Count Henry. 'This won't help your man Cild but it's a gift for your son. I hope you find your wife safe and well when you go home,' said Henry, and slipped a pound bag of silver into Ralph's hand.

Five

The Revelations of St John
and Others
February–March 1100

The next day the snow, which had been for a long time hovering on the edge of a thaw, went over the cliff with a rush. The forest tinkled with dripping boughs; fields turned to lakes, paths and ditches to swift rivers. Rivers became torrents of black and ice-green water, bursting banks, making quagmires out of meadows, sweeping away yet more sheep and cattle. And sickness again broke out.

One of its first victims was Ralph. It was a cough and fever like the one he had had at Fallowdene. He took to his bed. Eventually someone called a physician on whose recommendation he was carried to the infirmary attached to Winchester Cathedral. The Infirmarian monks knew their work and he began to recover. He was among the fortunate, but not among the grateful. For to what, he wondered, had he come back?

Meanwhile, Father Ilger of Minstead was far from being the only priest in the land who had to paddle to reach his church; nor was he alone in drawing ominous comparisons between the present dismal conditions and those described in the Revelations of John as foreshadowing the end of the world.

And Count Henry seethed, for there was no getting through the twenty miles of floods between Winchester and Chenna's Tun. Where, despite the existence of Edith, he now greatly wished to go.

The sea, surprisingly, was calm. Richard of Fallowdene's ship, the *St. Edith*, was taking a risk in plying the English Channel so early in the year but Richard was generally regarded as lucky and sometimes he and his skipper leant on that luck. Sailing from the mouth of the Loire, the *St. Edith* put into Southampton to drop a few passengers before going safely on to Chichester. It was not the sea, but the last leg of the journey, from Southampton to Winchester, by barge up a swollen and ill-defined river, which almost succeeded in drowning the embassy from Aquitaine and the courier from that knight errant Duke of Normandy, Robert Curthose.

They were not quite drowned, but arrived drenched and half-frozen, the barge having run aground twice on what should rightly have been fields instead of river bed, so that they had to wade for it to lighten the load before the vessel could float again.

The embassy retired straight to its quarters to thaw out but Curthose's courier, once dried, fortified with mead and clad in clean woollens, presented himself to Rufus in the hall without more delay, to announce the glad tidings that Duke Curthose, tired of his crusading fervour, was on his way home.

Having paused in Sicily on the way, in order to get married.

'He's coming back!' Henry thundered. His current squire, a quiet young man by the name of Godfrey, busied himself with cleaning his master's weapons. He unobtrusively collected up one or two daggers from a table, and put them out of sight. He also moved to the far side of the table. Henry was a generous master in some ways but when he was angry, the man who had thrown Conan from the tower at Rouen would suddenly appear and wise servants were wary of that man. Henry in one of his black furies was incalculable.

'Why the bloody hell,' roared Henry now, 'couldn't he die in the Holy Land like our grandfather did? The place is hot, enemy-infested, disease-ridden, full of snakes, and do any of them get him? No, by God! What gets him instead?' demanded Henry rhetorically of the air. 'A woman! He goes and gets *married*!'

'It's natural, sir,' ventured Godfrey.

'I know it's bloody natural! I'd like to marry, too!' Henry informed him. Godfrey, who knew about Edith, looked sympathetic.

Curthose's wife, according to the courier, was the daughter of one of the great Norman houses which had taken root in the Mediterranean lands. She was well-dowered enough to redeem Normandy – Rufus hadn't been entirely pleased with the news either – and she was beautiful, young and nubile.

Curthose could reasonably expect an heir quite soon. And where, after all, would that leave Henry?

Henry had sunk onto a bench, jamming his clenched hands between his knees. It had only needed Curthose to die abroad, leaving Rufus as his heir. He would then himself have been next in line and even while Rufus lived, could have become, say, governor of Normandy. And as he had once said to Rufus, that rise in status would have brought him Edith. He could have insisted. The barons would have backed him because he was all the succession there was. The thought of Edith, lost now perhaps for ever, turned him sick. It was like poison on a sword-edge. Curthose coming home, with a legitimate son a likelihood!

He lurched to his feet. He must have action, must give himself something different to think about or burst. Or let out his savage thoughts into words which someone might report to Rufus. 'Godfrey, are the floods down enough yet to make getting to somewhere in the Brockenhurst direction possible?'

'Only just, I should say, sir.'

'I'll try,' said Henry.

Odd, he thought sourly as his horse floundered, splashed and slithered to the Tun, that it should in a sense have been Edith who finally sent him there. He was fortunate in finding Sybil not among the other women, but on her own side of the stream, alone and out of doors, dragging hay from the byre. He dismounted, recognising her instantly but startled to see how blue her eyes were. The firelit forest hadn't shown him that.

Sybil, straightening up quickly, had recognised him too. She opened her mouth and closed it again. She did not know what to say.

'I heard you had been ill. You are Sybil, wife of Ralph des Aix, aren't you?'

'I . . . yes, my lord.' What she had recognised, in one dizzy instant, was the face of the Stranger in the Wood.

423

But she could see from his clothes and his horse that he was someone of note.

Henry had never been in the habit of hiding his identity. 'I am Count Henry, brother of the king.' She began to sink into a curtsey but he put out a hand to stop her. 'Last time we met, you were not so formal. No need for formality now, either.'

There was an awkward moment while they studied each other. Sybil was shaken by the exalted nature of the lover who had materialised out of the dance in the forest. Henry was thinking: yes, she's thin and careworn and dirty. None of these peasants wash themselves or their clothes in winter, though I can understand why they don't wash clothes; they've nowhere to dry them. I've been in that position myself, living hard in Normandy. But this filthy hovel! The magic's gone. There's no challenge here to Edith. Yet there's beauty under that skinny scared look. Suppose it were brought out again? I'll never be without women on the side, not even for Edith. Besides . . .

'You had a son at Candlemas?' he asked.

'Yes. He's to be called Gervase. My husband had a cousin of that name, who did something to give him a start in life.'

'Ralph wasn't home much in April and May last year,' said Henry bluntly. 'I know that. So is Gervase mine? Or don't you know?'

'I . . . he's yours, sir,' Sybil whispered and then looked frightened.

'I haven't come to take him from you. But I want to see him. He's thriving?'

'Yes. I was the one who nearly died. In here.' She led him into the dreadful place which was her house. The baby lay in a cradle, rather beautifully carved, a contrast to his shabby surroundings. She lifted him out. He promptly began to roar. There was a dark fuzz on his head.

'Feed him if he's hungry,' said Henry. 'I've seen more of you than that, remember?'

Sybil silently did as he said. 'Who carved the cradle?' Henry asked, seating himself on a stool.

'A man here at the Tun, called Oswin. He's clever at such things. My lord . . .'

'Yes?'

'Are you truly one of us? *You*?'

As much for her peace of mind as anything else, he said: 'Yes. But I keep it very secret. You must never tell anyone. Think of the scandal.'

'I'll keep the secret.' Sybil was visibly trying to put Count Henry, brother of the king, into the same skin as a member of her familiar peasant cult. 'Why have you come?' she asked. 'To see Gervase?'

'Not entirely.' They examined each other as they sat in domestic fashion on either side of this humble fire, like a married pair. Despite the difference in their backgrounds, they were linked through the baby; there was an intimacy. 'You're having hard times here,' said Henry. 'I've given your husband a gift of silver – in congratulation for the birth of his son.' They both smiled. 'But I want to ask you again what I asked you in the Forest. If you wish to leave this place and live under my protection, I will take care of you. You can come with me now. But the choice is yours.'

'I'm grateful,' said Sybil. 'But . . .' She found it hard to explain herself but Wulfhild would have understood. Sybil's wildness had been only the mental equivalent of a foal's fluffy coat. Her true nature had emerged at last and she was the daughter of Wulfhild, who liked familiar earth beneath her feet and familiar people around her. Even Chenna's Tun, though it was not Fallowdene, and certainly Ralph, who had brought her here in the first place out of kindness, felt safer than an unknown future with an unknown Count Henry.

'I'd be only a kind of secret in your life,' she said. 'You'll marry one day, some great lady. Then where would I be? And there's Ralph . . .'

Who had forced her to go to the Wood against her will. 'He matters to you?'

'He'd break in pieces if I left him. Anyway, I don't want to leave him. I . . . oh, Ralph!'

Taking him completely by surprise, Sybil burst into tears. Her flow of milk evidently ceased, for Gervase began to bawl in unison. 'I can't bear it!' Sybil wailed, and rocked back and forth, half as if to soothe the

425

howling baby, but half in the age-old fashion of those in
the depths of grief.

'What can't you bear?' He came to her side and put his
arms round her. 'Quietly. What's the matter? Tell me.'

'He's going to die!' Sybil sobbed. 'Ralph's going to die
and I can't bear it. You don't understand.'

'What don't I understand? What do you mean, Ralph's
going to die? He's been ill this winter but I hear he's
recovering.'

'I know. I don't mean that. But you said did he matter.
He's my *husband*!' She meant: *I have rejoiced in the shape
and warmth of his body.* To Henry she could not say those
words but he picked up her meaning. He longed thus to
rejoice in Edith's body. 'I follow. Go on,' he said.

'I can't bear thinking of him wounded, or frightened,
or . . . or . . . dead. I want to hide my eyes from thinking
of it. I know he's been ill and he's getting better but it's
still going to happen, I know it is. Oh, *Ralph*!'

Henry rose, removed what was after all his own son
from Sybil's grasp, deposited the screaming, crimson-
faced infant in its cradle and carried the cradle outside.
Had he had any doubts about Gervase's parentage, he
thought, the brat's temper would be evidence enough. He
came back and sat down beside Sybil again. 'Now then,'
he said. 'Tell me what this is all about. If I can do anything, I will.'

'You can't.'

'*Tell me*!'

He listened, not in surprise (he had heard something of
this mentioned in the Wood at Beltane, he recalled,
thinking of the exchange between the Stag King and the
worshipper with the high-pitched voice), but with in-
creasing anger and distaste. This cult should be destroyed,
he thought. It had given him a night's magical adventure,
but it was no more than devil-worship, intrinsically evil
and extremely dangerous. Sybil, still weeping although
more quietly now, said: 'Oswin, the man who made
Gervase's cradle, *he* says it's all stupid, that the Tun is
only one small place and it's the whole world that's in
danger. The priest at Minstead says the horsemen of the
Apocalypse are being let loose and that hunger and dis-

426

ease are here already, with war and death, all our deaths, just behind. It'll be the same everywhere. So what use will it be just to kill Ralph? How can he stand for the whole world? Oswin says he's just one ordinary man and all he represents is the Tun. But . . .'

'Your Oswin's right. It would take a god or a full-scale king at the least, to save the whole world.'

'But the others don't understand. They can't . . . they don't know there is any world outside. Most of them haven't been further than Lyndhurst. If that far, even.'

He stayed for some time, telling her that wild talk was mostly just wild talk, that a few warm months in the summer would put a stop to it all. He added firmly: 'But if by any chance, for any reason, you ever do find yourself alone, I'll take responsibility for you and Gervase. I'll see his future is provided for and yours as well. I'll find you another husband if necessary. A better-off one. Tell me something. Does Ralph know Gervase isn't his?'

'Yes. But we rarely speak of the parentage of the Children of the Wood, even if we know it. It's hard for the men sometimes. We don't make it harder. I shall never speak of you to anyone. I'll never tell anyone you're one of Herne's people. That's what you are thinking about, isn't it?' He nodded and she added shrewdly: 'It would be your word against mine, wouldn't it, and how much would mine weigh in that balance?'

Henry laughed. 'So be it. But remember my offer of help if ever you need it. I shall keep track of the Tun, indeed. You can rely on that.'

Taking his leave, he kissed her, but circumspectly, because he knew she did not wish for anything more. Sybil watched him ride away, feeling shaken in a new fashion. Before, she had been simply afraid for Ralph and afraid of a future trapped in the Tun without him, unable ever to go home to Fallowdene for she would never be welcome there now except as a brief visitor.

Henry, unwittingly, had opened up a new horizon of dread, a future in which there was no Ralph and she was not forced to stay in the Tun, no, not that, but handed instead like a helpless package into the power of some unknown man, to face an unknown future in which,

427

somehow, Fallowdene seemed to be further away than ever, a lovely dream from which she had been roughly wakened, and which would never come again.

Henry knew nothing of this and as he rode back to Winchester was not in fact thinking of either Sybil or Gervase.

Like St. John, Henry had become the recipient of a revelation.

'The sun's out. The lavender walk is sheltered from the wind,' said the Infirmarian to Ralph. 'There are benches. You could sit there for a while.'

It was March and the lavender wouldn't be out but the prospect of the open air was welcome. He had inhaled so much herbal steam and swallowed so much horehound cordial that aromatic vapours seemed to fill his head. He went out, shocked to find how weak his illness had made him. He was glad to sit on the bench and enjoy the sun on his face. He was still sitting there half an hour later when the Infirmarian appeared, bringing company, and said: 'Sir Ralph, you have a visitor.'

'Count Henry!' said Ralph, coming to his feet.

'Sit down. I'll sit with you. How are you?' enquired Henry, waving the Infirmarian away.

'Nearly well, thank you, my lord. I shall go home in a day or two. But . . .'

'To Chenna's Tun?'

'Yes. My lord, it was kind of you to come but I didn't expect . . . can I serve you in some way?'

'Oh yes,' said Henry. 'I hope you really are feeling better, by the way. I have a shock for you.'

'Oh?'

Henry smiled. It was an uncomfortable smile; the mouth curved humorously but there was a hard gleam in the brown eyes. Conan of Rouen and Abbess Christina would both have recognised it. 'Your . . . antics, shall we say? . . . in the forest on May Eve and, presumably, Lammas – that's another traditional date, I think? – have been witnessed,' said Henry, and waited with interest for Ralph's reply.

'I beg your pardon?' said Ralph politely. Not a muscle

twitched in his olive-skinned face. But Henry, watching keenly, saw that the sallowness of ill-health had nevertheless deepened.

'You, and others presumably of the Tun and its neighbours, are worshippers of Herne, a cult in which the devotees mask themselves as goats and stags and celebrate life's simpler pleasures in delightfully down-to-earth ways. You deny it?'

'I have not the remotest idea what you're talking about, my lord,' said Ralph briefly.

'Excellent. A man who can keep his own counsel can probably keep mine, too. Very well. But you must answer one question frankly. Have you heard that the end of the world is supposed to be at hand?' enquired Henry. He would have used the same tone to ask whether Ralph had heard the latest lovesong.

'Of course. Has anyone not heard it?' said Ralph. 'Every parish priest in the land seems to be preaching about the day of wrath to come.'

'And do you believe it, yourself?'

Ralph was silent a moment. Then he said: 'Do you know, I wonder sometimes. When year after year the crops fail first from one cause then from another. When people and animals fall ill and die and the skies pour water on our heads summer and winter alike.' He gave Henry a shrewd look. 'But I doubt if you believe it, my lord.'

'No. I don't. But plenty do. The Christian priests have been recommending repentance and crusading as means of averting catastrophe but I gather that priests of a – shall, we say, a pagan persuasion? – have advised a different approach. Sacrifices of propitiation, in fact. Sacrifices of, well, stags. Am I right?'

Ralph did not answer. The two of them stared steadily into each other's eyes, each intent on reading the other's thoughts while concealing his own. Silently conceding that the wordless duel was a draw with no points scored on either side, Henry said: 'The stags in question are of purely local fame which is very foolish. Simple people tend to imagine that their own village or hamlet is the centre of the world but of course it isn't. The threat, if there is one, involves all the world. What effect can even a

429

large number of insignificant deaths have on the power that decides the fate of all the lands and people that there are? Mighty crises need mighty solutions, don't you agree?'

'It would be uncivil of me, my lord, to say that you are talking as though you had gone out of your mind but . . .'

'Do I sound like that?' asked Henry pleasantly. 'Never mind. Just let me talk a little more. Your man Cild. I have no power to order his release, as things stand. The Sheriff of Hampshire has the discretion to free him but he won't use it unless the king commands him and the king won't.'

'May I ask where all this is leading?'

'We're nearly there. It's quite simple. I'm making you an offer, Sir Ralph. Cild's freedom, whole and sound, is part of it. Together with that, I also offer you the safety of your woodland cult. You may dance and copulate in a damp forest clearing to your heart's content as far as I'm concerned though I'm sure it can't be good for this bronchial tendency the Infirmarian here says you have. But your local priest won't approve if the details are laid officially before him and nor would the Bishop of Winchester, who will know very well how to go about stamping such practices out. On top of that, I'm prepared to give your manor, which I gather is in desperate straits, financial help until harvests improve. All in return for just one service, which you may perform yourself or through others – it's all the same to me.'

'And that is?'

'The danger *may* be real,' said Henry, 'and perhaps a propitiary sacrifice *is* the best hope of averting it. Who can say? But it needs to be a sacrifice of sufficient value. For a whole world nothing less than an anointed king is adequate, or so it seems to me. Cild's freedom, the safety of your cult, my silver, they're all yours if when my brother Curthose sets foot again in Normandy, King Rufus is already under the earth and his crown is on my head. I'd suggest a hunting accident,' said Henry thoughtfully. 'One of my brothers died that way; these things do happen. And it would be in keeping with the nature of Herne, would it not?' He observed, mildly, that Ralph was gaping at him. 'I do have some sort of right to that crown,' said

the man who had thrust Conan from the walls of Rouen
Castle, who had long ago crossed the chasm which separated most men from the act of cold murder. 'I am the
only one of my father's sons who was born in England,
the only one born after Father became a king. Think
about it,' said Henry, getting up, preparing to leave. 'I'd
suggest next Beltane,' he added casually over his
shoulder. 'There's a fourth item for you in my bargain,
after all, isn't there? It's worth it to you to hurry it along.
Your own life's at stake as well. You don't really want to
die as a Beltane sacrifice yourself, do you?'

'You were listening!' said Edith furiously to her aunt.
She shut her mouth hard after the last word. In
arguments with Aunt Christina, the words one actually
said resembled the island tops of submerged mountains.
She wondered if her aunt sensed the unsaid ones, most of
which were epithets. 'Jealous old bat!' was the unspoken
rider to the accusation of eavesdropping which Edith had
just levelled at the Abbess of Romsey. Even with
Henry's protection, she couldn't risk saying it aloud.
  'It is my duty to watch over you,' said Christina coldly.
'The woman Saehild will never enter here again. I was
remiss in allowing her to come three times before I
discovered her purpose. You have been forbidden to
communicate with Count Henry and I shall see that in
future the order is obeyed. You are to stay in Romsey
and put thoughts of lust and worldliness out of your
head. You may as well accept it, Edith. You will never
see Count Henry again. Your future lies in the life of
religion.'
  'It does not,' said Edith recklessly. 'It was just as well
for you that I had no violence to report to Saehild. If I
had, Henry would have found a way to deal with you.
Touch me and I'll see he hears of it somehow. Then
you'll wish you hadn't. I will never take the veil and you
can't make me!'
  'Count Henry is an obstinate, unbridled, immoral
young man and no good influence on you.'
  'You're terrified of him,' said Edith proudly. 'And you
know as well as I do that he'd come if I needed him.

431

He'll wade through blood to get his way. He'll come one day and take me away to marry him.'

Her mother, the saintly Margaret, would have been horrified. But as several people had already recognised, Edith was Malcolm of Scotland's daughter too, and very little had horrified Malcolm.

Six

The Holy Executioner
May 1100

At dawn on the first of May, 1100, before he prepared for the May Day hunt, Ralph des Aix had himself shriven. He did it out of habit, as though before a battle, although he had come straight to Winchester from the Beltane gathering. His confession, to say the least of it, omitted several important things, and was made in the presence of an intention which would have had the priest, had he known, considering exorcism instead of absolution.

He went out of the chapel of the Winchester palace into a mist-hazed morning which promised to be fine. They might have a better harvest this year and then he would see more flesh on Sybil . . . and at that he halted his thoughts, so roughly that if his thinking had been a horse, he would have jagged its mouth. It was so very easy to *forget* . . .

The Keeper of the Walk and his beaters were already at the kennels and the hounds, leaping and baying at their enclosure fence, had sensed sport to come.

'The deer we marked yesterday are in the cover south of the Long Glade,' Ralph said to the Keeper. 'We want them driven into the glade for a standing shoot. The wind's westerly so place yourselves to the east. No one is to interfere with the Twelve Acre Wood to the west. There are hinds there. They'll be in calf.'

When the Keeper and his men had gone, Ralph fetched a bucket of well water and went back to the poky quarters he shared with three others. There, he washed all over including his hair, and shaved meticulously.

He would have liked privacy but although most people were now in hall or stable, one of his room-mates came in. This one witness to Ralph's extreme and chilly ablutions, however, was only Sir Brian of Little Dene, who was in Winchester on knight service with de Warenne. He had recognised Ralph, of course, and knew that Ralph had

433

married Sybil. But he merely thought that Ralph had taken on a girl of bad reputation for the sake of a pretty face and probably a dowry, and was therefore either a wantwit or a cunning bargainer, and in neither case did Sir Brian consider the matter his business. He had offered, civilly, to carry news of Sybil home with him when he went, but he had little interest in her or Ralph. He glanced at the bucket but all he actually said was: 'I'm trying out a new crossbow today. Want to see it?'

Ralph, thankful that there were no probing questions, was happy to discuss crossbows. He could hardly tell Brian that today he must go scoured from head to foot with no trace of impurity about him, to provide a human sacrifice for Herne.

He was thankful too that Richard was not here. Normally, Richard would have been on duty along with Brian, but this time, according to Brian, Richard had bought himself out in order to attend to business at home. Richard would certainly have asked questions.

He put on clean clothes and went to the hall for some food. He could not afterwards remember what he ate. He was outside, waiting by his saddled horse, when the principals came out.

Henry was not with them. Henry had arranged to be elsewhere this morning, although Ralph did not suppose elsewhere was actually very far off. Rufus however came striding from the hall side by side with the chief members of the visiting Aquitainian embassy, and talking over his shoulder to Richie and to Walter Tirel, who had lately arrived from France. Perhaps to fill as best he might the void which Helias had left, Ralph thought. Tirel's brother-in-law Gilbert Clare followed, slight and fairhaired still. Many fairhaired men darkened with time but Clare would fade from pale gold to silver. All were combed and glossy, dressed for a May Day outing, and light of heart as boys.

He bowed formally as Rufus approached and Rufus, amiable enough as long as Ralph stayed correctly within the character of Knight Huntsman, said: 'Well, des Aix, have you some sturdy pricket buck for us today?'

'We shall manage a kill, I trust, my lord,' said Ralph.

*

434

It was still early as they rode out of Winchester into a forest fresh with dew and birdsong. Ralph rode close to Rufus and Tirel, who were discussing the Aquitainians. A valuable treaty had apparently been offered. Rufus talked easily, without stammering, a man who was sure he would see tomorrow.

It was hard for Ralph to keep his mind on his duties. Richie, spurring up alongside him, spoke twice before he realised that the boy was addressing him. 'Can I go with the houndsmen this morning instead of shooting? Stagbane hasn't seen sport in weeks.'

The big hound was running beside Richie's horse, nose hopefully questing along the ground, stern up and waving. 'We'd like to help rouse the game instead,' said Richie.

Stagbane's manners hadn't noticeably improved with time and an animal so undisciplined would not have been kept in the regular pack. But the boy had at least had the courtesy to ask, making up for his hound. Some youths in Richie's place would have ignored Ralph's authority. 'Yes, you can, but keep him in order. He ran amok last time and had half the pack off chasing a hare instead of a deer.' Ralph drew rein. 'We dismount here.'

Horses trampling through the wood might disturb the quarry too soon. They were left tethered, in the care of grooms, and Ralph led the way to the shooting stand on foot. They emerged in single file into a long grass-grown glade, fringed with bushes and shadowed by the massive trees beyond them. Using signs and very low-pitched speech, Ralph positioned the hunters. He put Rufus and Tirel in the best places and because of their acquaintanceship, gave Brian of Little Dene quite a good place too, not far from Tirel. The shaftbearers stood behind their masters, ready to hand arrows or, in case of crossbow enthusiasts, to prepare a second bow while the other was in use.

Brian's squire was his son. He was slow getting into place and Tirel and Rufus, who considered crossbows cumbersome, made silent fun of Brian, Tirel's pointing finger tracing the path of an imaginary speeding deer while Rufus strove fumblingly to load an invisible cross-bow and then gazed blankly about him in search of a quarry which had gone. Then young Brian came hastening up with the spare crossbow, and Brian jabbed a thumb at him and laughed. Differences of rank did not vanish in the hunting field but they were lessened; there was a levelling camaraderie. Rufus and Tirel grinned back.

Ralph, carrying his own quiver as he always did, had placed himself where he could see the Keeper at the end of the glade. He raised a hand and saw the Keeper repeat the signal for the beaters, out of sight beyond the thicket. Shouts and crashes began in the distance and hounds spoke. A jay sent up with a raucous cry of warning.

He stared in front of him, across the new grass to where the wall of bushes, just coming into leaf, was veiled in green. The first deer, as always, was not there at all one moment and bounding through the glade the next. Arrows sprang and the deer fell, kicking, a shaft standing up from its body. A second deer raced down the glade. No one was watching Ralph. He lowered his bow and stepped back, into the concealment of the undergrowth.

On a floor of damp leafmould, he passed noiselessly behind the line of archers. He saw Gilbert Clare shoot and miss and heard him swear. He saw Brian of Little Dene justify his choice of weapon by planting a bolt in the side of a buck, saw Rufus and Tirel simultaneously flatten their green-clad shoulders as they drew. It was dreamlike. He had come through the day so far on habit, performing familiar tasks automatically, just as when he had heard Mass that morning. Now all that was over and the real world in which men shot at deer and then went home to dinner must recede from him for ever.

Nothing was left now but the dull ache in his belly and the heavy thudding of his heart. He set one foot before the other with enormous care, renewing his choice at every step. He left the glade behind and went downhill, through oak and hornbeam, across a stream and then uphill, in among the great oaks of the Twelve Acre Wood which he had said the hunt must leave alone. There was another glade in the heart of the Twelve Acre, a very narrow, secret one. He saw it through the trees, a glint of bright green with a straight swordblade of sunlight thrusting down into it.

The bitterness he felt against Rufus these days still fell short of desiring to kill him. That was monstrous. He couldn't do that. Not even to save Cild or to propitiate Herne, let alone to salve his own insulted feelings.

Yet it seemed to him that a death, someone's death on this Feast of May, had been demanded. When the call for it came so insistently, through the voices of Herne's people, and from Count Henry alike, was a death not inevitable? So he must take it on himself.

For a knight to flee from danger was forbidden. He must not falter. He would walk through the glade to the far end. That was all he need do. It would be quick. He had thought first of managing alone, of simply running into the path of the shooting hunters. But he had seen in battle what happened to a man who was hit in the wrong place. To expose himself to random shots was more than he could contemplate. He had let Herne choose him an executioner and Herne had chosen well. Osmund was a fool yet he had this one talent, standing out from his general inadequacy like a tower on a plain: he could aim straight.

It was the best Ralph had been able to think of, to escape the trap of irreconcilables into which Henry had flung him, and to meet what he himself had begun to believe or fear were the commands of the Huntsman.

Strangely, he could understand Henry. He, Ralph, had known what it was to be a younger son, forced to fend for himself while his senior took the inheritance he would have handled better. He only wished Henry had not picked on him as a tool.

He had laid his plans before the Lodge, in a secret conclave at Easter. The women had not been there. Sybil knew nothing of it. He could not tell her this. The worst thing of all, the most weakening and unmanning, was knowing that he would not see Sybil again.

If there were truly magic in sacrificial blood, if Herne's favour could truly be bought in that fashion, perhaps Cild might somehow be set free. But he hoped Cild would not be Sybil's future. His own jealousy apart, it had occurred to him that Cild was probably the man whom Sybil had once tried to tell him she feared. Well, at least he would never have the pain of knowing.

The glade was peaceful, apparently deserted. A blackbird piped and a wood dove's tranquil voice replied. Nothing could have seemed less alarming.

He had never done anything harder than walk forward into it.

He had left the trees behind. He was in the open. He felt alone but he was not. Other Kings of the Wood, though not in living memory, had done this. They were with him now, an unseen escort, their resolution supporting his frailty.

Herne, Lord, Skyfather, Huntsman and Quarry, trinity of which the Christian trinity is only a pallid reflection, receive the offering. The throne in the clearing, the antler crown, the genuflexions, the kissing of feet, are for this; not homage paid to any man unearned but given to him who will lay down his life for his followers.

For the Tun, for Cild if your power can reach into Rufus' dungeons, take my life, freely given. I 'come to you, to Herne, the Holy Executioner. And I am myself Herne, the Stag and the Quarry. There is a rustling, high up in the branches that arch over this narrow glade. (In the branches?) Will I see the arrow coming? How much will I feel? When will it come? Oh God, oh Herne, when will it come . . .?

The rustling grew louder, became a splintering groan and Osmund, like an outsize windfall, tumbled out of an oak tree and landed at Ralph's feet. A broken branch came with him and the bow he had been holding cracked in half beneath him. He sprawled there, winded.

Fear and acceptance were drowned immediately in rage. He might have known. He should have known, since the moment Osmund drew that straw. 'Good,' everyone had said, 'Herne is wise, Osmund is the best shot among us.' Osmund was in all other respects also the clumsiest one among them. Trust him to break the branch he was crouched on, and his bow as well. Osmund always broke everything: pots, pans, ploughshares, *everything*. Through Ralph's head shot a thought as cynical and irreverent as any remark he had ever heard Rufus made, that the Horned One had buggered it right up and no mistake.

'You wantwit!' he snarled, yanking Osmund to his feet.

'The branch broke!' gasped Osmund unnecessarily. He leaned on Ralph, waggling his left foot uneasily to and fro.

'What the devil were you doing up a tree in the first place?'

'He said he felt safer with the hunt so near.' Penna had stepped out of cover. Faintly, in the distance, they could hear the baying and shouting of the hunt. 'He was afraid they'd come this way after all.'

'Take my bow!' Ralph snapped at Osmund. 'Here! Go on! You've got to do it. There's no way out.'

They gazed at him in admiration. They did not know about Henry, only that their King had made himself an offering to save the Tun's harvests. He could only hope that when he was dead, Henry would leave the Tun alone. 'What are you waiting for, Osmund?'

'My ankle's hurt.'

'In the name of the Horned One and Herne Hunter, I command you. Dear Christ,' said Ralph, relapsing into everyday language, 'I've been counting off the days of my life like beads on a bloody rosary for weeks and you're complaining of a *twisted ankle*? Take the bow, take it! Stand where you are. I'll position myself.' He shoved the weapon roughly into Osmund's reluctant hands and walked off quickly, hurrying towards death to keep himself from fleeing from it. He marked a clump of grass at the right distance from Osmund, reached it and spun round. *'Now!'*

Osmund drew. Don't look at the shaft. Don't think of shock and pain and darkness. Look for the last time at the bright grass, the woodpecker drilling bark high above. Osmund, what are you waiting for *now*?

From the woods to the east, from the midst of the hunt's dull hubbub, there rose up a scream.

It did not come to them as loud, but to travel so far so clearly it must really have been very loud indeed and they knew it. It went on and on, unbroken except for the whooping punctuation of air indrawn by someone too overwhelmed by terror and agony to pause for breath. Osmund dropped his weapon. *'What's that?'*

'Pick that bow up!' shouted Ralph.

'I can't, sir, I can't!' Osmund was distracted, flapping

439

his large hands, jerking towards the sound every time the distant screams crescendoed. 'I can't shoot you anyhow, it isn't right, it isn't real, I didn't know it 'ud be like this and oh dear God what's that *noise*?'

Ralph ran to him and snatched the bow up himself. 'You've ruined it all . . .!' The screams were making demands on him too, dragging him towards them. He left Penna and Osmund where they were, found himself running back to the hunt. The hideous noise was dying down, losing itself beneath a distant chorus of shouts. He dodged through the trees, jumping the stream, and arrived breathless in the Long Glade. A knot of men were huddled round something that lay in the middle, that kicked spasmodically and whimpered and frothed blood. Other men stood in groups, whitefaced and whispering. Half a dozen houndsmen, with leashed dogs, came hurrying through the trees and discovered Ralph without surprise. No one had apparently noticed his absence. 'Lost him!' one of them said. 'He got to his horse and got away, and his squire with him.'

'Who?' demanded Ralph. From the corner of his eye he saw that he had been followed; Penna was peering timidly from the bushes.

'The fool that did it, of course! That Brian of Little Dene or wherever it is.'

The thing in the midst of the glade had ceased to jerk. The men round it were moving back. One could see the tawny hair tumbled in the grass. Penna came right out of the bushes, stared wide-eyed and said fearfully: 'It's the king, ain't it? I've seen him out hunting afore. It's the king!'

'It's not the king, there's the king,' Ralph snapped. Rufus had been one of those crouched round the victim. He was standing up now, bulky and unmistakeable, with Tirel at his side.

'It was the king's nephew,' said the Keeper, coming up. 'Who are you?' He looked Penna up and down. He was English but considered himself a royal servant and a cut above the peasantry. 'Heard the noise and came to see the fun, did you? Amazing, the number of people there always are skulking in the woods. Why aren't you at your

440

ditching?' But he spoke without malice, his mind full of more shocking images than mere villein idleness. 'He got a crossbow bolt in the guts,' he said to Ralph.

It was the thing he himself had feared. 'How did it happen?' Ralph whispered.

'His dog ran out of control, came dashing into the clearing after a buck, right into the path of the shooting. The boy was shouting and whistling but the damn dog wouldn't come so the lad just ran out after him, tried to grab him. Just as that fool Sir Brian let fly.'

'Christ!' Ralph walked across the clearing. Richie lay twisted, shoulders this way, hips the other, hands clutched round the short bolt stub that protruded from his navel. The grass all round was spattered with blood and vomit and excreta. But it was over now. The hazel eyes, staring at the sky, were glazed.

Nearby, Rufus stood crossing himself. Tirel had a hand on his shoulder. Ralph turned away. Returning to Penna, he found Osmund there too, having caught up despite his limp. 'He's dead,' Ralph said bleakly. It was difficult to believe. Richie, that slightly feckless, but good-humoured, courteous boy, who had loved his dog and loved hunting, dead on a May morning. When it ought to have been Ralph . . .

'He looks so like the king, so like,' Penna whispered. 'So that's what's wanted.'

'What?' said Ralph.

'That's what's wanted!' Penna's voice rose and Ralph shook a warning head. 'That's why Osmund couldn't do it,' Penna persisted softly but with force, his eyes distended with a dreadful and contagious knowingness. Involuntarily, Ralph and Osmund drew close to him. 'Don't you see?' Penna whispered. 'It wasn't meant it should be you, sir. The Horned One don't take what He don't want. I see it now. It's the king of the land must die for the land, not the king of one wood. The Horned One knows what he's about right enough, and He'll have what He wants, mark my words, He'll have it!'

They stared at each other, enclosed in a bubble of sickly excitement. Ralph's knees had begun to tremble uncontrollably. For more than a month, he had been

441

awaiting death. Now it had withdrawn from him and he felt weak, as if half his blood had gone with it. Behind him, Richie's body was being lifted up, carried away. In front of Ralph, the ancient colonnades of the forest led the eye from trunk to trunk into the green shadows and bird-haunted fastnesses where lives went on which had nothing to do with humankind and cared less for human loves or hates, guilts or terrors, than for a broken twig.

But he, Ralph, was part of the forest. He had sat upon the log throne and worn the antlers. He had offered himself as the Quarry. And been passed over. In favour of what other?

For someone's life was forfeit. It did not even occur to him now to think otherwise. And the someone must be a consecrated king, whether his crown were of horn or gold. Only a king could make the offering. Richie was not eligible. Richie could be no more than the finger of Herne, pointing at the chosen one. 'No,' he said wordlessly inside his head, to the wide eyes of Osmund and Penna, to the sweet, unpitying woods of May. 'No, not that. Not me. I will not. I will not wield the knife of sacrifice. He has used me badly but we were lovers once.'

Leaves rustled. He was not even thinking of Henry's threats when the woods whispered to him: *You are Herne.*

When he entered the hall it was hushed. The May Day feast was cancelled. Henry came out of a side chamber. He had apparently been writing. There was ink on his fingers.

'An unfortunate accident,' he said. No one was near enough to overhear them. 'What went wrong? I find it hard to imagine, but clearly something did. You have till Lammas. So has Cild.'

Ralph had heard enough legal Latin in his time with Rufus to be familiar with its common terms and Henry of course would be used to them.

'*Fiat*,' said Ralph, and walked on.

442

Seven

Rumour
Summer 1100

It was a summer of rumour, of tales drifting pollen-like through the air until by mid-July they had spread from end to end of England and beyond.

The whispers began among Herne's followers. The Purkisses, the charcoal-burners who roamed the New Forest, also talked to a northward-bound minstrel, and to an itinerant pedlar, whose beat then took him on through Dorsetshire to Devon. A Breton horse-dealer, visiting Winchester to buy English brood-mares, exchanged the Sign of the Five-Pointed Star with the mares' owner and took interesting gossip home with him. It was in Brittany that the first whisper began on the Continent, that the Horned One had decreed that King William Rufus of England, that least Christian of rulers, should not outlive Lammas.

For the worshippers of Herne to speak of it except among themselves was forbidden, but rumour began to spread beyond them all the same. A few knowing words dropped in an alehouse by a customer who had overindulged in its wares; an unwise sentence or two exchanged in a street where unauthorised ears could hear; it needed no more.

Garbled versions eventually reached the ears of a number of parish priests, including Father Ilger of Minstead, who duly climbed into their pulpits and delivered sermons declaring that if that mighty sinner King Rufus did not mend his evil ways, the devil would assuredly carry off his soul to hell. Rufus did nothing to hinder the process, since he held a truly disgraceful midsummer banquet in Winchester to which every whore in the town, of either sex, was apparently invited.

A monk from Gloucester, visiting the Bishop of Winchester to deliver a treatise on medicine which had been commissioned from Abbot Serlo, heard gossip which so horrified him that he used his knowledge of the Five-

Pointed Star to learn more. And then went back to Winchester in an agony of guilt. His name was Brother Mark but he had been born Ketel of Chenna's Tun. He had taken the Oath of Quittance and might not speak of the Wood. But he now began to suffer from nightmares and shouted in his sleep so wildly that the Infirmarian was called to prescribe and Abbot Serlo asked to see the patient.

The abbot enquired the substance of the nightmares. The Oath of Quittance did not stop a man from repeating his dreams. Listening, Abbot Serlo became alarmed. God had many ways of speaking to men. Dreams were one of them.

'The king expects to pass Lammas at Malwood, hunting,' Ralph said to Oswin. 'You must bring arrows to sell, plenty, all sizes, your very best workmanship. But this time don't give them barbed tips. Just clean sharp points.'

'No barbs?' Oswin repeated. A barbed arrow would stay in the wound, hampering the flight of an injured animal, making it easier to bring down.

'No barbs,' said Ralph firmly. This kill must be clean. If he failed to kill at once, then let the victim heal. A barbed arrow dragged from a wound did monstrous damage; men injured thus often died in the end, but horribly.

Oswin's eyes had widened. He had understood.

Flambard had now bought his mother a fine house in Winchester as well as the one in London but he had never managed to dissuade her from telling fortunes on the side. The girl who visited her at the end of July wished to know if she would ever marry her sweetheart. Flambard's mother poured a drop of oil into a silver cup of water and sat, warming the cup between her palms, and watching the rainbow swirls of the oil upon the water. Then she said she was sorry but the power was not working today, and she could not take money for a pretence.

The girl went away disappointed and Flambard's mother sent for her son. Rufus had after all advanced Flambard to greatness. She owed her houses and her servants in the first place to the king. She had a debt to pay. If she could. If Flambard would co-operate.

'. . . it may be too late anyhow,' she said frankly to her

444

son. 'I told you, you should have let him marry when he had it in mind. A married man, a family man, the hounds couldn't touch. Don't know why. Maybe you do. But that's how it is. The dangerous time is Lammas. You've got to *try* to save him, whatever. You owe him that.'

Flambard opened his mouth to say: 'Nonsense!' but did not say it because he had after all known his mother and her oil-patterned water, for a long time.

In one hour from now, Rufus was to set out for Malwood, where Ralph des Aix had finished the refurbishments. The arrangement had almost been changed, for he was shortly to leave for Aquitaine. The embassy had done its work. Their duke, inspired by Curthose's example, wished to go on crusade and raise the money by mortgaging one of his provinces to Rufus. Rufus would have cancelled Malwood and been on his way already, except that a steady south wind was preventing him. He had decreed therefore that the Malwood hunt would go ahead as had been planned before the deal was closed. The Aquitainians could come with him, along with his brother Count Henry, and his friends Walter Tirel, FitzHamon, Gilbert Clare and a number of others. They would kill deer, and wait for the wind.

But while it held, Rufus too was held, captive in the forest whose images of glade and stag had filled the scrying cup.

Flambard's mother had said *Lammas* and this was Lammas Eve.

Rufus clattered into the forecourt of Malwood on the afternoon of August the First, Lammas Day, twenty-four hours later than he had intended, and in a temper so bad that it had infected his whole entourage and Henry, who as the king's brother might by cheerful conversation have offset Rufus' grim taciturnity, was himself silent.

If the Lammas hunt brought forth what he hoped, he would need to send letters at short notice to bishops and barons throughout the land and he had the drafts in readiness in his saddlebag. He had prepared them personally last May Day, thanking the saints that although all the Conqueror's sons had been taught to write, he was the

445

one who had kept in practice. He felt as though the leather bag that bumped his horse's flank was full of burning charcoal. When they reached Malwood, he was first off his horse, striding indoors ahead of the rest, carrying the bag himself.

Rufus stayed in his saddle for a few moments, scowling at the staff who had come out to meet them. 'Well, here we are! A day late but what about it? It rained half yesterday, anyway. Don't all gape as if the lot of us had two heads each. Take the horses!' He dismounted at last. Ralph, who had been coming over from the Tun each morning for two days, hurried forward and Rufus looked him up and down. 'What are you looking so glum about? I'm the one who was held up in Winchester by a pack of fussy Aquitainians wanting to put footnotes to the footnotes on this treaty of theirs. In the end I brought 'em with me. We're still not finished. When we are, if ever, I hope you'll show us some good sport. They want to prove what good shots they are. They're said to be marvels.'

'I hope to please you and your guests, my lord.' Ralph found that he was staring at Rufus, who was staring back in surprise. He dragged his gaze away.

'Good. Well, what are we all standing about for? I want my dinner. And some good wine and plenty of it.'

He stumped indoors. His chamberlain, Herbert, followed. Gilbert Clare, coming next, remarked: 'I hope the wine's potent. It might soothe his nerves. We don't know what's wrong with him. He keeps grumbling that the Aquitainians kept him in Winchester but they didn't; he kept himself there, nit-picking over an agreement he's making with them, and raising a lot of questions everyone thought were settled. The envoys have been dying to hunt. They're getting restive.'

'There's some good Burgundian in the cellar,' said Ralph, 'or so I believe. That may get him into a better mood.'

It didn't.

The quarrel which broke out between Rufus and Tirel during the after-dinner drinking started, absurdly, because Rufus announced that when he reached the pro-

446

vince of Poitou, which he was leasing, he would keep Christmas in its capital of Poitiers and after that had further plans and Tirel, quite mildly, said: 'Hadn't we better get to Poitou first? It's landlocked so we'll have to go via Maine and Anjou. Maine's quiet now but Helias is still unsubdued. He's never given an oath of fealty and . . .'

Rufus turned scarlet, lumbered to his feet, hammered a fist on the table and then shook it under Tirel's nose. His other hand actually hovered near his knifehilt. Suddenly, they were all on their feet, Tirel blinking in disbelief.

Then the effort of violent movement sent the wine fumes into Rufus' head and he flopped back into his seat. The envoys from Aquitaine gazed tactfully into space. 'Help me with him,' said Tirel to FitzHamon and Ralph, who at the first sign of trouble had sprung to Rufus' side.

Tirel and FitzHamon lent a shoulder each to their sagging lord while Ralph held doors open and Herbert Chamberlain, who had dealt with this sort of thing before, kept pace armed with a basin. But they got the king into his chamber before he said: 'Going to be sick,' in slurred tones. When it was over, they put him to bed. He curled up at once and shut his eyes.

'He'll have a hell of a head in the morning,' said FitzHamon. 'What he got through would float all his ships for the Aquitaine enterprise!'

'Poor devil,' said Ralph, sounding as if he meant it.

'But what's the matter with him? What did I say?' They all shook their heads and Tirel, with a shrug, glanced at the doorway beyond which the meal was still in progress and snapped: 'I'm tired of this dinner. I'd like to get to bed myself.'

Malwood, standing on the scooped-out top of its mound, was cramped and Ralph's efforts had made little difference to that for there was no room for much extension.

The place was therefore crowded, even though most of the court's usual ornamental hangers-on had been left behind. Henry and Rufus had the only separate chambers, which opened off the hall. The rest dumped themselves that night on pallets strewn haphazard about the hall itself, even Tirel and Herbert, since the king had not asked either for company. When the time came, they all slept quickly, except for Ralph. Although he had been up the previous night at the Lammas festival, Ralph could not sleep.

Like the Old One in Helias' forest, Ralph found himself glad of a substitute victim. It was not doubt which troubled him as he watched the stars move across an unshuttered window. He had felt no doubt since that moment in the clearing where Richie died. After all, he was demanding nothing of Rufus that he had not been willing to give too. He was instrument, not user. He would slay the sacrifice, but Herne had chosen it.

What troubled him were the details. He now desired to survive, to go back safely to Sybil and the child, the infant boy who was so blessedly unlike Cild, in fact so unlike the flaxen Tun folk altogether that he sometimes thought that the child was truly his, born early or a little late. The boy would have dark eyes like his own . . .

But if he were to see that child grow, were to hold Sybil in his arms again, were not to be killed or spend the rest of his life in sanctuary in a monastery as Brian of Little Dene looked like doing, the fatal arrow must not seem to come from him. He knew who he wanted as a scapegoat but that individual had, most inconveniently, failed this evening to buy any of the shafts Oswin had brought to sell at Malwood.

He had told the folk of his Lodge, at another hasty special conclave: 'Lammas will see a sacrifice. Ask no more questions.' Trusting him, they had obeyed. But Oswin understood that the arrows he had been asked for were part of the Lammas scheme. And those arrows, some of which he had also given to Ralph, were beautiful, and fit for the highest purpose, and distinctive as Oswin's work always was.

This was important. It was essential, firstly, that both slayer and scapegoat should use arrows which Ralph himself had demonstrably not made. They must also use identical arrows. The scapegoat therefore *must* be one of Oswin's customers but since the right man hadn't co-operated, then – who?

He gnawed his lip. It was all proving so difficult. First

Malwood was nearly cancelled altogether and hardly had that anxiety passed before the courier came to say that Rufus, though bound for Malwood, was delaying his arrival. Would it matter, that the perfect date, the First of August, had slipped by? Would Herne have expected him to do something about it and if so, what? And *why* the delay when according to Gilbert Clare there was no reason? Had Rufus somehow been warned . . .?

The hoarse yell from the king's chamber shot him and all the others off their beds as though the pallets had caught fire. They milled in the darkness, grabbing for weapons, lunging for the king's door. 'What is it? What's wrong? My lord . . .!'

'Lights!' Rufus was shouting on a note of panic. Herbert kindled one. It showed Rufus upright on his bed. The open door joined forces with an open window to make a draught and the hangings billowed in the gloom. FitzHamon, stark naked and brandishing a sword, rushed round the room, banging them with the flat of the blade. 'More lights, more, more!' Rufus ordered. Flints were struck. Someone came with a branched candelabra in each hand. Rufus gasped audibly with relief as the shadows withdrew before it. FitzHamon, having found nothing behind the tapestries but plain timber walls, became aware of his unprotected condition and demanded a robe. A page, observing that they were all in much the same state, sensibly came running with an armful. Outside, somebody was reassuring the envoys that no one had been murdered. 'But what *happened*?' Tirel reiterated loudly.

'I was riding the night mare.' Rufus' eyes were still searching the corners of the room as if he expected to find spectres there. 'But I never had a dream like that before.'

'If you tell it, it may disperse,' said Tirel helpfully.

They wrapped their robes round themselves and stood by the couch. The air was chill. In well-conducted monasteries, at this hour, monks were chanting Matins. But in the forest, the mist was coiling in and out of the trees, hinting at shape and form and then dissolving. What shapes of impending menace had crept from the woods to enter Rufus' sleeping brain?

'I dreamed I was ill,' he said huskily. He was still half

449

under the influence of the dream and, Ralph suspected, of last night's Burgundian. 'Just as I w . . . was seven years back, in Gloucester . . . a physician came to bleed me b . . . but he . . . he . . .'

'Better tell it,' said Tirel in practical tones.

'I knew him,' said Rufus. 'It was Brother Philip from St. Stephen's; I knew him as a boy. He had no scalpel. He plunged a crossbow bolt into my belly! And the blood came out of me all right, Holy Face, how it came out! You've seen men beheaded in battle? How the blood gushes? It plumed out of me like that and went up and put out the sun. I was inside a room but the sun was shining above me just the same. I . . . it . . .'

'You dreamed of your nephew,' said FitzHamon calmly. 'You saw him die, my lord. The wine made you dream.'

'I shan't sleep again tonight, nonetheless.' Rufus's face was still haunted. 'My head aches. Herbert, brew me something for it. All of you stay here. Tirel, you play chess with me. Fetch a board, someone.'

Chess was hardly a game for a half-drunk man with a headache to play in the small hours. But it served a purpose. Rufus grew slow and bored after a while and said impatiently: 'Oh, leave it. We'll finish the game tomorrow. I might sleep after all. But leave the lights and bring in your pallets.'

Herbert said, as the king fell asleep: 'I put a soothing potion in the headache brew.' He added uneasily: 'I once dreamed I was at a burying and my father died suddenly the week after. I hope this wasn't a portent.'

'Well, don't suggest that to *him*!' said FitzHamon.

'No,' Ralph agreed sharply. 'Don't!'

He was certain now that the king, by some means or other, knew that danger was close. All his anger against Rufus had gone. What must be must be but there was no longer any hatred in it. He did not want Rufus to believe in his danger, not only because it would put him on his guard, but also because it would make him suffer.

If he died in terror, Ralph would pity him and carry that pity like a barbed arrow in his own flesh, for the rest of his life.

Eight

A Day in the Death of
King Rufus
2nd August 1100

Ralph afterwards remembered the last day of King Rufus'
life as the most frightening day of his own, its burden of
dread greater even than on the morning when he thought
he was himself to die.

It was also the strangest day of his life. As he moved
step by step towards its terrifying conclusion, he felt
himself surrounded by forces he could not see. The task
was there and he was powerless to refuse it, but nor had
he power to overcome the succession of obstacles which
weirdly interposed themselves between him and his intent. As when it was rumoured that Rufus would not come
to Malwood at all, as when he came after all but one day
late, Ralph could only wait, a passive instrument, for the
outcome of an unseen struggle.

'Do you believe in Herne?' Sybil had once asked him,
curiously.

'Believe?' he said. 'I have believed enough, for long
enough, to make Herne real. Things do become real if you
believe in them enough. Then they take hold of you.'

Herne had hold of him now, as strongly as the divinity
of Christ and the love of God had hold of such men as
Father Ilger and Archbishop Anselm. And was as real.

He rose, noiselessly, at the first lightening in the east,
dressed and went quietly down the stairs, through the
lower hall where the lesser guests and the indoor servants
still snored, and out. The outbuildings were just
emerging, colourless shapes, from the darkness. The last
stars were fading and ground mist still drifted up from the
forest. The air smelt sharp and cold but there was a milky
feel beneath the tang; a fine, clear day lay ahead. The
recent rain had cleared. An omen?

He made his way to the outer enclosure where the

Keeper's cottage stood. The Keeper of the Malwood Walk came out, together with his son, to whom he was teaching the business. They offered Ralph some food but his knotted stomach couldn't imagine ever accepting food again. He refused with thanks and led the two of them down to the wicket in the outer palisade. Beyond was a moveable wooden bridge which they pushed across the ditch. They went over, into the forest.

For two hours they moved quietly along the rides, seeking fresh deer slots. They paced along a wide glade in the Hoar Woods where, Ralph said, he would place the royal hunters. *That* tree, said Ralph to himself, marking a stout oak which stood alone. He would recommend the king to stand beneath it. And there, under that tall ash, he would place himself. His stomach clenched again.

They returned to find a bustle of saddling-up in progress. There were curious glances towards Ralph. There were cult men from Truham and Minstead here. He had not said much at the Lodge, but he had said enough and the air was full of a secret waiting. One of the Purkisses, arriving with a donkey-cart full of charcoal for the ever-hungry kitchens, gave him in passing a long hard look from blue eyes ringed in brilliant white.

He must not fail.

'We only need the king to come out,' he said with studied lightness to Oswin, who was still at Malwood, as he tethered his horse outside the stable. He glanced towards the hall. There was no sign of Rufus yet and the morning was beginning to pass.

'Where's he got to, then?' said Oswin.

'I wish I knew,' said Ralph uneasily.

Rufus woke in the sane daylight, to the positively friendly – because familiar – greeting of a still-lingering drinker's headache. Well, movement and open air would shake that out of him. He felt better, free from the fermenting shadows of the night. Ahead of him lay a day's hunting and . . .

And at that, his mind balked like a bad-tempered mule. It had been Ranulf Flambard, the most normal man he knew, who in the commonplace surroundings of the main

452

courtyard at Winchester Palace, with a sparrow taking a bath in a puddle and a cat hopefully stalking it, had said: 'My lord, don't hunt at Lammas. It's dangerous.'

'*Dangerous*? What are you talking about?'

'I've heard a rumour.'

'What rumour?'

'The source isn't important. But I think . . .'

'*What rumour*? Come on, Flambard, the truth!'

'My mother,' said Flambard reluctantly, because he knew Rufus would have it out of him in the end, 'has had a vision.'

'Your *mother*?' Rufus could still hear his own gruff amusement. 'The witch?'

'She's not a witch. She's a good Christian woman . . .'

'She can be a Christian or a paynim for all I care. I'm still not interested in her visions.'

'. . . .who happens,' said Flambard, 'to have a gift, of a sort well-attested in the Bible.' Rufus started to walk away but Flambard kept pace with him. 'She saw a hunt, in a forest. She said the time was Lammas, don't ask me how she knows. But you were the quarry and a shaft was trained on your heart. And there have been other rumours; you know there have.'

'Yes, yes, tavern talk about some mad secret society trying to avert the end of the world. Stirred up by a lot of mad priests and their sermons. No doubt your mother has heard all that too. The priests haven't tried to kill the rumours, I notice. Most of them don't like me and quite earnestly believe that one day I'll incur the wrath of God in some more or less unmistakeable form. But I didn't expect this sort of talk from you. Bishop of Durham you may be, but must you go right over to the enemy and wallow in priestly superstition?'

'I haven't and I'm not. I think the threat is real – though I'm not sure what quarter it's actually coming from.'

Rufus snorted.

'I also think,' said Flambard with determination, 'that if there is a threat, from God or man, Lammas is a likely moment for it. The date, I believe, has a significance to certain – er – groups of people. And your Lammas hunt would provide an excellent opportunity, in any case, for an accident by virtue of being a hunt, never mind about the date. Your brother and your nephew both died while hunting, remember.'

'So what do you suggest I do, Flambard?'

'Don't hunt at Lammas. Don't go to Malwood. You've almost cancelled it once. Cancel it in good earnest. Aren't there some details of the Aquitaine treaty which could bear further discussion, even if the wind doesn't change to let you sail?'

'You should have mentioned the treaty first. I might have listened then.'

'Perhaps I should. I was clumsy. Men become clumsy when worry bedevils their judgement.'

Rufus looked at him. 'You mean it, don't you?'

'Yes, my lord. I do.'

'Very well.' Rufus made a brisk, irritated decision. 'Tomorrow is Lammas Day. We'll stay here, spend it in conference, and go to Malwood the next day, unless the wind lets up. Does that content you?'

It was in fact true that the treaty could still warrant discussion. He could not make a show as temporary ruler of Poitou let alone crunch through Maine and Anjou to get there without spending a good deal of money and laying some complicated plans.

But the day spent on such mundane affairs also pushed back the world of Flambard's sorceress mother, of rumours and unseen threats. Some new and exciting possibilities inherent in the treaty occurred to him and began to shape themselves into a scheme. He became once more king, campaigner and knight and these aspects of him were angry with Flambard for cozening them with nonsense. He had set out for Malwood in the evening in a temper. And here at Malwood, the world of visions had invaded; not the scrying bowl of Flambard's dreadful old mother this time, but the very mind of Rufus; king, campaigner and knight, notwithstanding.

Such diversions as hunting offered no refuge now. Hunting meant the forest and it was here that the danger lay.

Rising, he stared out over the trees which encircled Malwood and knew with shame that he did not want to hunt in those woods from which his brother and his nephew had both been carried dead, the one with his windpipe smashed and the other with a crossbow bolt through the belly.

He was horrified, knowing how his father would have condemned such a cravenness. But it made no difference. He looked at the treetops and shrank. He could not do it, could not force his feet to take him out there among them, or compel his tongue to order the hunt to proceed.

He turned to FitzHamon, who was dressing. 'We didn't bring those envoys along just for a hunting party,' he said. 'There's still a few things to discuss. We half-touched on them last night when Tirel wouldn't let us finish. The envoys have some work to do before they start enjoying themselves.'

'My lord will not hunt this morning,' said the squire who had been sent out to inform the huntsmen. 'He is caught up in matters of business. You're to hold yourselves in readiness to hunt later, perhaps. But for the time being you may unsaddle the horses and return the hounds to their kennels.'

Silently, shaken, Ralph also looked towards the sea of treetops below Malwood. With his mind, he said: 'Herne?'

'It can't be done,' said Henry exasperatedly. 'And why we're sitting here arguing about it as if it might, instead of using this excellent hunting weather, passes my understanding. We've been over and over it. It's impossible!'

From the start of the meeting, he had declined to sit. Now he began to prowl restlessly about the hall. The two Aquitainian envoys who were present nodded. They had been protesting from the start, when Rufus unveiled his scheme like a piece of vast and incomprehensible sculpture. The senior of them, a pious and engagingly unworldly individual melodiously known as William Sans Sang because he was so pale that he seemed bloodless, said patiently: 'Count Henry is right. It's too grandiose.'

'It's far too grandiose!' Henry's angry prowl brought him back to the table. 'Knock out Maine and Anjou, keep

455

Christmas in Poitiers – as if it were merely York! – and then as if all that weren't enough, you announce that you intend to keep Curthose out of Normandy too! I'm not poor-spirited, Rufus, that's an insulting thing to say. I think it would be a very good thing if Curthose is not allowed to redeem Normandy. We'd gain, frankly, and so would the Normans! But we may not even be able to manage the first part of the plan, let alone the rest! I'm talking practical sense. *Have* we ever really conquered Maine? What if we meet a strong resistance? I know you get angry if anyone says so, but Helias *is* still there, still refusing to make any kind of terms. As for taking Anjou at the same time – words fail me!'

'I agree,' said Gilbert Clare.

'Especially,' added Sans Sang with emphasis, 'now that Fulk of Anjou has married his son to Helias' daughter. The two of them will assuredly combine.'

They were repeating themselves and were growing bored. Rufus, however, was becoming furious. 'I am sick, *sick*, of the suggestion that it's beyond me to master Maine!' He glowered at them, head lowered. No one spoke. Several avoided his eyes. 'My plans allow for the difficulties,' said Rufus loudly. 'We challenge Curthose only after Maine and Anjou have been dealt with. If we move quickly we can – we *can*, gentlemen! – see to them both and have Normandy embattled, with its chief lords on our side, before Curthose gets home from his nice long travelling honeymoon. What's wrong with you all? Only a moment ago, I outlined an attractive agreement which could well win over Fulk without a fight, no matter who his son has married. Why don't you listen? Were you all asleep?'

'No, my lord,' said FitzHamon. 'But Fulk and Helias must know our plans by now. No one can assemble a fleet the size of ours in secret. Fulk will treat any advances with suspicion.'

'Helias was preparing for further war against you, sir, before we even left England,' said Sans Sang. 'He was casting about for new allies, apart from Fulk. He's been a widower for years but he's not yet forty; there was talk that he was considering remarriage, to some lady with

456

powerful relatives. He's said to have remarked that it's a shame our Duke's daughters are too young. One of them, Agnes, promises exceptional beauty, you know. Helias is a good-living man but he much appreciates beauty in women.'

The manner of Rufus' life was widely known but Sans Sang was one of those individuals whose piety and unworldliness protected him from certain kinds of knowledge as though he were a snail and they his shell. Oblique allusions, half-heard sentences which would have told much to less pure or more experienced minds had passed him by. When he saw Rufus' face change as though some expunging agent had wiped out the king's usual expression of cheerful pugnacity, leaving a blank, Sans Sang was visibly bewildered.

In the tight silence, FitzHamon and Gilbert Clare studied the tapestries, while Henry threw himself into a seat and sat there, scowling and taut, as though he might at a signal spring to arms. They, if not Sans Sang, knew what Rufus' imagination was showing him: Helias, with a lovely woman in his arms.

Rufus stared inimically round at them. 'We're all hungry. We'll take dinner early. We'll resume these talks tomorrow.'

The council adjourned, with relief.

Over dinner, Rufus, after being silent for a long time, said: 'We might hunt after all, when we've done with eating. You can demonstrate your marksmanship to our Aquitainian friends, Tirel. Let's hope no accidents interrupt the sport this time.'

'We had heard,' said Sans Sang courteously, 'that Sir Walter Tirel is an exceptional shot. We must try not to disgrace ourselves.'

'Are they going?' Oswin almost whispered it, coming up as Ralph led his horse out for the second time.

'Yes. Someone said something to upset him, judging from the talk at dinner. He wants some sport to blow it away. What's that you're carrying?'

'Six arrows. I want to present them to the king. I thought . . . a sort of courtesy.'

457

If you were going to have an animal put down, you petted it first. 'All right, go on in. You may make a few more sales while you're there.'

It was not every man of the Tun whom he would unhesitatingly send to make a personal gift to the king but Oswin had been selling arrows to the royal hunting parties for years. Also, he had a natural poise, the result of lifelong competence in everything he did (Osmund would have dropped things and fallen over someone's feet). He left Oswin to get on with it, busying himself with an examination of his horse's shoes. He must cultivate ordinariness today as though it were a harvest on which his life depended. No one, afterwards, must be able to say: That man des Aix was behaving rather oddly, the day the king died, wasn't he?

Besides, he wanted to think. He had that one last choice still to make.

He wondered, as he had done last May Day, how it was possible to be so leaden with dread and yet continue to move steadily towards the source of it. Within half an hour now, he would have made that choice; he would be one step closer to his terrible destination, and for all the shrinking within him, he would make that step, and all those that must follow.

Not many of them now.

Oswin came back, excited. 'Do you know what he did? You'll never believe that he said!'

'Did he tip you? He does that sometimes, you know that.'

'No! I said the arrows were a gift in honour of his first visit to Malwood and he examined them and said they were the best workmanship he'd ever seen!' Oswin had gone pink and shy, like a girl with her first compliment. 'And then he passed them to my lord Walter Tirel of Poix – he wouldn't buy any of my shafts yesterday! – and told my lord Tirel to make good use of them. In front of everyone, he told my lord Tirel that they were the *best* . . .' Oswin stopped short. 'What is it?'

Ralph found that he was staring past Oswin, towards the treetops of the forest, and brought his gaze back. 'You'll understand later,' he said.

For Tirel was the man he would have chosen. The king's friend, who could reasonably be given a shooting stand close enough to Rufus. The man who had once ousted Ralph in the king's affections, to whom Ralph had for years been perforce polite. A man who, furthermore, had the dubious Gilbert Clare for a brother-in-law (Gilbert Clare might have put anyone up to anything). The roof was on the house and Herne had put it there. Tirel's fine markmanship, thought Ralph, with a sudden, savage delight, would be remembered now for ever.

Rufus would come out at any moment. Ralph's guts were still knotted but there was a lightness in his limbs and his heartbeat had quickened. It was going to happen. At least, if Rufus would only come before anything else could go wrong, a sudden change in the weather, an urgent courier recalling him to Winchester or . . .

A mild hubbub at the gate, where someone – it looked like a monk – was apparently trying to gain entry, suddenly increased in volume. The monk's voice, raised to a shout, carried across the courtyard.

As one who receives a blow in the stomach, Ralph heard the brown-habited figure demand to see the king at once, because he had come to save King Rufus' life.

Mercifully, no one was looking at Ralph. All eyes were on the monk, who was now attempting to push past a couple of burly guards. One of them nodded to a third, who ran for the hall, reappearing a moment later with FitzHamon. The monk recognised FitzHamon's aura of authority and made for him. The guards let him do so. He caught at FitzHamon's sleeve. 'I must see the king! I tell you it's life and death!'

Ralph's hands bunched into fists. Herne leapt and raged in him like a fire. FitzHamon was asking something. The monk replied. 'Abbot Serlo? You're from Gloucester? Very well, come with me.' FitzHamon hustled the monk towards the hall.

'No!' muttered Ralph, as though the very strength of his feelings could negate opposition. 'No, no, no!' Did the monk actually know something and if so, what? If not, then what on earth did this mean? With Oswin behind him, he followed to the threshold of the hall, arriving in time to hear FitzHamon announce to Rufus that 'this man insists on seeing you', and to see him push the monk, who fell on his knees, landing beside Herbert Chamberlain, who was crouched at the king's feet, fitting skintight boots on them, as Rufus sat in a chair.

'Oh, get up,' said Rufus testily. 'I don't want rows of people prostrating themselves in front of me as if I were a heathen idol. What is it this time?'

'He wants to tell you his dreams, my lord,' said FitzHamon exasperatedly, producing instant merriment from Henry and Tirel, who were both standing close to Rufus. But across the room, Henry caught Ralph's eye and in his face, anger and desperation were mingled.

'You've had enough of other men's nightmares? You think this monk and I should just share with each other?' Rufus enquired jovially of FitzHamon. But his voice was up a pitch or two. Ralph folded his arms to hide his crossed fingers while he breathed a silent prayer. 'Oh Herne, we are so near. Don't let it go wrong now.'

'Dreams are just dreams,' said FitzHamon. 'But this man – no, be quiet, Brother-Whoever-You-Are, I'll tell it! – he comes from St. Peter's in Gloucester, Abbot Serlo's abbey. Serlo sent him, apparently. I have a great respect for Abbot Serlo, as you yourself have, my lord. I thought his message had better be delivered, although when you hear it . . .!' FitzHamon's sentence trailed off into a snort.

'All right, what is the message?' Down the hall, Rufus' eyes too sought Ralph's and seemed to be seeking reassurance, as though at some time recently they had glimpsed some less than comforting expression there. Ralph lowered his gaze quickly.

'The message,' said FitzHamon expressionlessly, 'is that he's had the same dream three nights running. My lord, he dreamed that you walked into a chapel and tried to eat a crucifix and that the figure on the Cross kicked you in the stomach. Serlo thought you should know.'

There was a moment of silence and then first Henry, and after him nearly everyone else in the hall, dissolved not merely into merriment this time but into guffaws. Ralph joined in. Red in the face and almost incoherent

460

with anger, the monk banged a clenched fist into his other palm and bellowed. When he was at last heard, the first word to emerge from the hubbub was: 'Danger!' The laughter quietened a little. 'There's danger to you, my lord!' the monk shouted. 'Signs and portents everywhere! My lord abbot agrees with me, the dreams have a meaning. He wants me to warn you!'

'Serlo shouldn't let his monks eat cheese for supper!' retorted Henry swiftly. The laughter broke out again.

'Has Serlo gone mad?' enquired Rufus. 'Does he take me for a peasant, doing this or not doing that according to the dreams of monks or old women?' His voice was hearty but his eyes were wretched. *He can't back out now*, thought Ralph, suddenly exultant. *He'd never hear the last of it. He daren't change any plan now, daren't refuse to hunt. They'd all remember Richie. I should have trusted Herne!*

'Give him a hundred shillings for his trouble, FitzHamon,' Rufus was saying. 'If Serlo won't let him keep it, it can buy Masses for my endangered soul. I'm going to hunt. Tirel's agreed to show our Aquitainian friends the meaning of a straight aim.'

He looked towards the open door as he spoke, rising to his feet now that Herbert's ministrations were over. This time, Ralph did not drop his eyes quickly enough. As they met the king's, he knew, too late, that they were blazing with triumph and with something more; with the intentness that fills the eyes of the hunter or the stalking cat, the instant before the kill.

And Rufus understood. Ralph saw the blood go out of his face as he identified his slayer, as he realised that the mercy he had refused to Cild was now in turn to be refused to him. But the whole court was laughing at the monk and jostling him as FitzHamon led him to a clerk who would pay him.

And Rufus, who could not now in honour veer from any course which he had set, must be seeing the darkness he had dreaded all his life, yawning for him like the mouth of a black tunnel towards which he must inevitably go. As the king came slowly down the hall, Oswin gripped Ralph's elbow. 'I know that monk! It's Ketel – you

461

administered the Oath of Quittance to him when you first came to the Tun! He went to Gloucester, yes, that's right!'

'Well, he hasn't broken the oath,' Ralph whispered. 'I think he's served it. Shh!'

With Tirel at his side, Rufus came level with them but went by without glancing towards them. He was making some remark to Tirel about the Aquitainians. '. . . mind you remember what I said, Tirel.'

'I will, my lord,' said Tirel, close at the royal shoulder. Tirel the scapegoat, to whom the king had given six new arrows from the Tun. The pattern is right, said Ralph's jumping pulses. He was immune to pity now. Herne was in their midst.

Rufus hesitated, once, just as they dismounted to walk, in single file, the last half-mile to the stand.

'Monks dream. So do kings,' he said abruptly to Ralph. 'That nightmare I had. It was ugly. That's a bad way to die, with a bolt through the guts. I saw Richie. The monk said the figure kicked . . .'

'Nothing of that kind is going to happen to you, my lord,' said Ralph quietly.

'I hope not,' said Rufus. As if the exchange had meant nothing, Ralph turned to Henry. 'My lord, would you care to lead a separate party to a different stand? The Keeper of the Walk will show you. That way everyone will have a fair chance of shooting. We have plenty of beaters.'

'By all means.'

'I thought that the king's party should include my lords of Poix and Tonbridge . . .'

'And FitzHamon,' put in Rufus.

'Of course. And with Count Henry . . .'

No one demurred at any of Ralph's suggestions. Smooth as an oiled key, the final arrangements slid into place. Henry, as he moved off, breathed: 'Cild,' so that only Ralph could hear him.

But Rufus had sensed their thoughts. His eyes fixed themselves for a long moment on Ralph's face. Then he walked ahead of Ralph, into the woods. He went proudly, as a royal stag should, even though Herne the Hunter was pacing on his spoor. As they went, the distance between them did not vary by as much as a stride's length. They were locked together now into a fixed pattern, twins and opposites, like light and darkness, until one of them should be dead. And on Ralph's brow was the weight of an unseen, antlered crown, as real as the weight of the kingdom's crown on Rufus.

From where Rufus stood under the oak he had been shown, he looked across a wide glade, broader than the one where Richie had died, with thin, gravelly soil, grass-grown, spread between two belts of trees. He could just see Tirel, about eighty yards away, half hidden by a clump of bushes. Ralph des Aix was nearer, motionless under a tall ash. In the distance, he could hear the beaters. These were the men, these the sights and sounds of a hundred other hunts. Everything appeared quite normal. Had he imagined it all, then: the ominous strangeness in Ralph's voice and eyes, the menace that since last night had seemed to fill the air like coming thunder?

Yes. Surely. This was an ordinary late afternoon shoot. Afterwards, there would be supper and in the morning, a further business session. He might well keep Christmas in Poitiers as he had planned.

He might even see Helias again.

But if he did, it would be only on the field of war. He knew now, finally, that even if they lived until the stars grew old, they would never be lovers. But for the despair of that discovery, made manifest to him through the innocent medium of William Sans Sang – who was somewhere out of sight down the glade now – they would none of them be in this glade at all. He would not have changed his mind at dinner. This hunt would not have happened and Serlo's monk could not have trapped him into it.

But it didn't matter. There was no danger. He had only imagined there was danger, nothing more. Hadn't he?

Over the forest, the afternoon was wearing away. The shadow of the oak ran out behind him across green-gold grass. The setting sun slanted through the wood in shafts of luminous, hard-edged haze, with a red fire behind it. The noise of the beaters was louder.

The first startled birds had gone up from the covert, wings whirring, giving out alarm calls. The first stag was there and gone so quickly that they missed him for he had vanished into the sun-haze before anyone could take aim. In the distance, Walter Tirel made a gesture that meant a rude word, and Rufus laughed.

Another stag broke, a smaller animal behind him. They bounded across the open ground, antlered heads thrown back. Rags of velvet still draped the crown of the bigger stag. Rufus brought up his bow to aim at him, but both of them, like the first, plunged into the bright haze. He swung round, trying to follow his target with his arrow-point, trying to get the sun out of his eyes.

He had just time to see Ralph's bow trained on him, just time to know that all his imaginings were after all the truth, before the shaft struck home.

It was not like Richie's death. Ralph had promised that and Ralph could keep his word because like Tirel he was a magnificent shot. The arrow took Rufus in the heart, spinning him round, tumbling him to the ground. It was not instantaneous and there was pain but not like Richie's. There was shock and loathing and disbelief, and then a swiftly-growing numbness and a sense of being borne away on a fast and swirling river.

He was still conscious when they all ran up. He had both hands clutched round the arrow in his chest. He saw them point at it. He heard Ralph say, in exactly the right tone of startled indignation: 'But that's surely one of the shafts my lord king gave to Sir Walter Tirel!' He heard someone answer bewilderedly: 'But did Tirel aim for a stag and hit the king by mistake then?' He heard Tirel's voice, appalled, exclaiming: 'No, all our arrows look alike. It wasn't mine!'

Rufus tried to say that it wasn't true, that Tirel was a victim too, that Tirel was his friend who had cheered him when he was miserable and would never harm him, that the man they wanted was Ralph, Ralph des Aix.

But Ralph was stooping over him, blocking out the others. The sun through the branches cast peculiar patterns on Ralph's face. He looked as though he was wearing antlers. This seemed so very extraordinary that Rufus found himself attempting to comment on it.

464

But he had already drifted too far and only a whisper came out and no one heard but Ralph himself. After that, it was too late.

And with that, it was all over. The composite dream in which Herne was real and Ralph and Rufus both his representatives, in which the king's death was a quest to be achieved no matter what the cost, to which all else in the world was subordinate, was broken.

There was only the body of a middle-aged man with thick pale ginger hair and a blunt-featured face which in life had been pugnacious and in death looked merely astonished.

It was difficult to think that he had ever been a king, still less the surrogate for a god.

And Ralph des Aix, gazing down at him while the hushed, shocked hunting party gathered round and Tirel, step by stealthy step, drew back to confer rapidly with his brother-in-law Gilbert Clare and then sprint for his horse and flee: had Ralph ever been King of the Wood, drawing Herne Huntsman's bow?

He could not now believe it. It was no longer real. The Wood was not real. He would never go to the Wood again, neither he nor Sybil. They would take the Oath of Quittance and be free of it. Let Oswin wear the antlers, or Cild, if he came back. The weight of the antler crown had gone from Ralph's brow and he would never feel it upon him again.

Epilogue

August
1100

'. . . we're almost done. A few lesser matters to deal with, that's all,' said King Henry to the clerk who was his secretary. The August evening was dimming but the new king, as his staff had found, was a glutton for work. 'I want an amnesty drawn up for some prisoners at present held in this city of Winchester. We're prepared to release them as a goodwill gesture, to celebrate our recent coronation. It is a unique gesture, naturally. The Forest Law will be pursued in all its rigour in the future. Draw up a proclamation about that, if you please.'

'Yes, sir,' said the secretary, who had been taking notes for hours and was getting tired.

'One of the men who will be released comes from a place in the New Forest called Chenna's Tun. He will no doubt go back there. He can act as guide to a courier we wish to send there. Take another note. The courier is to go to Sir Ralph des Aix, tenant of Chenna's Tun in Hampshire, taking the first instalment of an annual payment of fifteen pounds in silver. Draw up a document making that official and put it for services rendered as the reason. We don't propose to state the reason in the document.' Henry raised his eyes to the clerk and there appeared on his face a fleeting, naughty grin which reminded the secretary strongly and startlingly of the king's dead brother King William Rufus, who had died before his time, no doubt by the hand of God as retribution for his godless life, and been brought back to Winchester in such unkingly fashion, on a donkey cart belonging to a charcoal-burner named Purkiss. 'It would be tactless to put any details,' said Henry blandly. 'Sir Ralph has a son. Only he's my son, if you follow. I can't allow a child of mine to be reared in poverty and the family is poor. Add to the document an undertaking that if Sir Ralph dies – he has a recurrent chest complaint –

466

we shall provide for the child and find a good marriage for the widow.'

The clerk scratched busily with his quill. Henry looked at the unexpressive tonsure thus presented to him and said: 'I propose soon to present the court with a most royal and lovely lady as my queen and in due course I hope to have a lawful prince to follow me. But one must pay one's debts.'

Certainly a man like Henry of England must. The two personalities within him, the Henry whom Edith loved and who had pitied Sybil, and the other, the relentless Henry who had thrust Conan and Rufus alike into oblivion, both acknowledged it. Their debts were very heavy and they would in time, no doubt, incur still more.

Henry had seized power, leaving his brother's body to others while he himself galloped to Winchester to wrest the keys of treasury from its staggered custodians, send out his prudently drafted letters and get himself to London and crowned within four days. He had ruthlessly overturned Rufus' will, snatching the crown from tardy Curthose. And soon he would have Edith.

To Edith he would give a position that would last all her life, and happiness, which would last for a while – until his roving nature took control of him again and Edith, living as a queen must amid a crowd of watching eyes, would keep a calm face all day and grieve at night, alone in her ornately-hung bed, wondering with whom he slept instead. He loved her and at the thought of her, his body stirred, but he knew himself.

'We've shocked you,' he said suddenly to the clerk. 'You think all this immoral?'

'My lord!' The clerk did not know how to answer. He took a deep breath. 'My lord, we all welcome your accession. Er . . . immoral is the word one might use of . . . of your predecessor's way of life.'

'King Rufus?'

'Yes. My lord,' said the secretary nervously.

Rufus, before his death, had dreamed of his own blood, spouting to darken the sky. Then Serlo's monk had come. And at the last moment, in the forest, Henry had heard his brother say to Ralph: 'That's a bad way to die, with a bolt through the guts.'

467

Had Rufus guessed? Or even known?

Had he walked, knowing, ahead of Ralph into the wood, because he was too gallant to withdraw because of dreams or suspicions? Had he stood there, beneath that oak, knowing that death was coming for him?

'My brother,' said Henry coldly, 'was as knightly, as royal, as a man can be and far braver than most. I am aware of the Church's opinion of him. But in my presence, never speak of him like that again. He died a king and if I can do as much, I shall be thankful.'